## ABOUT THE AUTHOR

Stephen Goldenberg studied Law at Oxford University and, subsequently, enjoyed a career as an English and Media Studies teacher in London schools. He has published books and articles on English teaching and broadcast on educational issues on television and radio. He has published three previous crime novels – *Stony Ground, The Lying Game* and *Car Wheels on a Gravel Drive* (the latter two published by Matador). He lives in London and South-West France.

Visit Stephen at
**www.stephengoldenbergauthor.com**

# THE DEATH

## OF AN

# INVISIBLE MAN

STEPHEN GOLDENBERG

Matador
9 Priory Business Park,
Wistow Road, Kibworth Beauchamp,
Leicestershire. LE8 0RX
Tel: 0116 279 2299
Email: books@troubador.co.uk
Web: www.troubador.co.uk/matador
Twitter: @matadorbooks

ISBN 978 1838595 388

British Library Cataloguing in Publication Data.
A catalogue record for this book is available from the British Library.

Printed and bound in Great Britain by 4edge Limited
Typeset in 11pt Stempel Garamond by Troubador Publishing Ltd, Leicester, UK

Matador is an imprint of Troubador Publishing Ltd

*To my parents, Lillian and Gus.*

"The artist must be in his work as God is in creation, invisible and all-powerful; one must sense him everywhere but never see him."

**Gustave Flaubert**

"O! Woe is me,
To have seen what I have seen. Seen what I see!"

**Shakespeare: Hamlet Act 3 Scene 1**

# An Extract from
# *The Autobiography of an Invisible Man*

## MY BEGINNINGS

I am unique. I can say with confidence that there is no-one else on Earth like me. I sense your scepticism, dear reader. Isn't every human being unique, I hear you say? Don't the discoveries of modern science (blood groups, fingerprints and, most decisively, DNA) prove that we are all unique individuals? My answer to that is – yes, we may be scientifically and genetically unique, but we live in tribes and it is our shared tribal DNA that connects us to others.

I am connected to no-one. I belong to a tribe of one.

Not only am I unique but I am also invisible. Not literally, like the H.G. Wells' character. Perhaps it would be more accurate to describe myself as a man in the shadows. In photos of the famous, I am standing behind them, slightly out of focus. That is, if I haven't been disappeared – airbrushed from history like all those purged henchmen in photos of Stalin.

And so, I am writing this autobiography to put the record straight and claim my rightful place in history before I die; or, as is more likely, before I am forcibly extinguished from the Earth. My other reason for putting all this down in writing is as a kind of mea culpa: a confession, a plea for forgiveness for my sins.

Let me start with my name – although that's not as simple as it should be. On my birth certificate, I am Hare

Yehuda Felatu. Most people know me as Harry Felatu. For a brief period, at the behest of my mother, I called myself Harry Weinstein. I soon abandoned that. Can you imagine a six foot six inch, dark-skinned man with Polynesian features introducing himself to you as Harry Weinstein? You'd think I was playing some kind of weird anti-semitic joke. Are you beginning to see what I mean by unique?

I was born in Cardiff in 1930. My father was Maka Felatu – a New Zealand Maori rugby All-Black star. My mother was Sarah Weinstein, the daughter of a prosperous Welsh Jewish family. In 1927, when the South African authorities refused to accept Maoris as part of the touring All-Black squad, my father protested by founding the New Zealand Maori rugby team which toured Wales in 1929.

Wales may not have been South Africa but, even so, back then, it wasn't easy to find lodgings for twenty black men in Cardiff, especially as the tour was being run on a shoestring. That's where my grandfather, Abel Weinstein, came in. Like many immigrant Jewish families eager to assimilate, he had decided that the best way to gain acceptance was through sport – and, in Wales, that meant rugby. He progressed rapidly from becoming a benefactor and director of his local club to being elected to the Welsh National Rugby Board. Thus, he was the one who organised lodgings for the Maori team among his fellow board members, including putting up my father and two others in his large house in Pontcanna. These Polynesian giants must have attracted a lot of attention as they were escorted round Cardiff by the diminutive semitic Weinsteins – one of whom was my then twenty-two year old mother.

Despite their wealth and their prominence in the local business community, the Weinsteins had socialist leanings and were benevolent employers. In their Cardiff clothing factory, which manufactured uniforms (mainly military), many of their employees were Afro-Caribbean immigrants from the Tiger Bay district. Although the Weinsteins were very prominent members of Cardiff's small Jewish community, congregated in Pontcanna, and attended the local synagogue on high holidays, they considered themselves to be largely secular liberal Jews. My mother was their only child and, unusually for the time and her parents' cultural background, she was brought up to be a strong independent woman. Her education was as important to her parents as it would have been if she had been a boy. She attended an exclusive private school for girls and went from there to Oxford University to study English Literature.

If they had known what was going to become of their daughter, I suspect my Jewish grandparents would have been far less permissive and, in hindsight, probably regretted they had not imposed more control over her.

In June 1929, she had just returned home from university clutching her first class degree when Maka and his Maori team-mates arrived at the Weinstein mansion. Her parents were proud of their daughter, boasting of her academic success to their Jewish neighbours whose own daughters were being brought up with the sole aim of turning them into good Jewish wives and mothers.

However, their pride camouflaged some niggling worries. One was Sarah's oft-repeated ambition to be a writer and journalist. They were all for her having a career but they had hoped and assumed that, with her qualifications, she would choose something far more solid and respectable. Their other concern was the series of non-Jewish boyfriends she had cultivated during her time at Oxford. Non-observant Jews they may have been, but that didn't mean that they would countenance a gentile son-in-law. Fortunately, she never brought any of these boyfriends home with her in the vacations and they'd only ever met one of them on a weekend visit to Sarah in Oxford. He was called Jolyon, an old Etonian and heir to a baronetcy, and they had to admit that he had a disarming toffish charm. Nevertheless, the next time Sarah returned to the family home her mother, Naomi, made veiled comments about the unsuitability of such relationships, referring to the traditional anti-semitism of the English upper classes. Sarah laughed this off, telling her mother that she was stuck in the nineteenth century. But their concerns were half-hearted. They realised too late that the young woman they had created was now beyond their control and they would just have to hope that good sense and tradition would somehow prevail. And, anyway, none of these liaisons with young non-Jewish men lasted very long or seemed anything other than youthful flings. Thus, the Weinsteins were optimistic that, now that she was home from university, she would settle back into their parochial Cardiff enclave and, in preparation, they had considered the merits of several young men in the local Jewish community as suitable husbands for their wayward daughter.

Amid all this scheming, it did not occur to them that there was any conceivable danger in inviting three strapping young Polynesian men into their household to live alongside their flighty daughter. However relatively non-racist the Weinsteins may have been, these Maoris were so other – so strange and exotic – that they might as well have been a different species or from another planet. Never in their wildest dreams could they have imagined their daughter taking up with one of them.

And so, when their organised outings with the Maoris to introduce them to the wider life and culture of Cardiff came to an end, unbeknownst to her parents, they were followed by more intimate assignations between Maka and their daughter. Exactly how, when and where these dalliances mutated into full sexual congress, I could not say. Whether it took place right under her parents' noses, in their own home, or whether it was in some seedy dockside hotel (where trysts between dark-skinned sailors and white women were regular occurences, no questions asked) or whether my conception was al fresco during that long hot summer of 1929, I cannot say. Unsurprisingly, it never featured in any conversations I ever had with my mother (my father having long gone by the time I was old enough to be curious).

By the end of August, Maka and his team left Cardiff for a brief tour of England and only returned for a few days in October before embarking on the long sea journey back to New Zealand. Whether the Weinsteins noticed Sarah's lingering goodbye to Maka as they saw them off at the bus station, I do not know. All I can say is that, when Sarah announced to them a few months later (about the time, I imagine, when it was becoming difficult to hide her burgeoning bulge) that she was pregnant, they were predictably devastated. She resisted their demands to be told the identity of the father and whether he was aware of her condition. Their natural assumption was that it must be one of her Oxford upper-crust beaus and they took a crumb of comfort in the belief that, once her condition was made known to the young man's family, they would be forced to agree to a speedy marriage to avoid a scandal. Of course, such a damage limitation exercise would not be possible if Sarah continued to refuse to name the culprit and, despite all their remonstrations, continue to refuse she did.

In the meantime, she had written to Maka to tell him the news that she was expecting a baby. If it was any other young woman in my mother's position, you would surmise that she was putting a brave face on it – that her assertion of independence was actually a veiled plea for her lover to jump on the first ship back to Wales and rush to her side. But, if that's what you are thinking, dear reader, it's because you didn't know my mother. And why should you? I've told you very little about her. It's time for me to put that right.

I've established that she was an Oxford educated independent woman who was determined to carve out a life and career for herself in direct antithesis to that desired by her parents. A young woman who was not going to settle for the easy life of a Jewish wife and mother in the cossetted surroundings of her family's affluent middle-class community. No – she was very much a product of the post-suffragette era – a part of the 1920s flapper society. Not that I want you to picture her as one of those Charlestoning young women with cropped hair, bright red lipstick and short flouncy dresses. She was not conventionally beautiful and photos of the time do not do her justice. Her attractiveness was more a matter of personality than physical appearance. She was of average height for a woman with a solid bosomy figure and long lustrous black hair. Her nose was slightly too big for her face, her lips were thin and pinched, her best feature being her wide brown eyes. She dressed fairly conservatively for the period, not adopting slacks until much later in life. No, it wasn't her appearance that cast her as a typical feminist in the mould of Virginia Wolf or Vera Brittain; it was her wit, energy and intelligence.

As I never really knew my father, it's hard to imagine what he saw in Sarah Weinstein. As a Maori growing up in an impoverished area of Auckland, I'm sure he would never have experienced a woman quite like her. It wasn't just that she was white and Jewish, although that would have been strange enough. In every other way, she must have seemed like a creature from outer space. Her domineering personality and scalding tongue would have sent most young Englishmen, especially those of the Jewish persuasion, scampering for cover. So, it's hard to conjecture why Maka Felatu didn't do the same. I guess that, growing up as a Maori in New Zealand was a battle – often literally as rival street gangs fought it out on the back streets of South Auckland. From my subsequent researches into his background, I discovered that my father had a troubled childhood and spent time in juvenile institutions for various crimes including assault and robbery. Like many young Maoris of his size and athleticism, he found salvation in rugby. But, even when he established himself as an international rugby star, he still had to contend with racist attitudes. Like my mother, he was never one to accept the status quo, thus fighting racism within international rugby by forming the all-Maori team. And so, it is only conjecture but, having had to overcome so many challenges in his life, perhaps he saw Sarah Weinstein as just another mountain to climb. Maybe he saw my mother as a fearsome lineout opponent who needed to be conquered. Yes, maybe that was it. After all, what triumph is there in wooing and dominating a traditionally compliant domesticated woman? Whereas, if he could disarm and win over a liberated forceful woman like Sarah, then that would be a battle worth winning.

So, just when my mother was giving up on ever hearing back from her Maori paramour, a letter arrived. It was eloquently written for such a poorly educated man. (I found it among my mother's belongings when I was sorting through them after her death. The fact that she had kept it all those years shows that, deep down, she was more sentimental than she seemed during her lifetime). In the letter, he expressed his love for her, his delight at the news of her pregnancy and, despite being half a world away, his determination to stick by her.

The letter must have come as a surprise to her. I don't think she ever expected to see or hear from him again. Although I've never seen the letter she originally sent to him, knowing my mother, I have always assumed that she did not send it out of any feeling of desperation – a lover's plea for him to return and be by her side. No, I believe she wrote it out of a simple sense of duty – even politeness. She would have felt he had a right to know that he was about to become a father.

If I am right, then what did she expect would happen when he received her letter? Certainly not that he would jump on the first available ship and return to Wales – which is indeed what he did.

Oh dear. I can see that, despite what I have told you about my mother, you are still sceptical. How could a young woman of her background and education get herself into such a situation? What was she thinking? Surely, I must be wrong. Her letter must have been a plea of impassioned love. She wanted him back. Surely, she must have wanted what would be best for the child – to be brought up in a secure family environment with two parents? Because, if this wasn't what she wanted, then wouldn't her family have had both the means and the connections, albeit that it was of course illegal, to arrange for a professional and safe abortion in a discrete private clinic? Wouldn't that have been a more sensible solution for the daughter of a wealthy family than bringing up a mixed race child on her own in 1930s Britain?

As I have already said, my mother never talked about any of this and I never managed to summon up the courage to ask her about it. But I've given it a lot of thought over the years and, knowing my mother as well as I do, I think the following assumptions are more than credible.

I think Sarah Weinstein knew exactly what she was doing when she had sexual relations with a Maori and got herself pregnant. It's no surprise that she was sexually attracted to such a strikingly handsome athletic figure. But it wasn't Maka that she wanted – it was his baby. I don't think she ever truly loved him or expected to see him again once he'd returned to New Zealand. Nor was she motivated by the desire to bring a new life into the world. She would have given short shrift to any suggestion that she was fulfilling some overwhelming biological urge to procreate.

No, this was not about Maka or their child – this was about herself. She was laying down a marker for her future – an action that would forever label her as different – a non-conformist, a rebel. Far from ruining her life and blighting her future, as it would have for most other young women at that time, she saw it as the making of her. How can I explain it? My mother was a woman who never took the easy option. She thrived on conflict and adversity. I can only illustrate what I mean by using a joke I remember from years ago. A wealthy man arranges to play golf with some business associates. When they get ready to tee off, instead of a bag of expensive golf clubs, he prepares to strike the ball with his umbrella. The other golfers are surprised but too deferentially polite to question him. He continues to use the umbrella for the whole round – for driving, chipping and putting. And, despite this handicap, he's the best player and easily wins the round. Back in the clubhouse, one of his associates can no longer remain silent and asks him about the umbrella. He explains that, throughout his life, he has excelled at everything he turned his hand to, whether it was sports, the arts or business. But he soon grew tired of winning and achieving all his goals so easily and so he started to handicap himself to make things more of a challenge – hence playing golf with the umbrella. The other men looked at each other, hesitant and somewhat embarrassed. Finally, one starts to speak.

"I hope you don't think I'm being too intrusive but how do you…what do you…"

"Not at all," he interrupts. "It's a question I'm often asked. The answer is – standing up in a hammock."

And that's the best way I can sum up Sarah Weinstein's life. Starting with my conception and birth, she tried to do everything standing up in a hammock.

Of course, my mother's prevarication over the father's identity could only continue for so long. Once she had given birth, her parents' speculations as to the most likely sire would be instantly thrown into confusion as they stared down at the infant's face. Whatever shock they had felt at receiving the initial news of their daughter's pregnancy would pale into insignificance at that moment. For how long would they stare in disbelieving horror at my chubby brown body before their brains would start to register the father's true identity – or, at least, narrow it down to one of three? Therefore, as her due date approached, Sarah dropped a double bombshell on her parents. First, she announced that she was moving to London to stay with her university friend, Lydia. Before her mother could utter her first words of protest, Sarah explained in her inimitably forceful business-like manner that Lydia lived in Bloomsbury, very close to the central Middlesex hospital which had a world-renowned maternity unit and she had already made arrangements to give birth there. As soon as her mother could get a word in, she protested that Cardiff General was a perfectly reputable hospital and, more importantly, she must realise how stressful and exhausting it was to leave hospital and return home with a new-born baby. It is then that she would need the support of her mother and her wider family. Staying with a friend in some squalid bedsit in London was not an adequate substitute. It was then that Sarah dropped the second bombshell on them. That was why she didn't want to give birth in Cardiff and bring her baby up in the Pontcanna family home. She did not want to see them, the rest of the family or their neighbours staring in barely disguised distaste at her black baby.

By the time I had been delivered into the world and was ensconced in the flat in Guildford Street, Bloomsbury, my father was still aboard ship halfway through the thirty-five day journey from Auckland. Life for myself and my mother in those first weeks after my birth was very different from that envisaged by my grandmother. The Guildford Street apartment was as far removed from her image of a squalid London bedsit as could be. My mother's friend, Lydia, was the daughter of wealthy Devonshire landowners who had bought the Bloomsbury apartment as a rarely used London pied a terre. It had three spacious bedrooms, two bathrooms, an enormous reception room and a separate dining room, a roof garden and a daily maid to look after all the cleaning, cooking, shopping and laundering. So, even the imminent arrival of a six foot six inch Polynesian man would not put an undue strain on the household.

When Naomi Weinstein answered the knock on the door of her Pontcanna house on a cool drizzly afternoon in June of 1930, the last person she expected to see on her doorstep was a towering Maori man, looking damp and uncomfortable in his brown gabardine raincoat, clutching a bulging carpet bag in his right hand. She stared at him in disbelief. He waited nervously for her to speak first.

"What are you doing here?" She finally blurted out.

It wasn't what he had been expecting. He thought it was obvious why he was there. He didn't know what to say. He peered over the top of her head into the hallway towards the staircase at the far end, hoping that Sarah would appear and rescue him from this embarrassing situation.

"I've come to see Sarah," he said, hoping that Mrs Weinstein would put an end to this awkwardness and invite him in, but all she did was stare at him as if struggling to make sense of what he was saying.

"Look, I'm really sorry about what has happened," he continued. If he had been nervous when she'd first opened the door, he was now growing positively panicky. Was it possible that Sarah hadn't told her parents that he was coming? Had she even told them that he was the father of her child? "I understand how you must feel about me... and about what's happened between me and Sarah, but I've come back to make things right. I promise you that I will do my very best to provide for Sarah and the baby."

She still showed no sign of inviting him inside.

"Sarah's not here," she pronounced bluntly. "She's living in London. She doesn't want us to visit. She doesn't want us seeing the baby." There was a catch in her voice. She was fighting back tears. "I don't think there's anything else we have to say to each other." She closed the front door.

Maka stayed where he was as if expecting the door to re-open. He could only think that she was lying – that she didn't want him having anything to do with her daughter and just wanted rid of him. Sarah must be hidden away somewhere inside the palatial six-bedroomed house. He glanced at the bay windows on either side of the front porch on the off chance that he might see Sarah's face staring out at him, but there was nothing – not even the twitch of a curtain. He walked around the side of the house, past the kitchen door, to the back and stood below what had been Sarah's bedroom window last summer.

"Sarah! Sarah!" But still no face at the window. No sound of a baby crying. He shouted out her name again and, this time, Abel Weinstein appeared from the side of the house glaring angrily at him.

"My wife has already told you that Sarah's not here. I think you should leave immediately or I will be forced to call the police."

"I know you must hate me and I've said how sorry I am for what's happened, but I've travelled thousands of miles to be here. I have a right to see my baby." And then a thought suddenly occurred to him. "Is it a boy or a girl?"

Abel Weinstein half laughed, half grimaced. "So, she hasn't told you. Typical. It's a boy. But you can't see him because, as my wife has already told you, they are not here." He enunciated those final words in a slow staccato voice.

Maka stood frozen to the spot not knowing what else to do or say. Abel Weinstein saw his confusion and his anger relented slightly, replaced with the merest smidgeon of sympathy.

"Have you been in touch with her?" He asked. "Did she know you were coming?"

"Of course," Maka said, still struggling to understand what was going on. "How else would I know she was having our baby?"

Abel stared up at him with growing sympathy. "And she didn't tell you that she's not living here anymore? That she's moved to London?"

"No." Maka paused, a puzzled look on his face, searching for an explanation. "Maybe the letter got delayed or lost in the post."

"Or maybe she cares as little for you as she does for her parents," Abel said. "Anyway, that's for you and her to sort out."

He turned to go back into the house.

"Wait. Do you know where she's living in London? Do you have an address for her?"

Abel turned around to look at him and heaved a sigh. He turned back to the house, went inside and returned a minute later and thrust a piece of purple note paper into Maka's hand.

"I won't ask you to send her our love because she's made it clear she doesn't want it. Good luck. You're going to need it." He turned sharply on his heels and went back indoors.

I have recreated the above scene in some detail to illustrate what was to be only the first of the embarrassments my father would suffer at my mother's hands on his return. However, I am not going to attempt to recreate the scene between Maka and my mother when he finally turned up at the door of the Guildford Street apartment the following day. Whether he was right about a letter from Sarah having gone astray and, therefore, it was a cordial reunion, the embarrassment of his trip to Cardiff explained away as a simple miscommunication, I do not know. My suspicion is that my mother had shown a calculated disregard for the father of her child and had either forgotten or not even bothered to inform him of her change of abode. Whatever the reason, it was clear evidence of her ambivalent feelings about him returning to be by her side.

Suffice it to say that, whatever the real cause of the misunderstanding was, it was an inauspicious start to our family life.

# Friday 26th September 2001

"Sorry for the delay, ladies and gentlemen. We're being held at a red signal while we wait for the train ahead to vacate the platform. We'll be on the move shortly."

Becky Stone sighed with exasperation and looked down at her watch. Typical. Just when she was at the end of a long and stressful day, was tired, hungry and thirsty and wanted to get home as quickly as possible. And to make matters worse, there was no charge in her phone so she couldn't even contact Richard to tell him she'd be even later than expected. She could only hope that he'd got home from work at the usual time and had a meal prepared and a bottle of red wine opened for whenever she finally arrived.

She'd spent the whole day enclosed in the stuffy British Library poring over documents for her research for an exhibition she was helping to prepare for the Museum of London. Her job at the museum was temporary – a kind of internship – the first job she'd managed to get since leaving university four years earlier in which she could put her History degree to use. If a full day literally sweating over often hard to decipher documents wasn't bad enough, she had then had to drag herself back to the museum for a meeting to update progress on the exhibition. Like all such meetings, several tedious pedants droned on and on about the work they were doing. Reluctantly, she was forced to admit that she had been one of them, but at least she had an excuse. She needed to take every opportunity to impress if she was going to convert this into a permanent position.

She had had to ignore the frequent, irritating comments from her parents, and sometimes even from Richard, that it was about time she gave up holding out for some non-existent job in which she could be a serious Historian and settled instead for a solid, and properly remunerated, career. How about teaching History in a secondary school? You could use your skills and learning doing that, couldn't you? And what could be more rewarding than passing on your passion for your subject to future generations? She would always close such conversations down as quickly as possible. No, sorry, not cut out to be a teacher. Not enough patience. What she didn't go on to say was that, whenever the subject of a teaching career came up, all she could think about was the History lessons in the junior years at her comprehensive where her enthusiasm to learn was too often frustrated by the bored, disruptive behaviour of some others in her class. Her saintly teacher, Mrs Peters, was the very soul of forbearance. That could never be her, Becky thought. She'd strangle the little bastards.

"Ladies and gents, may I have your attention. I'm afraid there's a problem on the train in front of us. Someone has been taken ill. It means we're going to be stuck here a while longer. I apologise for the inconvenience. I'll keep you updated on developments."

Great. It was at times like this that Becky wished she lived anywhere else but London. She even felt nostalgic for her childhood home in Harrogate, although she only had to think back to the last tedious weekend she'd spent there visiting her parents to realise that she was so much better off where she was now – even with the frustrations of London Transport and the unaffordable housing. She looked around the carriage at the other passengers. They all seemed far less flustered than her – several of them on their mobile phones telling their loved ones they were stuck on the train. She needed to calm herself down. Find a distraction to vanquish the boredom and make the time go quicker. She reached into her bag to get out the novel she was reading but found herself scanning the same opening paragraph of the chapter she was on several times. She realised she wasn't going to be able to concentrate and put it back in her bag. Instead, she reached across the back of the seat and retrieved a discarded *Evening Standard*. She very rarely bought or read the *Standard*, finding it a tedious rag with precious little news in it and only occasionally picked one up if, like now, it had been left on the train. Even though it was now two weeks since the horrific terrorist attack on the Twin Towers in New York, it was still frontpage news. Becky couldn't help feeling that, as major an event as it had been, the media were now milking it for all it was worth. How many times did they need to repeat that film of the planes flying into the buildings? It was losing its shock value. The more she saw it repeated on the TV News, the more it was starting to look like a scene from an aliens attacking New York science fiction movie. She flipped through the inside pages of the paper in the hope of finding something to keep her occupied for a while, even if it was only to see if there was anything on television later that she could sink mindlessly in front of when she finally got home.

Skipping through the endless celebrity gossip and page after page of adverts, she almost missed the one interesting news story tucked away at the bottom of an inside page. It was the headline that grabbed her attention – 'Francis Bacon Model Found Dead'. It captured her interest because, coincidentally, the exhibition that she was researching was on the history of Soho and the specific period she had been assigned was the 1950s-1960s artistic scene centring round the likes of Francis Bacon and Lucien Freud. Unfortunately, the report was short on details and there was no accompanying photograph.

*Police were called to an address in Harlesden in the early hours of Wednesday morning when a passer-by out walking his dog found a body on the pavement. It has been identified as that of Harry Felatu, a single man in his sixties living in a third floor flat above where his body was found. Police are treating the death as suspicious although it would appear that Mr Felatu died in a fall from his open bedroom window. Harry Felatu was best known as a friend of the British painter, Francis Bacon, and had been a model for several of his paintings.*

Becky re-read it slowly as if a more careful perusal might elicit more information. What she realised was that she had a double connection with the story. Not only her research but also the location – she lived in Harlesden. She wondered exactly where the body had been found. She hadn't noticed any police activity on her way from the flat to the station that morning but then Harlesden covered a wide area. She swirled the name Harry Felatu round inside her head for a while to try and find a spark of recognition. It wasn't the kind of name you could easily forget. She tried to sift through her memory of all the documents, videos and photos she'd looked at in recent weeks to see if she could summon up some reference to this mysterious character, but it was no use. She'd need to trawl through them again in the British Library.

Just as she was tempted to get her laptop out of her bag and start checking through her plethora of notes and documents, the driver announced that the platform was now clear and apologised once again for the delay. The train chugged forward into Kensal Green station. Now Becky had a more urgent reason than simple sustenance to hurry home.

"Why don't you come and sit down and relax? You've

been stuck all day in front of a computer screen. Give yourself a break. I wouldn't mind but they're paying you bugger all for all this research you're doing. They can hardly expect you to be still at it at ten o'clock at night."

Becky was sitting at the dressing table in their bedroom googling Harry Felatu when Richard came in, attempting to drag her away. By the time she'd got back to the flat, he'd already eaten and her share of the lamb stew was being kept warm in the oven. She'd consumed it quickly, barely exchanging a word with Richard before disappearing into the bedroom with her laptop and a large glass of red wine. Richard had been expecting her to join him on the sofa in front of the *News at Ten* and it took him a while to realise what she was doing.

"So, what kind of day have you had, Richard?" He said mockingly as he watched her unresponsively clicking away on the laptop.

"Oh, I'm sorry." She finally looked up from the computer screen. "I didn't mean to ignore you. It's just that I spotted something strange while I was stuck on the train – something that might have a connection with my work."

She reached down into her bag and fished out the copy of the *Evening Standard* and turned to the news item. "Have you heard anything about this?"

"I've heard about it in general but why would I be interested in a row about some rich arseholes excavating a basement in Kensington?"

"No, not that. The story at the bottom of the page."

He browsed through it. "Okay. So, it's somewhere round here. No. I can't say I've heard anything but then why would I unless it was actually in this street?"

"Don't you see the connection?" Becky was tired and realised it was making her tetchy. "Sorry. I didn't mean to snap at you. I'm so wrapped up in all this stuff. It's my research on Soho. Francis Bacon and all the other artistic habitués of the drinking clubs. The article says that this man was connected to Bacon but I've never heard of him. I'm just trying to google him to see what I can find."

Richard gave a theatrical sigh. "Because, I suppose, at midnight all the internet references to this man will suddenly disappear like Cinderella's coach and horses. Surely it can wait until the morning. You're tired. You need your beauty sleep."

"I'm not going to spend long on it. There's very little to look at anyway. You go to bed if you want. I'll join you shortly. You know how it is when something really captures your interest like an itch you just can't resist scratching?"

"No, I can't say I do but then that's because I'm me and not you" He bent down and kissed her on the forehead. "I guess I'll see you in the morning."

It was at times like this, when she was so wrapped up in her own interests, that she seriously questioned how she and Richard were still together. They were so different. He was a science graduate and, although they had some things in common – a love of hill walking and adventure sports – when it came to matters artistic and literary, there was very little common ground. She was an avid consumer of Victorian novels and heavy historical tomes whereas Richard never read much beyond crime and science fiction potboilers. She had long ago given up trying to induct him into high culture. His only response to the one opera she'd dragged him along to was "that's three hours of my life I'll never get back". But then that was also one of the things that first attracted her to him – his honesty. Most people would consider him too honest. Not worth asking him what he thought of your new hairstyle if all you wanted was some insincere flattery. Instead, Richard would study it forensically from every angle before making a pronouncement that, even if it wasn't wholly negative, would include the minuses as well as the pluses. She would often sum him up to her acquaintances as a typical Yorkshireman, although she feared that southerners might interpret it as code for a misogynist. Fortunately, despite his northern bluntness, he was soft and affectionate – and, as a bonus, very good-looking.

Anyway, they were still together and, when she considered the seemingly more compatible relationships entered into by her university chums, none of which had lasted, she felt there might be some truth in the old adage that opposites attract.

Before Richard interrupted her, she had discovered, to her surprise, that there was an entry for Harry Felatu on Wikipedia, the recently set up online encyclopedia, so, once he had departed, she turned her attention back to the laptop and clicked on the entry on the Google search page.

*Harry Felatu (a.k.a Hare Yehuda Felatu) born in 1930 in Bloomsbury, London. His father was the New Zealand Maori rugby all-black Maka Felatu and his mother, Sarah Weinstein, was from a wealthy Jewish family. His parents met when his father was on a rugby tour of Britain. His parents split up shortly after his birth and Harry was brought up by his single parent mother.*

*He was educated at the Royal Grammar School High Wycombe and, after the end of the war, he left home and went to live in London, taking up a variety of occupations including night club bouncer and racing tipster, At six foot six inches tall and weighing two hundred and fifty pounds, he was an imposing figure who soon attracted attention when he began to frequent the Soho drinking dens in the early 1950s. He was befriended by the painter, Francis Bacon, who made use of him as both a model and a bodyguard. He has been identified as the figure in two Bacon paintings – 'Polynesian Man in a Headscarf' and 'Reclining Naked Blackman'.*

*His only other claim to fame is as the author of a novel 'An Angel in the City of Sin'. Set in Soho, it is a kind of female rake's progress, also described by one critic as 'Fanny Hill for the twentieth century'. It tells the picaresque story of Mary Cregan, a young Irish girl, coming to London as an au pair, who gradually descends into a life of debauchery leading to her premature death. With its realistic depictions of Soho's lower depths mixed with elements of drug and alcohol infused fantasy and mysticism, some later critics championed it as a precursor of magical realism. Because of its explicit sexual content, no British publisher would touch it, but it was published in 1956 by the Olympia Press in Paris and gained some notoriety though few sales.*

*It was republished as a Panther paperback in 1968 and, this time, found a cult following within the London underground hippy scene. This brief period in the spotlight culminated in an appearance on an early edition of Late Night Line Up on BBC2 where he was interviewed live about his novel by a young Joan Bakewell. No tape of the interview survives but it is rumoured that Felatu was drunk and the interview was brought to an abrupt close.*

*From the 1950s to the 1980s, he continued to be a regular in the Soho pubs and drinking clubs such as The Colony Room, The Coach and Horses and The French Pub, still mixing with members of the artistic community.*

*For most of his life Felatu has been a figure in the Soho*

*shadows – a hanger-on, an exotic ornament. Little is known about his life since then although it is believed that he is still living in London.*

Other google references either referred to his novel (two second-hand copies were available through Amazon from an independent bookshop in San Francisco) or to his father's rugby career. There were also numerous images of Francis Bacon paintings that were said to feature him, but no actual photographs of Felatu.

Having spent the past month trawling through acres of print and hundreds of photographs of Francis Bacon, Lucien Freud and their bohemian friends, she was certain that she'd seen no reference to Harry Felatu – and his wasn't the kind of name or appearance that was easily overlooked. On the other hand, there were so many weird and wonderful characters propping up the bars in places like the Colony Room, the York Minster and the Coach and Horses that even a giant half-Jewish, half Maori man might go unnoticed. And the Wikepedia entry had suggested that he was 'a figure in the shadows'.

Anyway, Richard was right. She was tired. Best leave it till tomorrow. Then, her first task would be to make a more thorough search through the documents at the British Library to see if she could find any reference to this man.

# An Extract from
# The Autobiography of an Invisible Man

## MY EARLY YEARS

I am still uncomfortably aware, dear reader, that, despite my earlier protestations, I am giving you a misleadingly negative impression of my mother and my relationship with her. Even at this early stage of my story, I feel it necessary to state in unequivocal terms that I always loved my mother and I bear no grudge against her either for the manner of my conception or for the part she played in banishing my father from my life.

To fully sympathise with her, you have to imagine what it must have been like to be Sarah Weinstein – an artistic intellectual young woman with a new exotic baby, living in the heart of Bloomsbury in the early 1930s. She must have felt she had been transported to paradise. Soon she was using her contacts from her time writing for the Oxford University newspaper to kick start her journalistic career in London. Within months of my birth, I would be sucking contentedly at her breast as she took tea with the likes of Vera Brittain and Winifred Holtby (who both lived around the corner in Doughty Street) while they discussed women's rights and the political situation in Germany. As I slept in my pram, she would wheel me around the local bookshops or I would be left in Lydia's loving capable hands while she researched her latest political diatribe in the British Museum Reading Room.

And so, it does not take much imagination to predict the effect that the arrival of a six foot six inch Maori rugby player would have on this idyll. Fish out of water. Bull in a china shop. None of these clichéd metaphors can adequately describe how out of place my father was in this female intellectual world. Not so much a fish out of water – more a fish drowning in water. I could paint you a more detailed picture of Maka hovering in the background among the bluestockings at my mother's Guildford Street soirees but I do not think it is necessary.

Again, I find myself in danger of giving you the wrong impression, dear reader. My father may not have had much of an education and certainly could not be called well-read, but he was literate and he was no fool. As I was to learn about him subsequently, during his travels with the New Zealand rugby tourists, he would take every opportunity to widen his horizons, visiting art galleries and museums wherever he went and familiarising himself with European culture. Even so, there was no hiding the fact that his social world was one of post-match male camaraderie, downing beers at the club bar, rather than tea and cakes at Bloomsbury literary gatherings.

When he thought he was going to be living in Cardiff, he had been proactive in sending a telegram to the coach of the Cardiff Blues rugby club asking if they would be interested in signing him for the following season. The reply was instantaneous. This was the 1930s so it was not common for the stars of southern hemisphere rugby to be playing in the UK, but the opportunity to have an All-Black in their team was too good to be turned down. Then, when he found himself unexpectedly relocated to London, Maka wasted no time in contacting the London Wasps who were equally alacritous in securing his services. This was very much the era of amateur rugby but, even in 1930, what later became known as shamateurism was already common practice. Although the club couldn't formally pay salaries to their star players, there were ways round this. Tobias Makepiece, the chairman of the Wasps' Board also ran his family's construction company, Makepiece Builders Limited, and he immediately hired Maka Felatu as a bricklayer at a very decent wage. It goes without saying that my father had no bricklaying skills and would never set foot on a building site.

Once pre-season training was underway, Maka was out of my mother's hair, spending increasing amounts of time at the Wasps' rugby ground and clubhouse in Sudbury, Middlesex. But it wasn't my father's arrival that was the chief disruption to my mother's halcyon days in Bloomsbury. Her stay in the Guildford Street apartment was only ever intended to be temporary. Even Lydia had only been allowed to use it for a brief period while she settled herself into post-university London life. Furthermore, I am fairly certain that Lydia's parents were not aware that she was sharing their London abode with an unmarried mother, her mixed-race baby and her Maori consort. So, when her parents announced they would be coming to stay in their Bloomsbury apartment, while there may have been room for Lydia to continue to live there, there was no way that my parents and I could stay. If it had just been my mother and I who needed rehousing, I'm sure Sarah would have found some way to stretch her meagre earnings from her writing to rent a scruffy garret somewhere in the vicinity, probably in dilapidated, but nearby, Kings Cross but, even with Maka's wage, it wouldn't be easy to afford a big enough flat. While my mother was struggling to find anywhere for us to live, my father (I believe without consulting her) announced that he had arranged to rent a small terraced house in Harrow – a convenient location for him, close to the Wasps' ground but, for my mother, a prospect that must have felt like being a Soviet dissident dispatched to the Gulag.

Despite her long and vociferous protests, she was forced to succumb to Maka's arrangement, having run out of time and alternative options. I suspect it was the first and last time that she allowed herself to be dictated to by a man.

This move was the beginning of the end for my parents' relationship. Sarah hated suburban Harrow. At every opportunity, she would bundle me into my stroller and join the serried ranks of early morning commuters on the train to Paddington from where she would head to Bloomsbury to spend the day with her friends. If necessary, she could leave me for the day with the likes of Vera Brittain or Winifred Holtby while she wrote her articles in the British Museum Reading Room. There were no such friends in Harrow that she could leave me with and there was no likelihood that she was going to make any. Whereas, in cosmopolitan Bloomsbury, a young woman with a coffee coloured baby, living with a giant Maori, was just one among a plethora of eccentric characters, in prissy conformist Harrow, wagging tongues and disapproving looks were the norm. It was a state of affairs that couldn't last.

Maka's first season with the Wasps started well but, after barely a dozen games, he picked up a nasty knee injury which was not only going to put him out of action for an extended period, but also threatened to end his career. From Sarah's point of view, what had, until then, been a difficult and frustrating existence, became unbearable. Maka was stuck at home for long periods and wanted to be looked after. He did not want Sarah gallivanting off at every opportunity to her bohemian friends in Bloomsbury. He wanted her at home, cooking his meals and being on call to meet his every need. Her response was typically combative – since he was going to be stuck at home all day, then not only could he look after himself, but he could also look after his infant son while she went to the British Museum to write her articles.

I was too young to remember the strife and unpleasantness that followed. I do not know what happened with the Wasps: whether, when it became clear that Maka's injury would sideline him for the rest of the season, Tobias Makepiece terminated his fictional employment with his construction company. All I do know is that, within six months of his arrival in England, Maka Felatu booked his passage back to New Zealand.

Identity crisis. It's one of those buzz phrases of the modern era. Everybody seems to suffer from it at some stage in their lives. Whether it's the crisis of masculinity in a world where women demand equality or gays and lesbians coming to terms with their sexuality or the dizzying variety of offspring from mixed race and religious marriages searching for a cultural identity as they grow into adulthood, it is happening all around us. All I can say to any of you out there who think you are struggling with an identity crisis is just pause as you read my story and imagine what it's been like to be me.

At least nowadays we have the sensible and politically correct term 'mixed race' to describe people like me. Back in the 1930s I was a half-caste – a misnomer suggesting that I was not a complete human being. And if, on top of a mixture of black and white, you stir in huge dollops of Maori and Jewish cultures, then my resulting confusion and otherness rockets off the scale. So, don't talk to me about identity crises.

Apologies for that short digression but I feel that it is especially appropriate at this point in my early life, Just as I was approaching my first birthday, I found myself fatherless

– and I would remain so for the rest of my life. Maka Felatu had removed himself to the other side of the world, never to return. I would never meet him again – never have a clear memory of him. His attempts to maintain contact were desultory. For a few years, there were birthday cards and the occasional Christmas present but, by the time I became a teenager, all communication ceased. I never questioned my mother about Maka. As far as I was concerned, I had no father. I have to say, as yet another defence of my mother, that she did what she could to keep some memory of Maka alive and never tried to hide my Maori antecedents from me. In fact, from the very start of my life, she made a conscious choice about my identity by specifying Maka as my father on my birth certificate and naming me Hare Yehuda Felatu. Mind you, as I grew older, I only had to look in the mirror and then look all around me to realise that I was different and to start asking questions. So, I guess, my mother didn't really have any choice. As I mentioned earlier, she briefly wrestled with the idea of renaming me Harry Weinstein when I reached my thirteenth birthday (a kind of secular alternative to a bar mitzvah, perhaps?), but she quickly rejected that idea.

Thus, I grew up with only a handful of mementoes of my father – my birth certificate, a framed photo of him in his all-black rugby kit and a rugby ball signed by the New Zealand team sent to me as a birthday present

Later in life, I tried to make contact with Maka and reconnect with my Maori roots but, by then, it was too late. He had died in Auckland in 1944 at the age of forty from liver failure due to alcoholism. He had married soon after his return to New Zealand and it was his widow, Emilia, who informed me of the details of his passing. He had restarted his rugby career but never fully recovered from his knee injury and only managed a couple of stop-start seasons playing for the Auckland Warriors before he was forced to retire. Like many sporting heroes of that era, he had made little money during his career and had no occupation to fall back on once it was over. Instead, his life revolved around the local bars where there were always rugby fans who would buy him drinks in exchange for listening to him recount the key moments in his career. Emilia did what she could to paint a picture of my father as a gentle giant – a kind and caring man. I took it with a pinch of salt, especially when she informed me that they had had a child together; Esther, my half-sister. I subsequently made some half-hearted efforts to maintain a correspondence with Emilia and Esther, but it soon fizzled out.

For the remainder of my formative years, it would be just me and my fiercely independent mother versus the rest of the world. Following Maka's departure, the immediate next step was to escape our stultifying, square pegs in round holes existence in Harrow and move back as close as possible to my mother's beloved Bloomsbury. This meant having to cram ourselves into a studio flat in the attic of a rundown terraced house in the Caledonian Road. Next, there was the question of how Sarah was going to find the money to support us. Her determination or, to put it more accurately, her downright stubbornness, to be independent and free from any family ties meant that she would not go to my grandparents for help even though, by then, they were doing everything they could to reconcile themselves to her situation and re-establish contact.

Instead, she worked hard to expand her journalistic opportunities, writing articles for a range of publications from the *Daily Herald* and the *Manchester Guardian's* women's page to *Peace News*. But the money she made from these articles only provided a meagre subsistence and she was forced to humble herself sufficiently to accept handouts from some of her wealthy Bloomsbury friends.

Despite this, my earliest memories are not of hardship or hunger but of a lively, stimulating sociable world. In elegant sitting rooms with walls festooned with oil paintings of severe, distinguished-looking men and women, I would spend happy hours squatting on Persian carpets playing with my building bricks and toy cars while Sarah and her friends sat nearby solving the problems of the world. While my mother was ensconced in various libraries researching and writing her pieces, I was looked after by a whole range of caring and affectionate bluestockings. They formed a dazzling extended family – a huge array of aunts and uncles to replace all my mother and father's relatives who I would never know.

Apart from those afternoons playing on the floor of those Georgian drawing rooms, my other vivid memories are of clutching my mother's hand tightly as we marched through the streets of London under a variety of multi-coloured banners surrounded by a familiar coterie of her friends. It might have been in support of the Jarrow hunger marchers or to agitate for women's rights or to protest against Italian atrocities in Abyssinia. There were very few socialist causes that my mother didn't throw her considerable energy into. As we marched along, surrounded by enthusiastic chanting crowds, banners fluttering in the wind, I would be patted on the head and fussed over. 'What a sturdy young chap,' my mother would be told. By then I was five years old and growing at a frightening rate. By the time I was nine, I was as tall as my mother, my father's genes obviously dictating my physical appearance. My mother's casual acquaintances or newer friends would be somewhat unnerved by me – by both my size and my skin colour: imagining that I was several years older than I actually was and, therefore, assuming that I must be retarded, they would give me pitying looks.

The one day that is imprinted firmly in my memory was the only demonstration my mother and I attended that was not made up of a small group of earnest socialists marching peacefully for some minority cause.

On this day, I was in the middle of the street being jostled and almost trampled on by a large crowd of angry shouting people. Minutes earlier, I had felt scared but secure in the midst of this tightly packed melee, clutching on to the belt of my mother's raincoat for dear life. But then, a phalanx of police, some on horseback, charged into the crowd wielding batons and, in the ensuing panic, I lost my grip and was suddenly on my own, being whirled round like a scrap of paper in the wind. I glanced all around but my mother was nowhere to be seen. Then the crowd parted in front of me and I found myself almost under the hooves of a rearing white horse being ridden by a snarling policeman swishing a long black baton in an arc just above my head. I was rooted to the spot, too scared to move, until I felt a pair of hands round my waist scooping me up from behind. They carried me out from under the horse's hooves and across the street into the shelter of a shop doorway. My rescuer was a squat, sweating, bald-headed man in a shabby blue suit. He knelt down to look into my terrified eyes.

"You alright, son?"

I nodded, tears pricking at the corners of my eyes. He looked me up and down as if checking for injuries. "You're a sturdy looking lad," he said. "Where you from?"

I couldn't reply. I was in shock – and, anyway, I couldn't remember where I was from.

"Do you speak English?" I nodded my head. "Are you here with your parents? Do you know where they are?" Again, all I could do was nod my head. No words would come. "Okay, let's get you somewhere safe."

He took me by the hand and led me through a back alley and along another street until we came to a building with a double doorway leading into a large hall. We stood in the doorway for several seconds surveying a scene which might have come from a Hieronymous Bosch painting. People with bloodied faces were sprawled across the floor, others were seated on kitchen chairs with their heads swathed in bandages, while some had their arms in slings. Women of various ages, shapes and sizes were bustling around with cups of tea. Soon I was seated in a corner with a piece of sponge cake on a plate in one hand and a cup of orange squash in the other. My rescuer had disappeared and an elderly plump woman with frizzy grey hair took control of me. She repeated much the same questions that the bald-headed man had asked, but I still couldn't respond.

It seemed an age before my mother arrived with her friend, Dorothy, and tearfully scooped me into her arms, smothering my face with her breasts. It was the only time I ever remember seeing her crying. She then turned to thank the woman who'd been looking after me. This was immediately followed by an altercation between my mother and the frizzy-haired woman. As far as I could make out, my mother had taken exception to the woman criticising her for bringing me to such a dangerous event and, presumably, either directly or by implication, questioning her parenting capabilities. I'm sure the woman was well meaning but Sarah Weinstein was always quick to assume that any criticism of her as a parent was actually a thinly veiled judgement of her morals as a single mother with a half-caste child.

And so, dear reader, there you have my small part in the Battle of Cable Street. It turned out to be, not only a seminal event in the history of the East End and the struggle against fascism in Britain, but also in mine and my mother's lives. However angry and defensive Sarah may have been in response to that old woman's criticisms, I think they must have made their mark. It was the last time my mother took me with her on a demonstration and, less than a year later, she abandoned our hand-to-mouth existence in the artistic milieu of central London and, reluctantly I assume, accepted the need to find a more financially and socially secure future for us.

# Monday 29th September 2001

The front door was opened by a bird-like woman with a candy floss bouffant of orange hair and a face so heavily caked in makeup that it formed an expressionless mask although, from the way she only held the door open a tiny crack, Becky assumed it hid a look of suspicion.

"Mrs Kaplanska?" Becky inquired.

"Yes," the woman said in a heavy Eastern European accent.

"I'm sorry to disturb you. I wonder if you could spare a few minutes. I'd like to speak to you about your recently deceased lodger – Mr Felatu."

"No. Sorry. I'm not speaking with the newspapers." She fired off the words as if she had become used to saying them and started to close the door. Becky leaned her arm against it to stop her. She had stood outside number 56 for several minutes trying to pluck up the courage to ring the doorbell. Now that she had done so, she was reluctant to walk away, even though she had doubts that this was either a good or a sensible idea.

"I'm not a newspaper reporter, Mrs Kaplanska, I'm a researcher. I work for the Museum of London and I have a particular interest in Mr Felatu as part of my research." As she spoke, she leaned more heavily against the door while, at the same time, fishing her museum identity badge out of her bag. She juggled around with the attached lanyard for a second before holding it in front of the pancaked face.

Mrs Kaplanska stared at the badge but continued to hold the door firmly in position. "We have already told the police all we know," she said. "He just lived upstairs. He was a tenant. We didn't know him much."

"I understand that," Becky said, grateful that the woman was no longer trying to push the door closed. "If I could just come in for a minute. I only have a couple of questions. However little you may know, it could be very helpful for my research."

She looked Becky up and down for several seconds, deciding whether to trust her and then opened the door fully and ushered her in.

Becky had spent as much time as she could spare during Saturday, after she and Richard had been food shopping and cleaned the flat, trawling through the research notes on her laptop and re-reading various articles and extracts she had photo-copied from books about 1950s Soho to see if she could find any references to a Harry Felatu. She had drawn a blank. And then, on Sunday morning, when she was in her local corner shop buying an *Observer*, she overheard the proprietor, Mr Khan, talking with another customer about the mysterious death of this strange man which had taken place just around the corner. When Becky went to the counter to pay for her newspaper, she joined in the discussion. Mr Khan, always keen to pass on any local gossip, divulged that the dead man had lived in Furness Road on the top floor of a house owned by the Kaplanskas. Mr Kaplanska, who was a good customer of his, placing a regular order for boxes of expensive Cuban cigars, had told Mr Khan all about the police investigation. With some subtle probing, Becky managed to get the full address from him.

And so, here she was, following the elderly Polish woman along the narrow hallway into a large sitting room jammed full of heavy, dark-stained wooden furniture and a faded brown leather sofa and matching armchairs. The room smelt of wood polish and an unidentifiable pungent flowery scent. As Becky perched herself on the edge of the not very comfortable leather sofa, a tall man dressed in a sharp grey suit with a red handkerchief, matching his red bowtie, poking from the breast pocket, came into the room.

"Who's this?" He barked at the woman.

"She works for…" She hesitated, trying to recall the identity badge.

"I'm a researcher for the Museum of London," Becky said. "I just want to ask a few questions about Mr Felatu." She held her identity badge out towards him.

"Huh," he said, not bothering to look at it but turning to the woman instead. "You're so gullible. You believe this nonsense. She's from the gutter press trying to dig up dirt." He turned back towards Becky and articulated his words slowly as if addressing someone mentally challenged. "We know nothing about this man. We regret we ever rented the rooms to him."

With his swept back grey hair greased flat on his head, horn-rimmed spectacles and pencil-thin moustache, he was the epitome of the distinguished gentleman – possibly ex-military, Becky thought. She assumed he was Mr Kaplanska and, judging by his air of authority and his aggressive manner, she expected his wife to be cowed by him but, when she turned to face him, Becky was surprised to see that she was quite the opposite.

"Victor, I have let her come in now, so please mind your own business and let us get on with our conversation. I thought you were going to the bank."

He was about to respond but thought better of it and just harrumphed his disapproval before executing a military-style turn and leaving the room.

"Never mind him. You were lucky it was me and not my husband who answered the door. He would have slammed it in your face. Now, what would you like to know?" Mrs Kaplanska slid back in the scuffed leather armchair, her feet dangling several inches above the floor.

"How long had you rented the upstairs to Mr Felatu?" Becky considered getting a notepad and pen out of her bag but decided it would make her look too much like a reporter.

"It must be nearly five years now."

"And can you tell me what he was like?"

Mrs Kaplanska hesitated for the merest second before answering. "He was very polite – an old-fashioned gentleman, if you know what I mean. When we first advertised the apartment, and he turned up, my husband and I didn't want to rent it to him." She paused as if waiting for Becky to ask another question but then continued. "Please understand, it wasn't because he was coloured. We're not prejudiced – although he was a bit…what is the word?"

"Strange, intimidating?" Becky offered.

"Intimidating. Yes. Scary. Being so big. You see, our policy was to rent only to young couples or women – never single men. They are more likely to be trouble. But he was not young and, like I said, very polite and well spoken. And he had the deposit in cash in his pocket."

"And was he a good tenant?"

"Oh yes. Always paid his rent on time. Never made any noise. He didn't have many visitors. Kept himself to himself – until this awful business, of course."

"So, he had some visitors? Do you think you could tell me about some of them? Describe them, perhaps?"

"No women," Mrs Kaplanska said before immediately adding, "not that we have any rules about women in the apartment. We may be old but we are quite modern – quite broadminded." She paused for thought. "There was one man who came a lot. About the same age as Mr Felatu. It seemed like he was his only friend. His name is Reznikoff.

I know this because he came to see us yesterday so that he could arrange to clear out Mr Felatu's things once the police have finished their investigation. This police investigation is most inconvenient. We can't do anything in the apartment. We can't clean it up and, of course, we can't advertise it for rent at all until this business is sorted out."

"So, apart from this Mr Reznikoff, were there any other visitors?"

"Not many people, as I said. Always men. There were two men who came together…let me think…it must have been two weeks ago. Very smart. In suits and ties. Not old. I think I had seen them here before, but they may have been different ones – just dressed the same."

"And did you know who they were? Did Mr Felatu talk about them?"

"No. We never talked much to him about anything. He minded his own business and we minded ours. They just looked like businessmen."

Becky wished she was a reporter. Then she would be better at this – know the right questions to ask to elicit that extra bit of vital information. Instead, she was trying to sound like the historical researcher that she was rather than a newspaper reporter or a policewoman. Nevertheless, she couldn't avoid asking the next question.

"Can you tell me what happened on the day he died? What you saw and heard?"

"We didn't see or hear anything," she said emphatically. "Fortunately, we weren't here that day. We were visiting my sister and her family in Reading. You can imagine the shock we felt when we got back. All the police and the yellow tape round the house. They wouldn't let us back in our own house. We couldn't believe it."

"And was there anything you noticed in his behaviour in recent weeks? Any changes? Did he seem depressed? Were there any signs that he might be planning to kill himself?"

"I told you. We hardly saw him except to say good morning when he went out the front door. Maybe we should have been more suspicious that he was so quiet and on his own so much." She flapped her hands in the air in a gesture of helplessness and frustration. "Yes. We should have been suspicious. We should have known there would be trouble. He was strange. Not normal. Now what are we going to do? If people know a man killed himself in the apartment then they won't want to rent it, will they? And then what will we do?" She shrugged her shoulders and waved her arms even more, her voice quavering on the edge of tears. Becky hoped she wasn't going to cry, picturing the gooey mess it would make of her face.

She gave her time to calm down before launching her next question. "Do you think there is any possibility that it might not have been suicide or an accident? Could someone have killed him?"

"Killed him? Murder, you mean?" Her voice rose to a higher pitch and her arms flapped more vigorously than before. "Who would murder him? You think he was murdered? Oh my God. I hadn't thought of that. Just imagine if me and Victor had been here. Maybe we would have been murdered too. Oh, I don't want to think about it."

"What's going on here?" Victor Kaplanska's looming figure had entered the room unnoticed behind Becky. He was staring at his distraught wife. "Young lady, how dare you upset my wife. I knew she shouldn't have let you in. I must ask you to leave immediately."

This time there was no reprimand from Mrs Kaplanska. She had pulled a handkerchief from her cardigan sleeve and gently dabbed her eyes. Becky didn't attempt to argue with Mr Kaplanska. Anyway, she couldn't think of anything else to ask.

"Thank you very much for sparing the time to talk to me," she said as she stood up to leave. "I'm really sorry if I've upset you."

"Just go," said her husband.

For the first time, Becky noticed that he had a heavy wooden walking stick in his hand which he now raised and waved dangerously close to her head.

She beat a hasty exit.

# Extracts from
# The Autobiography of an Invisible Man

## MY EDUCATION

"I think I can...I think I can...I think I can...I think I can."

Do you remember, dear reader, those first books your mother read to you as a child? If you do, then I'm sure some of you, like me, will remember *The Little Engine that Could*. It was one of those children's stories with a message designed to provide moral guidance for the rest of your life. My mother read it to me so often that the binding fell apart and she was constantly having to tape it together. Its story of the plucky little engine struggling, and succeeding, against the odds to pull the heavy train up a hill encapsulated how my mother was trying to bring me up. She knew life was going to be tough for a dark-skinned Jewish boy growing up in 1930s England. She anticipated the numerous obstacles that I would have to overcome to succeed in life – obstacles way beyond those faced by white Anglo-Saxon Christian boys. And so, she was always on the lookout for suitable books to read to me – books with a message about how to succeed against the odds. Books like *The Little Engine that Could*.

As a middle-class Jewish intellectual, it was no surprise that my mother would surround me with books. It was the first stage in her plan to turn me into a human version of *The Little Engine that Could*. She was determined that I should learn to read before I started formal schooling. Her reasoning was simple – as an oversized black six year old, on arriving in the classroom, I would face instant prejudice from both teachers and pupils. The teacher was bound to assume that I would conform to the standard stereotype and be of below average intelligence, therefore, my mother intended to dispel such low expectations as soon as I sat at my desk for my first reading lesson. I can picture her imagining with gleeful satisfaction the stunned look on my infant school teacher, Miss Eardley's, face when she placed the 'Dick and Jane' early reader in front of me and I read every word of it out loud to her.

And my mother's plan succeeded. Well, sort of. I arrived at infants' school having mastered the basics of decoding written language. Sadly, I have no memory of that moment when I showed an amazed, normally waspish Miss Eardley my precocious reading skills. Actually, there's a simple explanation for why I have no memory of it: it never happened. What did happen is that I deliberately subverted all my mother's hard work by keeping my advanced reading ability under wraps until my classmates had caught up with me and had started to decipher their first words in those early readers. Even at such a young age, I was sceptical about my mother's advice on how to succeed in life. She thought that I would stamp out any prejudice before it could arise by showing those around me that I was academically superior to them. Although I never attempted to discuss it with her, I surreptitiously rejected her plan. My reasoning was simple. I already felt physically very different from my classmates so why would I want to make myself stand out even more by being intellectually different.

My apologies, dear reader: I realise I have jumped ahead of myself. Here I am, sat in my infant classroom, at the start of my education and yet I haven't told you where I am.

From my previous chapter, you will naturally have made the assumption that I am in cosmopolitan King's Cross or Bloomsbury. You would be wrong. I am in a school in a village just outside impeccably white, prim and proper High Wycombe. How did Sarah Weinstein and I come to arrive there, you may ask? To be honest, I am not entirely sure. My assumption is that, after the aforementioned Battle of Cable Street incident, my mother was forced to seriously reconsider our situation – in particular, how she could earn enough money to support us both without having to rely on handouts from her wealthy friends.

As a result, through yet another of her Bloomsbury contacts, she was offered a job as a columnist and reporter for the *Bucks Examiner*, a local newspaper based in Chesham. This provided her with a small but regular income which she could supplement with her occasional contributions to publications such as the *Daily Herald* and the *Manchester Guardian*. Having already explained how difficult and frustrating Sarah found it living in suburban Harrow and how desperate she had been to return to her beloved Bloomsbury, you can imagine the enormous wrench it must have been for her to make this move to the Home Counties. Nevertheless, she bit the bullet and so, that is how you find a gawky six year old me squatting perilously on my tiny infants' classroom chair at Saint Paul's Church of England school in Wooburn Green on the outskirts of High Wycombe surrounded by thirty-four milky white-skinned open-mouthed children.

I am not going to spend much time reminiscing about my primary school years because, to be brutally honest, I remember very little about them. What most people tend to remember about their early school years are either the very happy times or very difficult, probably fraught, experiences. And that's the reason, I think, that I don't remember very much – because I was neither particularly happy nor unhappy at Saint Paul's and I have no really bad experiences to relate.

After their initial wariness, not to say downright fear, of the giant black boy who had suddenly appeared in their midst like some mythical ogre from an ancient fairy tale, they gradually became accustomed to my presence and, most importantly, realised that I was harmless. They became friendly. Well – almost. None of them became close friends. I was allowed to join in their playground games but I was never invited round to tea or to their birthday parties (although I suspect this was more to do with their parents' prejudices than their own). No, my chief problem at primary school wasn't the children or even the teachers. In fact, the teachers were very good to me and tried their best not to make me feel out of place (probably because they were relieved that such a hulking presence in their class was so polite and well behaved). The problem was my mother.

I recently read a report in the newspapers about so-called 'tiger mothers' who, I believe, are usually Chinese. Well, Sarah Weinstein was a tiger mother way before they even existed. If I could think of a more ferocious beast than a tiger then that would be an even more apt metaphor for my mother – but I can't think of anything more suitable. She was a frequent visitor to the school, either to speak to my class teacher or, more often, the headmistress. I never knew exactly what these visits were about except that I was sure that they couldn't have had anything to do with something untoward that had happened to me in school at that time or anything that I might have inadvertently told her, because I was very careful to tell her as little as possible, being only too aware of how easily the smallest hint of something not quite right at school would send her scurrying the following morning to the headmistress's office. In fact, these visits probably took place far more frequently than I was aware of. Since my mother was now a freelance writer working from home, it was very easy for her to abandon her typewriter at any time of the day and march through the school gates.

The only meetings that I was all too aware of, were the formal yearly ones – the parent-teacher consultation meetings – because she always insisted that I attended those with her. By the end of my first year in the school, my mother was well known to all the school staff whether they had taught me before or not. And so, as we took our seats opposite Miss … or Mrs … , whoever my class teacher was for that year, I would see said teacher start to wilt. This teacher, a domineering, sometimes scary, presence in the classroom, was suddenly diminished and cowed in anticipation of what was about to unfold in front of her. All these meetings followed a similar pattern. The teacher would begin by praising my behaviour (always exemplary), my politeness (ditto), my friendliness and gentleness with my classmates ("he's always so helpful") and …

It was at this point that my mother would interrupt. It would go something like this.

"Miss …, you don't have to tell me what my son is like. I live with him seven days a week. I know how well behaved and polite he is. That's the way I have brought him up. This place (she would turn and wave her hand theatrically round the hall) is not a social club or the boy scouts. It is, I believe, a school, so could you please inform me about his academic progress for which you are responsible and leave me to take care of his social and emotional development."

The teacher would then look even more discomfited and start to utter bland generalities about my progress in English, Mathematics and the various other areas of the curriculum. However hard they tried to praise my work and talk up my abilities, this was bound to be followed by a 'but'. In the history of education, there has never existed a student who, according to his or her teacher, didn't have room for improvement. But this was never good enough for Sarah.

"Miss … ," she would say, interrupting the teacher in full flow. "Are you not aware that you have an exceptional child in your class – namely, my son? (This time the hand waved at me as if inviting me to take a bow). "He could read and write before he even started at this school. Your job now is to nurture and enhance those exceptional qualities and it seems to me that, at present, you are failing to do so."

I won't go on. I trust, dear reader, that I have given you the gist of it. These consultations always took place in the school hall with all the teachers seated at tables placed round the edge with rows of chairs for the waiting parents and their offspring in the middle. My mother was not a softly spoken woman. Her voice never rose in anger. She was certainly never abusive. But her strong and strident voice could be heard across a wide area of the hall. It didn't take much for my mother and I to draw attention to ourselves. As I have pointed out repeatedly, we made a strange pair. The over-sized, shy dark-skinned boy and the small, white, effervescent mother

My mother's criticisms of the school and its teachers were always subtly worded. She would never directly accuse the teachers of racism or suggest that they might have lower expectations of me academically because I was an overgrown black boy. However, even without making such accusations directly, there was always something in her tone of voice and her skilful use of language that would have left them in no doubt that that was exactly what she was accusing them of.

At one point in my primary school career – I think it must have been when I was 8 or 9 – I overheard part of a conversation between my mother and her friend, Ana (bear with me, dear reader, I'll come to Ana shortly), in our kitchen. I was listening outside the door. After Sarah had launched into her habitual tirade against the school, she paused and, as if the thought had only just occurred to her, suggested to Ana that it might be a good idea if she removed me and undertook my schooling at home. After all, she continued, both you and I work from home so we could work together, taking it in turn to be in charge of his lessons. We are both very well educated and intelligent women – almost certainly far better educated than his teachers – so why shouldn't we be able to do a better job? I didn't stay to hear anymore, probably too horrified but, since nothing more was ever mentioned about the idea, I can only assume that, as was so often the case, the more sensible, practical and less volatile Ana must have talked my mother out of it.

Apologies for making another jump back in time, but I feel I should return briefly to the pre-school period and my mother teaching me to read with all those children's picture books with uplifting messages. She had not only searched for books like *The Little Engine that Could* but also ones that featured characters that I could relate to – namely, mixed race or black children. It will come as no surprise to you, dear reader, that very few such books existed in 1930s England – perhaps a few American ones, although they were not easily available. And so it was that Sarah Weinstein, never one for sitting back passively and waiting for things to change, made another key decision that would have a major effect on our financial future. She decided that, since there were no children's books reflecting the lives of people like us, she would write some of her own

Her first attempt was an instant success. *The Shareosaurus* was the tale of a mild-mannered, small and ungainly dinosaur who manages to persuade the tyrannosauruses, brontosauruses etc. to stop fighting each other and live together in peace and harmony. Once again, her university connections in the publishing world put her in touch with the Oxford University Press who snapped up the story and teamed her up with an illustrator, Ana Geisler, a Jewish refugee recently arrived from Vienna. Sarah quickly followed up this first book with *The Dog that Couldn't Bark* and *David is Different*, the story of a small black boy struggling to overcome prejudice, make friends and gain acceptance when his family moves from the inner city to a small rural town. A steady stream of books followed, all illustrated by Ana. Ana and my mother made such a perfect team that, before long, Ana's frequent working visits to our Buckinghamshire cottage became ever lengthier stays, until she moved in permanently. In the space of a few short years, Sarah Weinstein metamorphosed from being a Bloomsbury rebel with a Maori partner and a mixed race son into Home Counties' almost respectability with a new female companion. Of course, it wasn't actual respectability because, as you will have guessed, dear reader, my mother was now in a lesbian relationship. You can choose your own cliché. Out of the frying pan into the fire would be the most obvious. Now I was not only the odd one out as an oversized black boy in a school full of white kids; I was also, unsurprisingly, the only one with two mothers.

Once again, I am aware that the way I am presenting this change to our life might be misleading. Although I am sure that our neighbours in Wooburn Green were just as conservative and prejudiced as those in Harrow, outwardly they seemed far more accepting of two women sharing a house than I suspect they would have been if my black father and white mother had still been living together. When you consider that it had only been forty years earlier that Queen Victoria had refused to accept that lesbians existed, it was no surprise that the naïve inhabitants of the Home Counties would make no such inference from two women co-habiting, especially when one of them had a child.

And I was as unperturbed as the neighbours by this new domestic arrangement. It will come as no surprise to you, knowing my mother as well as I now hope you do that, no sooner was she sharing her bed with Ana, than she sat me down and explained the situation in the simple and direct manner that was her stock-in-trade. Sometimes men and women loved each other and lived together, she told me, but it was equally possible for two men or two women to fall in love and share a bedroom. So, from now on, I should consider Ana as a second mother.

As hard as I tried to search my memory for any negative reactions upon being told this – confusion, distress, resentment – all I can remember is being happy, even happier than I had been before Ana's arrival. I liked Ana. I liked her a lot – mainly because she was not Sarah Weinstein. In fact, in many ways, she was the opposite of my mother, both physically (she was tall, slim and fair-skinned) and emotionally (she was laid back and completely unneurotic). Before long, if I had any problems at school or any worries in general, it would be Ana I would go to for help and advice rather than Sarah because I knew that she would listen calmly and not rush into precipitate action, such as dashing to the school to confront the Headmistress. Plus, she was more affectionate and tactile. I think the problem for my mother was my size. I think she found it off-putting that I was now nearly as tall as her. It didn't mean that she stopped loving me, it was just that I must have now appeared to be too big for cuddles whereas Ana, being much taller, didn't have any difficulty with my size.

Every Saturday, my mother, Ana and I would go on a ritual shopping trip to High Wycombe town centre finishing up with my favourite bit – a visit to Ponti's ice cream parlour. Even though we must have seemed an odd trio, I cannot remember being stared at although, perhaps, it was because I had become so used to it over the years that I no longer noticed. High Wycombe may not have been the multi-cultural town it is now but, even in the late 1930s, there was a small Asian community.

The one time I did feel distinctly uncomfortable was when we attended the annual ceremony of the weighing of the Mayor outside the town hall. I don't know if they still keep up this ritual but, in those days, at the beginning and end of the Mayor's year in office, he would be weighed in public and the town crier would announce in a stentorian voice either 'and no more' or 'and some more'. I cannot remember which it was at the end of that particular year but, to my acute embarrassment, after the announcement, my mother shouted out 'you were a fat bastard before and you're still a fat bastard'. A policeman politely asked us to leave.

The pain was excruciating and I instinctively raised my hand to my stinging ear in a vain attempt to soothe it away. I should have been used to it by now. Such casually inflicted pain was a regular occurrence at the Royal Grammar School High Wycombe.

Sorry for any further confusion, dear reader, but I've made another unannounced leap forward. I am now eleven years old, we are in the midst of the Second World War and I have left the cosy ambience of Saint Paul's primary school for the infinitely more fraught world of the Royal Grammar School. As my time at Saint Paul's was drawing to an end, my mother was adamant that my educational future had to be at the prestigious grammar school and so she persuaded Mrs Toms, my primary school Headmistress, to put my name forward as a candidate to take the entrance exam. My mother was particularly impressed that T.S. Eliot had been a teacher there some years earlier – a fact that ensured that I have spent the rest of my life avoiding reading any of his writing. On this occasion, Ana fully supported her and they took turns every evening, in the run up to the exam, in putting me through a couple of hours of intensive coaching. Although I hated these sessions and came very close to openly defying both my mothers, it worked.

In the first week of September 1942, I made the tortuous first journey to my new school (two bus rides and a long walk), looking every inch the overgrown schoolboy in my navy blue blazer with red piping, my stripy school tie and my undersized cap balancing precariously on my oversized head. I was nearly six feet tall and towered over my classmates. I was not only uncomfortable in my already too tight uniform – I must have had a growth spurt since A.H. Jones, the school outfitters, had struggled to find clothes in my size – but also in my new surroundings. The very buildings were intimidating and the teachers terrifying. Added to all that was the fact that I knew hardly any of my fellow pupils. A few of my Saint Paul's classmates had arrived at the school with me, but I didn't count any of them as friends.

Although I couldn't say that I enjoyed my time at primary school or had any, what you could call, close friends there, compared to the Grammar School it was heaven. The Royal Grammar School would turn out to be purgatory. And so, I hope that explains why I have opened the account of my time there with the sadistic assault on me by Mr Jones, our Maths teacher. Before you jump to conclusions, I should explain that this was in no way racist on the teacher's part even though I was the only black boy in the class. I had simply been the latest boy to experience Mr Jones' unique form of punishment which he called 'elastication'. He had a desk drawer full of elastic bands of assorted lengths and thicknesses and, when he spotted one of his pupils misbehaving in some way or not paying attention, he would select one of a suitable size to fit the crime, approach the offender and twang it against his ear. During every lesson at least half the class would be twanged.

Very rarely were you given any reason for the infliction of this painful punishment. I can only remember one occasion when a boy was given advanced warning. Mr Jones interrupted his explanation of how to multiply fractions, walked behind his desk, moved his chair against the wall by the side of the blackboard, stood on it and drew an x with a piece of chalk in the upper corner.

"Tell me boy," he said to a small blond lad sitting in the front row when he had climbed down from the chair. "What is so fascinating about the place I've marked?"

"Nothing sir," replied the confused boy.

"Then why have you been staring at it for the last five minutes?" The twang of elastic band on ear swiftly followed.

Mr Jones was not alone in inflicting such punishments. He was just the most inventive in his choice of weapon. On occasion, (perhaps when there wasn't a suitable sized elastic band to hand) he would resort to the more common or garden methods used by his colleagues such as throwing chalk or blackboard erasers at our heads. However, unlike most other teachers, he never whacked outstretched palms with rulers or used the even more prosaic clip round the head with an open hand. It is a wonder that, to my knowledge, no student ever seems to have suffered a serious injury from such regular sadism. For our part, we students accepted it as part of school life as, I assume, did most of the parents. The exception, of course, would have been Sarah Weinstein, but I was careful never to complain to her about these punishments. I even resisted divulging these painful experiences to Ana for fear that she would tell my mother which would inevitably lead to an embarrassing confrontation at school between her and Mr Jones.

I can only remember one instance of student rebellion during my time at the school. Mr Timson, the Latin master's favourite punishment for talking in class was to make the culprit spend the rest of the lesson standing at the front of the classroom facing the wall with his hands on his head. Brian Bennet spent almost every Latin lesson in the aforementioned position until, one day, he must have had enough and, when Mr Timson was facing the rest of the class and could not see him, he turned to face us, took two pieces of chalk off the blackboard ledge and stuffed them up his nostrils. Most of us were too shocked to react to this comically thrilling act of defiance but a few boys burst out laughing and, by the time Mr Timson had delivered the flat of his hand to the side of their heads, Bennet had removed the chalk and turned back to face the wall.

I don't know much about modern day schools or their students but, from what I read in the newspapers, I suspect that our behaviour was, for the most part, exemplary and our occasional misdemeanours piddling in comparison. In those days, you didn't have to do much, or anything, to incur punishment. Get caught staring out the window – thwack. Not sitting up straight enough in your chair – slap. Peering at the boy sitting next to you – thump. Not quick enough to answer a question fired at you – wallop. Tie crooked – clout. Drip ink from pen nib onto exercise book – smack.

Despite their brutality, most of our teachers were viewed with affection. They all had nicknames related to their initials. Mr Jones was Pilgy because he was P. L. Jones and Mr Herbert was Torj as he was T. O. R. J. Herbert. The exception was the Headmaster, Mr E. R. Tucker, who was called Boss. In fact, it was a sign of a lack of respect, if not downright dislike, for a teacher not to be given a nickname.

If my life in the classroom was full of pain and misery, it wasn't any better outside. In truth, there was very little open racism. I was simply ostracised by the overwhelming white majority. An unofficial apartheid developed in which I was thrown together with the small band of Indian pupils and the one African boy. As the only black pupils in the school, he and I were sometimes referred to as Bosambo, the name of the Paul Robeson character in the recently released film *Sanders of the River*. The more obvious 'nigger' or 'darkie' were seldom used. Myself and an Indian boy called Sabir Ali were the only non-whites in our class and, as if we were joined at the hip, we automatically sat together in every lesson. In the gym changing room, we occupied the pegs in a far corner, several yards away from the rest of the class, as if we had been quarantined.

My mother was a confirmed atheist and had shown little interest in her Jewish heritage until a combination of her relationship with Ana Geisler and the outbreak of the war changed things. As horror stories of the treatment of Ana's remaining family in Vienna and that of other Jews in Hitler's growing empire reached her, she reclaimed her Jewishness as an act of solidarity rather than any rebirth of religious belief. And so, when filling in my entry form for the Royal Grammar School, under the heading 'Religion' she wrote 'Jewish'. The upshot of this was that my segregation from the other pupils was exacerbated. It meant that I was excused Religious Education lessons and was instead sent to the library. Along with the twenty or so other Jewish boys, I was also excused morning assemblies. Instead, we sat in a classroom doing private study in silence under the supervision of Mr Sullivan who, I assumed, was the only atheist teacher in the school. May 12th every year was Founder's Day when normal lessons were suspended for a day of special events. First there was a morning service at the local church from which, naturally, myself and the other Jewish and Asian boys were excused. We stayed at school and it became traditional to play a game of cricket. I was always the last to be chosen when the designated captains picked their teams. Even in this already ostracised group, I was an outsider. My Jewishness was frequently challenged or directly refuted by the other Jewish boys. Despite their badgering, I refused to explain my heritage assuming, I'm sure correctly, that it would have only provided further ammunition for their disdain.

During my first two years in the school, I was mostly ignored by the other students. Even the name calling and racist nicknames were only muttered behind my back. They were too wary of me. I was strange looking and I towered over them. But, as they got to know me better, their fear diminished. The catalyst for this came at the start of the third year when my recently appointed housemaster, Arby (A. R. B.) Collinson, called me into his office. I sat nervously in front of his desk, assuming that the only reason I would have been summoned to see him was because I was in some kind of trouble.

"Felatu. I wanted to talk to you about the check-up you had last week with the school nurse."

All pupils were examined by the school nurse at the start of every year. I say 'examined' but it was more a simple matter of weighing and measuring us, checking blood pressure and listening to our chests. Mr Collinson was turning over the pages of a cardboard covered file in front of him on the desk. I assumed it contained my school records.

"Her report suggests that you are perfectly fit and healthy," he continued. He paused as if expecting me to contradict this statement.

"Do you have any health problems?"

"No sir."

He sat back in his swivel chair and pressed his fingers together. His brow furrowed as if he was deep in thought. "This is a bit awkward, Felatu," he said hesitantly. "I don't want to cause any problems between you and your mother."

I hardly knew Mr Collinson. He'd only joined the school at the beginning of that term and this was the first time he'd spoken to me. It didn't sound like I was in trouble but, beyond that, I had no idea what this was all about.

"It's just that, looking at your records, to be specific the entry form your mother filled in when you joined the school, she wrote in the health section that you suffer from chronic asthma and, therefore, should not take part in outdoor sporting activities."

This was true. My mother had never encouraged me to take part in sporting activities and I never complained, realising, from an early age, that my size rendered me clumsy and uncoordinated. I was particularly keen to avoid ball games. In those days, there was no competitive sport in junior schools so my non-participation in such activities was not an issue. However, when I was informed that I had a place at the Royal Grammar School, my mother sat me down at the dining room table with the school entry forms in front of her and explained why she was including in the health section what she described as 'our little white lie'. The school, she explained, was mad about sport, in particular rugby, and, once they knew who my father was, they would have huge expectations of me as a sportsman. I would be put under great pressure. She knew that I hated sports and, therefore, she was using this small subterfuge to protect me from these misguided expectations. At the time, I was happy to go along with it. Of course, once I started at the school, I realised that it had a downside. It was one more thing that marked me out as different. On Wednesday afternoons, while my classmates muddily piled into each other on the rugby field, I stood wrapped up like a mummy on the sidelines watching.

"You obviously don't have asthma, Felatu. In fact, I doubt there's a fitter, healthier, more strapping lad in the whole school," Mr Collinson continued.

I hunched down in my chair looking away from him, trying to shrink myself into puniness.

"Are you a rugby fan, Felatu?"

"No sir," I replied truthfully.

His eyes narrowed as if he was in sudden pain.

"In my youth," he said, "I was a very good rugby player. In fact, I played several times for England. I once had the honour of playing against the New Zealand All-Blacks – against Maka, your father. He was a fantastic footballer. Virtually unstoppable once he got into his stride. You must be very proud of him."

I gave a half nod. I still wasn't sure where all this was going.

"You see, Felatu, at the Royal Grammar School our aim is to ensure that every boy reaches his maximum potential – academically, artistically and athletically. Because of your mother's wishes, we are not able to achieve this for you. When it comes to sporting achievement, you have immense potential with your inheritance from your father – your size and powerful build – potential that is going to waste."

There was another awkward silence while he looked me up and down, presumably admiring my potential.

He then sat forward and thumped his hand on the desk making his pen and pencils, and me, jump. "I'll stop beating about the bush. It's the start of the inter-House rugby competition in two weeks' time and I want you to play for Disraeli (purely coincidence, I'm sure, that of the four school Houses, this was the one I had been placed in). Now I know your mother won't approve but I don't see why, for the time being at least, she has to know. We can see how you get on in the House matches and, if you are as good as I'm sure you will be, we could look at drafting you into the school junior first fifteen. At that stage, we would probably have to tell your mother but, by then, I could tell her just how good you are and I'm sure she wouldn't want to hold you back from reaching your true potential."

Mr Collinson had never met my mother. I could have spoken up then and there – explained to him, with the utmost respect, exactly the kind of woman he would be dealing with – but I remained silent. He looked at me, awaiting a response. When he didn't immediately get one, he spoke again, this time more falteringly than before.

"Okay, I'm not going to force you to play rugby, Felatu. That decision has to be yours, so go away and think about it. If you feel you have to, then talk to your mother about it. If you decide you want to play, and you're happy to keep it a secret from her for the time being, then come back and let me know."

Immediately after I had left his office, I realised I didn't need to think about it. I was now old enough to understand how my mother's mind worked – how she wanted to bring me up. For her, there were other things in my heritage that were mixed as well as the obvious one of race. I had inherited from my parents a perfect combination of intellectual and physical prowess. At least, it should have been a perfect combination. But, for Sarah Weinstein, it wasn't a combination, it was a dichotomy. It was not mind and body, it was mind versus body, and she was determined that my rapidly growing body should be subordinate to my mind. Up until that moment in Mr Collinson's office, I had been happy to go along with that but, as I walked away down the corridor towards my maths lesson, I had an epiphany. Here was a chance to break free from the stranglehold my mother had over me and assert my independence. To decide for myself who I wanted to be or, in this particular instance, who I didn't want to be. I no longer wanted to be the outsider – the misfit. The only thing that Sarah could have done in the first two years at the grammar school to make me more isolated would have been to send me to school every day with long curly side locks, dressed in traditional Maori costume with 'alien' stamped on my forehead. Most of the things that set me apart from my schoolmates I couldn't change, but here was the one thing I could. My mother was the archetypal non-conformist and she had forced me to be the same. Now, at last, here was my chance to conform. I turned around, marched straight back into the office and announced my apostasy.

Thinking back to this decision, I now realise that I had another motive aside from my desire for acceptance. Academically, I was not doing that well. Now that I was in my middle years at the grammar school, it was becoming clear to me that I was never going to be much better than average in my studies. And, for my mother, average would never be good enough. I was never going to fulfil her expectations, therefore, if I was doomed to be an intellectual disappointment, why not give that other side of me – my body – a chance to achieve? She would still be disappointed but, maybe, just maybe, she would find some solace in my sporting achievements.

Two weeks later, on a cold Wednesday afternoon, as I lay face down in the mud with several smaller boys piled on top of me, I wondered what on earth I had been thinking. I had somehow managed to erase from my memory my cack-handed infant fumblings during playground games and persuaded myself that, as a powerfully built, six feet plus adolescent, things would now be different. After all, this was rugby, a game that, as far as I could gather from many hours stood watching from the touchline, was more about brawn than skill. Even Tubby Lomax, a fat boy in my class who was hopeless at all other physical activities, was a star forward in the first fifteen. Sadly, I was no Tubby Lomax. I rarely managed to hold on to that ridiculous oval ball when it was flung in my direction and, when I did, I was too lumbering and slow to escape speedy opponents who, by sheer weight of numbers, would cling on to me and bring me crashing to the ground. I may have had the size and the weight but I lacked one other vital ingredient – aggression.

I mentioned earlier how my mother found my size embarrassing. If there had been a medical procedure available by which I could have been shrunk, I'm sure she would have gone for it. If she couldn't shrink me physically, then her alternative was to shrink me psychologically. She made it clear to me, from an early age, that I should never use my size and strength to bully or dominate others. Sarah Weinstein was a militant pacifist – a contributor to *Peace News* – and, while I was allowed some boys' toys like model cars, trucks or aeroplanes, toy guns and soldiers were strictly forbidden. Nor was I allowed to read action adventure comics or go to see war or cowboy films. I was to be the archetypal gentle giant. The problem was that gentle giants do not do well on the rugby field.

And so, dear reader, my rugby career was a short and inglorious one. On the plus side, my mother never found out about it. On the minus side, the rest of the school either witnessed it or were subsequently told about it. Until then I had only been subjected to the occasional instance of name calling, and even that tended to be from a distance and under the breath, Although I had never shown any sign of aggression, my sheer bulk made my fellow students wary of me. Whereas the Asian boys in my ghettoised circle were frequent victims of bullying, I was left alone. But not anymore. Seeing boys half my size pounding me into the dirt and stamping all over me on the rugby pitch emboldened the school bullies. They realised I was not just an easy target; I was the perfect target. The most common thing you can say to belittle a bully is 'pick on someone your own size'. Bullies generally pick on smaller boys thereby risking being labelled cowards. So, picking on somebody as big as me made them instant heroes – Jack the Giant Killers, Davids slaying Goliath. If my time at the Royal Grammar School had been miserable before, it was doubly so now. I was picked on and goaded daily: challenged to fights and then jeered at as yellow or a pussy when I refused to engage in fisticuffs with boys who barely came up to my chest.

It all came to a head in the middle of my third year at the school. A red-haired, pale-skinned, freckly faced boy called George Wormald had just joined the school. As well as having to endure the normal taunts for being a 'newbie', he was mocked for his appearance. He desperately needed some way he could ingratiate himself with his fellow pupils. At first, he tried to be one of the gang by hanging round on the periphery while the bullies cornered and taunted me in the playground. But, on one particular day, he must have decided that being a hanger-on wasn't going to gain him any kudos. He needed to promote himself into a bully-in-chief.

"How's your mother, Felatu?" He said as he sidled up to me outside the toilets during morning break.

"None of your business," I said.

Five of my regular tormentors had gathered behind Wormald, content to be the audience on this occasion.

"I just wondered if she was still on the game," he said. The boys behind him were smirking.

I didn't reply. I had no idea what he was getting at. In my social isolation, I was ignorant of most playground argot. 'On the game' was a phrase that had no meaning for me.

"I believe she comes from Cardiff, your mother." He turned to grin at his compatriots. I don't know how he'd come across this information about my mother, but it was obvious that this was a persecution that had been prepared earlier. "I know Cardiff quite well I've got an aunty who lives there. I guess your mother must have lived round the docks?"

I still couldn't see what he was getting at. My isolation from the other boys had rendered me a very naïve fourteen year old.

"She must have made quite a lot of money from all those black sailors. I bet she doesn't even know which one of them's your daddy."

Now I knew what he was on about. The other boys were nudging each other and sniggering. I could feel my cheeks getting hot although I was dark-skinned enough for my blushes not to show.

Wormald pressed up close to me. "So, you must be the son of a whore." One idiot behind him chortled loudly.

"Shut your face, Wormald," I said. Normally I avoided responding, but this was worse than anything that had previously been said to me and the fact that it was coming out of the mouth of this weedy, freckle-faced, new boy made it even worse.

"Make me," he replied, now standing on tiptoe trying, and failing, to thrust his face into mine.

I stared him down but did nothing. Even with such extreme provocation, I managed to hold any aggressive instincts in check. And then, he punched me surprisingly hard in the stomach. It knocked the wind out of me and I doubled over. My face was just above his and, as his punch forced me to bend forward, my forehead made contact with his nose. I sank to my knees clutching my stomach and gasping for breath while Wormald simultaneously collapsed in a heap by my side, holding both hands to his face, blood pouring between his fingers.

Seconds later, Mr Thomas, one of the P.E. teachers, arrived on the scene.

"What's going on here?"

I was still gasping for breath and Wormald was holding his face and whimpering. The blood was now flowing down his white shirt front.

"It's Felatu, sir," said a weaselly dark-haired boy called Atherton. "He attacked Wormald. I think he's broken his nose."

Thirty minutes later, Wormald and I were standing in the Headmaster's office. Mr E. R. Tucker (Boss) was seated behind his massive oak desk staring with distaste at the bloodied Wormald before shifting his gaze to me with an equally disparaging expression. By now I had fully recovered from the punch. Wormald was still gulping down sobs. His face had been cleaned up by the school nurse but his nose was very red and swollen. His nostrils had been plugged with wads of cotton wool and the blood on his shirt front had dried.

I won't go into a detailed account of the interrogation that followed. Suffice it to say that Wormald testified that I had been the aggressor and attacked him – and his testimony was confirmed by his fellow bullies – the only witnesses to the incident. Also, according to Wormald, the attack was unprovoked. I said nothing in my defence. Why? I'm sure you must be asking, dear reader. Well, if you were the Headmaster, who would you believe – the weedy pasty-faced lad with a broken nose, covered in blood, or the tall strapping black boy with not a mark on him? Judgement was duly pronounced, Wormald was dismissed and E. R. Tucker reached into the cupboard behind his desk and produced his cane.

In retrospect, I wonder whether, subconsciously, I made no attempt to defend myself because I was happy for it to be believed by the rest of the school that I had initiated this vicious attack on poor innocent Wormald. Whether or not that was my actual reasoning at the time, the fictitious version of the attack spread around the school and had the desired effect. From that day onwards, I was feared and avoided – someone it would be unwise to pick a fight with.

After the administration of my punishment, E. R. Tucker announced that he would need to speak to my mother about what had happened. I feared that far more than I had my caning. But my accidentally violent act proved to be a turning point, not only in my school life, but also at home. My mother never met with Mr Tucker. The following morning, it was Ana who sat by my side in front of the Headmaster and listened to his warning that, if there was any repeat of the unprovoked violence that I had inflicted on George Wormald, I would be expelled from the grammar school. Ana, of course, knew me well enough to realise that I was not capable of such an unprovoked and vicious attack. She had asked me repeatedly to tell her what had really happened during our journey to the school that morning, but I remained silent.

If my mother had known about the incident, she undoubtedly would have forced the truth out of me, but neither Ana nor I ever told her about it. It so happened that, about the same time that I had been bent over the Headmaster's desk the previous day, my mother was being taken by ambulance to High Wycombe General Hospital. She remained there for a week 'undergoing tests', Ana told me.

Sarah Weinstein had always been a driven woman, working hard at whatever she turned her hand to. Since her success as a children's author, she and Ana had been churning out new books while, at the same time, she had been in even greater demand as a journalist. And if all that didn't occupy enough of her time, after the start of the war, she had thrown herself energetically into the anti-fascist movement, in particular supporting organisations publicising the plight of the Jews in Nazi occupied Europe. Like most other teenage boys, I was too absorbed in myself and my own problems to notice any changes in my mother. If I had paid more attention, I would have noticed how much weight she had lost and how much more lined and drawn her face was. The explanation she and Ana gave me for her sudden hospital admission was that she had been overworking and was suffering from exhaustion. I accepted it without question although, at the back of my mind, I couldn't help wondering what these tests were that the hospital was administering.

Once she had come home from the hospital, life seemed to continue as normal. Sarah threw herself back into her numerous activities and any misgivings I had were dispelled until the school holidays when, being at home all day, it could no longer be kept secret from me that my mother, accompanied by Ana, was paying regular weekly visits to the hospital. I was told nothing except that the doctors were still carrying out 'routine tests'. Of course, I knew that there was more to this than they were telling me, but I colluded with my mother and Ana in ignoring the elephant in the room. It was only when my mother started to retreat to her bed in the early evening (she had always been something of a night owl) and frequently took afternoon naps, that I was forced to recognise that there was nothing routine about what was happening. The life force that had been Sarah Weinstein was slowly grinding to a halt.

Nevertheless, I was still kept in the dark until the point at which she was spending more time in bed than out of it. Then, on one snowy January morning, I was summoned to my mother's bedside. I guessed what was coming. She came straight to the point – reverting to the pre-illness, brutally honest Sarah Weinstein. She had terminal cancer. The doctors had estimated that she had six months to live but they'd said that six months ago and she was still here. She was determined to fight it and cling to life for as long as possible, but I needed to know the truth. She hastened to reassure me that, if she ended up losing her battle, there were arrangements in place for Ana to continue to look after me. After all, Ana was very much a second mother to me already, wasn't she? I agreed that she was. Well, in that case, it will be a smooth transition for her to become your sole mother.

It was only a month later that she lost the fight. I met my maternal grandparents for the first time at the funeral. I never knew whether it was my mother recanting on her deathbed and requesting their presence or whether it was solely Ana's decision. Of course, back in the 1940s, Ana had no legal status as my mother's partner and, therefore, no right to become my guardian despite that being my mother's wish. It should have fallen to my grandparents, as my only living relatives in Britain, to take responsibility for me. I do not know for sure if they attempted to challenge that section of my mother's will, but I doubt it. What they did do is arrange with Ana for me to stay with them in Cardiff over the Easter holidays. It's possible, I suppose, that they intended this as a test run before I would make a permanent move there. If that is what was intended, it was a failure. It was an uncomfortable experience for all three of us. I remember very little about it other than being stuck in the house, bored, for most of the time. Don't get me wrong, they were perfectly hospitable and catered to my every need, but it was more as if I was a short stay house guest than their long-lost grandson. They were constantly asking me questions about myself, about how I was doing in school, what my favourite subjects were, what I wanted to be when I grow up, but their tone of voice registered politeness rather than any genuine interest in finding out more about me. And, all the time, their body language radiated discomfort. The visit was never to be repeated, although my grandparents did stay in sporadic contact through birthday cards and presents. My theory is that they couldn't come to terms with the sudden emergence into their lives of a giant black grandson. The blood connection may have been there, but it was too diluted. If they had been able to get to know me as a baby or small child, it might have been easier but, by then, it was too late. They were too old and frail and set in their ways and I was too bizarre. I should have provided them with a connection to their lost daughter. Just by looking at me, they would be reminded of Sarah. But, of course, I bore very little resemblance to my mother. I would always be a cuckoo in their nest.

I am aware, dear reader, that I have expressed very little emotion at my mother's death. It was true that having Ana there, moving relatively seamlessly from her role as my second mother to my sole guardian, was a great help. It also helped that we were able to share our grief. But, ever since I could remember, it had been me and my mother battling against a potentially hostile world and, at times, it had been a tough fight. Ana was a more than adequate substitute, but she could never be a complete replacement. I was safe and secure but in shock for a long time afterwards.

My disengagement from my studies had been growing even before my mother's death, but now I had no reason to continue with the struggle to fulfil her ambitions for me. In June of that year, I was due to take my School Certificate exams and I had little confidence of success. On the morning of the first exam, as I got off the bus and turned down the lane leading to school, I was confronted by the sight of a crowd of boys blocking the school entrance at the end of the road. They were standing in front of a police barrier and, as I mingled with them, I soon picked up from their excited chattering that a bomb had dropped on the school the night before. Even from my towering vantage point at the back of the crowd, I couldn't get a clear view of the school buildings, or what I imagined might remain of them, but I could smell and breathe in the dust and acrid smoke that still hung in the air. After a while, Mr Tucker appeared with a megaphone and announced that we should all return home and our parents should telephone for further information about when lessons could resume.

For the first time in my life, I thought there must be a God. He had saved me from humiliating failure in my exams and, in his infinite wisdom, destroyed the place I had grown to hate.

Sadly, this new-found religious faith was short-lived. Within two days, we received a phone call telling us that school was returning to normal the following day, including the resumption of the School Certificate exams. A V1 rocket, aiming for a target in central London, had overshot by some distance and landed in the playing fields next to the school. Apart from shattering the school windows at the front of the building, there was no structural damage.

As distressed as I still was by the death of my mother, when the envelope with my inevitably disappointing results landed on the doormat, I was relieved that she wasn't around and it was Ana who opened it. Unlike what I assumed Sarah's reaction would have been, Ana was all understanding and reassurance. It was not surprising, she said. I was still in mourning for my mother. How could I have been expected to concentrate on my studies. I would do much better in next year's retakes.

My heart sank. That meant staying on for another year at the Royal Grammar School and then, if I passed my school certificates, and that was a big if, staying on another two years to take my Highers. The thought of that filled me with horror and despair.

# Tuesday 30th September 2001

"Hi Guv. Do you want the good news or the bad news?"

"I don't want any fucking news. I'm busy enough as it is."

DC Ethan Edwards stood in front of the Inspector's desk clutching a sheath of papers in his right hand. Detective Inspector Madeline Rich continued to click her mouse and stare at her computer screen. Ethan stayed where he was, nervously passing the sheath of paper from hand to hand.

"Okay." Maddy Rich sighed and turned her attention away from the screen and towards Ethan. "How about the good news – as if I don't know the answer."

"There isn't any good news," Ethan grinned.

"Of course there isn't. Just like there isn't any such thing as good luck. Do you know that song – *Born under a Bad Sign*?" Maddy said.

Ethan shook his head.

"Of course you don't. You're barely out of fucking nappies. It contains my favourite line in blues music – 'if it wasn't for bad luck, I wouldn't have no luck at all.'" She half-sang it in a poor imitation of a gravelly-voiced black blues singer. "And, I'm afraid to say, it's the same with news. As far as this office is concerned, it's always bad news. So, Cowboy, just give it to me straight."

When Ethan Edwards first joined the CID team at Paddington Green six months earlier, he was asked how he got a name like 'Ethan' and, when he replied that his parents were film buffs and had named him after the John Wayne character in *The Searchers*, they started to call him

Cowboy and the name had stuck ever since. It taught him an important lesson – tell your colleagues as little as possible about either your past or your personal life.

"It's about that suspected suicide in Harlesden. Just got the autopsy report." He tossed the stapled sheets of paper on to the desk.

"Aha," Maddy said. "The death by defenestration. Don't get many of those in twenty-first century Paddington."

"The death by de-what?" Ethan looked puzzled. In the short time he'd been working for her, Ethan had grown used to Inspector Rich's habit of wrong-footing him by throwing out random non-sequiturs. It was usually her way of showing how much more knowledgeable and better educated she was.

"Defenestration?" She repeated, pausing to give Ethan time to recognise the word, while knowing that he wouldn't. "It means death by being thrown out, or throwing yourself out, of a window."

"There's a word for that?" Ethan still looked puzzled.

"Yes. It used to be a common occurrence in years gone by. Often a way of getting rid of disagreeable courtiers or politicians. But also used, in more recent times, in police states, to rid themselves of awkward dissidents. You know the drill. We were just asking him a few questions when he tried to escape by throwing himself out of the window." She paused as if considering whether to continue with the lecture. "Anyway. This autopsy report. You obviously know what it says so why don't you give me the gist – although I can probably guess what's coming."

"It's only interim, but the pathologist says that the cause of death was major trauma to the side of the head causing serious brain damage. She thinks it was caused by a blow from a blunt instrument and not by the fall from the window. In other words…"

"He was dead before he fell out the window. So, we're looking at a murder case. Great."

"As I said, Guv, it's not a hundred per cent certain. The forensics team are going back to the scene to do another check just to be sure he couldn't have hit his head on anything before he hit the pavement. Apparently, there are some railings…" He was interrupted by the buzzing of his mobile phone. He removed it from his jacket pocket and glanced down at the screen. "This could be what we're waiting for. D'you mind?" Maddy waved her hand stoically at him.

"Edwards," he said and then listened in silence for thirty seconds. "Okay. Thanks for getting on to it so quickly." He pocketed the phone and gave Maddy Rich a resigned look. "Definitely no sign of his head having hit the railings or anything else on the way down. They were pretty certain of that anyway, as the body wasn't close enough to them when it was found."

Maddy Rich clicked her mouse and turned her attention back to the computer screen as if she had lost interest in the whole subject.

"So…" He waited a few seconds for her to say something. "Where do we go from here?"

Despite her seeming lack of attention, Maddy's reply was instant. "Go back and interview that old couple that own the house – what was their name?"

"Mr and Mrs Kaplanska. But we've already spoken to them. They were away from home at the time of the…" He was about to say suicide before correcting himself, "murder, so they didn't see or hear anything."

"We need to question them more thoroughly about this man – Felatu. Try and find out if they know anything about his friends or acquaintances. Details of any visitors. Whether they ever heard him having arguments with anybody. Whether he showed any signs of being nervous or stressed in recent weeks. Stuff like that."

"Okay guv, I can do that."

"Also, wasn't there something about a friend who was going to sort out his belongings?"

Ethan reached into his inside jacket pocket, took out a notebook and flipped over several pages. "It's a Mr Reznikoff. He lives round the corner in Paddington. DC Adams interviewed him. He wasn't very helpful."

"Well we need to talk to him again. Maybe once he knows his friend was murdered, he'll realise that he's got more that he can tell us. What about family?"

"As far as we have been able to ascertain so far, he doesn't have any, although we're still looking into it. I know it's not very helpful, guv, but he seems to be a classic example of a loner – an old guy living on his own with almost no family or friends."

"'Seems' is not a word I like, Cowboy." Maddy was still focussed on the screen and started tapping on her keyboard. She stopped abruptly and looked up at Ethan. "Wasn't there something about him having connections with the art world? He was a painter's model, wasn't he?"

"Yes. For Francis Bacon. The guy who did all those weird paintings of people with twisted faces."

"I'm well aware who Francis Bacon is," she said brusquely. "He was gay, wasn't he? Not that I want to go too anti-gay on this but there might be some leads there that we can follow. We need to pull all this together. I'll call a team meeting for later this afternoon so we can get this investigation properly organised."

"Right then. I'll get started on those interviews." He turned towards the door.

"Oh. Before you go." Maddy picked up the pathologist's report and waved it at him. "Does it give any indication of time of death?"

"Yes. They reckon he must have been killed only a very short time before he went out the window. About two thirty in the morning."

"So – not a lot of people around at that time of night. Did we do a door to door with the neighbours?"

"We knocked up the immediate ones but we didn't expect to get much from them when we thought it was suicide. If any of them had seen him throwing himself out the window, we assumed they'd have phoned the police."

"Fine, but now it's a murder case we need to do a door to door along the whole street plus all the houses that back on to it to see if anybody saw or heard anything. And we need to put out a request for information from anybody who may have been in the vicinity at the time."

Ethan Jones stood still, a pained look on his face.

"Was there something else?" The Inspector said. "Because there's a lot to do. No time to stand around staring into space. You need to saddle up and get on your horse."

"There is a lot to do," Ethan said. "We're going to need more manpower."

"Of course we are. It's a murder investigation." Maddy Rich paused. "Oh, I forgot. This must be your first murder?"

"Yes."

"Don't worry. Leave it with me. There'll be a full team in place for the meeting this afternoon. But we don't need to wait for that, so get going. Chop chop." She waved her hand at him and turned her attention back to the computer.

Becky Stone sat at the formica–topped table in David Reznikoff's spartan kitchen. It was like a room from the 1950s that she remembered seeing on a school visit to the Geoffrye Museum, all painted wooden units with chrome handles, a noisy water-heater mounted above a stone sink and a Baby Belling gas cooker. Despite its down-at-the-heel retro appearance, the room was clean and tidy. No piles of dirty dishes in the sink or splashes of food residue on the work surfaces that you might expect to find in the kitchen of a single elderly man. No unpleasant smells of damp or decay, just the faint odour of fried food.

David Reznikoff stood on tiptoe reaching into a cupboard for a tin of biscuits to go with the two mugs of tea he had just poured. He was not much over five feet tall with wire wool tufts of frizzy grey hair surrounding a bald dome. He had a large nose, thin lips and slightly bulgy eyes. The top buttons of his check shirt were open revealing a thatch of grey chest hair. A pot belly overhung his brown corduroy trousers which clung precariously to his narrow hips and small buttocks.

"So how exactly can I help you, Miss Stone?" Becky had been surprised by his refined upper-class accent which didn't go with his scruffy appearance and modest accommodation.

"Well, as I've already told you, I'm doing this research for the Museum into Soho in the 1950s and, when I heard the news about Mr Felatu's death and his connections with the Soho artistic scene, I was intrigued. His wasn't a name I'd come across in my research."

"Aha. Soho. The stories I could tell you about that time, Miss Stone. They would make your hair curl." He gave her an impish look as he put the tray with the mugs of tea and the plate of biscuits on the table.

"You were around Soho at that time as well?" Becky said. "Is that when you first met Mr Felatu?"

"Yes. I was a young journalist at the time. I'd just been taken on by the *Daily Express* to be one of the writers for the William Hickey column. I was also a bit of an artist myself."

Becky shifted her gaze to two abstract paintings, both featuring similar overlapping waves of colour, on the wall by the kitchen door.

He noticed her looking at them. "Yes, those are two of mine," he said. "As you can see, I'm no Picasso." She was about to say something mildly complimentary but he carried on talking before she had a chance. "I had some minor successes – sold a few paintings – but I couldn't make a living from it. That's why I fell back on the journalism. My connections with the art world took me to the Soho drinking clubs. They were the ideal place to pick up lots of juicy stories for the column."

"And what was Felatu's connection with all of that? How important a figure was he?"

He bit into a shortbread biscuit, giving himself time to think about his answer.

"He was a very small fish – if you'll forgive me for using a rather unsuitable metaphor to describe such a giant of a man." He chuckled to himself. "If it wasn't for his size and his exotic appearance, you'd hardly have noticed him." He paused, holding the remains of his biscuit half-way to his mouth. "I'm sorry, Miss Stone, but I don't really understand why you want to know about all this. I know you say it's for your research, but I can save you a lot of time and energy by simply telling you that Harry Felatu played very little part in the events of that time."

"Yes, I know that – otherwise, he'd be better known but…"

"Are you from the police working undercover? Or perhaps the secret service?" He interrupted through a mouth full of biscuit crumbs.

"What?" Becky was taken aback. "No, of course I'm not. I showed you proof of my identity."

"Hmm. If you're working undercover, Miss Stone, then of course you're going to be provided with documentation that shows you're somebody else." David Reznikoff narrowed his eyes, looking at her inquisitively, while brushing crumbs from his lips. "You do know he was murdered, don't you?"

"What?" Becky nearly spit out a mouthful of tea. "The police have already said they think it was suicide. What makes you think he was murdered?"

Reznikoff scraped his chair back, got to his feet and walked over to the window. There wasn't much of a view, just the backs of the tenement flats opposite.

"As I said before, I don't really know who you are, Miss Stone, and I'm not sure that it's advisable for me to talk to you about Harry. It could be dangerous – for both of us."

Becky was feeling a mixture of intrigue and exasperation. David Reznikoff was coming across as something of a drama queen. He seemed to be enjoying himself at her expense; playing some kind of game with her. She should have realised as soon as she met him that it was a stupid idea trying to get information from him. He was a lonely old man relieving his boredom by playing court to a young woman and telling her tall tales. He probably had no connection at all with 1950s Soho.

"The reason I think he was murdered," he continued, still with his back to Becky, staring out the window, "is because he told me he probably would be. He told me there were people out to get him. People who wanted him dead. He didn't say exactly who they were. To be honest, you never knew what to believe with Harry. He was something of a fantasist." It takes one to know one, Becky couldn't help thinking. "Oh yes. He could spin a good yarn. Sometimes, I don't think he even knew himself whether what he was saying was the truth or something he'd made up."

"So, he might just have been being paranoid when he talked about people wanting to kill him?"

"Possibly. Who can say?" He said, turning round with a rictus grin on his face.

"And you're sure he didn't give you any indication of who these people were – these people who wanted to kill him?"

"No, not in so many words. He just hinted that they were high ups – well connected. Politicians. Lords. Even Royalty."

"But you don't have any indication of who these people might be – any actual names?"

"No. I'm afraid not."

Becky was finding his ingratiating tone and fixed grin increasingly irritating. She tried a few more questions which elicited no further information before deciding she'd had enough. Time to put an end to the game.

On her journey home, Becky took her notebook and pen from her bag to jot down a summary of what she had learnt from David Reznikoff. She stared at the blank page for a minute or so, pen hovering, before putting them back in her bag. There was nothing to be gleaned from Reznikoff's ramblings, she decided, other than his melodramatic announcement that Felatu may have been murdered – and then he couldn't offer any evidence. It was time she gave up this wild-goose chase. It was clear that Harry Felatu was just a minor hanger-on in the 1950s Soho bohemian set. She needed to get back to her proper research, even though she was beginning to find it somewhat mundane. Just the usual Soho suspects – Francis Bacon, Lucien Freud, John Minton et al.

The reason she'd been so keen on investigating Felatu was not only the coincidence of him living, and dying, round the corner from where she lived, No, it was much more about her trying to put her own stamp on the exhibition – to come up with something new, something unknown, something original, something that would get her noticed –

something that would persuade the Museum curators that, once her internship came to an end, she would be worthy of a permanent post. That was still her aim, but she had to accept that Harry Felatu was not going to be her magic passport to success.

"You're home early. What's happened? Did your laptop crash? Cup of tea?" Richard called to her from the kitchen.

She tossed her bag on to the sofa, slumped down next to it and kicked off her shoes.

"I should be asking you the same thing," she said, looking at her watch. "It's only 3.30. What are you doing home at this hour? It's too mild for the school's heating to have broken down. You haven't been given the sack, have you?"

Richard stood in the kitchen doorway and held up his hands in mock supplication. "You've got me bang to rights. Got caught having sex with a sixth form girl in the stock cupboard."

"That's not funny. You shouldn't joke about things like that."

"Well, I'm gratified that you're so confident I'm joking." He gave her a pained look. "Becky, you're so wrapped up in yourself and your work that I don't think you listen to a word I say. I wasn't at school today. I was at an exam board meeting which finished at 2.00."

"Oh yes. Sorry. You did tell me. And I will have that cup of tea."

He grinned and retreated to the kitchen.

"It was the same for me," she called after him. "I was only in the library this morning. Then I went to see this friend of Harry Felatu's. I didn't stay long. He didn't have much to tell me."

Richard reappeared with the mug of tea, slid a coaster across the wooden coffee table and put the tea down in front of her.

"That's a pity," he said. "Especially now it's all got so much more intriguing."

Becky was just about to take a sip of her tea. "Sorry. What are you talking about? What's intriguing?"

"You know. The news about Felatu." He sat next to her on the sofa. She still looked puzzled. "You haven't heard?"

"Haven't heard what?"

"It's been on the News. I was just listening to Radio London in the kitchen. The police have announced that it's now a murder inquiry." Becky nearly choked, just managing to swallow her mouthful of tea in an exact repeat of her actions an hour or so earlier in David Reznikoff's kitchen when he'd made the exact same statement. "They're now saying it wasn't suicide, it was murder and they're asking for anybody who might have any information to contact them."

Becky put her mug back on the table without looking, tipping it clumsily on the edge of the coaster, spilling tea across the tabletop. Richard raced into the kitchen and, returning with a kitchen roll, tore off several strips and carefully mopped the table, trying to prevent any spillage on to the Persian rug.

"You look like you've seen a ghost," he said when he'd finished mopping up. "You've gone very pale."

"That's probably because I have," she said. "Seen a ghost, that is."

She proceeded to tell Richard what David Reznikoff had told her earlier that afternoon.

# Extracts from
# The Autobiography of an Invisible Man

## I RETURN TO THE BIG SMOKE

It's a warm sunny Sunday morning in the Spring of 1947 and I'm being swept along by the jostling crowds in Ridley Road Market. I extricate myself from the tide of people to stop at interesting looking clothes stalls and rifle through the racks of shirts and trousers with little hope of finding anything of interest, chiefly because I have no money to spare or clothing coupons, but also because, now that I am an almost fully grown adult, it's impossible to find anything to fit my six and a half foot frame. Eventually, I manage to disentangle myself from the throng and make my way to the food stalls. Ana has given me a shopping list and some money and coupons.

My sincere apologies, dear reader, but you will probably realise by now that I quite enjoy disorientating you – although it's never for long. Yes, I am back in London. Ana and I have abandoned High Wycombe. I had had to put up with almost another year of misery and disappointing reports from the grammar school before I finally managed to persuade Ana to let me leave school. And then there was nothing else to keep us in Wooburn Green. Ana and my mother had made very few friends there and, now that my mother was no longer with us, Ana was lonely and in need of a more vibrant social life. Some of her old Viennese school friends had managed to escape the Nazis and now lived in

East London so Ana arranged for us to move into the top floor of a terraced house in Hackney. The bottom floor was occupied by Irma, one of Ana's oldest friends, her husband, Erich, and their infant daughter.

I was only too happy to escape the tedium of Wooburn Green and rekindle those early memories of London life with Sarah. Even the constant noise and clouds of dust as bulldozers and men with shovels cleared debris from the bombsites couldn't dampen my enthusiasm for the city. At every opportunity I would explore my mother's old Bloomsbury haunts – the bookshops, libraries and cafes – and walk around the East End markets.

It had been far from easy for me to persuade Ana to let me abandon my futile attempt to retake my school certificate exams and leave the Royal Grammar School. She took her guardianship of me very seriously and was worried about my future. Once I had announced that I intended to leave school, she naturally demanded to know what I planned to do instead. I had no answer. The truth was that the only thing I could think of as a future career was to become a writer. Not surprising, I suppose. It's not unusual to want to follow in your parent's footsteps and my only notion of the world of work was seeing my mother sat at her desk each day scribbling her newspaper and magazine articles and her children's stories. But there was no way I could tell Ana that I wanted to be a writer because I had no idea whether I had any talent. English had been my favourite school subject (in so far as I had a favourite) and I continued to write stories even after I left school, but I never showed them to Ana. They were buried at the bottom of my underwear drawer. I knew they weren't very good. And anyway, Ana had changed since my mother's death. I have already explained how seriously she took her responsibilities as a surrogate parent; so much so that she had cast aside her previous artistic bohemian existence and adopted a more sober, conservative lifestyle. Gone were the slacks and baggy mohair pullovers to be replaced with tweed skirts and crisp white blouses.

She had been entrusted with the responsibility of guiding my path to adulthood by Sarah and I think she felt she had already fallen down on the job when I failed my school certificate exams. So, her first response to my request to leave school without retaking them was a firm no. Of course, my mother would have wanted me to follow in her footsteps and go to Oxford or Cambridge, but both Ana and I knew that that was never going to happen. I was regularly summoned to the sitting room to discuss the various ways in which I might be able to continue my education and gain some qualifications so that I could pursue a respectable profession. The idea that I might want to be like her and Sarah and become a bohemian artist of some kind would have been an anathema to her. She was very patient with me – far more than my mother would have been. As I politely rejected each new idea that she would come up with, each college course that she suggested, she would merely shrug her shoulders and go off in search of further possibilities. In desperation, she even wrote to my grandfather in Cardiff to enquire whether there was any possibility that I could be taken on as a trainee in the family clothing business. She never informed me of his response (although I'm sure it would not have been enthusiastic) and, anyway, I rejected the idea as soon as she informed me that she had sent the letter.

Once we had moved to London, there were a lot more options open to me. A stream of college prospectuses and adverts for apprenticeships and trainee schemes littered the dining room table. Finally, Ana's persistence and her heart-felt concern for my future wellbeing wore me down. I hated to keep disappointing her and seem ungrateful for all the efforts she was making on my behalf. I felt obliged to accept one of her suggestions and, for some unfathomable reason, it was to apply for a course in Accountancy and Book-keeping at Sir John Cass College. While it may have been debatable whether English was my best subject at school, Maths was undoubtedly not my favourite. As Ana helped me fill in the application form, I guess I went along with it because it gave me a temporary respite from her constant pressure to make a decision about my future. I say a brief respite because I couldn't see how they could possibly accept me onto the course. I had neither the qualifications nor the aptitude for it. And yet, within a matter of weeks. I was attending my first day at the college.

There had been no entrance test and so my demonstrable lack of mathematical aptitude was no obstacle to my being offered a place. Bear in mind, dear reader, that this was the immediate post-war period and thousands of young men were returning to civilian life having had their education curtailed by the war. There was an urgent need to get them all into employment or training and there was no point in asking for qualifications that they hadn't had the opportunity to acquire while they had been away fighting. Although I hadn't been in the armed forces, I somehow slipped in unnoticed alongside them.

"You're a big fucker, aren't you? More a gorilla than a monkey."

I'd left Ridley Road and was wending my way through the backstreets around Kingsland Road Station on my way back home. I was enjoying the feel of the August sun on my face, probably daydreaming; definitely not taking in my surroundings. That was how three burly men in almost identical uniforms of dark trousers and black polo neck shirts had approached me from behind and now had me surrounded, pressed up against a high brick wall. The one who spoke first was not much older than me. He had thin greasy fair hair brylcreamed flat against his skull, a thin rat-like face and a wispy pubescent moustache.

"Where you from?" He continued. "You don't look like one of them African bastards."

"I'm from London," I said in as calm a voice as I could manage.

He turned around and gave a gap-toothed grin to his mates. They burst out laughing.

"Oooh, get the posh voice. Who does this nigger bastard think he is, Lord Muck?" He turned back to face me. "Don't give me that, sunshine. You don't get a tan like yours in London." The grin disappeared to be replaced by a twisted snarl as he stood on tiptoe and thrust his face as close as he could to mine. His breath stank of cigarettes and fried breakfasts.

"You should go back to where you come from, sonny. You ain't wanted here." This time the words were spat out by a fat middle aged man with a sweat-covered bald head and a stubbly jowly face. As he spoke, he pushed himself closer to me, shoving me back against the wall.

I had a vision of being back in the school playground being confronted by George Wormald. I briefly considered whether, this time, I should use my head deliberately rather than accidentally or hit him over the head with my string bag full of the fruit and vegetables I'd purchased in the market, but I was too scared. There were no teachers around to come to my aid and there were three of them. And then I noticed out of the corner of my eye that the fair-haired one had what looked like a wooden club in his hand.

Before I could say or do anything further, the fair-haired lad plunged forward, his head butting me in the chest, slamming my back painfully against the wall. He dropped the club and crumpled in a heap at my feet clutching the side of his head. Simultaneously, the bald portly thug was flung sideways and fell on his back at the kerbside. The other member of the gang turned and started to run off down the street. Sprawled against the wall, I put my hands up to my face to protect myself as I was now confronted by three other men, this time in check shirts with rolled up sleeves rather than black polo necks. All three had, what looked like, bunched up newspapers in their hands – the weapons I assumed they had used to attack my assailants.

One of them, with dark wavy hair and a swarthy complexion, kicked the fair-haired youth, sprawled on the pavement at my feet, in the stomach and then wrenched him upright by his trouser belt. He hit him again across the head with the rolled-up newspaper. The other two were kicking the fat man as he curled into a foetal position by the roadside.

The fracas was over in a flash and the two beaten men were allowed to stagger painfully to their feet and stumble off down the street shouting obscenities once they'd put sufficient distance between themselves and their attackers.

"Dirty Jew bastards. We'll get you back for this," was their parting shot as they disappeared round a corner.

"Are you alright, son?" The man with the wavy hair asked me. "I'm Morris." He held out his hand and I shook it hesitantly.

"I'm Hare," I said.

"This is Gerald and this is Leonard." I shook hands with the other two men. "Where are you from Harry?"

"I'm from London. I live near here. Hackney."

Morris smiled. "No, I mean where are you from originally?'

There was that question again. I was destined to be asked it all my life. "It's complicated," I said. "But I was born in London."

"Well, never mind that," he continued. "I'm sorry about those fascist bastards. They were trying to hold one of their meetings in the market, but we made sure that wasn't going to happen. Fortunately for you, we could see they were up to no good, so we followed them just to make sure they left the area without causing any trouble. If they get the chance, they often try to vandalise Jewish businesses, smash their windows and such like."

"Why? Who are they?" I said.

"You haven't come across them before?" Gerald asked, raising his eyebrows. "I'm surprised. A big fella like you. Forgive me for saying so, but you do stick out like a sore thumb. I'm surprised you haven't been targeted before. The BUF?" I must have looked puzzled. "The British Union of Fascists. Fortunately, they make themselves fairly conspicuous with all their black gear."

They took me back to Ridley Road and bought me a cup of tea in the market café. All three of them were regularly greeted by name as customers drifted in and out while we sat and drank our tea and talked. They told me that they were part of an organisation called the 43 Group. It had been formed by Jewish ex-servicemen who were determined that, having fought in the war and defeated the Nazis, on their return to civilian life in London, they were not going to sit back and watch home grown fascists spread their antisemitic poison. The 43 Group now numbered around three hundred and their purpose was to disrupt and destroy the British Union of Fascists in every way possible but, in particular, by using violence. Their favoured weapon was the rolled-up newspaper, usually concealing a wad of cardboard or a wooden stave. The police didn't immediately recognise it as a weapon.

Once I knew who they were, I felt safe and confident enough to answer Morris' initial question and explain my Jewish and Maori antecedents. They were fascinated and plied me with questions. Before I took my leave of them, they invited me to their next meeting the following Thursday at the nearby Maccabi House.

At first, I wasn't sure that I wanted to go. I have previously established my peaceful dovish demeanour, my only ever act of violence being that unintended one in the school playground. What help could I be to an organisation that prided itself on its strong-arm tactics? But then I thought back to my narrow escape from the gang of fascist thugs. I was no longer living in the genteel surroundings of Wooburn Green. I was now roaming the mean streets of East London. Gerald was right. I was a very conspicuous target for the racists and fascists. I needed to toughen myself up. And so, from that Thursday onwards, I became an active member of the 43 Group – a regular participant in their weekend skirmishes with the blackshirts.

On that first Thursday evening, I joined Gerald, Morris, Leonard and half a dozen others sat around an oblong table in a meeting room at Maccabi House. I was nervous, still doubtful that I belonged there. After the initial introductions and the serving of coffee, they started to plan the following weekend's activities. It was typical of all the subsequent Thursday evening meetings I attended. There was no agenda and no Chair. The discussion was haphazard and frequently drifted away from the immediate purpose and into more general arguments about current political issues. Most of them were supporters of the Atlee Government, although a few were communists and took issue with some of what the 'allegedly' socialist government was doing. I listened and said nothing. Despite my mother's engagement with feminism and socialism and her increasing anti-fascist activities in the years before her death, I had little interest in politics.

On that particular evening, the conversation revolved around the recent hanging of two British army sergeants in Palestine by the Irgun, the Jewish terrorist organisation, in retaliation for the execution of three of their members by the British.

"It was regrettable but necessary," Morris pronounced. "The Atlee Government is doing everything it can to back out of the promises it made to the Jews. When push comes to shove, they'll cave in to the Arab States and desert us Jews if they think that's in their best economic interests. We have to learn from our past mistakes. We'll never get anywhere by sitting back passively and waiting for things to be given to us because of guilt feelings about the concentration camps. Now, at last, we're standing up for ourselves."

Gerald shook his head disapprovingly. "Morris. Surely you can see that there's a difference between standing up for your people and carrying out vicious murders? For God's sake, one of those sergeants was Jewish."

"More fool him for serving in the British army in Palestine," said Morris.

"Anyway, you're wrong about Atlee," said Amos, an earnest young man with a wispy beard and shiny blue yarmulke which gave him the appearance of a rabbinical scholar. "He's on the side of us Jews. He's already said that he supports the principles of the Balfour Declaration."

"If that's the case, why has he let that antisemite Ernie Bevan be in charge of it?" Morris responded.

"How is Bevan an antisemite?" Leonard interjected.

"Well, how about when he made that comment about the Jews of Europe pushing to the front of the queue?" Said Morris. "Not to mention when he implied that Jews were black-marketeers who hoarded fuel."

"Okay, okay guys." Leonard raised his hands in the air in an attempt to bring the meeting to order. "We're not here to argue politics. Enough of this talk. We need to plan some action. And, whatever the rights and wrongs of those Irgun assassinations in Palestine, it's starting to create a lot of trouble for us Jews here. There are antisemitic attacks breaking out all over the country. My cousin Daniel phoned me earlier from Manchester. There's been a lot of trouble in Cheetham Hill. The synagogue's been attacked and dozens of Jewish shops have had their windows smashed. I'm going up there this weekend to see the situation for myself. If anyone wants to come with, they'll be welcome. Fortunately, things haven't been so bad yet in London, although Hendon synagogue's walls were graffitied last night. The usual stuff – "Hang the Jews" and "Jews – Hitler was right." I propose that some of us go to Hendon this Shabbos to add some extra security."

"Agreed," said Leon, a tubby middle-aged man with curly grey hair. "That's my sister's local shul. I'll organise a few men to go with me."

"The other issue is Sunday morning," said Leonard. "The fascists are holding a rally in Victoria Park. We need a commando group to go and deal with them. Are the rest of you up for that?" There were grunts of affirmation from round the table. "We'll need a few more, of course. About a dozen of us should be enough." He turned to look at me. "How about you, Harry? Are you up for it? It'll be a chance to break you in."

"Yes. Fine."

"Great. If you could stay behind after the meeting, I can give you a bit of rudimentary training."

The training was pretty basic. Their principle rule of combat was – you do not wait to be attacked, you take the fight to the enemy. Despite most of these Ashkenazy Jews having inherited their race's small stature, they made up for their lack of a physical presence by being tough, wily and determined. They had all been trained in armed and unarmed combat during the war and several of them were keen amateur boxers. So, it was obvious why they jumped at the chance to sign me up to their quick reaction commando cell. Of course, I refrained from telling them that, despite my size, I was something of a softy. The quick reaction commando cell was a small group who could be transported at short notice by volunteer black cab drivers to any weekend Mosleyite gatherings. Once there, they would use a twin-pronged attack to carve a way through the crowd to the platform and beat up the speakers. Because I was so conspicuous, they kept me in reserve, my job being to hang around at the back of the crowd and either rush through as reinforcement if the fight was threatening to turn against them or to intercept any fleeing fascists and ensure they didn't evade a beating.

My metamorphosis from non-violent shrinking violet to a meter out of regular thrashings could be traced back to that playground incident with George Wormald. I had been loath to admit it to myself at the time but, even though my bloodying of Wormald had been accidental, I had still found it exhilarating. I especially enjoyed the fear it had instilled in the other bullies.

A few weeks before my first encounter with the 43 Group, one of Ana's cousins had paid her a visit. He was a sickly, cadaverous young man. One evening, after dinner, he volunteered to do the washing up and I joined him in the kitchen to do the drying. In preparation, he rolled up his shirtsleeves to reveal a row of numbers tattooed on his lower arm. I asked him what they were but he was reluctant to speak about them. He muttered something about his imprisonment by the Nazis. I asked Ana about it the following day and she told me that he was an Auschwitz survivor. Although Ana's Austrian relatives and friends were equally reluctant to discuss their horrific experiences, my connection to them provided me with a more personal, and much more visceral, sense of what the concentration camps had been like. And that made it much easier for me to be prepared to discard my pacifist past and join up with such a militaristic group. And, in addition, I was propelled by another, subconscious, motivation: the same thing that pushed me to make several important decisions in my life – the thought that my mother would be looking down on me and would approve of what I was doing. She may not have wanted me to deploy my size and strength in sporting activities, but I hoped that she would approve of me using my physical attributes for such a worthy cause.

My first outing with the 43 Group that following Sunday morning was typical of how I would be spending most of my weekends for the next couple of months. A dozen of us gathered outside Maccabi House, chatting away amiably until three black cabs pulled up and we clambered in. The atmosphere on the journey to Victoria Park was all light-hearted banter, more like we were off on a day trip to the seaside than heading for a violent confrontation. We were dropped off in a back street near one of the park entrances and then strolled off in different directions, either in pairs or on our own, so as not to attract any suspicion when we arrived at the gathering in the middle of the park.

There was a crowd of about a hundred milling around a makeshift platform of beer crates. There were about a dozen men in the familiar black outfits at the front of the crowd, the rest looking like individuals and families out for a Sunday morning stroll in the late-August sunshine. As had been pre-arranged, I remained at the back of the crowd trying to look as inconspicuous as possible. As the first speaker climbed onto the crates and started to harangue the crowd, I could see various members of our group easing their way through to get closer to the front. At a signal from Leonard, two of them rushed on to the platform, grabbed the speaker and threw him down on the grass. The others had manoeuvred themselves behind the other black polo-shirted individuals and attacked them with their rolled-up newspapers before they had a chance to go to the aid of their orator comrade. It was all over within a couple of minutes. I observed several of the younger fascists pushing their way through the crowd to escape the violence. As I watched them weaving their way in my direction, I thought back to my abortive rugby career at school. It wasn't only my lack of aggression that rendered me useless, it was also my lack of manoeuvrability. When speedy and agile opposition players ran towards me with ball in hand, they would skip past me as if I wasn't there, my long arms flailing at thin air. My bulk and clumsiness meant that I was almost as slow at changing direction as those enormous oil-tankers. As I positioned myself to block off their escape route, I focused my attention on a young man with greasy dark hair and large sticking out ears. Fortunately, he was so busy looking over his shoulder to see if he was being chased, that he ran straight into me. I grabbed hold of him, shoved him to the ground and delivered several hefty kicks to his stomach, pulled him back on to his feet, slapped him round the face several times and then allowed him to scamper off. I then made my way back to the park gates where the cabs were waiting to ferry us home.

As I have already said, this was the first of a number of such 'commando raids' I participated in and, I have to admit, dear reader, that I enjoyed this unleashing of my violent side. I loved seeing the look of fear in the fascists' eyes and hearing their howls of pain as I towered over them, pinning them to the ground and grinding their faces beneath my boots.

Of course, I kept my 43 Group meetings and my weekend forays with the quick reaction commando unit secret from Ana. Even when she vented her anger and disgust at witnessing a group of blackshirts distributing pamphlets in Petticoat Lane Market, I held my tongue.

Our success in disrupting these BUF rallies was as much down to the ineptitude and sheer stupidity of the fascist bully boys as to our own careful planning. Because they suspected that they would be refused, they never applied for official permission to hold their rallies and, therefore, there was very rarely any police presence. They also believed wrongly that, by holding their meetings in this secretive guerrilla fashion, anti-fascist organisations like ours wouldn't have any advanced warning and, thereby, be able to disrupt them. Unfortunately for them, the 43 Group had a mole within their organisation.

My own involvement in these commando activities was difficult at first. Even allowing for the plan to hold me in reserve well to the rear of the gatherings, I was still an easily recognisable figure. However, with the arrival of less clement Autumn weather, I was able to disguise myself with a large hat and wrap my face in a voluminous scarf.

We rarely had the opportunity to attack Oswald Mosley himself as he had taken something of a backseat since the end of the war and, on the rare occasions when he did speak at public meetings, his security was very heavy. Instead, we targeted his unofficial second-in-command, Jeffrey Hamm, a typically tall, blond, blue-eyed Aryan. Hamm's favourite Sunday pulpit was outside Jack Straw's Castle in Hampstead and we regularly disrupted these meetings, on one occasion routing his bodyguards and giving him a thorough beating.

My final adventure with the 43 Group was to be the most audacious. We all met up every Wednesday evening in the Fox and Hounds pub on the Whitechapel Road for a few drinks. One Wednesday, as we were leaving the pub after last orders, Morris took me aside and told me that they had something special planned for the following day. He asked me if I'd be interested in taking part. He refused to give me any details when I asked and this made it sound intriguing. It was a college day but I could easily skip off. My attendance had often been erratic. So, I agreed to meet up with them at Maccabi House the following morning.

As well as providing meeting rooms for Jewish organisations such as ours, Maccabi House was a Jewish social and sports club and, on that Thursday morning, volunteers were busy arranging sporting activities for the coming weekend. Morris was in the small office at the rear of the building with Gerald and Leonard. There was one chair and a cluttered desk with a telephone on it.

"Come in," Morris said, "and close the door behind you."

I had to squeeze up close to Leonard and Gerald, leaving just enough room to shut the door.

Once he was convinced that no one outside could hear us, Morris picked up the phone. "It's supposed to be used for arranging the club's sporting activities and social events," he said to me with a knowing wink, "but I think you could call what we're about to do a kind of sport."

He dialled a number and waited as it rang.

"Hello. Is that Mr Jeffrey Hamm?" Again, he looked up at me and winked mischievously. "This is Inspector Beasely calling from Stepney Green police station. I'm phoning you because I have received information from one of my sources that there is an attack planned on your offices. I believe it is due to take place this afternoon."

Morris grimaced and held the receiver a few inches away from his ear. We could hear a loud, angry voice, presumably Jeffrey Hamm's, coming from the receiver, although we couldn't make out what he was saying.

"Well, I'm sorry you feel that way, Mr Hamm," Morris said once the angry voice had subsided. "I'm aware that you have complained before about the lack of protection we have given you in the past against these – 'yid bastards', as you call them, but that's why we're offering you protection now. At two o'clock this afternoon, several of my officers in plain clothes will pay you a visit. I don't want to send uniformed officers as we don't want to forewarn or scare off your would-be assailants. We'd like to catch them in the act." He paused while the voice at the other end of the line sounded off again. "Okay Mr Hamm. Let's just agree that it's better late than never. We'll see you this afternoon. Goodbye."

That afternoon, six of us arrived at the British Union of Fascists' office on the first floor of a terraced house in Roman Road, Hackney. A short stocky young man in blue workman's overalls let us in the front door. As we followed him to the top of the stairs, Morris told me to wait on the landing outside the office door and stand guard. Then he stood on tiptoe and whispered in my ear. "Give it a minute or so and then you can come in."

Morris had provided himself with a not very convincing imitation police i.d. badge but, fortunately for us, the fascists were too stupid to ask for any identification. The door was left ajar so I could hear what was being said.

"It's good to see you, officers. As I said to your boss, it's about time you gave us some protection against these Jewish thugs. You do little enough to protect our open-air meetings …"

At this point, I stepped into the open doorway. Jeffrey Hamm was standing up in front of a large oak desk. The young man in the overalls and another, older man in the traditional black polo neck attire stood on either side of him. Hamm's jaw dropped when he saw me standing there. He was temporarily at a loss for words but then he found his voice. "What's that black bastard doing here? How did he get in?" You could almost see the cogs in his tiny brain turning over. "Hold on. I recognise him. He's one of them. Don't just stand there. Arrest him." He glared at Morris and then at Leonard until it slowly dawned on him what was going on.

I won't go into all the gory details except to say that the office was thoroughly trashed, Hamm's two henchmen were tied up and dumped in a broom cupboard and Hamm himself was pushed to the floor and kicked and beaten unconscious.

By the early1950s, the fascists were in retreat in the East End, only continuing with occasional meetings down in Brighton. The 43 Group's work was done and they disbanded. I still met up with some of them for a Wednesday night drink but, as time wore on, I gradually lost contact.

In the meantime, I had somehow managed to finish my course at the college despite my palpable lack of enthusiasm and my erratic attendance. I had learned just about enough to enable me to squeeze through the final exams. Looking back on it now, I can see that the excitement and danger of my weekend activities with the 43 Group must have helped me through the weekday boredom of my book-keeping studies. I was still living with Ana in Hackney and, as a trustee of my mother's estate, she provided me with a weekly allowance from it. It was ample for my meagre needs, but I still felt duty bound to earn my keep by getting some kind of job so I could pay Ana something towards my board and lodging. And so, I took a job as a bookkeeper with a Hatton

Garden jewellery business – a job I was only given because the owner was another member of Ana's extended family.

When I look back on my life, I find myself searching for those key moments, those turning points. My mother's death, my adoption by Ana and our subsequent move to London should have been major turning points but, at first, little seemed to change, until I joined the 43 Group. Until then, my life had been more or less solitary. As I have already explained, I had no close friends at school. I had always felt isolated by my bizarre heritage and exotic appearance. From my early childhood onwards, it had always been my mother and I versus the rest of the world. Any parent is protective of their child but, because I was so different, Sarah was extra, if not over, protective. If she had still been alive when I reached my maturity, I'm sure I would have struggled to free myself from her apron strings. While Sarah Weinstein would have fiercely challenged anyone who attempted to stereotype her as a typical Jewish mother, in many ways that is what she was. She was a smothering, outsized personality – flamboyantly extrovert. My natural response was to become the opposite – to retreat into my shell. And, even though she was now gone and Ana was a very different character – far less controlling – initially, nothing changed. I stayed in my shell.

Then came the 43 Group. It was as if a part of me that had been locked away in a cupboard had suddenly been let out. Not only my angry violent side, but also a more outgoing, social side. I now had friends and compatriots. These sorties across London in our fleet of black cabs gave me a purpose in life – a cause; and, more importantly, a sense of excitement and adventure. And so, when it came to an end, I was left in limbo. Which way was my life now going? Would I simply drift back into my mundane existence as the anonymous clerk tucked away in the back office of the jewellery store, perhaps summoning up the courage to ask Stella, the pretty brunette shop assistant, out on a date and eventually settle down with her, or someone similar, and start a family? Or was there some way I could continue to pursue the more adventurous life I had found as part of the 43 Group?

The answer came out of the blue one Sunday morning as I wandered among the crowds browsing the market stalls in Petticoat Lane. A heavy hand fell on my shoulder from behind and a deep mellifluous voice boomed at me.

"Hello young man. And which tribe do you belong to, if you don't mind me asking?"

I turned and stared dumbfounded at the exotic figure in front of me. He was almost as tall as me and he was black. But it was the way he was dressed that struck me dumb. He wore a towering headdress of red white and blue feathers, a colourfully embroidered waistcoat over a white shirt with puffy sleeves and a tartan sash round his waist supporting silky billowing pantaloons. As I continued to stare open-mouthed at this strange apparition, he grinned, revealing a prominent gold tooth flashing in the sunlight like an image from a toothpaste advertisement.

"Do you speak English?" He enunciated slowly.

"Yes," I muttered.

"I asked you where you are from." He articulated each word carefully, assuming I was finding it difficult to understand him.

"London. I was born in London." It was my habitual and only answer to that question.

He threw back his head and bellowed with laughter, his ostrich feathers fluttering as if he was about to take flight. "Let us go somewhere where we can talk. I want to know more about you. I believe myself to be the most exotic creature in England, but you come close to challenging me."

Here was another turning point – a passport into an alternative, and more exhilarating, world. Over a cup of tea, we told each other about our respective backgrounds. Mine was true but, as I discovered later, his was a fantasy. As we walked through the East End streets together, he was constantly greeted with smiles, waves and friendly banter. He called himself Ras Prince Monolulu and claimed to be descended from Ethiopian royalty. He said he was a prince of the Falasha tribe who were black Ethiopian Jews. That explained the Star of David sewn on his waistcoat. He also claimed Scottish ancestry, thus the tartan cummerbund.

Once we had exchanged backgrounds, he made me a proposition. He made his living as a racing tipster (or turf adviser, as he preferred to be called). He spent his working life roaming the East End streets, offices and factories selling his tips and attending racetracks across the Home Counties, especially Newmarket, Kemptown, Epsom and Ascot. He needed an assistant: someone who could carry his money for him and act as a protector. Despite his size, he had been attacked and robbed on a couple of occasions. It was not only my size that made me ideal for the job, but also my appearance which would fit in well with his own. He decided that I could be a Fijian prince and he started describing the kind of costume he envisaged me wearing.

The following Saturday we sat side by side on the train to Newmarket. Having spent my whole life up until that moment trying to make myself as inconspicuous as possible, a not inconsiderable task for someone of my size and appearance, it came as a relief to be sat alongside a man who went to such extravagant lengths to exaggerate his weirdness.

Like my involvement with the 43 Group, this was only going to be an occasional evening and weekend activity. I was not about to give up the day job. In fact, my mundane job as an accounts clerk in the little office at the back of the jewellery store, was made bearable by these new out of hours adventures, as they had been by my forays with the 43 Group. My only hesitation about accepting the Prince's offer had been the costume. Whilst I was happy to render myself more conspicuous by accompanying this outrageously flamboyant black man, I felt it a step too far to go the whole hog and allow him to dress me up in tribal gear. After this first trip to the racetrack, I relented a little and agreed to drape one of his multi-coloured cloaks over my plain white shirt and black trousers, but I refused to wear his mock-up of a tribal headdress.

Although I had no interest in horse-racing or gambling of any kind, I was happy to be his silent partner – his bagman cum bodyguard – trying to look austere and regal as I trailed around at his shoulder.

"I gotta a horse! I gotta a horse!" He cried out as we moved through the crowds. "I gotta horse to beat the favourite."

Everyone seemed to know him and he exchanged banter with the regular racetrack goers as they passed by.

"Take a tip from a black man. He'll bring you luck."

He charged ten shillings for a tip. They were written on scraps of paper tucked into brown envelopes and, every time he handed one over, he would repeat the mantra – "if you tell anyone else, it will lose."

I never knew how he came up with his horses – he kept his methods close to his chest – but he obviously had a method and he must have had a reasonable ratio of success because he had no problem selling his tips and, more often than not, to the same returning customers. Either that or he was such an accepted and colourful part of the race going ritual that the spectators were as happy to spend money on his tips as they were on purchasing a beer or a pie.

But not everyone at the racetrack greeted the Prince with cheery smiles and friendly banter. The official racecourse bookmakers often eyed him with scowls. I soon realised why he had wanted my extra muscle at his side.

Some weekday evenings I would accompany him as he made his rounds of East End pubs and clubs repeating the same slogans and selling plenty of tips. And so it was that, one Friday night, I went with him as he ventured further afield, touring the pubs and private drinking clubs of Soho.

This was to be the start of the next, and most radical, turning point in my life.

# Monday 5th October 2001

Edelstein and Partners Solicitors were situated in a small but very plush suite of offices on the second floor of a Georgian town house at the back of Kingsway in Holborn. As DC Ethan Edwards entered the reception area, he was surprised at how opulent the offices were. He shuffled his backside squeakily on the multi-seat white leather sofa and his scuffed black boots sank into the grey shag pile carpet. There was a Gaggia coffee machine softly humming and bubbling with a fresh brew on a table next to the sofa with a plate of luxury chocolate biscuits beside it. A range of newspapers and magazines were neatly fanned out on an onyx coffee table in front of him. There were impressionist style landscape paintings lining the walls. They did not look like reproductions.

Ethan didn't know what to make of it. It must cost a pretty penny to hire one of the partners in this law firm, even if it was only to draft and administer your will. A man like Harry Felatu, living in cheap threadbare rooms in a Harlesden back street would hardly have been at home in these surroundings, Ethan thought.

"Detective Jones. I'm Martin Edelstein." An overweight man in a pin-striped suit with a reddish face and thick black hair streaked with strands of grey held out his hand. Ethan stood up and shook it.

"If you'll follow me to my office." He turned and led the way down a short corridor to a frosted glass door with his name etched on it.

"I understand you are here to ask me some questions about Harry Felatu. Of course, I'll do everything I can to be of assistance. It's a shocking business. I can't say I knew Mr Felatu well – in fact, I only met him once and that was a good five or six years ago. It was my late father who dealt with Mr Felatu's business. Even so, I was very shocked to hear that he'd been murdered. Do you have any idea who did it?"

"It's early days but I'm sure we'll get the culprits," Ethan said as he lowered himself into the chair next to Edelstein's desk.

There was a large box file on the desk in front of Martin Edelstein which he flipped open. "So, how can I help?" He leaned back in his swivel chair and rested his hands on his ample stomach.

"Well, to start with, I'm a bit mystified as to how a man like Mr Felatu came to hire you as his solicitor." Ethan waved his hand around the spacious, luxuriously furnished office. "I don't imagine you come cheap."

Martin Edelstein tilted his head back and laughed, his double chin wobbling. The laughter mutated into a guttural cough. Recovering himself, he adopted a more serious expression.

"I'm sorry. I know this isn't a laughing matter. It's just that, despite appearances, Harry Felatu was quite a wealthy man."

Ethen stared at him sceptically. "Wealthy? Are you sure? But how? I mean – he didn't live like someone with a lot of money."

"From what my father used to say about him, I can well believe that." He paused, stroking his chins. "I suppose he would have been what one could call an eccentric millionaire – a bit like Howard Hughes. Although maybe that's not such a good example. Hughes only looked like a tramp. He lived most of his life in a penthouse suite in one of his luxury hotels with servants."

Ethan didn't know who Howard Hughes was and didn't want to waste time finding out. "I think you'd better explain to me where all this money came from. He doesn't seem to have had much of a job or career that we can ascertain. Was he a gambler?"

"No, Mr Jones. It's very simple. He inherited it. His mother was a children's author. She made a good living from her books while she was alive but, since her death, the books have remained in print and, during the 1960s and 70s, they became very popular. The money from them went into a trust fund for Harry Felatu as her only descendant."

Ethan sat in silence, staring into space. This changed everything. Instead of the apparently motiveless murder of a down-at-heel elderly recluse, this was now about a man with squirreled away wealth, bringing into play the commonest motive there was for murder.

"So, I understand that you have a copy of his will that you can give me?"

Edelstein reached into the box file and withdrew a stapled document. "I'm afraid that, if you're hoping for some black sheep in the family who's been left a small fortune and, therefore, has ample motive to bump him off, you are going to be disappointed." He handed over the will.

"So, who has he left the money to?"

"Apart from the trust fund paying him a modest monthly stipend on which I presume he lived, the rest of the money was used to fund a range of charitable causes and he has confirmed, in the will, that they will all continue to be funded after his death. They are all listed in there. Quite a few of them are bursaries set up with various colleges and universities to provide scholarships for underprivileged black and mixed-race children. He's left no money at all to any living individual." Martin Edelstein smiled. He seemed to be enjoying the look of dismay and disappointment on the young detective's face.

"Can I take this away with me?" Ethan waved the will at him.

"Of course. Be my guest. I presume you have spoken to Ana? Although I don't suppose she could have been of very much help to you. I believe she's still alive, although I don't know if she's fully compos mentis."

"Ana?" Ethan stared blankly at him. "Sorry but I'm not sure who you're talking about."

"Ana Geisler. She was Harry's guardian. She looked after him when his mother died. Initially, she had money provided from the trust fund to look after Harry but that ceased to be payable to her once he reached maturity so she certainly wouldn't have had any motive to kill him." He smiled mischievously. "But then, she must be in her nineties and I believe she's pretty much house bound so I guess that rules her out as a suspect."

"Do you have an address for her?"

"I should have. I'll get my secretary to dig it out for you."

As Ethan walked back to Holborn tube station, there was an extra bounce in his step. This was his first murder case and it was beginning to get very interesting.

"Miss Stone. How are you?"

Becky was walking across the forecourt of the British Library when her mobile rang. She didn't recognise the number but the voice was familiar.

"Sorry. Who is this?"

"David Reznikoff. You said I should contact you if I had any further information that you might be interested in. Well, I've just remembered something about Harry that I didn't mention when we met last week."

Becky's heart sank. She knew as soon as she had given him her mobile phone number that it was a mistake – an opportunity for him to pester her; to play more of his annoying games.

"Thank you for phoning, Mr Reznikoff but I've decided not to pursue my interest in Mr Felatu any further. I felt that it was just leading me down a blind alley. I've decided it's best left to the police."

"Seriously?" He sounded disappointed. "Even though you now know he was murdered? Well, it's your decision, of course." There was a moment's silence but, before Becky could end the call as speedily and politely as possible, he continued. "Why don't I give you my piece of information anyway and then you can decide whether you want to do anything with it or not?"

Becky took a deep breath. Against her better judgement, she didn't terminate the call. "Okay. Go ahead."

"What I forgot to tell you, Miss Stone, is that Harry does have one living relative. At least, I'm fairly certain she's still alive."

"Yes," said Becky, still not sure why she was continuing to listen.

"After his mother died when he was a teenager, he was brought up by her partner – a woman called Ana Geisler. She'll be in her nineties now."

Becky had that same feeling she got when standing at the coffee shop counter staring at the cakes and trying to resist temptation. "Can you spell her name for me?" Becky balanced her bag on a low wall and removed her notepad and pen while he spelt out the name. "And do you have any contact details for her?"

She could picture his slyly grinning face, happy to have reeled her in again. "I'm afraid not. All I know is that she lives in Hampstead."

"And who is that, may I ask?"

Richard had appeared unannounced at her shoulder as she was googling Ana Geisler. She could detect the hint of suspicion in his voice. "It's none of your business. And I wish you wouldn't creep up on me like that. It feels like you're spying on me."

"Sorry. I just came to ask if you wanted a cup of tea. If I'd have known you were emailing your secret lover–"

She turned and looked up at him. "It's just somebody connected with my research if you must know. I only contact my lover by phone."

"It's something to do with that murdered man, isn't it?"

Becky didn't respond. She left the cursor hovering over one of the entries for Ana Geisler waiting for Richard to leave her alone. Instead, he put his hands on her shoulders and started gently massaging them. "Oh Becky, you're way too young to be playing Miss Marple. You really should leave this to the police. It's none of your business."

"No, it's none of YOUR business. I don't want a cup of tea, thanks. Now leave me alone."

He let go of her shoulders and moved round the desk to face her, a censorious look on his face.

She sighed. "Look, I know I said I wasn't going to pursue it but I've received some new information and I know I'm being stupid and I should forget about it and leave it to the police but it's like an irritating itch that I just have to scratch. It'll probably come to nothing. Once I've scratched it, it'll probably go away. But I do have to scratch it."

Richard echoed her sigh. "I guess I should know you by now. Your stubbornness. Like a dog with a bone. It annoys the hell out of me at times, but I guess it's also one of the reasons I love you." He bent down and kissed her on the forehead.

"And I love you too. Now, fuck off."

As Becky stood outside Bullingham Mansions, she had that familiar feeling of aspirational envy. Despite its arty-farty middle class trendiness, she would have loved to live in a mansion block just next to Hampstead High Street. Even with its creeping gentrification, Harlesden was no contest. Maybe one day, she mused, before pushing such thoughts from her mind and pressing Ana Geisler's entry buzzer.

"Who is it?" Barked a suspicious sounding foreign accented female voice.

"I've come to speak to Ana Geisler. It's about Harry Felatu."

"Are you the police?" The voice sounded even more distrustful.

"No, I'm not." Becky wondered whether she was speaking to Ana Geisler. She didn't think so. The voice sounded too young.

"Are you a journalist? Ana is not speaking to any journalists."

"No, I'm not a journalist either. I have a personal interest in Mr Felatu and I just want to ask her a few questions." This was stupid, Becky thought. She should never have come. She should have followed her earlier instincts and heeded Richard's advice.

"You must understand that Miss Geisler is very upset by what happened to Mr Felatu. She does not want to speak to anybody."

Before Becky could interrupt to apologise for bothering her and then beat a hasty retreat, a faint voice in the background, presumably from somewhere inside the flat, interrupted the woman on the entry phone. It sounded like another woman. Becky couldn't make out what she was saying, although she did hear the woman on the entry phone's reply.

"I'm only trying to do what's best for you. I'm supposed to be looking after you." She sounded even more irritated than she had when speaking to Becky. Then there was a further indistinct response from the voice in the background.

"Okay, you can come up," the exasperated woman muttered, while pressing the entry buzzer.

Becky, on the point of turning away, not expecting to be suddenly granted entry, was only just in time to push open the heavy glass-panelled door before the buzzer stopped. When she stepped out of the lift on the second floor, she was facing the open door of number 23 and an annoyed looking middle-aged woman with long straight blond hair, her arms folded underneath her ample bosom. She looked like a Headmistress waiting to upbraid a naughty pupil. She looked Becky up and down as if still making up her mind whether to let her in or not.

"I have told Ana that I do not think this is a good idea. She is elderly and very frail and she does not need to be upset anymore."

"Oh, for goodness sake, Magda," said a strident middle European voice from inside the flat. "I've already told you that I'm happy to speak to the young lady. Please let her in."

Magda raised her eyes to the ceiling before stepping aside to allow enough space for Becky to edge carefully past her. On the far side of the elegant oak-panelled entry hall, a very thin woman with tightly curled grey hair and tortoise shell glasses sat in a wheelchair.

"Please come into the sitting room. I'm Ana Geisler." Her voice was that of a much younger woman.

The sitting room was the size of Becky's whole flat. The walls were festooned with art works, mostly portrait drawings, and the furniture was all heavy wooden antiques. One wall was crammed floor to ceiling with books and the whole room had a musty library smell. Through the open door at the far end came the sound of clattering crockery as Magda noisily made tea.

Once Becky had explained who she was and how she had come to be tangentially connected with Harry Felatu, Ana Geisler leaned forward in her wheelchair. She had a long body but her shoulders were hunched over. Her wrinkled face was very pale and her blue eyes were watery. She nodded her head and smiled wistfully.

"Ah. Poor Hare." She heaved a sigh. "Before I say anything else, please allow me to apologise for Magda. We have been together for nearly forty years and she means very well. She is very protective of me – a bit too protective at times. I told her to let you in because I like to talk to people and I don't do very much of it these days. Once you get to my age, most of your friends and family have died and you don't get much opportunity to meet new people. In fact, Hare was the last remaining person in my family."

"I'm very sorry for your loss. Maybe you could tell me something about him."

Ana spent the next ten minutes giving an account of her relationship with Sarah Weinstein, Sarah's death and her subsequent life in London as Hare Felatu's guardian. At that point, Magda interrupted, bringing in a tray of tea things including a plate with two slices of apple strudel. She took her time unloading the tea things from the tray on to the glass-topped coffee table while glancing suspiciously at Becky before leaving the room. While Becky poured the tea and placed slices of strudel on to willow patterned plates, Ana continued.

"I loved Hare just as much as if he was my own son, but I have always felt that I let Sarah down. I didn't take care for him as well as I should have done." She looked pensively at Becky. "Do you have any children, Miss Stone?"

"No, I don't."

"Me neither. I imagine bringing up children is difficult even when they're your own, but trying to be a mother to a teenage boy who isn't yours – that's very tough. And Hare was a very troubled young man. No surprise really when you consider his background and the fact that he lost his mother at such a young age." She paused and dabbed her eyes with an embroidered handkerchief which had been tucked in the sleeve of her blouse.

"I'm sure you did your best," said Becky reassuringly.

"Maybe. Maybe not. Very soon he was an adult and there was not much I could do. I tried to offer advice – steer him on the right course – but, like most young people, he wasn't going to listen to a fuddy duddy like me. He was going to go his own way."

"Did you see him very often?"

"In the early days, soon after he left home, he would often come to visit but it got less and less over the years. He didn't like me criticising his life – the people he was mixing with. Eventually, he just stopped telling me anything about what he was doing. I suppose because he knew I would disapprove."

"And when did you see him last?"

"It must have been about six months ago. He took me out to lunch."

"And how did he seem?"

"He was fine. As usual, he didn't want to talk about himself. We mainly reminisced about the old days. I'm afraid that's what us old people tend to do."

"I'm sorry to have to ask you but – have you any idea why he was murdered? Any idea who would have wanted to kill him?"

"No. I have no idea. As I said, I knew very little about his life. I only know he mixed with a lot of…how can I describe them?" She paused and looked round the room as if trying to find inspiration in the pictures on the walls. "A lot of undesirable people. Low lifes. Criminals – some of them."

"Do you have specific people in mind?"

"Not really. You obviously know about all that Soho crowd he used to mix with. I'm an artist myself," she said, waving her hand in the direction of the drawings on the walls. "I knew some of them. Met them at shows and in galleries. They had talent but they led unpleasant lives. I wouldn't want you to think I'm prejudiced. Homophobic." She pronounced the word with exaggerated care. "Is that the word for it?" Becky nodded. "I am lesbian myself so how could I be? In my day, we had to be more careful – more reserved in our behaviour. No shows of affection in public. But now anything goes. I warned Hare. I told him they were not to be trusted. They were not real friends."

"You talked about criminals," Becky said, as Magda re-entered the room carrying a vacuum cleaner. She walked past Becky and into the hallway. Becky avoided her eyes.

"I don't know much about it. I just heard rumours. I often asked Hare about the sort of people he was mixing with. Some of them, I think he was doing work for. He never answered. The police asked me the same question but I couldn't help them either. My only surprise is that he survived as long as he did. I was always worried that he would come to a bad end, especially when he would go a long time without contacting me."

After they had finished their tea and strudel, Ana showed Becky some of her artwork, including drawings of Sarah Weinstein and Hare as a boy. She led Becky across to the bookshelves where she pulled out some original editions of Sarah's children's stories featuring her own illustrations. While Becky leafed through the books, Magda's hoovering and general clattering about could be heard in the other rooms. Despite her partner's hostility, Ana seemed to bask in Becky's company and enjoyed having an audience to whom she could reminisce. For her part, Becky loved listening to such a vibrant ninety plus year old even though she had little useful information to impart about Harry.

It was another dead end. Becky left Bullingham Mansions resolving that this really would be her final attempt to investigate the mystery that was Harry Felatu.

# Extracts from
# *The Autobiography of an Invisible Man*

## THE SOHO YEARS

It was on a rainy November evening in Soho that I trailed behind Prince Monolulu as he pushed through a scuffed wooden door below a sign for The Colony Room and climbed a narrow dimly lit staircase. The flock wallpaper was peeling at the edges and there was an unpleasant smell; a mixture of damp and mouse droppings. At the top of the stairs, we passed through a padded door into a long, narrow, smoky bar half full of drinkers, mostly male.

"Well, if it isn't my very own Prince Charming. How are you, cunty?"

"I'm fine, Muriel. And may I be permitted to say that you are looking particularly lovely this evening?" Prince Monolulu bent down to kiss her outstretched hand.

I turned to face the woman he was speaking to. She was perched on a stool next to the entrance as if guarding it. Her shoulder length dark hair was swept back from her forehead and tucked behind her ears. She wore a floral-patterned summer dress. One bare arm leaned on the bar, her raised hand holding a cigarette, her face tilted upwards, her dark brown eyes staring inquiringly at me.

"Fuck me, cunty. Are you real? Am I seeing things? Did your mother get fucked by an Easter Island statue?"

"Oh, do shut up, Muriel." It was a man at the other end of the bar with a pock-marked face wearing a grubby sheepskin jacket. "Leave the boy alone. You'll frighten him away. It's about time we had a bit of youth and beauty in this hole."

"Alright Mary. Keep your cock in your trousers. I've already made up my mind." She turned her dark probing eyes back towards me. "You can be an honorary member of my establishment. Mind you, with someone of your size, I might have to build an extension." She turned back to the group of men at the other end of the bar standing round the man in the sheepskin jacket. "It makes a change to have a real man in here rather than all you nancy boys." She swivelled her head back towards me. "You are a real man, aren't you, Tiny?" She emphasised the word 'real' and narrowed her eyes flirtatiously.

"Watch yourself, young fella. Muriel likes you. That's unheard of. I'd get out of here if I were you before she gets her hooks into you," said a balding man with black-rimmed glasses and a very pink face nursing an almost empty wine glass at a small table in the corner of the room.

"Nobody asked for your opinion," Muriel said. "It's about time you opened your bean bag, Lottie, and bought yourself another drink."

The pink faced man stood up and sidled over to me. He introduced himself as David Archer. He was well spoken and smartly dressed in a dark blue suit and red tie although, on closer inspection, the jacket cuffs and elbows were frayed and the lapels stained. He bought us both glasses of red wine. For the next fifteen minutes, while the Prince toured the room chatting familiarly to the drinkers and selling the odd tip, I introduced myself to the half a dozen men gathered around David Archer and the man in the sheepskin jacket. I gave as brief an explanation as I could about myself. For that fifteen minutes, I was the centre of attention for this motley, mostly inebriated, crew. As very much of an introvert, this sudden attention should have felt uncomfortable, and yet it didn't. And, when the Prince had finished his business and was heading for the exit, I was reluctant to go with him.

The following week, the Prince and I returned to The Colony Room, only this time, when he had finished his tour of the bar, I did not leave with him.

It was as if I had been trapped in a spider's web. It's difficult to describe the addictive charm of the place. It had nothing to do with the sticky green walls or the tatty bamboo fronted bar above which a row of bedraggled potted plants on a shelf struggled to survive, suffocated by the clouds of cigarette smoke. Nor was it the dim lighting preserved even in the middle of the afternoon by the drawn, threadbare, floral patterned curtains. It was partly Muriel and her stream of foul-mouthed put downs, but mainly, for me, it was a feeling of acceptance – of being part of an exclusive and outrageous club. It was similar to the feeling I had had when I was part of the 43 Group. Similar, but different. Then we had a simple pro-active purpose and, once that purpose had been achieved, the friendships and camaraderie quickly evaporated. In The Colony Room, there was no purpose other than to exist – to be yourself. It was packed with renegades, artists, aesthetes and bon viveurs. A safe haven for weirdos and eccentrics. A place where my own strangeness was accepted. The very lack of purpose attracted me. For some time, I had been searching for a purpose in my life and, at last, I had found it. My purpose was to have no purpose. It felt strangely liberating.

And also, if I am to be completely honest, dear reader, once again there was the ghost of my mother hanging over me. Despite the fact that she had been dead for nearly ten years, I still felt that I must be a disappointment to her. I still felt that I needed to win her approval. Although it didn't look as if |I was ever going to become a writer or an artist myself, I rather pathetically believed that, if she could see me mixing in artistic circles, she would be proud. In this small way, I was aping her lifestyle. She had been happiest when she had been subsumed into the intellectual life of the Bloomsbury village. I would now find some contentment by being a part of the bohemian community in the Soho village.

And it wasn't just about a desire to blend in with this louche company. I soon found that I could be accepted by them while maintaining my individuality. And I was flattered that I had my own nickname: Muriel's use of 'Tiny' stuck, while she called everybody else either 'Mary' or 'Cunty'. The only other exception to this was the man who was the centre of attention for the crowd round the bar on my second visit – a man Muriel called 'daughter' while he always referred to her as 'mother'. He was plumpish with a pear-shaped face and reddish cheeks – like a debauched cherub, as I once heard somebody describe him. That night his hair was combed back from his forehead and glistened with what I later discovered was brown Kiwi shoe polish. He wore a black polo neck jumper under a grey herring bone suit. Like Muriel, he always seemed to have a cigarette scissored between his fingers.

I edged nearer to him at the bar to catch what it was he was saying that was captivating the others.

"Oh, I remember that woman. She was called Marlene." His voice was an odd mixture of refined Mayfair and East End mockney. "Before they carted her off to the looney bin, she used to regularly call the fire brigade. When they arrived and naturally asked her where the fire was, she would lift up her dress and show them her cunt. "Here," she would say."

"Was she the one who used to be a hostess at the Coconut Grove?" It was the man with the pock-marked face who had been the centre of attention on my first visit. "We used to call her the buggers' Vera Lynn. She was always flashing her private parts."

"Oh John, I think you'll find they ceased to be private a long time ago," said the debauched cherub.

"Sorry dearie, you can't come in. It's members only." It was Muriel's booming voice addressing a young man in a black leather jacket who'd just stepped through the entrance. Everyone at the bar turned to stare at him, entertained by his embarrassment.

"Oh. Well, could I just use your toilet?" Said the young man.

"When I said 'members only' I wasn't making an exception for your cock. Now piss off."

As the young man beat a hasty retreat, I turned back round to come face to face with 'daughter'. He was staring up at me with an astonished look on his face.

"I haven't seen you here before." He tilted his body sideways so he could peer round me towards Muriel. "Who is this vision of exaggerated butchness, mother?"

"That's Tiny," said Muriel. "I've just made him an honorary member."

He leaned back to face me. "Well hallo Tiny. It's a pleasure to meet you." He held out a limp hand. "I'm Francis Bacon."

"Hare Felatu," I said, shaking his hand. At the time, I had no idea who Francis Bacon was.

"Well, I think we should all celebrate such an illustrious and decorative new member," he announced turning to Tony, the barman. "Champagne for all my real friends, real pain for my sham friends."

Over the next few years, I would grow used to Francis ordering bottles of his favourite tipple in this same flamboyant manner.

My introduction to The Colony Room and its bohemian habitués was to change far more than just my social life. Two weeks after my second visit there, I had tendered my resignation to my boss at the Hatton Garden jewellers and ended what had anyway been a somewhat lukewarm relationship with Stella, the pretty dark-haired shop assistant I'd been fantasising about marrying. After my introduction to the bohemian life of Soho, my proposed future as a bookkeeper in a jewellery business married to the attractive but uninspiring Stella had become deeply unenticing.

On my third visit to The Colony Room, David Archer, the middle-aged pink-faced man who had bought me a drink on my first visit, told me that he had just opened a bookshop and café in nearby Greek Street. With his cut-glass accent, slight stutter and penchant for tweed jackets, he looked and sounded like one of Bertie Wooster's eccentric uncles. His conversation was often hard to follow due to a combination of the stutter and his habit of changing topic mid-sentence. As he was telling me about the bookshop and his plans to turn it into a gathering place for poets and writers, I realised, after managing to decode a lengthy convoluted sentence, that he was offering me a job. I told him that I had no experience of working in bookshops or the retail trade in general, but he dismissed my reservations with a wave of his good arm. (Sorry, I forgot to mention that he had a withered arm). Before I could respond any further to his offer, he had moved the topic of conversation on to Dylan Thomas. He told me he had met the Welsh poet when he first arrived in London and had published his first collection of poetry. Then there was another abrupt switch of topic. There was a studio room in the attic above the bookshop. I could move into it rent free, if I wanted. He would count it as part of my remuneration for working in the bookshop. And then the topics melded together –

Dylan Thomas had been a previous occupant of this studio flat.

And so it was that, one week later, I had a new job and a new home. Ana was not best pleased about either the home or the job. Why give up a solid, well paid, respectable career to become a shop assistant? I had told her as little as possible about my recent dalliances in Soho, although I had mentioned my meeting with Francis Bacon (now that I had discovered who he was), since I thought that, as a fellow artist, she would have heard of him and would be impressed. She wasn't. She had met him at a recent private gallery viewing and had found him as self-indulgent and louche as his paintings. Although she had to reluctantly accept that, at twenty-three, I was old enough to make my own decisions, she begged me not to get involved with Francis Bacon and his crowd. I owed a lot to Ana for looking after me when my mother died and she had always been like a second mother to me so, not wanting to upset or worry her, I agreed that I would keep well away from the motley crew at The Colony Club. I hated lying to her, but I guess that's what children do when seeking to appease their parents.

After the routine drudgery of my book-keeping job, closeted away day after day in the tiny backroom office of the Hatton Garden jewellery store, working in the Greek Street bookshop was liberating. I need not have worried that my complete lack of experience as a bookseller or any other kind of salesman would be a drawback. Nobody else working in the shop, including David Archer himself, seemed to have the slightest idea of how to run such an establishment. Here is an example from my first day.

A bearded man in a duffel coat comes up to me at the sales desk clutching a copy of *Nausea* by John Paul Sartre.

Bearded man: Could I buy this, please?

Me: Yes (while looking at the inside flyleaf). That will be five shillings and sixpence, please.

David Archer: (appearing at my shoulder and taking the book from me): Oh, I'm terribly sorry. This book's not for sale. It's for display purposes only. You could try Foyles or Better Books in Charing Cross Road. I'm sure they'll have a copy.

Man exits shop looking bewildered.

And this was a regular occurrence when David was present in the shop. It gradually dawned on me that he saw it more as a lending library than a shop and was reluctant to sell any of the books.

The café in the rear of the shop was run by a voluptuous Rubinesque woman called Henrietta who doubled as an occasional model for the painter, Lucien Freud. As you entered the café down a short flight of stairs, you were confronted by a life size photograph of Henrietta in the nude, filling an alcove. Like the bookshop, the café was run on very unorthodox lines. First thing every morning, Henrietta would go around the corner to the upmarket French patisserie in Dean Street and buy a stack of cakes, pastries and filled baguettes which she would then sell in the bookshop café for less than she had paid for them.

A frequent visitor to the shop and café was the man with the pock-marked face and scruffy appearance who I had met at The Colony Room that first night. I soon got to know him better. He was John Deakin – a photographer – and David Archer's boyfriend. Theirs was not an easy relationship to understand. While David was the most affable, kind and generous man, Deakin was mendacious and malevolent. He would lounge around in an armchair at the back of the shop delivering a steady stream of bitchy sneering remarks, principally directed at David who, for the most part, ignored them.

On one occasion, David and I heard a furious shouting match, and the sound of furniture being sent flying, coming from the direction of the café. When we arrived to see what was happening, Henrietta was hurling obscenities, and a mille-feuille, at Deakin, who rapidly retreated, his face flecked with splotches of cream and what could have either been jam or his habitual bloodstains from that morning's shaving cuts. It transpired that this assault on Deakin was prompted by her discovery that he had been selling nude photos of her, that he had taken for Lucien Freud, to passers-by on the streets of Soho for ten shillings each.

Although it could not be said that this new job was boring, after my first week I was very doubtful that it would last much longer. There was little money in the till at the end of each day and the café must have been running at a huge loss, especially taking into account the numerous impecunious would-be poets who frequented it and were allowed to consume copious amounts of coffee on credit. I voiced my worries to Adil, a young Indian, and a minor poet, who worked part-time in the shop. Oh no need to worry, he replied. David's a very wealthy man. He owns half of Wiltshire.

If the day job was bizarre, my evenings were no less unusual. I frequently spent them in The Colony Room where Francis Bacon grew increasingly more attached to me. He was such an outgoing vivacious personality, unleashing constant streams of gossipy stories, that it was hard to fathom what possible interest he could have in such a dull introvert as me. I broached this one day with David Archer who looked at me with raised eyebrows.

"My dear young fellow," he said. "Your naivete is utterly charming. Francis is a homosexual but, like a lot of queers, he's none too keen on the company of other queers.

He craves the company of butch heterosexual men like you. What he's hoping is that he can convert you, so watch your back – no pun intended."

Francis himself told me that the reason he liked me was because I only spoke when I had something that was worth saying. Most of the time, he was surrounded by people who rabbited on interminably even though they had nothing to say that was worth listening to. I was a refreshing change.

Two weeks after I first met him, he invited me to his studio in South Kensington. My only previous experience of an artist's studio was Ana's attic room in our Wooburn Green house where she worked on her illustrations for my mother's children's books. It had been a surgically clean and tidy space with an uncluttered desk, an easel, shelves with neat rows of books and cartons of paper and walls decorated with framed examples of her artwork. Francis' studio could not have been more different. It was on the first floor of a mews cottage. The bare floorboards were covered in piles of paper, discarded dirty rags and sponges, squeezed out paint tubes, old paint-spattered cashmere sweaters, empty champagne cartons and old copies of *Paris Match*. The picture window was curtained with a grubby beige blanket. The walls were festooned with a kaleidoscope of pinned up images – photos of wild animals, boxers and Nazi leaders, a painting of Christ carrying his cross and a range of other reproductions by the likes of Goya, Velasquez, Degas, Van Gogh and Michelangelo. In the tiny gaps between these images, there were finger smears of multi-coloured paint. When I expressed my surprise at the squalid state of his studio to one of Francis' friends one evening, he told me that, about a year ago, there had been a period of several weeks when the studio was pervaded by a revolting smell. Eventually, the cause of the smell was discovered when Francis, searching for something in a far corner of the studio, uncovered a pheasant carcass that he'd bought some time ago with the intention of including it in a still life.

Francis dragged a wooden kitchen chair from amidst the debris and asked me if I minded sitting still while he sketched me. It was to be the first, but not the last, time I modelled for him. While he worked at his easel, he told me about his childhood and youth growing up in rural Ireland in candid detail, much of it a tirade against his reviled father. He described how his father had once caught him, when he was a small boy, dressing in his mother's underwear and had him horsewhipped by his Irish grooms (his father was a racehorse trainer). He peered at me from behind his easel and grinned. I believe he was trying to see if I was embarrassed by these revelations. Since my skin colour didn't allow for very visible blushing, he was none the wiser.

"The thing is, Harry," he said, "what my father didn't realise was that he was doing me a favour. Ever since then, I have positively enjoyed a good beating." He paused, still staring intently at me. "I would imagine a strapping young man like you must be a beater rather than one of the beaten." I made no comment. "If you like, I could help you make some money out of your muscle. For starters, I myself would pay you to give me a good whipping. Or, if you'd prefer that it was less personal, there are parties that I could take you to where there are men who would pay you a pound a lash."

I thanked him for the offer but told him it was not my style. Despite my size and strength, I said, I did not indulge in violence. Although I shared many confidences with Francis and gave him a reasonably detailed account of my own life, I refrained from telling him about my activities with the 43 Group.

The following week, first thing on Monday morning, just after I had arrived for work in the bookshop, the phone rang. It was Francis sounding uncharacteristically agitated.

I could barely hear him as he was whispering into the receiver. "Harry, I need your help urgently. Can you come over to the studio post haste?"

"Why? What's wrong?"

"Never mind. You'll find out when you get here. I'm sure David will be able to hold the fort for you in the shop."

When I arrived at the studio, I was let in by a barefoot Francis clad in a kimono style silk robe. One side of his face was bruised and swollen and he had a smear of blood on one ear.

"He's in the bedroom," Francis whispered, gesturing over his shoulder.

"Who is?"

"How the fuck should I know. It doesn't matter who he is. I just need you to get rid of him."

He was a heavily tattooed merchant seaman who Francis had picked up in a pub in Wapping the night before. Apparently, the man had pandered somewhat overenthusiastically to Francis' desire for rough sex and now he was refusing to leave. Fortunately, my simply appearing at the bedroom door immediately changed his mind without me having to resort to strong arm tactics.

From that morning on, there were numerous other occasions when Francis would call on me as a kind of bodyguard cum enforcer. Although he did not dress particularly flashily and did not own an expensive car (or a car of any kind since he couldn't drive), he always wore a Cartier gold watch which he said helped to attract rough trade. On one occasion, he was so worried that the young tough that he'd picked up off the streets and brought back to the studio, was going to rob him, that he hid the watch under the bedroom carpet only for the man to tread on it as he came back from the bathroom.

One time, after I had stepped in once again to rescue Francis, I hesitatingly criticised him for his attraction to these guttersnipes, warning him that, sooner or later, I would either not be available or would arrive too late to rescue him and he would come to a bad end. As he stood in front of the bathroom mirror camouflaging his latest bruises with makeup, he agreed with me and vowed that he would renounce his regrettable taste in men. Of course, he never did. His attitude was summed up for me one evening at dinner in Wheeler's, his favourite restaurant, when the waiter was about to remove the wine decanter from our table and Francis grabbed it back and poured the remains into his glass.

"But sir, those are the dregs," the waiter said.

"The dregs are what I prefer," Francis replied.

It is only now, looking back on my life, that I can begin to understand why I embraced The Colony Room lifestyle and felt flattered to be treated as a friend by a bunch of people who would have been labelled as undesirables by decent, so-called, civilised society. My initial attraction to them is easily explained. Their rebelliousness, their otherness, their rejection of, and open hostility towards, the stultifying conformity of 1950s English society was immediately appealing to someone like me – a young mixed-race man who, however hard he tried, would never fit in to that staid white Christian notion of Englishness. Neither could I relate to the new minority ethnic groups that were pouring into London at that time. Having been raised by Sarah Weinstein among her upper-class literary Bloomsbury circle, I had nothing at all in common with London's growing West Indian community other than, like them, not being white. As I said at the beginning of this autobiography, I was the only member of my tribe.

And yet, in that demi-monde of Soho watering holes, among the crowd of artists and eccentric hangers-on who surrounded Francis, I found a home – a kind of substitute family.

Before long, my days in the bookshop became almost as boring as those in my tiny office behind the jewellery store had been. The difference was that now the boredom was due to having nothing to do rather than the routine drudgery of the book-keeping work. And so, I began to use the time to write. I still doubted I had much talent but, unlike earlier in my life, I was now surrounded by a wealth of intriguing raw material – a panoply of fascinating characters who I started to incorporate into an account of Soho life which became my novel *An Angel in the City of Sin*.

Meanwhile, my relationship with Francis was changing. I was no longer just a model and part-time artistic muse; I was becoming even more of a protector. Apart from picking up young men for rough sex, Francis' other vice was gambling. He was a regular visitor to the gambling club, Crockfords. Although he travelled everywhere by taxi, on the nights when he went home with his pockets stuffed with winnings, he became fearful of being attacked and robbed and so (remembering the similar role I had carried out for Prince Monolulu) he would ask me to accompany him. I had no interest in gambling and felt uncomfortably out of place standing behind Francis at the blackjack table in suit and tie, like the proverbial wallflower at the ball. Unlike The Colony Room, The Coach and Horses, The French House or any of the other drinking dens I regularly accompanied Francis to, Crockfords was populated by tedious zombies with dead eyes and brains fixated on the next card, spin of the wheel or roll of the dice. The one exception was a small young man with a dark complexion, frizzy receding black hair, a beaky nose, thin lips and bulgy eyes who plonked himself down next to Francis at the roulette table one evening.

"Good evening David. And, before you ask, no I can't lend you any money." Francis spoke without turning to look at the young man, his eyes focused on the roulette wheel.

"Good to see you too, Francis. I'm fine thanks. Quite flush at the moment so I've no need of your money," the young man said in a refined accent.

"Well, you must want something."

"Hallo. Who's this?" The little man had turned his head and was staring up at me. "I presume he's with you, Francis. What do you call him? Mr Whiplash?"

"His name's Harry Felatu. He's a friend of mine." Francis delivered the introductions in a weary monotone. "Harry, this is David Reznikoff. He's a man to be avoided at all costs. He's even more of a user than I am and that's saying something."

"How do you do, Harry." Reznikoff stood up and shook my hand. "Ignore Francis. He wouldn't want to admit it but, secretly, he's very fond of me. I'm harmless. I'm just a crazy mixed up yid."

"Alright David. Get to the point. You must want something."

"Well Francis, as it happens there is something." He smiled impishly at both of us. "I'd like to invite you to the opening night of a new club of mine. It's called Al Capone's. It's in the East End, near Cable Street. It's a jazz club. There'll be great music – and dancing."

"David. You know I hate jazz – and dancing. The only reason anyone dances is as a prelude to sex – and I'm a hopeless dancer, so why would I want to show myself up?"

"God Francis. You can be a real killjoy. Forget about the dancing. There'll be plenty of champagne and a great mix of people. And you can bring Mr Felatu with you." Reznikoff looked up at me admiringly. He obviously assumed I was Francis' boyfriend.

"And I presume this event will be extensively reported in the gutter press?" Francis turned around to address me. "That's another reason to steer clear of Mr Reznikoff. He writes, or more accurately, spews out vile calumny, for the William Hickey column in the *Daily Express*. Just another of Lord Beaverbrook's whores."

"Remind me never to ask you for a reference, Francis." Reznikoff was staring at me intently as he spoke. "Mr Felatu. Or may I call you Harry? Could I have a brief word with you in private?" I glanced down at Francis whose attention was focused on the next spin of the roulette wheel.

David Reznikoff led me over to an empty blackjack table well out of earshot of Francis.

"Listen Harry," he said. "I do genuinely want you to come to this opening night, but I also have an ulterior motive. The whole attraction of this club is going to be its edgy atmosphere. It's going to be a kind of West meets East. The posh Mayfair set mixing with East End cockney rough diamonds. The problem is that I want it to feel dangerous and edgy but without any actual danger. That would only frighten off the Mayfair types. So, I hope you won't be offended, but you'd be an ideal person to provide a bit of security. Not a formal bouncer. I've already hired a couple of those to be on the door. Just to be a sort of presence around the bar and the dance floor. Of course, I'll pay you."

I hardly needed the money and I was not at all interested in extending my career as a heavy but, as with so many other things I have ended up doing during my life, it offered me yet another new experience.

Alongside joining the 43 Group, teaming up with Prince Monolulu and meeting Francis Bacon, it would be another turning point in my life – one which, in retrospect, I'd have done better to avoid.

# Friday 9th October 2001

Becky was working from home, tidying up the final pieces of research for her section of the Soho exhibition, when her mobile phone rang. This time she recognised the number immediately. David Reznikoff. She put it back on the desk, intent on letting it go to voicemail, but then she changed her mind. Better to answer it and tell him in no uncertain terms that she did not want to speak to him nor did she want him to contact her anymore.

"Miss Stone. Becky. I can't tell you how relieved I am to have got through to you. I'm sorry but you're the only person I could think of to call. The only one who can help me." It was spoken in one breathless rush, giving her no chance to interrupt. She could barely make out what he was saying. He sounded like he was about to burst into tears. "I'm in trouble and I need your help urgently."

"Mr Reznikoff. Calm down. I don't see how I can help you. As I've already told you…"

"No, you don't understand. This is serious. I'm in trouble. Please."

Becky's resolve was starting to waver. She so wanted to stick to her initial intention and tell him firmly that she was no longer pursuing her interest in Harry Felatu and, therefore, had no wish to have any further contact with him, but he sounded so scared, so vulnerable. Nothing like the garrulous schmoozer of their previous conversations. Nevertheless, she determined to keep her voice as firm and distanced as possible.

"Mr Reznikoff. If you could just tell me as calmly as possible what this is about, then I'll be better able to see if there's anything I can do for you."

"I can't talk about it on the phone." He was now whispering as if afraid that someone might be listening. "Where are you, Becky?"

She was irritated by him using her first name, but she didn't feel it was the right moment to mention it. "I'm at home – I'm working from home," she added, putting the emphasis on the word 'working'.

"That's good. You're not far away then. I need you to come round to my flat. When you get here, you'll see for yourself what my problem is. I promise you this is not a wind up. If there was anyone else I could ask, but there isn't. You're my only hope."

Becky was trying hard to maintain her scepticism. She knew what an accomplished fantasist he could be and, therefore, was inclined to believe that this could all be an elaborate performance. But if it was a performance designed to lure her back in, then she had to admit it was a very convincing one. His panic sounded genuine. Not for the first or last time, when it came to David Reznikoff, she let her soft-hearted side overrule her more hard-headed instincts.

"Alright. I'll get to you as soon as I can."

"Oh, thank you, Becky. You're a mensch."

No sooner had she pressed the buzzer than she heard his footsteps scampering down the stairs. What little hair he had was sticking out in unruly tufts as if he'd just woken from a troubled sleep. One side of his face was red and slightly swollen and his shirt tail was hanging out of his trousers.

"Thank you so much for coming." He leaned forward, grabbed her jacket sleeve and gently pulled her through the doorway. "Come upstairs and see for yourself."

At the top of the stairs, he stood aside and let her lead the way. On her first visit, she had been surprised how neat and tidy the flat was. Now it couldn't have been more different. She was greeted by a scene of carnage. There were shards of broken crockery on the floor by the kitchen units, books were scattered over the living room carpet, some lying open with their pages fanned out. Cupboard drawers had been pulled out and left upside down on the floor, their contents strewn around.

"You've had a break-in?" Becky said. "Have you called the police?"

"No, Becky. It wasn't a break-in. I had visitors. Two men. They did this."

"I don't understand." Becky moved round the room as if it was an obstacle course, stepping carefully to avoid the things on the floor. "Did they take anything?"

"No. They didn't find anything. At least, not what they were looking for."

"Sorry." Becky stopped and looked at him. She was having trouble figuring out what he was saying. "Did you know these men? Do you know what they were looking for?"

"Yes – I mean no, I didn't know the men. But yes, I know what they were looking for. They were looking for anything belonging to Harry. They wanted to know what I'd taken from Harry's flat. Whether I had any papers of his. Any documents. I told them I didn't have anything but they wouldn't listen. They threatened me – slapped me. Then they searched." He stretched out his arms as if he was conducting an orchestra and gesticulated at the debris.

Becky started idly picking up books and putting them back on the shelves. "Have you any idea exactly what they were looking for? Why they were so interested in Harry Felatu?"

"No. I have no idea."

"Look – you really must call the police. It doesn't matter whether they've taken anything or not. This is a crime – and they've assaulted you."

"No. I can't call the police. There's no point. They won't be able to do anything." He paused, thinking about what he was going to say next. "When I say I don't know who these people are, it's the truth. However, I do know who they are not. They are not criminals. I'm not saying that they are police exactly, but they are officials of some kind. Somebody else – somebody important – must have sent them. Calling the police will just make things worse. More dangerous for me."

Becky was beginning to wish she hadn't come. At least she now knew that his panicky phone call had been no act put on for her benefit, but what he was now telling her made no sense. Just paranoid ramblings.

She picked up a pile of magazines from an armchair and, seeing nowhere to put them, dumped them on the floor before sitting down.

"Mr Reznikoff. There must be things you're not telling me. You say you don't know who these men are or what they're looking for, yet you do know that they're not criminals. And you're suggesting that somebody else has sent them. Either you are going to have to be up front with me and tell me what you do know or I'll have to leave because, at the moment, the only way I can think of to help you is by calling the police."

David Reznikoff sighed. Then he reached down, pulled a kitchen chair upright and sat on it wearily. He put his hands on his head and ran his fingers through his already tousled hair.

After another thirty seconds, Becky felt she had to break the silence. "Can I make you a cup of tea? You're still in shock. Sweet tea might help."

"Yes. Thank you," he muttered.

While Becky put the kettle on, washed up a couple of unbroken mugs that were lying in the sink and searched among the jumble in the cupboards for tea bags and sugar, Reznikoff started to talk.

"After they finished going through the flat, they started to question me. They asked me how I knew Harry and what I knew about him. That wasn't difficult. I could answer those questions. Then they asked me when I'd last seen him and whether I knew any of his other friends. Again, no problem. But then they asked me if I had any of Harry's belongings. Did I know where all his stuff had gone. I told them the truth – that I'd cleared out the flat. There was nothing of any value. It all got thrown away. They wouldn't believe me. That's when they started slapping me around, threatening me. I kept telling them I didn't know anything else. Then they stopped hitting me and told me that, if I came across any of Harry's property or knew the whereabouts of any of it, I should let them know. I said – but I don't know who you are. How can I get in touch with you? They said, don't worry, we'll be keeping in contact with you." He gave her a pained look. "Becky, they said it like it was a threat."

"And you're sure they didn't say exactly what it was they were looking for?" Becky was pouring the tea.

He scratched the top of his head. "They may have said something about documents. Papers of some kind. They weren't specific."

"You said you thought they were some kind of officials – not criminals. What made you think that?" Becky put the two mugs of tea on the kitchen table and sat opposite him.

"They were very smartly dressed. Expensive suits. Haircuts. They were educated. Posh accents."

Becky sipped her tea and stared at Reznikoff who sat with his hands clasped round his mug avoiding her gaze.

"This is still not making any sense. I know I'm starting to sound like a broken record, but your only option is to call the police."

"They specifically warned me not to go to the police." He turned his frightened eyes towards Becky. "These were probably the men who murdered Harry. If I go to the police, they won't hesitate to kill me as well."

"Okay." Becky took a deep breath. "If you don't know exactly who these two men are, you must have some idea of why they are so interested in Harry Felatu. There are still things you're not telling me. Why would anyone want to kill him? And why, even after his death, are they still interested in him?"

David Reznikoff swallowed the rest of his tea, put the mug down and gave Becky a long hard look. He opened his mouth and then closed it again as if having second thoughts about what he was going to say.

"Okay." He sat upright and composed himself. It seemed to Becky that he was preparing to make some kind of confession. "You must understand, Becky, the 1960s was a strange time in London. Especially in the circles Harry and I were moving in. It was a time when all the old traditions of British society – all the old hierarchies – were crumbling. In particular, you had the two extreme ends of society coming together. Some of the lower classes were moving upwards and some of the upper classes found it exciting to dive down into the lower depths. The middle classes dominated everything and they were despised by both the rich and the poor. And so, increasingly, those at the bottom and the top started to get together. They found they had a lot in common. A hatred of conformity and a love of adventure. A rejection of conventional morality. Both groups embraced immorality – especially when it came to sex."

"Mr Reznikoff." Becky's patience and her sympathy for his plight were beginning to wear thin. He was now sounding much more like his old swaggering self. "I know I wasn't alive in the 1960s, but I am a historian and I do know something about the period. So, maybe if you could just finish with the lecture and get back to answering my question."

"I'm sorry, Becky." He looked at her with a theatrical hangdog expression. "If you could just bear with an old man and his reminiscences for a minute or two, I can assure you I am getting to the point. The point being that, at that time, Harry and I had a lot of connections with both groups of people – the East End criminals and the upper crust. I lost track of Harry in the mid-seventies but, by then, he was mixing with a lot of very influential people. Not only socialising with them but also giving them a bit of a helping hand from time to time."

"Which people are you talking about? Can you be more specific?"

"I'd rather not at the moment. Suffice it to say that there were politicians and members of the aristocracy. Even members of the royal family."

"And what sort of things did he do for them?"

"Again Becky, I can't really say." Becky was about to protest but he held up his hand to stop her. "It's not because I don't want to tell you. It's because I don't know for sure. You see, the difference between me and Harry was that I'm very talkative. You've probably noticed that." He gave her an impish grin. "I love to gossip. Some people would say that I can be indiscreet. I don't know when to keep my mouth shut. Back then, my big mouth got me into a lot of trouble. Harry was the opposite. He could keep a secret. He didn't spread gossip. People felt they could trust him. Nobody trusted me."

This time Becky did manage to interrupt. "This is all very well but I'm not sure it's getting us anywhere. You're still not answering the most important question. Why would anybody want to kill him?"

He shrugged his shoulders and held his hands out in a gesture of supplication. "I know this is frustrating for you – it is for me as well – but all I'm saying is that I think, maybe, Harry got a bit too involved with somebody rich and powerful. Maybe he knew too many secrets about these people and that's why they had him disposed of."

Becky stood up, grabbed her bag from the back of the chair and slid it over her shoulder.

"This is all very interesting," she said, sounding more frustrated than interested, "but I still have no idea how I can help you. It seems to me you only have two choices. Either you call in the police or, if you really know nothing else, you lie low and hope that it will all go away. Either way, I don't see what else I can do to help you."

"Please Becky. Just sit back down for a minute. I have something I need to show you." He waved his hand at the chair she had been sitting on and stood up gingerly, clutching his right hip with his other hand and wincing. "I have one thing that they didn't find."

He gave her a conspiratorial look, then picked up the kitchen chair he had been sitting on and, weaving his way around the debris until he reached the bookshelves, he stood on the chair and, reaching up to the top shelf, took down one of the few books left on it. He brought it back to the table and placed it in front of Becky. She recognised it immediately. *Soho in the 1950s* by Daniel Farson with a famous cover photo of Francis Bacon, Lucien Freud and other artistic types sitting round a table at Wheeler's Restaurant. She had browsed through it for her research.

"Open it to page 164," he said.

Becky flipped through the pages. Page 164 contained a half page photo of a man wearing a guardsman's beaver skin hat, a military jacket and a kilt, holding a baton and marching with his head tilted upwards in front of a brass band. The caption described it as a 1957 Soho street festival. The man wasn't identified but Becky immediately recognised him as a young David Reznikoff.

"Very fetching, Mr Reznikoff," she said with more than a hint of sarcasm. "Any particular reason, other than vanity, for showing me this?"

"The book arrived in the post a couple of days ago. Harry sent it just before he died. At first, I couldn't understand why. I already have a copy. But there was a note attached telling me to turn to that page, so I did. You can still see the marks on the page." He leaned over and pointed. "He had taped an envelope to it." He stood up again and weaved his way across the room to a small loose-leaf table by the window and picked up an old oak desk tidy which had been turned upside down, its envelopes, pens, pencils and paper clips scattered across the tabletop. He pressed a small catch on the back and a hidden drawer appeared. He removed a brown envelope from it, returned to the kitchen table and placed it on top of the open book in front of Becky.

Once again, she was irritated by his blatant theatricality. He would have made a good, if old-fashioned, stage magician, she thought, pulling rabbits out of a hat.

"Open it," he said.

Becky did so, sliding out a single sheet of paper which she unfolded. It was from a storage company in St. John's Wood addressed to Hare Felatu. The letter thanked Mr Felatu for using their services and for his cheque for the first six months rental of a safety deposit box. At the end of the letter, there was a code which he would need to use whenever he wanted to access his box. Once she had read it, Becky looked up at Reznikoff who was smiling at her.

"Was there anything else?" She said. "Any letter from Harry explaining why he sent you this... or explaining what's in the box?"

"No. Nothing. But it could be important. This might be what those men were looking for. I was going to go there tomorrow and check it out."

"And I suppose you want me to go with you," said Becky with a sigh of resignation.

"No. I want you to go instead of me. Those men. They might be having me watched. I'm worried that if I go there, they could follow me. That's why it's better if you go on your own."

There was a twinkle in his eyes. Becky's first instinct was to politely refuse to help him any further and walk away. But, at the same time, that sensible voice inside her was being drowned out by a growing buzz of excitement. This was a mystery that she was going to find it hard, if not impossible, to walk away from. As Reznikoff stared imploringly at her, she could see that he knew he was sucking her in.

# Extracts from
# The Autobiography of an Invisible Man

## THE GANGSTER YEARS

It was a Thursday evening in The Colony Room and everyone was talking about the opening night of David Reznikoff's Al Capone club.

"It's supposed to be fancy dress – like we're all in 1920s Chicago. I hate fancy dress. What on earth can I go as?" Said David Archer to no-one in particular.

"Go as yourself – a bald-headed old cunt." It was Muriel Belcher, perched as usual on her stool at the far end of the bar.

"And what are you going to go as?" I asked Francis. "A gangster's moll?"

"What makes you think I'm going?" Francis said. "Do you know who the most boring people in the world are?"

"No," I answered, even though he was now speaking to the whole room. Conversation ground to a halt as everyone waited to hear what Francis would say next.

"It's a toss up between the stuck up English upper classes and cockney gangsters and their blowsy women. And both of those will be at the opening, so of course I'm not going." He turned to Jock, the barman, and ordered another glass of white wine. "And I would strongly advise you not to go either." He had turned back to face me. "David Reznikoff is a walking talking disaster area. Everything he touches turns to shit. Last year, he decided to open a fish restaurant on Gerrard Street. The only problem was that it had no kitchen. A bit of a problem for a restaurant, you would have thought. But it was no obstacle for David. He had a simple fish and chip shop menu printed. His immaculately attired waiters would take the orders and then rush out the back to a nearby chippie, get the order as takeaway and then bring it back to the restaurant, decant it on to the best bone china plates and serve it up to the clientele for exorbitant prices. You can imagine how long that enterprise lasted."

Francis received his glass from Jock before continuing the character assassination. "When he first arrived in Soho and still had all his hair, people used to mistake him for Lucien Freud. He quickly took advantage and started to charge his drinks to Lucien's bar bill. He only stopped when Lucian found out and had him beaten up."

"That's an occupational hazard for David – getting beaten up," said John Deakin, propping up the bar next to Francis. "He will persist in trying to ingratiate himself with all those East End thugs. He ends up owing them money and then they have him done over. I think he secretly takes after you, Francis. He must enjoy it."

Nevertheless, the following Saturday night I walked through a rain-sodden, debris-filled courtyard off Cable Street and up a steep iron staircase to the entry to the Al Capone club on the first floor of an old warehouse building. I was dressed in my prince of wales check suit, a striped kipper tie and black patent leather shoes, trying, and failing, to look like a 1920s Chicago gangster and feeling very uncomfortable. Even the largest size off-the-peg suit barely fitted me so there was an acre of white shirt cuff protruding from the end of my jacket sleeves, my trouser turn ups appeared to have had an argument with my shoes and my eighteen inch shirt collar was too tight round my neck to button up.

It goes without saying, dear reader, that I had ignored Francis' warnings and, instead, had adopted his philosophy of life. He once said to me, "I want an extraordinary life – to go everywhere and meet everybody". He liked to be constantly moving between extremes of squalor and opulence. He once took me with him to the Smithfield pubs in the early morning when the only customers were the meat market porters and butchers in their blood-stained aprons. I asked him why he liked going there He said he enjoyed walking past all the hanging carcasses and the bloody counters. "This is what life is like. We're all on our way to becoming dead meat."

His favourite Shakespeare quote was "life is like a tale told by an idiot, full of sound and fury, signifying nothing."

Thus, that evening, I was looking forward to meeting new people, both from the gutter and Belgravia, with the added attraction of a soupcon of danger. Just possibly, I would be living on the edge.

But, as I stood at the side of the dance floor, feeling awkward and out of place, watching young wealthy socialites attempting to jive to raucous jazz music from a six-piece band squeezed onto a narrow stage at the far end of the cavernous room, a gaggle of uncoordinated flailing arms and twirling legs, I soon realised the place was about as dangerous and edgy as a women's institute jumble sale. The room was large enough for the different social groupings to keep well away from each other. The group nearest the long bar, judging by their braying voices, floppy hair and champagne flutes were the Mayfairites. On the far side of the room, nearest the exit, was an area crammed with dilapidated sofas, cane dining chairs and small wooden bistro tables. It was occupied by burly men in tight-fitting Italian mohair suits with short brylcreamed hair and women in off-the-shoulder satin gowns with towering bouffants and thick make up. Either this was their notion of 1920s Chicago fancy dress or these were the East End gangsters and their molls. By the side of the stage, there was a small group of West Indian men and women, possibly friends of the band, watching the bright young things gyrating around the dance floor, making no attempt to hide their disdainful looks.

David Reznikoff was flitting about from group to group like an anxious butterfly, finally landing amongst the gangsters. As there seemed little chance that I would be called upon to quell any outbreak of trouble in such an anodyne atmosphere, I retreated to the bar and ordered a large glass of white wine. As I turned back round to survey the dance floor, David Reznikoff appeared at my side.

"Going well, don't you think?"

"If you say so," I said, making no attempt to hide my boredom.

"Well anyway, it seems that you have attracted the interest of some friends of mine. Let me take you over and introduce you."

Before I could say anything, he had set off towards the gathering of gangsters. I reluctantly followed him as he edged between some swarthy Mediterranean looking men until we emerged into a space in front of a scuffed red velvet sofa on which two identical men in similar double-breasted suits with tightly knotted ties sat side by side, like mirror images, their hands resting on their knees. They were silent, impassive, staring up at me in a disturbingly forensic way. I felt uncomfortable but made an effort not to show it. I assumed they were judging me – trying to work out exactly who, or what, I was. Although I hadn't known him for long, it was the first time I had seen David Reznikoff appear uneasy.

"This is Harry Felatu," he said, fluttering his hand in my direction. "Harry, this Reggie and Ronnie." He paused apprehensively before adding, "The twins," as if this would render them instantly recognisable to me.

Neither of them said anything. They continued to look up at me – or, more accurately, to look inside me.

Eventually, David broke the silence. "He's a very interesting mixture is Harry…"

"Shut up, David." It was the twin on the right who spoke. I had no idea which was Reggie and which Ronnie. He was softly spoken with a pronounced cockney twang. "You're not from round here, are you Harry?" It might have been a joke, but he said it without a trace of irony and no-one around him so much as smiled.

"Well, I used to live in Hackney but I wasn't born round here, if that's what you mean." I was preparing myself for some kind of racist jibe.

"That's good." It was still the one on the right talking. The only distinguishing feature that I could make out was that he had a slightly thinner face than his brother. "You see, we're looking for new people to work for us. Different sorts of people. We're getting a bit cheesed off with all your typical East Enders and we like the look of you. So, how about you come and do some work for us?"

"I'm sorry to disappoint you," I said, assuming that it was my size and muscle they were interested in, "but I think you've got the wrong impression of me. I'm only doing this job tonight as a favour to David. It's not what I usually do." David turned his head towards me and screwed his face into a look of mild pain.

"Mr Felatu. Harry. I think you may have a mistaken impression of us," continued the talkative twin. "I assume that you think we're some kind of dodgy geezers and we want to take you on as a heavy. How do you know it's not your brain we're after?" This time the sarcasm was obvious. He nudged his brother and smiled. The other twin showed no change of expression. "Who exactly do you think we are? You don't want to believe things you hear people saying about us."

"I haven't heard anybody saying anything. I don't know anything about you." I thought my reply might annoy him. He obviously expected everyone to know who they were, but there was no change of expression.

"That's good. So, if this isn't what you normally do, what else do you do?"

"I work in a bookshop."

"There you are, Ronnie. I told you he was an intellectual."

David Reznikoff was looking increasingly agitated as he glanced from the twins to me and then back again.

"I tell you what, Harry. You give our offer a bit of thought. Not too much though." I detected a sinister tone in his voice. "When we've got some work for you, we'll let David here know so he can pass a message on to you."

"No problem, Reggie. I can do that," said David. Before I could offer any response, he grabbed me by the sleeve. "Harry, I need you to give me a hand over by the bar," he said while hurriedly dragging me through the crowd away from the twins.

"What do you think you're playing at?" He hissed as soon as we were out of earshot. "You don't say no to Reggie and Ronnie."

"But I think I just did – or tried to."

"Listen to me, Harry. They're dangerous. If they ask you to do something for them, just do it. I'm sure it won't be very much – and they pay well."

The conversation dragged on for several minutes, David trying in every way he could to persuade me how important it was to cooperate with the twins while I remained non-committal. David finally gave up, saying he'd contact me as soon as he heard anything from them.

During the following week, I learned a lot about the Krays. Everyone in The Colony Room, including Francis, knew about them and most had lurid stories to tell.

"They are the epitome of the gutter," said Francis, "but there's nothing wrong with the gutter. As you know, I spend a lot of time living in it myself. And, as people in the gutter go, the Krays are a cut above most of them. You have to admire their chutzpah. About a year ago, they broke into my studio, stole a couple of my paintings and then offered to sell them back to me. At a very reasonable price. They could have got a lot more if they'd offered them to private collectors. So, I bought them back. Otherwise, I have had very little to do with them. If you want to know more, you should talk to Lucien Freud. He's bosom buddies with them. I believe he gets them to take care of his enemies for him – and, as we all know, Lucien has plenty of enemies."

The conversation around the bar swiftly shifted from the Krays to salacious stories about Lucien Freud, during which Francis grabbed my jacket sleeve and pulled me to one side.

"It's just occurred to me what the twins might want you to do for them. Ronnie has a penchant for young boys so it may be that they just want you to do a bit of pimping for him." Francis made it sound unexceptional. "They've probably heard that you do favours for me and they must think that that includes supplying me with young men."

"Well, I certainly won't be doing that." I was careful not to sound shocked or prudish. I always endeavoured to appear unshockable in the presence of Francis and the other Colony Room regulars

For the next few months, I heard nothing from David Reznikoff or the Krays. I had assumed that they had forgotten about their offer to me. In the meantime, David Archer had been hawking my novel around various publishers without success. Until he arrived in the bookshop one day clutching a large brown envelope which he handed to me.

"Victory at last," he said with a wide grin on his face. "It's a publishing agreement for your novel with the Olympia Press."

"The Olympia Press?" I didn't want to sound ungrateful, but I had only barely heard of the Olympia Press and couldn't call to mind selling any of their books.

"It's owned by a man called Maurice Girodias. He's based in Paris but he publishes English language stuff. Often things the British and American publishers won't touch."

"You mean pornography?"

"Not exactly. Just somewhat risqué stuff. Samuel Becket, Henry Miller, *The Naked Lunch*, *Lolita*. I would stock more of his stuff but they're hellish to import as customs and excise seize most of them."

I tried to remain calm but I was quite excited. It had been achievement enough to have managed to complete the novel. I hadn't expected anyone to want to publish it. I took the contract out of the brown envelope and signed without bothering to read it.

In the following months, I waited for the royalties to start pouring in while continuing to work in the bookshop. The ironic truth was that, on the day David had arrived in the shop brandishing the publishing contract, I had been intending to hand in my notice but, not wanting to seem ungrateful after all that David Archer had done for me, I now decided to postpone my resignation.

Six months after publication the royalties were trickling, rather than flooding in. Only a select few radical bookshops stocked Olympia Press titles, if they could get hold of them. I discovered David was right. H.M Customs and Excise regularly seized their Paris shipments and burned the lot, including some quite innocuous titles.

Despite my pride in being a published novelist, I kept my book a secret from Ana fearing she would disapprove of its content. I couldn't help but wonder what my mother would have thought of me. Most of what I had done since leaving school, I'm sure she would not have approved of, but I was confident that she would have been proud of this.

Although it was evident that I was not going to make my fortune as a writer, I nevertheless decided that it was now time to tell David Archer that I was leaving the bookshop and, therefore, vacating my garret flat above it. I moved to a larger, though equally shabby, flat above a fish and chip shop in Paddington. The rent was cheap enough for me to be able to live on the monthly allowance that I received from my mother's trust fund. Although I still spent most of my time in and around Soho, it felt like I was living out in the sticks. I could now understand exactly how my mother had felt when she had been forced to leave her beloved Bloomsbury. I'd hardly travelled a great distance – just a half an hour or so on the tube or bus to reach my usual haunts – but, nevertheless, it put a bit of a dent in my social life. Since splitting up from my first serious girlfriend, Stella, the jewellery shop assistant, I had had several dalliances with various young, and not so young, artistic women, and artists' models, who either hung around the Soho drinking scene or visited the bookshop. They tended to tire of me quickly when it became clear that I had no artistic credentials and very little money. Now my romantic life became even more limited. These women were moths attracted to the bright lights of Soho and were not keen on being dragged off to the anonymity of Paddington. And, even if I managed to lure them back to my seedy flat, the smell of fried fish was not much of an aphrodisiac.

"I've been looking for you for the past week. Where the fuck have you been? David told me you'd left the bookshop." It was David Reznikoff buttonholing me one evening at The Colony Room bar a couple of weeks after my move to Paddington. "The Twins have got a job for you. I promised them I'd let you know and they've been getting very impatient. Boy, am I glad I've found you. Any longer and my knackers would be nailed to a coffee table."

"I don't really need a job at the moment, David. If you like, I can go and tell them myself."

"For fuck's sake, Harry. Are you pulling my leg? I hope you are. I've told you before, you don't say no to Reggie and Ronnie." Others round the bar had halted their conversations and were listening to us with amusement.

"Sounds like another beating for you, Davey my lad. Or will it be a broomstick up the arsehole? Anyway, enjoy."

"Shut up, John. Mind your own fucking business," David said to a smirking John Deakin before turning back to me. "It's a simple enough job. There's a film being shot on the streets of the East End and they just want you to help out with a bit of crowd control while they're filming." He looked pleadingly up at me. Now that I'd heard more about the Krays, I was sure his fear was genuine and I felt sorry for him. I kept him on tenterhooks while I mulled it over. It was true that I didn't need a job, but I did have a lot of time on my hands and the thought of being present on a film set was enticing.

"Alright. Tell them I'll do it."

The change in David Reznikoff was instant. His habitual cocky, assured self replaced the wheedling individual of the past few minutes.

"I'll go and tell them now and then I'll meet you back here tomorrow night to give you the details."

A small middle-aged woman in a baggy white raincoat and navy-blue slacks, a knitted woollen cap perched on her head, was bellowing through a megaphone. We were in a narrow back street in Stepney and the scene they were filming involved a short buxom actress, a headscarf perched precariously on her bouffant blond hair, wheeling a pram. As I stood watching the extras being marshalled and cameras and lighting rigs wheeled into place, I was approached by a heavyset swarthy young man in a shiny dark grey suit.

He peered quizzically at me. "You must be Harry." He spoke broad cockney but with a hint of a foreign accent. I subsequently discovered that he was nicknamed Maltese Tony. "There can't be many other people that look like you."

"Yes, that's me. Harry Felatu."

"Tony Lambros. Pleased to meet you." He shook my hand.

"I was told to meet Reggie and Ronnie here. Where are they?" I was looking up and down the street as I spoke.

"They're not here. They've left me in charge. They don't get on with her." He jerked his thumb over his shoulder in the general direction of the woman with the megaphone. "She's the director. She's got a foul mouth on her. The Twins can't stand women swearing – or dressing up like men. They've got very strict morals."

There were a number of other Mediterranean-looking men in suits who, I later learned, were Greek Cypriots, patrolling the barriers that had been set up at both ends of the street. Tony and I joined one of the groups. We spent the rest of the day gently ushering away any over-curious spectators while watching the same short scene between the blond pram pusher and a bald tubby window cleaner carrying a ladder over his shoulder, repeated over and over while the woman with the megaphone barked obscenities.

During the many quiet periods of the day, when we were stood around with little or nothing to do, Tony filled me in on what it was like working for the Twins. He told me that they were surprisingly quiet and very shy. Old-fashioned gentlemen is how he described them. Very polite to women and the elderly. They never swore and never boasted about themselves. But don't be fooled by all of that, he warned me. They watch and listen to everything. Nothing gets past them. They can always tell if you're lying. He then proceeded to tell me a series of shocking stories he'd heard about them to show me how dangerous and violent they were despite their outwardly calm demeanour. I suspected at the time that these were mostly apocryphal, designed to bolster the Kray's reputation and spread fear and respect. Several of them concerned murders they had either committed themselves or ordered their henchmen to do for them. As an example of the twins cunning, he explained how they had become friendly with an East End undertaker who would dispose of bodies for them by putting them in the coffins of other deceased persons awaiting burial or cremation in his funeral parlour.

I made no comments during these monologues, not sure why Tony was telling me all this. I was minded to suggest to him that, if the Krays were as dangerous as he said they were, it might not be advisable for him to be telling a complete stranger like me all these incriminating stories, but I held my peace.

As the film crew were wrapping up at the end of the day, packing their equipment into vans, the director approached me.

"Ever done any acting?" She asked in a deep croaky voice, looking me up and down.

"I can't say I have."

She continued to study me, moving either side of me, presumably checking out my profiles. It reminded me of the way Francis would look at me from behind his easel when I used to model for him.

"Well, that doesn't matter. You don't need to be an actor for what I have in mind for you. I like the look of you. I'd like to use you in a scene we're filming in a couple of days' time. Are you up for it?"

I told her I was and, two days later, we were filming in a cellar nightclub in the Mile End Road. The scene involved a fight breaking out in the club between two of the characters. Naturally, I was typecast as the bouncer who steps in to separate them and escort them out to the street. I was even given two lines of dialogue which I managed to deliver to the satisfaction of the feisty director. Ronnie and Reggie were present for the filming. Apparently, they owned a stake in the night club.

"That was very good, Harry. I like your style," Reggie said to me when the shooting of the scene was over. By then, I had learned to distinguish between the twins. As well as being infinitely more talkative, Reggie was also the slightly thinner of the two. "Let's just hope you're as good in real life situations," he added with a conspiratorial wink.

Whilst this was the beginning and end of my acting career, it was only the start of my involvement with the Krays.

# Monday 12th October 2001

Becky spent most of the morning zigzagging around London on trains, buses and on foot as if trapped in a pinball machine. She started by getting on a train at Harlesden and went to Baker Street. From there, she caught a bus to Oxford Circus. Then she walked along Oxford Street, went into John Lewis and walked swiftly through several departments before leaving by a side exit, circling back around and heading west towards Bond Street station, going in and out of several shops on the way. At the station, she took a Jubilee line train to St. John's Wood.

At every twist and turn of this circuitous journey, she looked all around her, studying as many of the faces in the vicinity as she could to see if she recognised having seen any of them in the course of her travels earlier that morning. She felt ridiculous doing this, but also somewhat excited.

Once she had agreed, in deference to David Reznikoff's paranoia, to go and check out Harry Felatu's safety deposit box, it dawned on her that she had every reason to be just as paranoid herself. If these mysterious men were having Reznikoff's flat watched, then they would surely have noted her visit and might have decided to have her followed as well. Thus, the reason for her now behaving like a character in a spy novel.

By the time she reached the end of her meandering journey, she was one of only four people getting off the train at midday at St. John's Wood. Having studied the other three carefully, she was confident that none of their faces was familiar from earlier in her travels and, anyway, one of them was an elderly woman struggling with two heavy shopping bags and the other two were giggling teenage girls in school uniform – so, unlikely to be mysterious hitmen in disguise. If she had been followed earlier that morning, then she had shaken them off. Despite recognising how absurd she was being, she couldn't help feeling pleased with herself; like a small child winning a game of hide and seek.

Becky had had a perfect, safe and secure, uneventful childhood and adolescence in middle class, genteel Harrogate. Her mother was a primary school teacher and her father a hotel manager. They lived in a modern, three-bedroom, semi-detached house in a quiet cul-de-sac. Rebecca was the good dutiful daughter. Her sister Judith, three years her senior, was the bad daughter – the rebel. Judith had been the perpetually whingeing baby who didn't sleep through the night until she was two years old. Rebecca had been the perfect baby. During her teenage years Jude, as she by then insisted on being called, had run the gamut of unsuitable boyfriends, drunken nights out, risqué clothing, a shoulder tattoo and numerous piercings – all of which, and a lot more besides, led to frequent rows with their parents. Many an evening, Becky would lay awake in bed listening to her parents, who had waited up for her sister's homecoming, chastising Jude as she came through the front door, plastered in make-up, and usually plastered by alcohol as well. It would always end in the same way. Jude would storm off upstairs to her room while her father would shout after her that she was grounded.

Jude was highly intelligent, showing a particular talent for art and design and, despite her wayward social life, she managed to scrape together three A Levels and, by dint of a successful interview and presentation of her portfolio, was given a place at Goldsmith's College in London. Her parents were surprised and delighted. As she packed her bags and set off for the Capital, they kept their fingers crossed that this would mark the end of her period of teenage defiance. Unfortunately, as Becky predicted quietly to herself at the time, Jude's first year at Goldsmith's turned out to be not the turning of a page in her life, but merely a continuation of her dissolute teenage years. She did little work, took a variety of drugs, got pregnant and then decided to have the baby and drop out.

Being three years her junior, Becky witnessed Jude's antics with a mixture of horror and envy. After each new misdeed by her sister, their mother would tut about it to Becky while they were both preparing the evening meal and then, invariably follow this up by praising Becky for her good behaviour and warning her not to be tempted to go down the same path as her sister. As she had always done, Becky dutifully complied. Her school reports were always glowing. At parents' evenings, her teachers would deliver the oft-repeated mantra "if only all our students could be like Rebecca". She had had the occasional friendships with boys at school but would have been hard-pressed to describe any of them as 'boyfriends'. She tended to end up with the nerdy academic types, not that she had much choice; the more dangerous ones that Jude had always gravitated towards showed no interest in the class swat. The bookish boys were safe and, however much, in the privacy of her own dreams, she may have hankered after the other sort, she was forced to accept that, in real life, the nerds suited her better. Once she reached the sixth form, things occasionally got a bit more serious but, apart from some snogging at the back of the cinema, sometimes accompanied by some fumbling and groping, once she said no these boys were too cowed and polite to go any further. In comparison with the reprobates her sister hung around with, they were eminently acceptable to her parents.

Even after she'd escaped home and arrived at the anticipated den of iniquity that was Manchester University, she managed to miss out on all the stereotypical excesses of student life. On her second day there, she stood behind a tall, curly-haired, dark-eyed Physics student in the queue to have their photos taken for their university identity cards. They got talking and quickly discovered that they were both from Yorkshire and had grown up barely ten miles apart – Becky in Harrogate and Richard in Otley. The similarities didn't end there. They liked the same music (they were both big Portishead fans) and the same films (especially Coen brothers' movies). A perfect match. So, he asked her out to the cinema. Within a fortnight, they were sleeping together. It was her first, and only, serious relationship and her first, and only, sexual partner. They remained together for the rest of their time at university. They were 'going steady'. Becky hated the phrase but was forced to admit that it was a perfect description of their safe, innocuous partnership. There had been no storm-tossed passion; no furious rows followed by reconciliation sex; no straying from the straight and narrow into other sexual encounters or even mild flirtations. Just steady. All those other men, all those illicit adventures she should have been having – the sowing of her wild oats, had been abandoned before they'd even got started so that she could 'go steady'.

Seven years on and they were still together. It wasn't that she was bored with him. He was good-looking, he made her laugh, he was romantic and devoted to her. They still shared lots of interests. Every now and then, when she was feeling down in the dumps, usually after another job application had been rejected, she would fret about her boring conventional life: regret settling into a serious relationship so young: regret opting for safety and security over adventure and risk: regret being the good obedient daughter: regret not being Jude. And then she would find herself casting surreptitious glances at good-looking young men on the tube – the kind with rugged features, unkempt, long hair and scruffy but stylish clothes. She fantasised about propositioning them and going off to a hotel for an afternoon of wild, no-strings-attached sex. Of course, it was never going to happen – although she had carried on a brief flirtation with a handsome Asian student who was on a work experience placement at the museum. They went out for a drink together, but Becky got cold feet and immediately put a dampener on things by telling him that she had a partner.

Sitting around the dining table at her parents' house in Harrogate the previous Christmas, she had tried to persuade herself that she was now the non-conformist rebel of the family because she and Richard were still unmarried and childless whereas Jude was there with her new, very respectable husband, Jason, a corporate lawyer, and their new baby, as well as her now ten year old son, the product of that dissolute first year at Goldsmith's. But it wouldn't wash. Despite their very conservative lifestyle, her parents were children of the sixties and, therefore, wouldn't dream of using the phrase 'living in sin'.

The reason that Becky had been mulling over all of this during her meandering travels that morning was obvious. It explained why, against her better judgement, against common sense and rationality, she had agreed to help David Reznikoff and had played that morning's absurd game of hide and seek around the streets of London. For almost the first time in her life, she was doing something that wasn't sensible; that wasn't what nice, staid Rebecca would be expected to do. She was flirting with danger – or, at least, potential danger. And, once she managed to put aside that feeling of foolishness, she realised she was enjoying it, even though, behind this growing feeling of excitement, she knew that it would more than likely turn out to be a wild goose chase. Even though she had Felatu's letter from Safestore Security with its entry code for the safety deposit box in her bag, she feared that, once the staff there saw that she was a petite young blond woman and not Harry Felatu, a six and a half foot dark-skinned seventy year old male, they'd refuse her access to it. But, as it turned out, there were no such problems. Once the young woman at the reception desk saw that she had the letter, she didn't ask for any other proof of identity: she simply tapped in the box number on her computer and then got an attendant to take Becky down a maze of corridors to the room containing the box.

A short while later, Becky sat on a bench on the almost empty platform at St. John's Wood Station with the contents of the safety deposit box on her lap. It was a sellotaped white cardboard shoe box. She was itching to open it but decided, reluctantly, to wait until she was in the presence of David Reznikoff. However, there was a clue to its contents. Written on the top in large blue felt-tipped capital letters was THE AUTOBIOGRAPHY OF AN INVISIBLE MAN.

Ethan Jones hovered hesitantly in the open doorway to D.I. Maddy Rich's office.

"Don't stand there like a lemon, come in," she said without taking her eyes off her computer screen. "I'm a bit busy so make it brief."

He walked into the office and stood awkwardly next to her desk. "Okay boss. Just a quick update on the Felatu case." He eyed the chair in front of him but, as she showed no sign of inviting him to sit down, he stayed standing.

Maddy finished what she was typing, took her eyes off the screen and gave him her full attention. "Okay, shoot."

He winced, assuming it was another joke reference to his 'cowboy' nickname. "We've been through all Felatu's trust fund documents and, to cut a long story short, they pretty much all seem to be what the solicitor said they were – namely, endowments to various educational charities or bursaries to kids from disadvantaged backgrounds to enable them to go to university."

"Is that it?" Maddy turned her attention back to her computer.

"No. Not quite. There is one exception." He looked down at the sheet of A4 paper he was holding "There was a one-off payment in 1986 of twenty-five thousand pounds to an account called 'Athos Holdings' in a bank in Vienna. We've googled it but we can't find any reference to 'Athos Holdings'. Of course, it's a long time ago and it quite likely no longer exists. It's just that it sticks out like a sore thumb. All the other grants easily fit in with the aims and purposes of the trust."

"Ah." She paused for a moment in thought. "You're sure there isn't also a 'Porthos' or 'Aramis' Holdings? Maybe even a 'D'Artagnan?'" She looked up at him with raised eyebrows.

Not for the first time in his conversations with the D.I. he was confused.

"Sorry," she said, seeing the puzzled look on his face. "I should make allowances for your youth. I would guess you weren't a great reader as a child. Probably spent all your time playing video games. 'The Three Musketeers'? A novel by Alexander Dumas?"

Something clicked in Ethan's brain. "Oh yes. I think I've seen the film. Lots of big hats with feathers and swordfights?"

"That'll be the one. Anyway, don't worry about it. I was just being flippant."

"Alright. So, should I go to Vienna and check out this 'Athos Holdings'?" He grinned at her.

"Of course, Ethan. I'll book you a business class flight and a suite in a 5-star hotel." She returned his grin. "First thing you need to do is go back and see that solicitor who administers the trust fund and see if he knows anything about this 'Athos Holdings'. So, on your horse, Cowboy. Or, if you prefer, on the bus, to the wild west of Holborn."

# Extracts from
## The Autobiography of an Invisible Man

### THE GANGSTER YEARS (CONT.)

"This is Harry Felatu, ma'am."

Feeling intensely uncomfortable in my inevitably too small hired dinner suit, I stared down at a beaming Princess Margaret.

I was a reluctant participant in the line-up at the Royal Film Premiere of *Sparrers Can't Sing* at the Empire Cinema, Bow Road. One of the producers had asked me to join on the end of the line of actors and the production team to be presented to the Princess and Lord Snowden. Initially, I turned down his request on the grounds that I was far too much of a minor participant in the film to be granted such an honour. That's when he told me that Princess Margaret had specifically mentioned, at the end of the screening, that she would like to meet me.

In deference to my mother's memory who (it will come as no surprise to you, dear reader,) was a staunch republican, I did not bow like the rest of the actors but merely tilted my head slightly.

"It's good to meet you, Mr Felatu. Such a small part for such a big man." Her smile remained fixed. I was unsure whether it was an intentional double entendre. "Well, it may have been only a bit part but you certainly caught the eye. Have you appeared in any other films?"

"No ma'am. I'm not an actor. I just happened to be working on the set and got roped in."

"And where exactly are you from, Harry?" Out of the corner of my eye, I could see her entourage, including Lord Snowden, queuing up impatiently behind her. She'd spent some time exchanging a few words with the stars and the director of the film but, starting up a conversation with such a non-entity as me, was obviously not the done thing.

"My father was a New Zealander, ma'am. A Maori." I decided it was best not to delay things further by going into a more detailed account of my antecedents.

"A splendid country, New Zealand. I very much enjoyed my visit there – four years ago, I think it was. Fascinating people, the Maoris. They performed the Haka for me. Such a strange dance. Part comical, part frightening. I imagine that you must be a very good Haka dancer, Mr Felatu."

"I've never actually been to New Zealand, ma'am. I was born in London. It's a long story." I was doing as much as I could to cut the conversation short and felt like turning to the queue behind her and shrugging my shoulders.

"Your Royal Highness, we should be moving on," said a tall thin bald-headed man with a bushy moustache as he leaned over her.

"I'd love to hear your full story, Mr Felatu, but unfortunately they think I'm holding things up so I'll have to move on – " she suddenly stood on tiptoe trying, I assumed, to get her mouth closer to my ear "– and speak to some very boring people," she whispered. "I hope there might be another opportunity in the future to hear your story." She beamed at me and then moved on.

The after-premiere party was held at the Krays' nightclub on the Mile End Road. Princess Margaret and Lord Snowden did not stay for it so there was no further opportunity that night for me to tell her about myself. The Krays never talked about their high society connections, but their henchmen had told me that they had met the Princess and Lord Snowden on other occasions. I couldn't remember ever having met Lord Snowden back when he was plain Anthony Armstrong-Jones, even though he had been a part of the wider artistic community surrounding Francis Bacon and Lucien Freud for several years before he met the Princess. Despite all their seemingly knowledgeable insider gossip, when the Princess's engagement to Armstong-Jones was first announced, it came as a surprise to The Colony Club regulars and Francis, among others, immediately trotted out a whole host of salacious stories about the society photographer's sexual relationships with both men and women.

My presence at the after-premiere party had a two-fold purpose: as well as being a bit-part actor in the film, I had been offered the job of co-manager of their Mile End night club by the Krays and I had accepted. At the time, it had seemed a sensible decision as, after leaving David Archer's bookshop, I was at a bit of a loose end. I salved my conscience by reasoning that, although I was being employed by these decidedly dodgy characters, it was a legitimate enterprise and they were not recruiting me for any of their more nefarious activities. I also persuaded myself that it would only be short term until I could find something else. My co-manager was an Italian dwarf called Mario. I subsequently discovered that our juxtaposition had been deliberately engineered by the Twins – a reflection of their warped sense of humour. They loved practical jokes and were fascinated by giants and midgets which explained their teaming me up with the diminutive Italian.

At this point in my story, I feel the need to pause. The need to explain myself, because I can sense what you are thinking, dear reader. So far, I have presented myself as a reasonably intelligent individual. And so, you must be asking yourself, what is this man doing, getting himself involved with the most notorious villains in London? Surely, he must have been able to see, despite all the half-hearted justifications referred to above, that nothing good would come of it? They are hard questions to answer. If I could go back in time and meet my younger self at that stage in his life, obviously I would have told him not to be so stupid. I could try and put it down to the impetuosity of youth, except that I was then approaching thirty-five years of age.

No. I can only explain my more dubious decisions by doing some backtracking to that day when my mother sat me down to tell me about her relationship with Ana. As I have already said, I was surprisingly unphased by the news. In fact, when she told me that, from then on, I was to treat Ana as a second mother, I was more than happy to do so. Let me remind you, dear reader: for me, Ana became a foil. Someone I could confide in when I was uncertain how my mother would react if I spoke about certain things to her. Ana was a patient and sympathetic listener. She would never fly off the handle. Having those two contrasting mothers worked very well for me.

But once Sarah had died and Ana became my only mother and no longer a foil, no longer a safe haven, but my only source of support, it somehow seemed like a betrayal to rely on her alone. It was almost certainly something to do with me growing up – becoming a teenager. Before, I knew that my mother's advice would be less like advice and more like instruction. She would tend to push me away from the safe and sensible route and nudge me towards the more risqué path. And I would react to my mother's extrovert exuberance by becoming the opposite: by shrinking into my shell. So, instead of seeking my mother's advice, I went to Ana, because she would give me safe practical guidance. But, once my mother was gone and I was reaching maturity,

I hankered after a more dangerous life. I now wanted to be like my deceased mother – more of a risk taker. So, I went less and less to Ana for advice. Told her as little as possible about what I was doing with my life until, eventually, I told her nothing at all.

Instead, I began to have long conversations with my mother. Although I have never been a superstitious or religious person, I started to believe that my mother could indeed communicate with me from beyond the grave. Of course, dear reader, I knew she wasn't really speaking to me. I hadn't gone mad. I knew it was just me speaking to myself, except with her voice. I persuaded myself that, if she had still been alive, that is what she would have said to me. And I so badly wanted her guidance – or, at the very least, her approval.

It is one of life's paradoxes that people who grow up with both their parents living, make every effort to escape from them and resist them having any influence over their lives whereas, orphans like me who no longer have the option of living under a parent's thumb, desperately miss that influence and often seek to replicate it, either through a surrogate, usually a husband or wife, or, as in my case, an imaginary presence.

Now that my nights were being taken up with my duties in the East End nightclub, I was spending considerably less time at The Colony, The French House and my other hangouts in Soho and, therefore, seeing much less of Francis. He had invited me to the press show for the retrospective of his work at the Tate, which had included one of his paintings of me, but, mercifully, there had been no more early morning or late night calls for me to rescue him from some young roughneck he'd picked up. The last call I received was to help him subdue his current boyfriend, an East End boxer, who was breaking up furniture and ripping up his clothes after they had had a falling out at his studio.

By then, his fascination with me had worn off. Any lingering fantasy that I would metamorphose into a sexual partner and pander to his masochism had now faded away. The new boyfriend seemed happy to fulfil these needs and, on the rare occasions when I did run across him, Francis often showed signs of having been roughed up. Anyway, by then I was beginning to find his wit less than sparkling as his conversation turned increasingly more maudlin. He told me on one occasion that he thought about death every day. He revelled in what he described as 'the edgy atmosphere of the world' – in particular, the threat of nuclear war. The world could end at any time, he would say. Whereas the rest of us had been appalled by the Cuban Missile Crisis, Francis had found it enthralling.

Apart from my stint as security on the set of *Sparrers Can't Sing* and my new position as co-manager of the Kentucky Club, I was rarely called on by the Twins to participate in any of their more dubious activities. On a couple of occasions, they asked me to accompany Tony, their Maltese lieutenant, on his missions. They refused to tell me what the purpose of these visits were but were quick to reassure me that no violence would be involved. They just wanted me there as extra security. It turned out that both of the initial trips I made with Tony were to rent boys. On the way, Tony told me that he was just collecting something from them and, in the unlikely event that they would be reluctant to give it to him, the Twins were confident that my presence alone would render the young men quiescent.

As we drove down the Whitechapel Road to one of the rent boys' rooms in Stepney, Tony was his usual garrulous self.

"This is one of Ronnie's set ups," he told me. "He

provides these rent boys to various of his upper-class associates. Members of Parliament, Lords, High Court Judges – those kind of people. Promises them it'll be very discreet. His aim is to get them to become regulars with the boys – sometimes even start up relationships. Then he gets the boys to collect evidence on them. You know, compromising things – letters perhaps or sometimes secret tape recordings. All stuff he can keep stored away for later use if necessary." He turned towards me and tapped the side of his nose. "Just in case there should come a time when he might need to call in some favours, if you get my meaning."

I didn't say anything. It confirmed my initial suspicion that my presence at these collections wasn't really necessary and that Tony had been instructed to tell me what the purposes of the visits were. While the Krays may never have boasted about their connections with high society, they were nevertheless keen that people knew about them. People like me. I think they felt that it would help to keep me hooked in to working for them and persuade me that they were much more than simple criminals.

And so, when I was asked to accompany Tony and two of his Maltese associates to a flat above a shop in High Street Kensington one Easter Monday morning, I naturally assumed it would be just another visit to a rent boy. To my surprise, the door was opened by a bleary-eyed David Reznikoff wearing a dragon-patterned silk dressing gown. Blinking in the early morning sunlight, it took him a moment to register who we were. Once he had, a look of panic spread across his face and he tried to slam the door shut but Tony was too quick for him and wedged his foot in the way while one of his accomplices shouldered the door open, sending David staggering backwards, waving his arms to try and steady himself before tumbling over at the foot of a flight of stairs.

"Behave yourself, David," Tony said, grabbing him by the arm and jerking him to his feet. "We just need to have a word with you."

That panicked look remained. David Reznikoff opened and closed his mouth, but no sound came out. I stayed standing on the pavement watching as Tony's mates took hold of Reznikoff's arms and marched him backwards up the narrow flight of stairs, his bare feet bumping feebly up the steps. I reluctantly followed them up two flights of stairs and into the second floor flat. It was dark inside. We had presumably woken him up. Tony walked across to the floor to ceiling windows and opened the curtains, revealing a narrow balcony with cast-iron railings and a view down to the high street. The other two pinned Reznikoff down in an armchair. His eyes swivelled in panic from one to the other of the Maltese men before fixing on me as I hovered uncertainly in the doorway. At last, he found his voice, albeit a barely audible croak.

"Harry. What's this about? There must be a mistake. I haven't done anything."

Before I could attempt any kind of reply, Tony stepped in front of me and stood facing him.

"You're right, David," he said. "You haven't done anything." He put extra emphasis on 'done'. "As usual, it's your big mouth that's got you into trouble. We're just here to teach you a little lesson. It's a message from the Twins. You've got to learn to keep that big flapper of yours shut." He nodded at his two henchmen who hauled David up out of the armchair and once again dragged him backwards towards a doorway leading to a bathroom.

"Please wait, Tony," he pleaded. His dressing gown had flapped open revealing his scrawny naked body. He was hanging limply between them, making no attempt to resist. "It's some kind of misunderstanding. It must be. If you'll just take me to see Reggie and Ronnie, I'm sure I'll be able to explain everything."

Tony was impassive. The two men dragged him into the bathroom and one of them kicked the door closed behind them.

Tony, noticing the look of disapproval on my face, shrugged his shoulders.

"Is all this necessary?" I said. "And why the fuck do I need to be here? Were they worried he'd be too much for the three of you to handle?"

"The Twins wanted you to come. You'll have to ask them why. You're a friend of David's, aren't you? I guess that might be the reason."

There were clattering and banging noises coming from the bathroom along with David Reznikoff's muffled cries.

"Reggie promised me there'd be no violence," I said.

"Don't worry. They're not hurting him. Not much anyway."

"I'm sorry, Tony. I don't want to be a part of this. I'm out of here." Before he could say anything, I'd turned on my heels and headed out the door and down the stairs. When I reached the street, I stopped and stared at the scene confronting me further up the road. There was the sound of beating drums. Marching up Kensington High Street towards where I was standing, was a phalanx of people hemmed in by two rows of police officers, completely blocking the traffic. They were carrying multi-coloured banners and chanting. As they got closer, I could hear the chants.

"1-2-3-4-5, keep the human race alive."

"Ashes to ashes, dust to dust, if the bomb doesn't get you then the fallout must."

At the front was a row of people with linked arms, a large black banner being held above their heads with the words 'March from Aldermarston to London' printed on it in large white letters. The one person I recognised in that front row, with his long grey hair fluttering in the wind, was the philosopher Bertrand Russell.

I thought about going back up to the flat and warning Tony of the large number of police in the street below, thinking that it might force him to abort whatever it was they were doing to David Reznikoff but, before I could move, I heard a noise above my head – a clanking sound. I stepped back off the pavement and looked up. I could see the backs of the two Maltese heavies out on the second floor balcony. They seemed to be struggling to lift something. As they turned around, I could see that it was a wooden kitchen chair with a naked David Reznikoff strapped to it. I watched in horror as they hauled it over the edge of the railings until David was upside down and I could see the top of his head. I was about to shout out, assuming they were going to launch him over the edge. Instead, they proceeded to use the sheets and towels with which they had strapped him to the chair to secure the chair legs to the railings, leaving David hanging down headfirst. His mouth was gagged although the noise of the rapidly approaching drums and chants from the marchers drowned out any attempts he was making to cry out. Something dripped down on to the pavement at my feet. Small red spatterings. I looked back up and could see the top of David's head. What little hair he had had been inexpertly shaved off, probably with a blunt razor. There were still one or two small black tufts of hair surrounded by cuts dripping with blood.

I was ushered back on to the pavement by a policeman as the march reached me and started to file by. I expected that, at any moment, somebody would spot the ghastly scene on the balcony above and point it out, but everybody's attention, including the police, was on the marchers.

There was a tap on my shoulder. It was Tony and his two friends.

"Come on, Harry. We're leaving."

I stared up at Reznikoff, still hanging from the balcony. "You're not going to leave him like that?"

"Of course we are," Tony said. "I told you we weren't going to hurt him – much. Just teach him a lesson. He'll be alright. Somebody'll spot him soon."

I shrugged Tony's hand off and started to walk back through the doorway up to the flat.

"Don't be stupid, Harry," he shouted after me. "You'll regret it. The Twins aren't gonna like it."

He started up the stairs after me but then thought better of it, not wanting to attract attention from the crowds out on the street. I walked up the stairs, straight through the living room and out on to the balcony where I quickly hauled the chair and David Reznikoff back over the railings and carried him into the room. I closed the window behind me not daring to look down into the street to see if I had attracted any attention, before I set about unstrapping his limp body. Once I'd untied and ungagged him, I fetched his dressing gown from the bathroom and helped him back on with it. He continued to whimper, too shocked to speak. I bathed the cuts on the top of his head with balled up clumps of dampened toilet paper. As I dabbed at the blood, I could feel the tension in my body as I expected that, any second, there would be a ring on the bell or a knock at the door announcing the arrival of the police. I started to think of a story I could tell them. It seemed impossible that, in all that crowd of people out on the street, no one had looked up and spotted a naked bloody man hanging from a balcony. But there was no knock or ring and soon the drums and chants of the demonstrators evaporated into the distance as they headed for their Hyde Park rally. Now the only noise came from David Reznikoff as he finally stopped sobbing, calmed himself down and began to thank me over and over again.

I went into the kitchen and made him a mug of sweetened tea.

"So, what have you been up to, David?" I said, setting down the mug on a wicker basket that served as a coffee table. "What's all this about?"

"You don't want to know," he said as he sipped the tea.

"You're right," I said. "I don't want to know."

As he drank his tea, it was as if it was a magic potion that returned him to his normal cocky self.

"So, Harry, you're working for Reggie and Ronnie now? Full-time, I hear."

"I'm just managing one of their night clubs. Nothing more," I said.

"Apart from your little excursion this morning." He grinned at me. I didn't respond. "You're playing a dangerous game, Harry. If you're not careful, you're going to get dragged into some very nasty stuff."

I remained tight-lipped. He then poured out a stream of gossip about the Twins and their criminal activities – the very same gossip, I assumed, that had got him into trouble in the first place. Incorrigible was the word that most readily came to mind when summing up David Reznikoff. Soon, apart from the crusted blood on his scalp, it was as if nothing out of the ordinary had happened and I had just popped by for a social call.

As I was leaving, he said, "I'm so glad you were here, Harry. I don't know how to thank you. I'll make it up to you some time."

"Yes," I said. "I won't hold my breath."

As I left the flat, I thought back to Tony's words – "the Twins aren't going to like it."

The following Saturday night I was working at the Mile End Road club as usual. I had heard nothing from the Twins or any of their associates about the incident with David Reznikoff so, when Ronnie entered the club accompanied by a pretty wraith-like young man with a mop of floppy blond hair, I stayed calm and avoided making any acknowledgement of his presence. He sat in his usual booth in a corner furthest away from the bar and summoned a waitress. I stayed by the bar watching out of the corner of my eye as the waitress took his order and then walked back across the almost empty dance floor towards me. Ronnie's eyes appeared to be following her but, once she'd arrived at the bar, it was clear that it was me he was staring at. There was the usual impenetrable look on his face – even more menacing for showing no emotion.

"Two double whiskies and soda, Eddie," the waitress said to the barman.

"Make that one double whisky and soda and a lemonade," I said to Eddie.

Eddie had turned towards the optics behind him but now turned round and stared at me, puzzled. Stella, the waitress, was about to say something but Eddie beat her to it.

"But Harry, it's Ronnie…"

"I know who it is," I said, not looking at him. "And I said make it one double whiskey and a lemonade."

When the drinks had been poured and placed on a small round tray with a bowl of peanuts, Stella picked it up gingerly as if it was about to explode and hovered by the bar, glancing nervously at me, presumably hoping that I might change my mind about the drinks order or maybe decide to take it over myself. After a few seconds, she reluctantly shuffled back across the dance floor to Ronnie and his young friend.

Thirty seconds later, Stella was back by my side at the bar. "Ronnie wants to talk to you," she said.

I sauntered over to the booth, Ronnie's eyes fixing me with his thousand yard stare as I approached.

"What's this, Harry?" Ronnie said, waving his hand over the drinks. "I ordered two whiskies." The boy with the floppy hair was grinning up at me, anticipating my imminent humiliation.

"Sorry Ronnie," I said, "but I believe your companion here is underage. I can't serve him alcohol."

"I'm sorry too, Harry. Just remind me who owns this club?."

"You do, Ronnie. But I'm the manager. You employ me, I believe, to serve yours and the club's interests. If this young man wasn't here with you but was on his own, I don't think you'd want me serving him alcohol and putting the club's licence at risk." Ronnie continued to give me that stare and the kid continued to grin inanely.

"Do you know what Reggie and me like about you, Harry?" He paused, giving me a chance to answer even though it was obviously a rhetorical question. "It's your crazy mixed up heritage. All those different bloods stirring around inside you. It shows that we have a lot in common. We're an odd mixture – me and Reggie – just like you. A bit of Eastern European Jewish, some Irish, some Romany gypsy. What we're not so sure we like about you is that you don't seem to be frightened of us. Everybody else is, so why aren't you?"

"Maybe I am," I said, endeavouring to appear as deadpan and unfrightened as possible.

"Well, you're very good at hiding it. Maybe now would be a good time to start to show it." He paused and continued to look me in the eye. "Anyway, that's enough of this for now. You go away and think about it. I came here to enjoy myself, not to get into an argument. We'll talk more about this some other time."

As I turned to walk back to the bar, Ronnie's teenage companion piped up in a squeaky voice, "here, what about my whiskey?"

"Shut the fuck up and drink your lemonade," Ronnie grunted at him.

At this point, dear reader, I would not blame you if you were feeling somewhat incredulous. If I were a biographer writing Hare Felatu's life story rather than an autobiographer, I would be pausing here to question just how fearless Hare Felatu really was. I would be finding it hard to believe that he could be so confrontational with the two most feared and violent men in London at that time – at any time: that he could seem so unflustered when facing up to them. If Felatu was telling me these stories himself, I would assume he was a fantasist who was just trying to 'big himself up'.

But this is me trying to look back at myself thirty years ago and even I find it hard to explain my behaviour at that time. It's possible that I had adopted the old adage that the best thing to do when under threat of attack is to show no fear – to face up to it rather than run away. But a more likely explanation is that I had inherited my fearlessness from my mother. She had always refused to bow down before anybody no matter how rich and powerful they were. If she could do that as a diminutive woman, then surely, as a towering giant of a man, I should be no less indomitable. Ultimately, what I had learnt from my mother, and from the many years it had taken me to come to terms with my own height and strength, was that it had nothing to do with size but everything to do with strength of mind.

I cannot explain why I ended up working for the Krays; only that they had wanted me and not the other way round. At the time, I felt, maybe wrongly, that I could walk away with impunity whenever I chose.

That promise of a follow up discussion, issued as a barely veiled threat by Ronnie, never took place. There was no further mention of either the drinks incident in the club or my rescuing of David Reznikoff that Easter Monday. If I thought about it at all, my reasoning at the time was that the Twins had more than enough hangers-on who were terrified of them and obeyed their every command. Maybe it was a welcome change to have someone who was not cowed by them. And, added to that, my lack of fear was no threat to them. Unlike their rival South London gangs, I was not looking to muscle in on their operations. In fact, I was adamant that I was not a criminal at all. Instead, I believe they wanted to hang on to me because they thought that I could be useful to them in other ways.

# Thursday 15th October 2001

On the tube journey back to Harlesden, Becky sat rigidly in her train seat, the box she had collected from Harry Felatu's safety deposit facility balanced on her knees, her hands spread out on top of it as if fearful that some small animal inside might try to escape. As she stared down at it, she was reminded of an old Hitchcock film that she and David had seen at the Manchester University Film Club in which a boy travelled on a bus across London with a parcel he had to deliver on his lap. What he did not know was that the parcel contained a bomb. That set Becky to wondering just how explosive the document inside the box might turn out to be. Initially, she had decided that, since she was merely an emissary collecting it on behalf of David Reznikoff, she should take it straight back to him.

Her first reaction in the storage facility, when she read the title on the box lid, 'The Autobiography of an Invisible Man', was one of disappointment. Having discovered from her earlier research on Harry Felatu that he had published at least one novel in his life, she assumed that this might be the manuscript of his latest work of fiction. And so, sitting on the platform at St. John's Wood Station at the start of her journey, she couldn't resist flipping open the box and having a brief perusal of the contents just to satisfy that initial fear/curiosity. It was a manuscript of about 200 pages written in elegant cursive longhand. A quick scan of the first few pages was enough to confirm that the 'Invisible Man' was no fictional character but Harry Felatu himself and this was indeed his autobiography. With a feeling of relief mixed with excitement and, for Becky, a rare effort of self-restraint, she closed the box and resolved to wait before continuing to read it.

However, once she was sat on the train, she had been itching to open it up and start reading through it although, like a government official transporting top secret confidential files, she felt she needed more privacy than in a busy underground train carriage before she opened it up again. And then, there was still that lingering fear, despite all the precautions she had taken earlier in the day, that there might be someone following her. It would have to wait until she was in the safety of her own flat.

Back in the flat, she made herself a cup of coffee while checking her mobile phone. There were three missed calls from David Reznikoff made while she was on the underground. He was obviously desperate to find out how she had got on. Her finger hovered over 'call back' but she decided to leave him to stew for a while. Instead, she carried her mug of coffee, a pack of digestive biscuits and the manuscript through to her desk. She hadn't eaten anything since breakfast and she would have liked to get some proper lunch but she was too impatient for any further delays. She took the manuscript out of the box and started to read. She had only reached page four when her phone rang. She knew who it would be without needing to look at the screen. As always, her initial impulse was to let it go to voicemail but she knew she wouldn't be able to put off speaking to him for long so she may as well get it over with now.

"Becky. Did you get there? How did it go?" His voice was tetchy and impatient.

"Yes. I got there okay. I've only just got back to my flat. I've brought…"

"Don't say anymore, Becky. Can you meet me this afternoon? We can discuss it then."

"Okay. I'm not doing anything this afternoon other than…"

"Right. How about in an hour? Say 3.30?" He seemed to want to cut the phone call short. Becky assumed he was playing safe in case his phone was being tapped. "Don't come to my flat. I'm still worried they might be watching me. Let's meet in that café that we met in before. Do you remember it?"

"Yes. That'll be fine."

"Don't bring anything with you. Just in case, if you get my meaning. I'll see you there."

The café Veneziana in Praed Street was the kind of budget greasy spoon that attracted local workmen, homeless itinerants and members of the small local Italian community. That Wednesday afternoon, there was only a mother with two small children and two workmen in paint-spattered overalls apart from Becky and David Reznikoff so there was no danger of them being overheard by any associates of the mysterious thugs who had terrorised him. Becky sat at a table furthest away from the serving counter while David collected their order. He made his way gingerly across the café carrying a tray with two cappuccinos and a slice of black forest gateau. He put the tray down spilling frothy liquid into the saucers.

"Are you sure you won't have anything to eat?" He said as he dug his fork into the gateau. "The coffee here is not the best, but their cakes and pastries are delicious – and cheap."

"No, I'm fine."

He glanced over his shoulder around the café, assuring himself that nobody was in earshot. Nevertheless, when he continued to speak, it was barely above a whisper. "Well. Tell me what you found."

Becky took a sip of her coffee. She was enjoying his impatience as she took her time to reply. It was a reversal of their usual roles. "There was only one thing in the safety deposit box. It's a manuscript. It's called 'The Autobiography of an Invisible Man'. I've only glanced at the opening few pages but it seems to be his own autobiography."

He looked disappointed. He scratched the bald patch on top of his head. "Nothing else?" She shook her head. "Are you sure? Have you looked through it all? Checked all the pages to see if there are any other documents buried inside it?"

"No. I haven't had time."

"You need to do that. It's possible that he's using the autobiography as camouflage like he used that Soho book to hide the safety deposit box letter. There could be something important hidden inside that he wanted me to find." He paused as the café door opened and a hunched over elderly woman with a shopping trolley and a mangy white poodle on a lead came in.

"Would you like me to give the manuscript to you? I feel maybe you should have it. After all, he intended you to have it," Becky said.

"No. You keep it. It'll be safer with you. After you've checked through it to see if anything else is there, you can read it if you want. I know all about Harry's life so I doubt there's much of interest in it for me – although you could let me know what he says about me. Plenty of scurrilous stuff, I'm sure."

They sat without talking for a while, drinking their coffees, before Becky broke the silence.

"So – where do we go from here?"

"When you get home, you check through the manuscript quickly and then let me know if you find anything. We need a code for when you phone me. I'm still worried somebody might be listening in to my phone." He sat back in thought for several seconds. "If you find something, say 'I've made a doctor's appointment for you'. If there's nothing say 'I've cancelled your doctor's appointment.'"

"Not very imaginative, Mr Reznikoff. How about 'the seagulls are flying over the trawler'?"

"Sorry Becky, but I'm not in the mood for joking. I'll wait to hear from you."

He stood up and was about to leave but then stood statue-like for a few seconds before sitting back down.

"I know you probably think I'm being paranoid but these people are dangerous and we both need to be cautious. I would suggest you don't keep the manuscript in your flat. Is there somewhere else you could read it?"

She almost laughed and was about to tell him that, yes, he was being paranoid except she saw the troubled look on his face and remembered the state his flat had been in.

"I suppose I could keep it in my locker at the museum and read it there," she said.

"I think that would be for the best." He got up and walked out of the café.

Becky watched him as he stopped briefly on the pavement outside and looked up and down the street before heading off.

# Extracts from
# The Autobiography of an Invisible Man

## MIXING WITH THE UPPER ECHELONS

"Let me introduce you to Harry Felatu. He manages the club for us. Harry, this is Bob – Lord Boothby."

The ultraelegant chubby man with slicked back grey hair sitting next to Ronnie Kray needed no introduction being instantly recognisable from his frequent television appearances. He was wearing his signature spotted bow tie and sporting a white carnation in his lapel.

"Pleased to meet you," I said, shaking his outstretched hand. I refrained from addressing him as your lordship. As I have previously mentioned, one of the things I had inherited from my mother was a refusal to defer to my supposed superiors. MPs, celebrities, assorted members of the landed gentry, regularly appeared in the club usually accompanying Reggie and Ronnie. When introduced to any of them, I endeavoured to be unimpressed even though Ronnie had complained to me on previous occasions about my lack of respect. It was no different with Lord Boothby.

"Good to meet you, Harry," he said. "I've heard quite a bit about you. All good, of course. From, among others, Princess Margaret – who appears to be quite a fan of yours." His mellifluous voice wrapped around me like wisps of shot silk. I was somewhat taken aback. It took a moment before the memory of our brief encounter at the film premiere came back to me.

"I'm surprised to hear that," I managed to say once I had regained my composure. "We only had the briefest of conversations."

"Well, brief it may have been, but you obviously made quite an impression. Look, why don't you join us. I'll order another bottle and we can talk further." He indicated a spare chair on the end of the table. As well as he and Reggie, there was a young man with short dark hair in a stylish midnight blue mohair suit sitting at the table holding a glass of champagne. I couldn't remember his name, but I recognised him as one of the twins' small time criminal associates.

"I have one or two things I need to see to in the office," I said. There it was again – an automatic refusal to kowtow to the nobility but then, out of the corner of my eye, I spotted the look of irritation on Ronnie's face. I hesitated before deciding that it would be prudent not to get into Ronnie's bad books over something as trivial as having a drink with one of his aristocratic buddies. "It'll only take a few minutes and then I'll be back over."

I remember very little of the subsequent conversation with Lord Boothby and his young companion. He did nearly all the talking – most of it, semi-amusing gossip about Princess Margaret – some of it complimentary and some vicious. At one point, he described her, with what I assumed was well-rehearsed alliteration, as 'a midget Maltese manicurist'. There was the occasional interjection from Leslie, the young petty criminal who I later discovered was Boothby's current 'bit of rough'. The conversation ended with Lord Boothby making a passing oblique reference to various problems he was having to confront and wondering whether I might be able to help him. He did not elaborate and I tried to be as non-committal as possible. As I got up to leave, he said he would be in contact in the near future.

There were no more visits to the club from his lordship in the following weeks and I didn't hear anything more from him, I suspect because, a week or so after our meeting, the *Sunday Mirror* printed a front page exclusive linking a well-known, but unnamed, member of the House of Lords with the Krays, intimating that there had been a sexual relationship and claiming to have photographs to prove it. Although he was not named, it was obvious that it was Boothby. The scandal rumbled on for a few weeks as Lord Boothby threatened to sue. The *Sunday Mirror* eventually backed down, sacked its editor, issued an apology and paid his lordship substantial damages.

After all of that, I assumed that he had decided to keep a low profile for a while and avoid any further connections with the Krays or any of their associates.

By this time, I was getting bored with working at the Mile End Road club and was considering whether to call it a day. Then, one evening, my mind was made up for me. Although their visits to the nightclub were becoming less frequent by then, the Mayfair crowd still occasionally slummed it in the Mile End Road. That particular evening, I was sorting out some paperwork in the office when I heard angry raised voices coming from the club. As I came out of the office door to see what the commotion was about, two middle aged men and two younger women walked briskly towards me on their way out.

"Disgusting. That bastard should be locked up, preferably in a loony bin," said the man at the front, simultaneously dabbing a wet patch on his suit jacket with a handkerchief. The woman behind him was shaking something from her elaborately coiffured blonde hair.

"Sorry. Is there a problem?" I said, moving in front of them.

"A problem?" Said the man. "There certainly is. It's that Kray nutter. He shouldn't be allowed in polite society."

"What has he done?" I asked, stopping myself from adding 'this time'.

"He was sitting above us on the balcony." It was now one of the younger women speaking in a voice so high pitched it was almost a squeak. "And he starts shouting down at us calling us 'bloody stuffed shirts' and then the next thing we know he's showered us with champagne. You can tell him we won't be coming back and neither will any of our friends."

"I suppose we should be grateful that it wasn't something else he sprayed on us," said the other young woman, at which her companion grimaced.

I didn't bother trying to apologise but stepped aside and let them continue towards the exit. Once they'd left, I headed back into the main club room and across the dance floor towards the wrought iron staircase leading to the balcony. As I got there, I met Reggie coming down. He stood in my way at the bottom of the stairs.

"Don't bother, Harry," he said. "Ronnie'll be alright. It's just that he forgot to take his pills today."

I'd frequently overheard the Twins' henchmen talking about Ronnie's mental health problems. Schizophrenia was often mentioned but I wasn't aware that he'd been having treatment or was on medication. I stood in silence for several seconds giving Reggie a disapproving look before I turned and headed back to the office to finish the paperwork. But, when I got there, I couldn't concentrate. This had pushed me over the edge. I needed to act before I had a chance to change my mind. It was bad enough working for a bunch of criminals but having to deal with one who was also insane was too much, so I headed straight back into the club. By the time I reached the balcony, the Twins had gone.

My next opportunity was when Reggie arrived at the club the following evening, I went up to him, all set to tell him that I was resigning but, before I could say anything, he started speaking to me.

"So, tell me, Harry. Are you free tomorrow afternoon?"

My immediate instinct was to say no I wasn't. This could only be an invitation to go along with their henchmen to another of their dodgy activities. Fortunately, they had not requested my participation in these 'visits' since the roughing up of David Reznikoff.

Instead, in one of my habitual bouts of stupidity, I hedged my bets. "I might be," I replied. "It depends why."

"We want you to come with us to visit this new nightclub that's about to open in Soho. We're going to have a share in the ownership and we'd like you to manage it for us. We thought you might like to give it the once over before you decide."

And so, the following afternoon there I was standing outside of The Hideaway Club in Gerrard Street, Soho, waiting for Reggie and Ronnie to arrive.

I am sure, dear reader, that you are thinking the exact same thing as I am now as I look back at myself thirty years ago. After all, I was no longer an impetuous youth; I was approaching forty. Having just made the eminently sensible decision to cut my ties with these hoodlums, why had I changed my mind? Well, I have to admit that my initial decision was only partly a moral one: it was also the very practical fact that I was fed up with all the travelling between my flat in Paddington and The Kentucky Club in the Mile End Road – especially the journeys home in the early hours of the morning. Therefore, when Reggie mentioned the new job in a club in Soho, my interest was piqued despite my earlier resolution. I was missing the Soho pubs and drinking clubs and so, the chance to work back in the area and reacquaint myself with these old haunts and the bohemian artistic community frequenting them was enticing.

The twins arrived accompanied by a small man with a pale freckly face and fluffy receding red hair wearing an expensive-looking camel-hair coat. Reggie introduced him as Eddie, their accountant.

As we entered the club, a tall thin man in his thirties came out of an office door behind the reception desk. He was dark-skinned with a large nose and thick black, fashionably shoulder-length hair. He did not look pleased to see us.

"Mr McGregor, I presume," said Reggie, reaching out to shake his hand. "Or can I call you Hugh?"

Mr McGregor kept his hands firmly by his side.

"I'm Reggie and this is…"

"I know who you are. What do you want?" His tone of voice was even more hostile than his demeanour.

Reggie lowered his hand to his side. "We've come to discuss a business offer with you. We'd like to offer you our services in this new venture of yours." He waved his hand towards the archway leading into the main club. "Of course, in return for us providing this support to you, we'd want a modest share in the business – shall we say twenty per cent?" There were sounds of hammering and drilling coming from inside the club. Hugh McGregor said nothing but just stood behind the reception desk looking impatient.

Undeterred, Reggie continued. "Let me be more specific. In return for this share in the business, we will provide you with a manager for the club." He turned round and flapped his hand in my direction. "Let me introduce you. This is Harry Felatu. He's a very experienced night club manager."

I stayed where I was, standing several feet behind Reggie, not bothering to extend a hand which would obviously be rejected. Hugh McGregor continued to look less than impressed.

"We will also provide you with a team of doormen and security guards," Reggie said.

"Let me stop you there, Mr Kray." He had a cut glass public school accent. "I'm not interested. However you try to dress it up, you are petty criminals running a protection racket. I was warned to expect you when I bought this place so I suggest you fuck off before I call the police."

"There's no need for foul language," said Reggie. "If there's one thing my brother and I can't stand, it's the use of expletives, especially from such an obviously well brought up young man like yourself. An old-Etonian, I'm led to believe."

"You should listen to my brother," Ronnie said. He had wandered over to the archway leading to the club bar and was watching a couple of decorators at work. "He turned back towards Hugh McGregor. "This is Eddie Smith, our accountant." He pointed at the red-headed man standing next to me. "If we could step into your office, Eddie can show you the financial benefits of the deal we're offering you. He's very kindly already drawn up the paperwork for you to sign."

"The deal you're offering me won't benefit me at all and you know it. It's not so much a deal, more extortion."

Despite my growing discomfort at the scene unfolding before me, I couldn't help but admire the man's calm implacability.

Ronnie stood and stared at him, his eyes like ray-guns in an old science fiction comic. I half-expected Mr McGregor to be reduced to a pile of ashes on the floor. Then Ronnie turned on his heels and walked through the archway towards the bar. He lifted the wooden flap and moved behind it and, in one smooth movement, with a sweep of his arm sent a row of glasses crashing to the floor. Then he picked up a whisky bottle from under the counter and swung it along a row of optics behind him, showering glass and alcohol everywhere. The drilling from the far side of the club stopped and the painters turned to watch what was happening.

Ronnie dropped the broken bottle neck, shook shards of glass and drops of liquid off his sleeve and walked from behind the bar back towards the club owner.

"You see. This is what could happen," he said. "But not if you have someone like Harry here managing the club for you – with our support, of course."

Hugh McGregor's dark complexion had turned several shades darker and redder. He was struggling to remain calm. "Just get out," he said between gritted teeth.

Ronnie took several more steps towards McGregor, clenching his fist.

"That's enough, Ron," said Reggie, putting a hand on his shoulder to restrain him. He turned back to McGregor and spoke in slow carefully enunciated words as if the man was mentally defective. "It's obvious that you're new to this night club business, Hugh. That's why you need us. We're old hands at it. You make a deal with us and you're getting genuine expertise. Forget all this nonsense you've heard about hoodlums and protection rackets. You've probably been watching too many James Cagney movies. Once word gets out that the Krays have a part share in your club, you won't get any trouble. So, what do you think?"

He was still remarkably calm. Upper class sang-froid, I would describe it as. "I think you've made a mistake. You're messing with the wrong person. I want nothing to do with thugs like you. So, for the last time, I'm giving you the chance to leave before I call the police."

Three workmen in paint-spattered overalls were now standing in the archway watching. Without any of us noticing it, Ronnie had picked up a small pewter art deco figure of a naked woman off the reception desk. I moved closer behind him prepared to restrain him if he attempted to swing it at the club owner, but Reggie beat me to it and grabbed hold of his sleeve. Simultaneously, he turned his head back towards Hugh MacGregor.

"I think you need a bit of time to think over our offer. No need to make a hasty decision. We'll give you a couple of days. We'll come back on…shall we say Friday… to talk it over again?"

Reggie tugged on Ronnie's sleeve. The statuette fell from his grip and bounced on the tiled floor. "Come on, Ronnie. Time to go. The man's busy. He's got a new club to get ready to open."

Reggie and Ronnie's ubiquitous canary yellow Cadillac with its whitewall tyres was waiting at the kerb outside, its engine idling. Reggie offered me a lift.

"No thanks," I said, trying to sound as if nothing untoward had happened. "I'll walk. I could do with the exercise." I don't know who I was angrier with – the Twins or myself. I had been incredibly stupid. I knew the Krays well enough by then to have been able to predict what was likely to happen. Still, at least it had served to confirm how right my earlier decision had been. I needed to get out before it was too late. No more prevarications.

"Look, I've been meaning to tell you for some time," I said. "I don't want to work for you anymore. I'm resigning."

Ronnie had already climbed into the back seat of the Cadillac. Reggie had hold of the door handle and was about to join him. He turned back round to face me.

"Come on, Harry," he said, in a cajoling tone of voice. "You don't want to worry about what just happened in there. He's just an arrogant upper-class twat. He'll come round when he realises what's good for him. And then you'll be manager of this place."

"Even if he does, I'm not interested. I'm moving on. It's nothing to do with what happened this afternoon. And it's not about you and Reggie. It's about me. I just think it's time for me to do other things with my life."

Reggie tilted his head to one side and stared at me, a hint of that Kray menace in his eyes. "Like I said to Mr MacGregor a minute ago, no need to make any hasty decisions, Harry. Give yourself time. Think about it." He patted me on the shoulder, gave me a lopsided smile and got in the car. They drove off and I turned in the direction of the Colony Club in bad need of a drink and some convivial company.

The following morning, I phoned Mario, the Italian dwarf and my co-manager, and told him I'd resigned and he was now in sole charge of the Kentucky Club. Then I waited nervously, expecting at any moment the knock on the door that would herald the arrival of Reggie and accompanying heavies to 'persuade' me to change my mind.

Later that afternoon, there was indeed a knock on my door but it wasn't the twins. It was two plainclothes police officers requesting that I accompany them to West End Central police station for questioning about a serious incident.

As I waited in the station foyer, a tall thin man in a pin-striped suit with thick-rimmed glasses and a bald head entered and introduced himself as Ernest Green, my solicitor. Before I could say anything, he hurriedly informed me that Reggie, Ronnie and Eddie Smith had already been arrested and questioned. He was the Krays' solicitor and they'd asked him to act for me as well. His advice was simple. I was to make no comment to any questions I was asked about the previous day's events at the Hideaway Club. It was especially important, he emphasised, that I say nothing that might incriminate Reggie and Ronnie. I told him that I wouldn't say anything to harm the Twins but I would not remain silent as I needed to defend myself as I had played no part in what had taken place at the club. He strongly advised me against this. Once I admitted I was there and witnessed what happened, the police would insist on knowing what I had seen. Best to say and admit nothing.

The policeman questioning me introduced himself as Detective Inspector Read. I confirmed my name and address and that I had been present with the Krays and Eddie Smith at the Hideaway Club in Gerrard Street the previous afternoon. When I was asked what had taken place between the Kray brothers and Hugh MacGregor, I said that I didn't know. The Krays had brought me along with them as prospective manager of the club and, while they were talking business with Mr MacGregor, I was walking around inspecting the place, including the renovation work that was going on. Inspector Read said that I must surely have heard the commotion at the bar when Ronnie smashed the glasses and optics. I replied that I hadn't heard anything. As I said earlier, I was inspecting the building work and there was a lot of noise from the drilling and hammering. I was asked a series of further questions about my association with the Krays. I told the inspector that my only connection was as a manager of one of their night clubs. He suggested to me that the reason I had accompanied them was that I was a six feet six inch tall thug there to back up their threatening behaviour. Of course, I denied that. The interview ended with Inspector Read formally charging me with demanding money with menaces. He informed me that I would be kept in custody overnight and attend a court bail hearing the following morning.

Ernest Green sat next to me throughout the interview looking grim-faced. Afterwards, he asked to have a few minutes with me before I was taken to a cell.

"It's a pity you chose not to follow my advice and say nothing but at least you didn't say anything too incriminating to yourself or, more particularly, Reggie and Ronnie. But I must warn you, you've made a bit of a rod for your own back. In court, the prosecution will grill you about how it was possible that you saw and heard nothing."

"Surely they won't have to rely on my testimony. The workmen witnessed everything. They're independent witnesses. They saw and heard everything."

Ernest Green gave me a pitying smile, as if surprised at my naiveté. "They know who the Kray twins are. And so, just like you, they saw and heard nothing. They were too busy in the club room sawing and hammering."

The next morning, I was taken back to the interview room instead of to the bail hearing. There, Inspector Read offered to drop the charges against me if I agreed to testify against the Krays in court. I said I would testify but I would only repeat what I had said in the previous day's interview because it was the truth. He asked me to wait outside. After a few minutes, he came out and told me they were dropping the charge against me and I was free to go.

I subsequently learned that Reggie and Ronnie had been refused bail and remanded in custody awaiting trial, having also been charged with demanding money with menaces. Although that meant that, for the time being, I could stop worrying about a visit from the Twins themselves, I should have realised it wasn't going to keep me entirely out of their clutches. A few days later, I received a visit from Tony and one of his Maltese compatriots. He informed me that, assuming I was going to be called as a witness, under no circumstances should I say anything that would be to the detriment of the Krays' defence. If I did, there would be dire consequences. He also told me that he was taking over my management duties at the club for the time being, but that Reggie and Ronnie were not at all happy about my resignation and would be discussing the matter with me further when their trial was done and dusted.

As hard as I tried to stop worrying about the whole sorry mess, I couldn't help but beat myself up over my pathetic failure to disentangle myself earlier from the Krays, not to mention getting involved with them in the first place. Fortunately, some good news arrived just in time to distract me from all of that. Out of the blue, I received a letter from a major paperback publisher expressing an interest in bringing out a new edition of my novel *An Angel in the City of Sin*. It was over ten years since its, decidedly unspectacular, original publication and I had presumed it was long forgotten. So much so that I had never been tempted to write another. They were offering me a miserly advance but promised that they would promote it heavily and were confident of healthy sales as they expected it to tap into the burgeoning hippy counter-cultural youth movements that had sprung up in recent years. In fact, my novel had only come to their attention because one of their young trendy editors had picked up a second-hand copy of the Olympia Press edition in Compendium Books in Camden Town and had been very impressed.

The Krays' trial was a damp squib. I stuck rigidly to my story, even under intense grilling by the barrister for the prosecution. The Twins' defence was that they had gone to see Hugh MacGregor because they were trying to interest him in investing in a project they were involved with in Nigeria. He had misunderstood the purpose of their visit and had grown unnecessarily belligerent which explained the accidentally broken glasses. There had been no mention of protection money. The jury were unable to reach a verdict. It should go without saying that the gossip surrounding the trial suggested that several of the jurors had been nobbled. The retrial that followed ended in their acquittal.

Despite the warnings that Tony had given to me, I neither saw nor heard anything from the Twins after they were released. They both went on holiday and, when they got back, Reggie got married. In the cossetted surroundings of The Colony Room, The Coach and Horses and The French Pub, I overheard occasional snatches of gossip about them. Feeling themselves untouchable after their acquittal, especially as pressure was put on the Metropolitan Police by Lord Boothby and other influential friends of the Krays to refrain from harassing them, they embarked upon a reign of terror. For a couple of years, my life was quiet and uneventful. I basked in the brief success de scandale of my re-launched novel, even receiving some attention from the newspapers and television, while re-establishing the routines of my Soho lifestyle, enjoying a sexual relationship with Elspeth, an upper crust young woman who was a friend and model of Lucien Freud's. I was back floating around on the fringes of bohemia, drinking far too much, and enjoying it.

It was only after the Krays had been arrested for the murder of Jack The Hat McVitie that I was hauled in for questioning by Detective Inspector Read and asked once again about my relationship with the Twins. He tried very hard to place me at the frequent parties in Ronnie's East End flat, especially the one at which Jack The Hat had been murdered but, this time, I could deny having ever attended such events with complete honesty. He told me that others present on the night of the murder had testified that I was also present. It sounded half-hearted to me and, since I wasn't called as a witness at their subsequent trial, it was obvious that he'd been 'flying a kite'.

Nevertheless, as the trial approached, I grew increasingly nervous, expecting that every ring of the doorbell would either be the police calling me in for even more questioning or the Krays' henchmen issuing either more dire warnings or actual beatings.

One evening, when I was sitting at the bar of The Coach and Horses somewhat the worse for wear, I was joined by David Reznikoff. I hadn't seen him for some time and was not surprised to see that he was attired in the full late 1960's hippy regalia of green velvet suit with flared trousers and floppy collared flowery shirt with a purple chiffon scarf knotted round his scrawny neck. His sparse black hair curled down over his shoulders.

"Let me get you another glass of red wine," he said. I nodded my acquiescence. He stared enquiringly at me. "If you don't mind me saying, Harry, you don't seem to be full of the joys of Spring."

"Maybe that's because it's only the beginning of March, David."

"Still, the weather's a bit Spring-like out there." He paused, still looking me up and down. "Or maybe you've been spending too much time propping up bars to notice what it's like outside?"

"You're right there. I much prefer spending time in the gloom inhaling the smoke and the smell of stale beer and the urinals. In fact, I'm so used to sitting in semi-darkness that I'm finding your peacock finery a bit dazzling."

He smiled and put a reassuring hand on my shoulder. "Come on. Tell your Uncle David what's wrong."

My normal instinct would be to tell David Reznikoff as little as possible, being all too aware of his propensity to shoot his mouth off to all and sundry, but I decided to throw caution to the wind. I needed someone to talk to. And so, I launched into a lengthy discourse on my dealings with the Krays over the past few years, most of which he already knew about. I concluded by telling him about my recent interview with the police and my fear that I would be dragged into the trial. But then, even if I wasn't, on the assumption that the Twins would somehow wriggle their way out of it and get themselves acquitted, I was worried that, once they were back on the streets, they would drag me back into their orbit.

He downed the rest of his wine and ordered two more glasses before responding. "Maybe I can help you out, Harry. After all, I still owe you for coming back to rescue me from my perils of Pauline moment on the balcony. I'm working on a film script at the moment. As it happens, the story has quite a close connection to the Krays. It's set in London's gangland and it's all about the links between gangsters and the rock music scene. Mick Jagger's been lined up to star in it." He could see that I was looking somewhat impatient. David had a habit of name-dropping. "Anyway, to cut a long story short, I'm having a bit of trouble with it…the script, I mean. Sort of writer's block. And this friend of mine has offered me the use of his cottage in Wales for as long as I like and I thought I might take him up on it. It's very picturesque, apparently. In the Brecon Beacons. The middle of nowhere. So, I thought that, if I could get out of the hurly burly of London for a while into a bit of peace and quiet, it might help me concentrate on the writing. So… why don't you come with me? Then you can get away from everything that's going on here. A sort of sanctuary."

My first reaction to his offer was to say thanks but no thanks. I'd always found David good company for the odd half an hour at a time but spending days or even weeks with him in an isolated country cottage was another thing entirely. On the other hand, he was right. It would be an escape, especially if I didn't tell anybody that I was going.

Two days later, after much meandering around narrow country lanes as I tried to navigate us using my non-existent map-reading skills, we arrived outside a worse for wear whitewashed cottage, surrounded by an overgrown garden, in the battered mini clubman that David had also borrowed from his friend.

The cottage was very rough and ready, the only heating being a wood-burning stove in the sitting room, but I didn't mind any of that. I had been used to a sparse way of life, even in the flats I'd lived in in London. Nevertheless, as soon as I arrived, I started yearning to get back to London. Like my mother, I had never been very keen on the countryside. Even the time we spent living in the village on the edge of High Wycombe could hardly have been called a rural existence. There were some farms in the surrounding area and plenty of well-manicured fields but we never ventured into them. Apart from my desire to escape the possible perils that faced me in London, the other reason I had decided to take up David's offer was because I thought it might be good for me to experience a dose of country living. However, within the first couple of days, my prejudices had been confirmed. The weather was miserable – cold, with early morning mists followed by drizzling rain for most of the rest of the day. Mud, mud and more mud – and the smell of manure. And, although I was supposed to be escaping from it, I felt the constant need for news of what was happening in London.

I sometimes accompanied David on his regular food shopping trips into the nearest small town and usually managed to pick up a newspaper, so I just about kept in touch with the progress of the trial. There was no television or radio in the cottage. I also tried phoning Elspeth from the phone box in the local village but, the only time I got through to her, she couldn't tell me anything about what had been going on as she said she'd been too busy, and not very interested anyway, to follow any of it. I tried asking her to come and stay in the cottage for a while, but she said she was too busy working on a new painting (she was a budding artist as well as a model). She grew increasingly impatient as I kept pressing her until she finally put the phone down on me. I had the feeling that, once I returned to London, our relationship would be over. It was the story of my life, dear reader. You may have noticed that I've told you very little about the women in my life. That's because all my relationships were very short-lived.

The only escape from the boredom of the cottage was to go to the local village pub for the evening. It was not a relaxing experience. The landlord was a grizzle-haired old man with a drinker's nose set in the middle of a thin, rodent-like, pock-marked face. On our first visit, he seemed reluctant to serve us, giving us a police style grilling on where we were from, where we were staying and what we were doing in that part of the world. Once he knew we were from London and which cottage we were staying in, it told him all he needed to know about us. We obviously fitted the stereotype of the many previous visitors to David's friend's cottage – effete London perverts.

It was a small one room pub, so it was hard to escape the regulars. The men looked like cartoon character yokels. They stared at us with open hostility. We couldn't have stood out more if we'd been aliens just landed from Mars – David with his long hair and hippy clothes and me – well, dear reader, I think you can picture by now how conspicuous I would have looked. I did briefly consider announcing to the whole pub that my mother had been born in Wales, but I suspect they would have thought I was taking the piss. On about our third or fourth visit, a couple of mini-skirted young women came over to talk to us. Apparently, they had met David in the village grocery shop a couple of days earlier and he had engaged them in conversation.

"So. You're the drummer then?" Said the younger of the two, flicking her fringe of dark brown hair flirtatiously out of her eyes. She had a pretty symmetrical face, although with too much make up for my liking. "That must explain the muscles."

As I stared at her in confusion, David leapt into the conversation. "I was telling Deidre and Gwen about the band when I met them the other day," he said, nudging my leg under the table. "Yes, Harry's the drummer, although he shares some of the vocals as well."

"Have you had any hits? Don't remember seeing you on *Top of the Pops*. What did you say the name of the group was again?" This was the chubby one with long auburn hair and glasses.

"The Green Dragon Cult. We had a minor hit. Got to about number twenty-five in the charts so we didn't quite make *Top of the Pops*. We've come to the cottage to write some songs for the new album. And we've got a new single coming out in a few weeks' time. We've got high hopes for that so I'm sure you'll be seeing us on the telly in the very near future." David's normal flamboyance was ratcheted up several notches. Apart from the clinking of glasses and the odd order being placed at the bar, the rest of the pub was quiet, everybody obviously listening to the London weirdo.

As far as possible, I stayed out of the rest of the conversation which mainly consisted of David telling the two young women about his friendship and numerous adventures with The Rolling Stones. My attention was only half on David's bogus blather as I was growing increasingly concerned at how all of it was going down with the local yokels. Badly, of course. Each new arrival would order their drinks and then turn and stare at our table before joining one of their friends who would mutter into their ear while the rest of them continued to watch us. Eventually, I intervened to cut the conversation short and get us both out of the pub before the men's resentment turned to violence.

As I headed for the door, David hung back at the table. "How about coming back to the cottage with us for a night cap?" He said to Gwen and Deidre.

I leapt back, grabbed his arm and flung him towards the door.

"Sorry ladies. Not tonight," I said. "We've got a very early start in the recording studio tomorrow. David must have forgotten. We need an early night."

On the drive back to the cottage, David berated me for cutting the evening short. He told me that both the women were well up for being groupies and I could have been well in with Deidre, the prettier one, who would have been only too happy to be able to boast that she had slept with a rock star. I didn't even bother to enquire what he, a gay man, would be doing with Gwen for the rest of the night while I was in bed with Deirdre. I said nothing, too intent upon hanging on grimly to the sides of my seat as David, driving far too fast in the pitch black, barely kept the car on the single-track road, almost ploughing into the fields on every corner.

At breakfast the following morning, I let rip, telling him that the locals were already unfriendly enough without him adding to it by his ridiculous story that we were rock stars. I insisted that, from now on, the village pub was out of bounds. If we wanted a drink, we'd have to drive into the town.

But, the following day, I realised that simply staying away from the village would not guarantee our safety. That morning, for what seemed like the first time in weeks, I awoke to the unfamiliar sight of a sliver of sunshine bursting through the gap in the bedroom curtains. I quickly washed and dressed and went for a stroll before breakfast. I'd barely got a quarter of a mile from the cottage before I passed a young farmer sitting on a style cradling a shotgun in his lap. I nodded a good morning at him, but he just stared at me and narrowed his eyes as I passed. A few hundred yards further on, there was another, older man, leaning against a gate also holding a shotgun. This time I made no attempt to acknowledge his presence. He looked daggers at me as I approached and brought the shotgun level with his hip, his finger on the trigger, pointing it in my direction at roughly groin level. When I went to see the film *Straw Dogs* a couple of years later, the story of Dustin Hoffman, the American Professor of Mathematics, and his young wife being terrorised by the men in a small Cornish village made the hairs prickle on the back of my neck, not so much because of the violent events on screen but more because of how closely it reminded me of our sojourn in the Brecon Beacons.

Thankfully, unlike in the film, the hostility of the farmers was just for show and went no further. And, anyway, the following week, on our regular trip into town for provisions, I went into the newsagents and felt a huge weight fall from my shoulders as the banner headlines in the national newspapers on the rack by the door all screamed out that the Krays had been found guilty of murder. I bought one and went immediately to the local tearoom to sit and read the details. They were to be sentenced the following week and, with the death penalty now abolished, they were certain to get life sentences. When we got back to the cottage, I packed my bag and asked David to drive me to the nearest train station. I expected him to protest and try and get me to change my mind, but he just nodded acquiescently. He'd also had his fill of rural Wales and so we drove back to London together.

The pile of mail on the mat by the front door of my Paddington flat was the usual mixture of bills and advertising circulars except for one letter. My full name and address had been typed very neatly on it and it was embossed with a Houses of Parliament stamp. When I opened it and pulled out the letter, a gold-rimmed invitation card fluttered on to the floor. I left it and unfolded the letter. It was on House of Lords notepaper and signed at the bottom by Lord Robert Boothby. In the letter, he said that he had seen me being interviewed on the television show *Late Night Line-up* and was reminded of our meeting at The Kentucky Club. (I have omitted to mention this television appearance, dear reader, as I did not cover myself in glory. In fact, it was an embarrassment that I had been eager to erase from my memory.) Ever since that night, he wrote, he had been meaning to re-establish our acquaintance. To that end, he had enclosed an invitation to a black-tie party at his apartments in Eton Square.

With the Krays safely under lock and key, I guess he now felt it was safe to fraternise once more with the London demi-monde, of which I was clearly still considered to be a member.

# Wednesday 21st October 2001

It had been two days since Ethan Jones last found the time to sit in front of a computer at Paddington Green police station. There were seventy-eight emails in his inbox awaiting his attention. As he only had fifteen minutes to spare before he'd have to be on the move again, he trawled through them as speedily as he could in search of the one or two that might be important. There were a few that he would need to check but could wait till later and, therefore, should not be instantly deleted, but only one that he was compelled to open immediately. It was a report, written in immaculate English, and much more detailed and thorough than he had expected, from Inspector Lukas Honig of the Austrian Federal Police. It was headed,

> *"Action on a request from the Metropolitan Police regarding the status of an account in the name of Athos Holdings held in the Vienna Central branch of Raiffeisen Bank."*

The rest of the report followed.

> *"I am able to confirm that, since it was opened in 1986, the only transactions to the above account have been one payment made in pounds sterling transferred into Austrian schillings, at whatever the exchange rate was on that date, from the account of the Sarah Weinstein Trust fund held at the High Holborn branch of HSBC Bank. That exact*

*same sum was then withdrawn in cash some time during the following week. I can confirm that there is only one named account holder – a Doctor Malcolm Harrison.*

*I have now visited Doctor Harrison at his apartment in central Vienna to interview him. Doctor Harrison advertises himself as a spiritual healer and hypnotherapist and has a consulting room in his apartment. He is forty-two years old and unmarried. He lives on his own. During our interview, he informed me that he has lived and worked in Vienna for the past fifteen years having emigrated from the United Kingdom. He confirmed that he was the registered account holder for Athos Holdings and that it was he who withdrew the money from the account and then paid it into his own personal bank account. He refused to answer when I asked him why the money could not simply be paid directly into his own account. All he would say is that it was all legal and above board and there was no question that it was anything to do with money laundering. He refused to specify exactly what the reason for the payment was other than that it was paid for services rendered to the Sarah Weinstein Trust Fund. Despite my repeated questions, he declined to say what those services were.*

*I did not pursue the issue of the bank account any further but, instead, asked if I could see Doctor Harrison's identification papers – in particular, his passport. He became flustered and uncooperative. He insisted on knowing what the purpose of my enquiry was. I told him I was not at liberty to divulge that information but, if he continued to be uncooperative, I would be forced to obtain a warrant to search his premises and to seize his identity papers. He continued to protest but finally agreed to show me his passport. On examining it, I discovered that, while*

*the photo was clearly Doctor Harrison the name on the*
*passport was a Mr Alexander Laxley-Young. I asked him*
*whether this was his real name and he confirmed that it*
*was. He said that he had changed his name on arriving in*
*Vienna for 'professional reasons' but refused to elaborate on*
*this. I asked him if he was a qualified medical practitioner*
*to which he replied that he had been in the UK but that*
*his qualifications were not recognised in Austria which is*
*why he had started up his current practice in alternative*
*medicine. I queried this, saying that, as I understood it,*
*all EU countries had reciprocal arrangements to recognise*
*each other's medical qualifications. Again, he declined*
*to comment. I terminated the interview at this point,*
*informing him that I may have to return to ask him further*
*questions depending upon how my enquiries developed.*

*I hope this information is helpful. If you wish me to carry*
*out any further investigations, please let me know. I am at*
*your disposal."*

Ethan returned to his home screen and stared into space
pondering on what he had just read. He had no idea whether
it had any significance, but it was definitely suspicious
and would require further investigation. He turned his
concentration back to the computer and went into the
police records site and started typing in Doctor Alexander
Laxley-Young but then saw the time in the bottom right-
hand corner of the screen and cursed. He had a meeting he
had to go to and he was already late. It would have to wait
until later that afternoon.

Becky was feeling frustrated. She had taken David Reznikoff's
advice and transferred Harry Felatu's manuscript to her
locker at the Museum of London. The problem was that

she was now finding precious little time to read it. As her team were embarking on the final preparations for the Soho exhibition, which was due to open in six weeks' time, she was either stuck at her desk working non-stop or involved in consultations with colleagues, even during her lunch hours. One thing she had managed to do with it so far was speedily leaf through all the pages, as David Reznikoff had suggested, to check whether Harry Felatu had hidden any other slips of paper, letters or documents with further messages that might provide a clue as to why he was killed or who his killers might have been. She hadn't found anything. In other snatched moments during coffee breaks or between finishing work and heading off home, she had managed to read the sections in which he described his childhood experiences. While they were interesting and entertaining, they were obviously not going to provide any clues as to his mysterious death. She decided that, when she next found some time to continue her reading, she'd skip to nearer the end where it was more likely that such clues would reside.

Her feelings about her continued involvement in the Felatu affair were veering about wildly. One moment, she would convince herself that it was all a wild goose chase: a mystery she was completely unqualified to solve. Richard had been right when he said she was too young to play Miss Marple. Best to leave it to the police. After all, it was likely to have been nothing more than a robbery that had gone horribly wrong or perhaps a case of mistaken identity, although how could anyone mistake such a unique, outlandish character as Harry Felatu for someone else? But then, seconds later, that thought would send her back to seeing it as a gripping mystery which, if she stuck with it, she just might be able to solve.

And so, she weighed up the evidence for about the hundredth time. Who would kill somebody by battering them over the head with a blunt object and then throwing them from a window to make it look like an accident? Surely that wasn't what burglars who had been disturbed after breaking in would do? And why would Felatu go to all the trouble of sending David Reznikoff his storage facility invoice hidden in a book? Why not simply tell him about his autobiography and where he had deposited it? And why stash a manuscript of your autobiography in a safety deposit box in the first place? And then, there was the raid on David Reznikoff's flat? Surely that was proof that there was something sinister about Harry Felatu's death? On the other hand, there was David Reznikoff himself – the fantasist, the games player. Who was to say he hadn't wrecked his own flat and beat himself up just to keep Becky's attention?

All of this was still whirling around in Becky's head when she arrived back at her flat that evening to find the front door open and voices coming from inside. She walked nervously across the small lobby to the partially open sitting room door. She could feel her heart thumping and realised that, despite all her attempts to dismiss Reznikoff as a fantasist and a drama queen, she was becoming just as paranoid as he was.

"Richard? Is that you?" She called out in a hesitant voice as she pushed the door open. "Why have you left the front door...?"

Richard, who was sitting in an armchair, turned to face her as did the young Asian woman in a police officer's uniform sitting on the sofa opposite him.

"Becky. I've been phoning you. This is police constable Begum." He flapped his hand at the police officer.

Becky was no longer paying attention to Richard or the police officer. Instead, she was looking around the room. The floor to ceiling bookshelves on the right-hand wall were in disarray with some books scattered on the floor, splayed open. The drawers in Richard's desk under the window were open. The contents of his always tidily organised desktop were now skewiff. It didn't look anything like as bad as the wreckage in David Reznikoff's flat and, if you didn't know how meticulously tidy Richard was (Becky had often suggested to him that he might have a mild form of OCD), you might have thought that it was simply the apartment of a very messy person.

Becky stood open-mouthed. Speechless.

"As you can see," said Richard, waving his arm around, "we've had a break-in. Well, not quite a break-in exactly. I got home about an hour ago. I let myself into the flat as normal and found all this. I've had a quick look round but I can't find anything missing, although you'd better check your stuff just in case I've missed something. They've been through your desk and the wardrobe and cupboard in the bedroom as well. I called the police straight away. PC Begum only arrived a short time ago."

Becky put her bag down and started taking her jacket off. Her mind was racing. She was struggling to take it all in, barely listening to what Richard was saying.

"Miss Stone," Officer Begum said. Becky was slowly clearing her head. She stopped staring around the room and focussed on the young Asian woman. "The mystery is that there is no sign of anyone actually breaking and entering. Your partner found the front door locked as usual when he got home and there's no sign that any of the windows have been broken or forced open. Usually, burglaries like this, during the middle of the day, are kids just looking for money or small valuables like jewellery."

"They chose the wrong flat then," said Richard, squeezing out a smile. "We have bugger all worth stealing. My only prized possession is my vinyl LP collection and I can't see anybody else being interested in that, although you could get quite a good price for some of them on Ebay. And as for Becky, she doesn't have any expensive jewellery – that is unless she's been keeping it hidden from me." He directed that last comment at Becky but she didn't seem to have heard him. She had gone back to looking around the room.

"Have either of you given anyone else a key to the flat? A neighbour perhaps who could look after it when you go away?" Officer Begum asked.

"No," said Richard. "We haven't lived here very long and we don't know our neighbours that well. I guess we should have thought of leaving a spare key with somebody but we haven't up till now."

"And how do you think they might have got through the main entrance door to the block?" Richard and Becky's flat was on the first floor of a small 1930s mansion block.

"They could have just rung one of the bells outside and said they were delivering something or they wanted to read the meters. It's been a bit of a problem in the past. Neighbours are always letting people in. We've put up notices by the front door about it but it doesn't seem to have made any difference," Richard said.

Becky still hadn't moved from her standing position by the doorway. She was now picturing the two men in sharp suits pressing all the buzzers outside the front entrance waiting for somebody to let them in.

"I've only had a quick look at the front door to your flat," the policewoman said, "but the lock isn't very sophisticated to say the least. Just a simple Yale. Not very secure."

"Well, that's our landlord for you," said Richard. "He's a cheapskate."

"Well, if you'll both excuse me," said the officer, "there's not much more I can do here at the moment. On my way out, I'll check with any of your neighbours who are in to see if they saw or heard anything and also whether any of them let any strangers into the building this afternoon. In the meantime, if you could let me know if you find anything missing or you come across any information about who might have done this, give me a call. Here's my card. If you need to claim anything on your insurance, I can give you a crime number for the insurance company."

After Richard had shown the officer out, he returned to the sitting room and stood staring at Becky.

"Are you alright? A stupid question, I know. It's obviously a shock. It's just that you haven't said a single thing since you came in."

"I'm fine. I just feel a bit disorientated," she said.

"Well, it could have been worse, I suppose," Richard said, glancing round the room. "They've left a bit of a mess but they haven't done any of those horrible things you hear about burglars doing. Leaving little calling cards." He stopped himself from saying anything more specific.

Becky still stood as if frozen to the spot and said nothing. Richard tilted his head to one side and gave her a quizzical look.

"Do you have an idea what this might be about?" He said. "This wouldn't be anything to do with that man's murder – the one you were supposedly investigating – would it? You're not still wasting your time with that, are you?"

"No. I've given up on that." Becky tried to sound unphased by his question, hoping there was nothing in her voice or her general demeanour that would give away that she was lying.

"Okay," he said, not looking totally convinced. "I'll go and put the kettle on and make us a drink, if I can find the cups and the tea. They've made a bit of a mess in the kitchen as well. While I'm doing that, perhaps you could check your stuff in the bedroom. Then, if there's nothing missing, I guess we can start clearing up."

By the time he got back to a desk at Paddington Green, it was late in the afternoon and, instead of immediately going off duty, Ethan spent some time trawling through police records and the internet for any information on Doctor Alexander Laxley-Young. There was quite a lot. Thank god for the internet, he thought. What did we do before it existed? The answer was that he didn't know. He was very much a part of the information technology generation. He scribbled down the bits and pieces he'd found onto scraps of paper and, when he had finished, he juggled the scraps into chronological order across the desktop and typed it up into a rough report.

Alexander Laxley-Young had been born in Edinburgh. Both his parents were doctors; his father had worked at the Edinburgh Infirmary and his mother had been a GP. He went to a feepaying school and then studied medicine at St. Andrew's University. He had subsequently trained as a junior doctor at St. Bart's Hospital in London and then joined a private gynaecological practice in Harley Street. It was during that period that he appeared on the police records data base. In 1983, he had been accused of indecent assault by one of his patients. She eventually dropped the charge but, shortly after, he was dismissed from the Harley Street practice. He was subsequently reported to the British Medical Association for misconduct. He was accused by the practice of misuse of prescription drugs for private purposes and of indecent assaults on two patients. After a formal hearing in front of the BMA disciplinary committee, he was struck off the medical register. It was a year after this that he left London for Vienna. It was at that point that he disappeared from the net apart from a recent website for his spiritual healing practice.

Ethan read through it again. There was no doubt that he was a suspicious, not to say rather unsavoury, character, but there was nothing that Ethan had found to connect him with Harry Felatu other than his receiving money from the trust fund. Somehow, he needed to find out what that money was being paid for. The only thing he could think of was to go back to Felatu's solicitor to see if he knew anything about Doctor Laxley-Young and why he had been paid such a large sum of money.

As Ethan was leaving Paddington Green, his phone rang. It was Martin Edelstein, Harry Felatu's solicitor. Ethan had phoned him a half an hour earlier to ask him if he had any further information on Athos Holdings. For example, could he confirm that the named account holder was Alexander Laxley-Young and could he find out exactly what the money was being paid for? Ethan was surprised to get such a prompt reply, although he was not sure whether it would be a good or bad omen.

"Mr Edelstein. Thanks for getting back to me so promptly."

"Yes. Well, I'm afraid the reason I can answer your questions so quickly is because, unfortunately, there's nothing I can tell you. As I said at our earlier meeting, it was my late father who set up the Sarah Weinstein Trust Fund with Mr Felatu and arranged all the payments and, although I've taken over responsibility for it, I've done very little except to keep it ticking over. I've had a quick skim through the original paperwork but it's all very basic. All I have is the date on which the payment to Athos Holdings was made and their account details in Vienna. There's no mention of this Doctor Laxley-Young or any reason for the payment. If you like, I could contact my father's former partner, David Levy, to see whether he knows any more. He retired seven years ago. Although, to be honest, I think it would be a waste of time as I'm sure he never had anything to do with the fund."

Ethan said that wouldn't be necessary and thanked him for his time before terminating the call. He then tried phoning his girlfriend, Anna, to see if she could meet him after work for a drink. He badly needed one and he didn't want to sit in a pub on his own. The call went straight to voicemail.

He was feeling a mixture of disappointment and frustration while, at the same time, annoyance with himself for feeling like that. He may not have been involved in detective work for very long, but it had been long enough to experience how often investigations just fizzled out. He'd convinced himself, when he decided to join the police force, that it was a pragmatic decision in no way influenced by any romantic notions of detective work as portrayed in all those supposedly gritty and realistic police series on television. However, once he'd been assigned to his first murder investigation, especially one as mysterious as Harry Felatu's, he couldn't help but feel excited. Nor could he prevent himself from fantasising about solving the case single-handedly and picturing the scene in Paddington Green where he was congratulated by Inspector Maddy Rich in front of his colleagues as they raised their office mugs to toast his success.

Maybe it would still happen but, as of now, it was looking very unlikely.

Once they had finished clearing up and had ascertained that there was nothing missing, Becky's initial shock began to wear off and she was forced to start thinking about what she would do now. There was only one obvious thing to do – tell the police everything. The full details of her attempted investigation of Harry Felatu's murder including her meetings with David Reznikoff, the invasion of his flat, the discovery of the safety deposit box letter and the retrieval of the manuscript of his autobiography.

But, two days later, she was still thinking about it, on several occasions holding her phone in one hand and PC Begum's card in the other, about to ring the number, before changing her mind. The problem was that, if she told the police everything now, she would also have to hand over the autobiography manuscript. Her main reason for delaying, she told herself, was that she wanted to read as much of it as possible before handing it over. Her reasoning was twofold. Firstly, she was still hopeful that she would find things in it that could be last minute revelatory additions to her section of the museum's Soho exhibition and, secondly, there might still be clues buried somewhere in it to explain why and by who Harry Felatu had been murdered. And so, during those two days, she grabbed every opportunity during breaks in setting up the exhibition, to read as much of it as possible.

On the third day after the break-in, during her lunch hour, she reached the chapter where Felatu recalls his time working for the Krays. She was both shocked and excited. Surely, this could be the connection she was looking for. Okay, it was a long time ago but maybe this explained why he was killed. He had been involved with one of the most notorious criminal gangs in London's history. Perhaps he had died as a result of some ancient grudge or long-delayed revenge?

But, as soon as she started to give it more thought, her excitement started to leak away. The Krays had been locked up since the late 1960s and, as she understood it, their gang had disintegrated with their trial and imprisonment. And anyway, how could she possibly investigate whether there were any remnants who might have still harboured a grudge against Felatu after all these years?

She sighed and, once again, reached into her shoulder bag for her phone. She was sitting in a basement café at Seven Dials in Covent Garden. There was no mobile phone signal. She sat staring at the screen. It had just occurred to her. There was another problem about going to the police. They would want to know why she hadn't reported all of this earlier. Would they be satisfied if she told them the simple truth – that she had entertained the stupid fantasy that she could solve the crime herself? That she was hoping that it would somehow raise her profile at the Museum of London and they would offer her a permanent position? Or would they accuse her of withholding evidence in a murder case? Might they even charge her? She didn't know enough about the law to be able to answer that question. She would have to google it when she got home.

And then there was David Reznikoff to think about. Although she wasn't sure that she needed to show him any consideration, she had to acknowledge to herself that, if she went to the police now, she would be putting him in the same position as her. He could equally be accused of withholding information in a murder case and, unlike her, he wouldn't have the mitigating factor of, at least belatedly, having voluntarily come forward with the information. Perhaps she owed it to him to warn him about what she intended to do. As she left the café and reached street level, she put aside her hesitations and phoned David Reznikoff. She knew it was yet another of her delaying tactics. She knew she was risking him turning on the charm and talking her out of it. But, at that precise moment in time, delay was what she was happiest with.

Since her last visit, David Reznikoff's flat had been returned to its pristine condition. Over the phone, she had told him about her break-in and so, they decided that they may as well meet at his flat as there was no need for any further subterfuge now that those sharp-suited young men obviously knew they were connected.

Becky turned down his offer of a hot drink. She already felt she was coffeed out for the day. He made himself a cup of tea and sat down opposite her at the kitchen table. She told him what little there was to tell about the break-in and concluded by saying that she now saw no alternative other than to go to the police, give them Felatu's manuscript and tell them everything that had happened – including his involvement. She refrained from mentioning her fear that she could be charged with withholding evidence.

He looked genuinely dismayed as she was describing the break-in.

"Becky, I'm really sorry I got you involved in this," he said.

"You didn't get me involved. I got myself involved. I'm just sorry I wasn't more persuasive when I originally told you to go to the police."

"It wouldn't have made any difference. What could the police have done? What can they do now? We don't know who these people are. There's no evidence that would help the police to find them. I doubt the police would even be very interested. Neither of us had anything stolen." He gave her a doleful look and slid his hand across the tabletop towards hers. She lifted her hands out of the way. She still wasn't sure what she thought about him. She veered between finding him creepily manipulative and rakishly charming.

"And if you give them the autobiography," he continued "how's that going to help? You've already said there's nothing in it to suggest why Harry was murdered." Becky lowered her eyes away from his. He leaned forward and reached across to grasp her arm. "You think you've found something?"

"I don't know. Possibly. Did you know that he used to work for the Kray brothers?"

"Ah." He nodded his head and smiled impishly. "Of course I knew. I introduced him to them."

She brushed his hand off and shook her head at him. "And you didn't think this was something worth mentioning? For God's sake, David. They were a mega criminal gang. Don't you think there could be some connection between them and his death?"

Reznikoff slowly shook his head. "Thirty years ago, they were. There's nothing left from those days. They're mostly either still in prison or dead. And the ones that aren't are making a healthy living from appearing in TV documentaries or writing their autobiographies. I can't see how it could have anything to do with Harry's death. If somebody from back then had been in contact with him, I'm sure he would have told me."

"So, you think that's another dead end?" Becky sighed. "Then all the more reason we should just tell the police what we know and wash our hands of the whole thing."

David Reznikoff stood up and walked round the table towards the window. He started to scratch his bald patch. By now, she was used to his mannerisms. There was something on his mind.

"What is it? What are you thinking?" She couldn't stop herself asking the question even though, at the same time, trying to tell herself she didn't want to know.

He turned towards her, walked back to the table and sat down. "Maltese Tony," he said enigmatically.

"What? Who?" Alarm bells rang for Becky. Was he starting to play games with her again?

"Maltese Tony. He was one of the Krays' chief henchmen back in the day. Harry knew him well. He served a long stretch in prison but, after he came out, I remember Harry telling me he still saw him occasionally."

"You think he might have something to do with all this?" Despite herself, Becky couldn't help but show some interest.

"I doubt it. He may not even be still alive. The last time I remember Harry talking about him, he wasn't very well. I think he said he was in a wheelchair."

"Okay, so that's another red herring." Becky got to her feet. "I'd better be going. I'm sorry, David, but, when I go to work tomorrow, I'm going to collect the manuscript and take it to the police. Whether they're interested in it or not, at least I can forget about it." She started walking towards the door.

"Wait, Becky." He grabbed hold of her jacket sleeve as she walked past him "Give it one more day. I'll make some enquiries. See if Maltese Tony is still around and, if he is, we could go and see him."

"But you just said you didn't think he could have anything to do with it." Not for the first time, she was exasperated.

"Probably not. But he still knows a lot of people from back then. It's a long shot but it's just possible he might know something. You've waited this long without going to the police. What will one or two days more matter?"

Becky stood staring at an abstract painting on the wall by the door. It was lots of loops and swirls of bright colours surrounding several disembodied eyes. There was something spookily similar about all her meetings with David Reznikoff. Whatever her mindset when she arrived, he always managed to change it by the time she left. It was like that film *Groundhog Day*. She should start calling him her Svengali, she thought, except there was nothing subliminal about what he did. It was all out in the open and she always fell for it.

# Extracts from
# The Autobiography of an Invisible Man

## A BRUSH WITH ROYALTY

As I fold my six foot six inch frame awkwardly on to a low leather sofa next to Princess Margaret, all I can think about is what my mother would say if she could see me now.

I am in Lord Boothby's opulent Eaton Square apartment. I look up and imagine my mother's ghost hovering next to the twinkling crystal glass chandelier above my head. I would like to think that she would be both surprised and proud, if she really were looking down on me, to see how I had progressed in my life since my miserable school days in High Wycombe. Having left behind my uncomfortable flirtation with the Krays, here I was mingling with the aristocracy and about to engage in conversation with a member of the Royal Family. But, of course, knowing my mother as well as I now imagine you do, dear reader, we can both agree that pride would be the last thing that she would be feeling. Disgust? Maybe not. Disappointment? Probably. More likely, a mixture of despair and annoyance that she could have brought up her son to become such a toady.

When I received the invitation from Lord Boothby, my first inclination was to ignore it. It would mean having to mingle with lots of VIPs. I would stick out like a sore thumb at such a gathering – physically as well as socially. And why had he invited me in the first place? From what I already knew about Boothby and his previous association with the Krays, he liked to mingle with the criminal classes. In the parlance of the times, he liked 'a bit of rough'. And that, of course, included his sexual proclivity for dodgy young men. Of course, I didn't fit into that category being no longer in the first flush of youth (actually having just entered my forties), even if I might still be considered a touch 'dodgy'. I had also heard rumours during my time at the Kentucky Club about the sort of masochistic practices allegedly enjoyed by his Lordship. Could it be that this invitation was somehow linked with that? I didn't know whether he was acquainted with Francis Bacon but maybe they had compared notes on their masochistic practices and my name had come up. It seemed unlikely as I had always politely snubbed Francis' suggestions that I might participate in such 'parties'.

In the end, it was because I couldn't imagine why I had been invited, that I decided to accept the invitation. After my initial relief, post the Krays' convictions, that I had had a lucky escape from the dangerous situation I had landed myself in, I was now finding my return to a quieter life rather boring. My visits to my old Soho drinking establishments were becoming less frequent. The old bohemian crowd had dispersed either to haunts elsewhere or into alcoholism or drug addiction or an early death. I had started to search for new adventures. Maybe this upper crust gathering would provide me with them.

I'd had no idea that Princess Margaret would be attending until I arrived at 1 Eaton Square to be greeted by Lord Boothby and offered a glass of champagne from a silver tray carried by a liveried flunky. Boothby immediately informed me of the impending royal arrival and said that she was especially keen to renew her acquaintance with me.

And so, here I was, sitting next to her Royal Highness on the leather sofa, trying to hunker down and make myself as small as possible next to the diminutive Princess. As if I didn't feel out of place enough, I was the only male present not in evening dress, although I was reasonably presentable in my new dark grey lounge suit purchased from the recently opened Edgware Road branch of a shop called High and Mighty. It was a welcome change to be able to buy something off-the-peg that fitted me and not to have to feel self-conscious about acres of bare arm and leg sticking out from the bottom of my jacket sleeves and trousers when I sat down next to the Princess on that sofa. I had been instructed by one of her party that I should address her as ma'am. My first thought, as I conjured up my mother's apparition hovering above me, was to ignore this protocol as a small act of rebellion to assuage some of my dead mother's imagined scorn. But it immediately struck me as childish petulance, so I ignored it.

The Princess was smoking a cigarette in a long black holder. Her skin was tanned and healthy looking, her dark hair swept upwards and back into an elaborately coiffed bun. She was wearing a pale green satin evening dress, low cut with frilly bows on the shoulders. Large double hooped earrings and a pearl necklace completed her elegant look. To say that I felt intimidated would be an understatement.

As soon as she started talking, she put me at my ease, reminding me of our meeting at the *Sparrers Can't Sing* premiere. I was amazed at how much she remembered of our conversation that night, including how she had expressed her desire to renew our acquaintance at some later date so that I could tell her more about myself.

"So now is your chance, Mr Felatu," she said. "You said your background was complicated. Well, we have plenty of time now. You can fill me in."

And so, I did, trying to make it as concise as possible. As I was describing my mother to her, she stopped me.

"She sounds a fascinating woman but, from what you are saying, it seems that she wouldn't have approved of me." She blew clouds of smoke in my general direction which, as a confirmed non-smoker, I was tempted to wave away but I restrained myself, not wanting to appear rude.

"Correct ma'am. She was a socialist. Definitely a republican, although she did mix in some quite upper-class circles." I went on to describe our time in Bloomsbury and her group of highborn literary friends.

"And do you share her views, Mr Felatu?"

"No. Not really. I'm fairly non-political. I fear I would be somewhat of a disappointment to her." I gave an involuntary glance up at the chandelier.

"Oh no. I'm sure she'd be very proud of you. Mothers nearly always are, no matter how their children turn out. Although, having said that, I fear my own mother is not too happy with me and far prefers my sister."

She was interrupted by one of her entourage leaning over her. "Sorry to interrupt, ma'am, but Lord and Lady Carnegie would like to pay their respects."

She waved her cigarette holder at him dismissively. "Yes, you are interrupting. I'm talking with Mr Felatu as you can see. If I have time, I will talk to them later."

She turned back towards me, at the same time removing the cigarette end from her holder and depositing it in an ashtray on the coffee table in front of us. As if by magic, a young male attendant appeared from nowhere, took a cigarette from a packet in his hand, inserted it into the long black holder, produced a gold cigarette lighter and lit it for her. She made no acknowledgement of his actions but continued our conversation.

"I am led to understand, Mr Felatu, that you are well acquainted with the London artistic community. In particular, the painter Francis Bacon?"

"Yes, we used to be quite friendly. He used me as a model for two of his paintings."

"I'm afraid I'm no great lover of his art or the man himself. I've never actually been formally introduced to him, but he was once extremely rude to me at a party we both attended." There was a pause during which she seemed about to elaborate but then changed her mind. "Do you know Lucian Freud? Now I do admire his paintings. I would quite like to meet him."

"I've come across him, ma'am, but I can't say that I know him."

"How about Picasso?"

"I'm afraid I've never met him." I suspected that this might bring our conversation to an end. She had obviously heard about my connections to the art world and perhaps assumed that I could introduce her to some of these artists. I therefore assumed I must be disappointing her. However, she showed no signs of getting up to leave but, instead, turned and signalled to a waiter who deposited another glass of champagne on the table in front of her.

"No, I've never met Picasso," she said, "but, apparently – ," she leaned in closer to me as if she was about to share a whispered secret, " and I was told this by his biographer – even though he's never met me, he has sexual fantasies about me. Even said, at one point, that he would like to marry me."

I said nothing. I couldn't think of any suitable response. I glanced round the huge open plan reception room at the groups of elegant guests quaffing champagne, nibbling canapes and chatting. In the far corner of the room was the only other non-white person apart from me. He was a middle-aged West Indian seated at a grand piano churning out classic show tunes and occasionally singing along in a low bar-room crooner's voice.

All the while the Princess and I had been talking, I had noticed out of the corner of my eye some of the guests casting glances in our direction disapprovingly while sharing whispered comments. I realised we were the centre of attention. The Princess showed no awareness of this, although I was sure she must have noticed it. In fact, although I had no evidence, it occurred to me that this might explain my presence at the party. It was well-known that Princess Margaret liked to defy convention and be outrageous – and what could be more outrageous than spending your evening shunning your wealthy and titled fellow guests to talk to and, I had to admit, flirt with, a very large dark-skinned man of dubious background and even more dubious reputation.

"My husband is something of a bohemian artist himself," she continued, "but he never introduces me to any of these interesting people. He thinks I come from a different world and that my world and theirs should never meet. He's probably right – although I can't say I like my world very much. I prefer theirs – and yours, Mr Felatu."

I was about to disabuse her that my life was at all interesting when she blew another cloud of smoke towards me and continued with her flow.

"It's the problem with being a member of the Royal Family. My sister, of course, has to live in the stuffy world of royal duty. She's surrounded by stuffed shirts and crusty old retainers. Since I am destined not to be queen, I try to avoid all that starchiness. I can break the rules. I can mix with the slightly sordid." I think I may have pulled a face at this point, assuming she was referring to me but, if I did, she didn't notice. "People who drink and smoke too much and live their lives at night. My sister, the Queen, represents all that is dutiful and good so, in comparison, I feel I have no choice. I am destined to be the evil sister." She raised her eyebrows and smiled archly.

At this point, the same young male retainer re-appeared, hovering awkwardly by the side of the sofa

"Oh alright, James. I'm sorry, Mr Felatu, but duty calls and, as much as I try to, I can't always avoid it. I'll have to go and talk to some boring people. It's been fascinating to hear your story. I hope we can meet again sometime soon."

I struggled to launch my elongated frame from its positon sunk into the soft cushiony folds of the sofa as she stood up to leave. To my, and I'm sure my deceased mother's, embarrassment, I involuntarily bent my head in the merest semblance of a bow.

After the Princess and her retinue had left the party, Lord Boothby buttonholed me.

"My word, you've made an impression," he said, as he sipped from a brandy glass. "I normally hate inviting her to these gatherings. She's usually so rude to everybody. Hardly talks at all. I've never known her to sit down and have such a lengthy conversation with anyone before. I'd love to know your secret." He gave me a conspiratorial smile as if it must be obvious to both of us why the Princess was so interested in me. "Anyway, thank you so much for coming. Rest assured that we will meet again soon." He transferred the cigar he was holding in one hand to the fingers gripping the brandy glass and vigorously shook my hand.

He was true to his promise, although it was over a year before we were to meet again.

As you may have gathered from the frequent lengthy gaps in my narrative, dear reader, there have been numerous periods in my life when I have drifted along doing very little with myself. Perhaps *Autobiography of a Layabout* would have been a better title for this manuscript – or, if I wanted to be more romantically generous to myself, *The Autobiography of a Flaneur*. The truth is that, since my young days working for the jewellers in Hatton Garden, I had never had what you might call a proper job. Assistant to Prince Monolulu, following him around the racetracks, pubs and clubs, muse/ bodyguard/model for Francis Bacon, night club manager for the Krays. None of them proper jobs. Even my spell at David Archer's Soho bookshop could hardly be considered proper as we were more a library and social gathering place than a shop and I hardly ever sold anything. This was partly the curse of my mother's trust fund. I had no financial need to find a proper salaried job. And add to that, the fact that I had no idea what I wanted to do with my life. I had no vocation. My book-keeping qualifications only led to the kind of office jobs that I found tedious. My ambition to follow in my mother's footsteps and become a writer had ground to a halt. After the brief success de scandale of my first novel, I had struggled for an idea for a second. And then, after the Krays' imprisonment, I started to write one based loosely on my experiences working for the Twins. But there was little interest from agents or publishers. It was too esoteric for them. They wanted me to write something more like a true confession than my actual Dante-esque story of a man drifting unintentionally into London criminal low life. David Archer was now dead and I had no other contacts in the book world so the manuscript lay under a pile of old bedclothes in the bottom of my wardrobe.

The early to mid-seventies was one of my longest periods of lassitude. I grew bored and started drinking too much. I had a series of brief relationships with women. They either found my drinking and general lack of ambition off-putting or they shared my indolent alcohol-infused lifestyle and we split up due to mutual loathing.

As for friends, I no longer had any close ones. Lots of acquaintances but no real friends. From my earliest schooldays right the way through the rest of my life, I have always been something of a loner. My justification for this is that I was too other – too different for people to be able to relate to me. But, if I am honest with myself, that is just an excuse. It is much more about me pushing people away than the other way around. I had enjoyed periods of camaraderie – times when I felt part of a group into which I could blend. The 43 Group, Francis Bacon and The Colony Room artistic set, the Krays' henchmen. But I now realise that this was a way of avoiding any real closeness or intimacy with specific individuals.

Of all the people I'd got to know since that first time I discovered The Colony Room and its regulars when I accompanied Prince Monolulu, the only one I had continued to have occasional contact with was David Reznikoff and that was more to do with accidental happenstance than any actual desire on both our parts to be friends. And, as it happens, it was another chance meeting with David Reznikoff that brought an end to this particular languorous period of my life.

I was drinking on my own one evening in The Coach and Horses in Soho after my then girlfriend, Debbie Richter, an occasional journalist, poet and full-time alcoholic, had walked out on me after yet another of our frequent rows. David spotted me hidden away at a table in a far corner and, carrying a tray with a gin and tonic for himself and another large glass of red wine for me, he deposited himself opposite me uninvited, a broad smile lighting up his face. He still sported a mauve chiffon cravat and his hair was slightly more sparse than when I had last seen him, but he was otherwise dressed more conservatively than in his earlier hippy faze in a fawn tweed jacket, blue denim jeans and a check shirt.

"Harry Felatu. How convenient is this? I've been meaning to get in touch with you for the past couple of weeks. How the devil are you?"

"All the better for seeing you, David," I said.

He ignored my patently ironic tone and continued with his usual breathless gush. "Not to beat about the bush, the reason that I've been keen to meet up is that I have a proposition to put to you. A business proposition." He paused and stared at me as if expecting some reciprocal sign of enthusiasm. When I didn't respond and instead glugged down the remains of my original glass of wine, he continued unabashed.

"Sorry. I forgot to ask. What are you doing with yourself at present? Perhaps you've got some project of your own on the go?"

"I think you know me well enough by now to know exactly what I'm doing," I said. "If I was an actor, I would say I was resting."

I had made the mistake during one of our lengthy boozy conversations while we had been holed up together in that cold damp cottage in the Brecon Beacons of telling David about my mother's trust fund. He now knew that I was a man of means. As soon as he mentioned a business proposition, I recalled some of his previous failed enterprises. The fish restaurant. Several nightclubs. A meditation centre that he'd opened in Shepherds Bush in partnership with a self-styled Indian guru after we'd returned from Wales which closed down after a couple of months when the guru made off with the remains of the money.

"Great. Then let me tell you all about it," he continued. I started on the glass of wine he'd bought me. I knew I should have stopped him in his tracks before he could even get started and told him I wasn't interested, but I harboured a modicum of affection for David which I was at a loss to understand. Most likely, dear reader, it was a result of what I told you earlier about my inability to form close friendships. Love him or loathe him, he was the only one of my acqaintances who was still here. And, to be honest, however much I suspected that he was about to regale me with yet another of his doomed projects, I welcomed his company and the chance to avoid another maudlin evening spent alone drowning my sorrows.

"I'm opening an art gallery in Mayfair," he said with a wave of outstretched arms and a beaming smile as if announcing that he'd just won a million pounds on the football pools. I said nothing but must have raised my eyebrows in scepticism.

"Okay, okay," he said, swivelling his hands, palms outward in a defensive gesture. "I know I haven't got the best track record in these sorts of ventures but I promise you, Harry, this is different."

"It's always different, David." I swallowed some more wine. Spending the evening getting drunk on my own was beginning to seem a more attractive option.

"No, no, Harry. This time it really is. I've already got the premises. It's perfect. In the heart of the Mayfair art scene. And I've got some financial backing. Have you heard of Nathan Myerson?" He didn't wait for an answer seeing the blank look on my face. "He's a wealthy financier and a serious art collector. We've even got an opening exhibition set up. John Minton's illustrations. You remember Johnny? He's just about to come back into fashion. Our exhibition will neatly coincide with a retrospective at the Tate."

The following morning, I met David and his benefactor, Nathan Myerson, at the gallery premises in Brook Street. Despite my reservations about getting involved with any David Reznikoff project, I have to admit I was intrigued. Partly because it offered me a way out of my present malaise, but also because it would put me back in contact with the London art world – a world I had become very attached to over the previous twenty years. In his pin-striped three-piece suit, Nathan looked as far removed from the bohemian art world as it was possible to get. David introduced me to him with glowing hyperbole. According to him, I was quite an expert in the world of modern art with an insider's knowledge. The names of Francis Bacon and Lucian Freud were dropped. I had even been friends with John Minton before his tragic suicide. (Not true, although I do remember being introduced to him one evening in The Colony Room by Francis).

After we had inspected the premises, David took me aside and proposed that my involvement could be more than simply being front of house in the gallery where I could name drop my artist connections to the wealthy Mayfair clientele looking to buy, which was the role he had proposed to me the previous evening in the pub. He suggested that I might like to invest in the gallery and become a partner with Nathan and himself. I told him I would think about it.

By the time I was sat at a window seat in Wheeler's Restaurant in Soho two days later waiting for my adopted mother, Ana Geisler, and her new partner, Magda, to arrive for lunch, I was, despite my earlier reservations, quite excited by the idea of being a Mayfair gallery owner and keen, if somewhat nervous, to float the idea to Ana. My occasional lunches with her had become less frequent over the years since I had left our flat in Hackney. I suspect this was because we shared a mutual feeling of guilt. I felt grateful for the way she had taken me under her wing after my mother's death and for the efforts she had made to encourage me to continue with my education. As a result, each time we met and she would ask me what I was doing with myself, I would feel that I had failed her when I could only reply 'nothing much'. For her part, I know she blamed herself, feeling she had let my mother down for not ensuring that I achieved more with my life. The only time I had previously approached one of our lunches together with as much enthusiasm as I was feeling on that day, was when I first told her of my association with Francis Bacon. As a fellow artist, I thought that, for once, I was doing something that would impress her. And so, her disdain for Francis – both for his work and his lifestyle – was a disappointment. During our subsequent lunches over the years, I either kept what I was doing a secret from her or told her as little as possible. For example, I mentioned working as a nightclub manager but not who I was working for.

And then there was a purely practical reason for me hoping that Ana would approve of this new project. If I were to take up David's offer and invest in the gallery then, as my co-trustee of the Sarah Weinstein Trust Fund, I would need Ana's agreement to release money from it for the investment.

When the two of them arrived at the restaurant, Ana and I were equally nervous. Me about her reaction to my news about the gallery and her about how I would take to her new partner. For my part, I found Magda rather cold and austere although, at the time, I put it down to her unease at being introduced to such a confusing remnant of Ana's past. (Regrettably, even after we got to know each other better, her dislike and suspicion of me continued and I was never able to warm to her). At first, Ana seemed sceptical about the gallery, plying me with a series of questions about the plans and my partners in the project. I had never previously mentioned David Reznikoff to her so I said as little as possible about him, concentrating instead on Nathan Myerson on the off chance that she might have heard of and be impressed by our association with the well-known philanthropist. As I fed her with more information, I could see that she was warming to the idea. And then, I attempted to seal the deal by making a totally unplanned and rather rash statement.

"I've told my partners that one of the conditions for us making this investment is that it will be called the Sarah Weinstein Gallery."

Three months later, the Sarah Weinstein Gallery was officially opened with Ana and Magda present for the lavish preview of the John Minton Exhibition. Although David and Nathan had already decided to call it the Meridian Gallery, it took surprisingly little persuasion to get them to agree to name it after my mother once I made it a condition of my investing in it.

Francis Bacon and Lucian Freud were among a whole range of illustrious artists attending and, for the first time in a long time, I knew that I had Ana's approval (and, therefore, by osmosis, my deceased mother's). As the champagne and canapes were being passed around, David Reznikoff appeared at my shoulder.

"It seems to be going well," I said to him.

"Going well? It's going fantastically. Do you know, Harry, we've already sold more than half of the exhibits? I've just been totting up our commission. Wait till you see the figures." He sounded as if he couldn't quite believe what he was saying. David Reznikoff and success had rarely been bedfellows.

As David melted back into the throng, Lord Boothby approached me accompanied by a tall willowy man with a bushy second world war R.A.F. pilot's moustache and a mop of wiry grey hair. He looked vaguely familiar but I couldn't place him. He wore a navy-blue blazer and slacks and a tie with a club crest on it.

"Harry. Good to see you again." Robert Boothby shook my hand vigorously. We hadn't seen each other since the party at his Belgravia apartment. "Let me introduce you to a friend and colleague of mine."

"Sir Richard Delacourt." His companion introduced himself while shaking my hand. "Just call me Richard." Now I recognised him. He was a Conservative backbench MP who had raised his profile in recent years by leading a group in the House of Commons opposed to our membership of the European Common Market. "Bob has told me quite a lot about you, Harry. I hope you don't mind if I call you Harry?" I immediately wondered what Lord Boothby could have told him. My past association with the brothers Kray, perhaps? It was still a mystery to me why his Lordship would have any interest in me even though, as I have previously outlined, dear reader, I had my suspicions. As if to dispel my puzzled expression, Sir Richard continued. "And one of the things he's told me is that you are quite a hit with a certain member of the Royal Family." He flashed me a conspiratorial smile.

So that's it, I thought. He's not so much interested in me per se as he is in my inexplicable friendship with Princess Margaret.

"The reason I bring that up," he said, "is that I am also a close friend of the Princess and I'm hosting a birthday party for her at my residence in Chalfont St. Peter in a month's time and I'd very much like you to attend, as I'm sure would Margaret herself."

"Thank you very much. It's very kind of you. I'd be delighted to attend." There was nothing else I could say. I still felt less than comfortable mixing with the aristocracy but, now that I was firmly ensconced as a denizen of the Mayfair art establishment, I would have to get used to it.

Then I felt a hand patting me on the back. I turned to see Francis Bacon beaming up at me with the face of a dissolute cherub, a champagne flute clutched in his right hand.

"Well, this is a turn up for the books. Harry Felatu, Mayfair Gallery owner. I'm impressed."

"I'll send an official invitation to you care of the gallery," Sir Richard said, clearly annoyed at Francis' interruption. "It's been good to meet you." He and Lord Boothby turned and started to walk away without acknowledging Francis' presence.

"And you're now well in with all the upper-class twats, I see," Francis said, loud enough for the two of them to hear as they blended into the crowd.

"Terrific exhibition," he continued. "I was always an admirer of Johnny Minton's work."

"Were you, Francis?" I said. "I seem to recall an occasion in The Colony Room when you poured a bottle of champagne over his head."

"Did I? Are you sure? Doesn't sound like me – wasting champagne. Uh oh." He tugged on my sleeve and waved his champagne glass towards a group of people standing in front of an illustration for *Alice in Wonderland*. "Watch out for her."

"Who?" I asked.

"The dumpy woman with the long blond hair in the knee length black boots. She's a spy – although I don't know whether it's me or you she's spying on."

"Sorry, Francis. You've lost me."

"She runs the Marlborough Gallery. Her name's Valerie Collins – Valerie from the gallery, as I call her. She's either here to stake you out as a rival or she's here to keep an eye on me. She has first dibs on my new work at present and she wouldn't want to lose me to a johnny come lately like you."

"And is that likely to happen?" I said, raising a quizzical eyebrow.

"Come now. Let's not get ahead of ourselves, Harry. You'll need to be a lot more established before you're able to snare as big a catch as me. Have you got any other exhibitions lined up?"

"As it happens, we're planning a retrospective of John Deakin's photographic portraits."

"Oh my. So, is it the gallery policy to only mount exhibitions of Soho faggots named John?"

I ignored the comment, noticing that, while Francis was still his old acerbic self, physically he was looking a lot older than when I'd last seen him. He'd abandoned the kiwi boot polish and let his hair go a sandy grey and his face was even puffier and more debauched looking.

As if he could read my thoughts, he said, "I feel like the great survivor. You know I always thought I'd die young but I'm remarkably healthy considering my lifestyle." He held up the champagne flute as illustration. "When I do finally go, I'll have to donate my liver to medical research. Yes, I'm still going strong which is more than can be said for John Minton or David Archer or poor old Johnny Deakin. Did you know, that bastard Deakin made me his next of kin? Not that he had anything to leave me. He did it out of spite. It meant that I had to be the one to go and identify his body. Mind you, it wasn't as ghastly as I thought it would be. You know what an ugly old sod he was? Well, in death he actually looked almost handsome."

"Well, I hope you'll come to his exhibition. There's bound to be one or two photos of you."

"Oh god, no. I hate seeing photos of myself – especially more recent ones. And I try and avoid looking at myself in mirrors these days."

"Well, they don't make mirrors like they used to, do they, Francis?" It was Lucian Freud who had sidled up behind him.

"There speaks a man who's yet to see the wrong side of sixty," Francis said. For the past thirty years, the two most celebrated modern English painters had veered between being close friends and deadly enemies. I wasn't sure what the current state of their relationship was although their initial interchange seemed cordial enough.

I decided not to hang around and find out. "Excuse me, but I have some business I need to attend to in the office. Thanks to both of you for coming."

I edged my way through the crowd and stood at the far end of the room for a few seconds surveying the scene. I glanced around the sea of faces, from the renowned art critics and journalists to the painters and artists and the politicians and peers. I spotted David Reznikoff fixing a red sticker to one of the illustrations. I felt something I hadn't felt for a long time – happy. A part of something I could at last be proud of. A bow-tied and black waist-coated waiter offered me a glass of champagne from a silver tray which I declined. I hadn't touched a drop of alcohol the whole evening – proof, I felt, that I was turning my life around.

# Monday 26th October 2001

The incident room at Paddington Green Station always felt overheated, both literally and metaphorically and, on an unseasonably hot late-October afternoon, it was even stuffier than usual with the winter heating automatically switched on and the sun streaming through the large picture windows which always stayed closed to shut out the traffic noise in the street below and on the flyover nearby. Despite there being an equal number of women officers in the room, it still had a permanent smell of male locker room sweat. Ethan took off his jacket and draped it over the back of a chair. The big whiteboard at the front of the room had two large photographs at the top: a very old and slightly out of focus one of Harry Felatu and a crime investigation photo of the house and area of pavement outside it where Harry Felatu's body had been found. There were three thick black lines emanating from Felatu's photo forming a spider diagram with three bubbles. One simply contained the words 'the Krays', another surrounded the name 'Dr Alexander Laxley-Young' and the third had 'the Sarah Weinstein Trust Fund' written inside it.

It had been exactly four weeks since Harry Felatu's murder and Maddy Rich had called a team meeting to update them all on the progress or, more accurately lack of it, in the investigation.

Ethan was about to cross the room to talk to one of his colleagues when Maddy Rich strode purposefully through the door clutching black and red whiteboard marker pens in one hand and a sheath of papers in the other. She walked in front of the board and turned to face the team. Her auburn hair was tied back in a tight ponytail accentuating her sharp-featured face. Ethan had now been working for her long enough to recognise that, when she wore her hair tied back in this way, it was because she wanted to look more business-like and authoritative.

"Morning all. You all know why we're here. We need to assess where we're at in this murder investigation. And, from the start, I'm going to be brutally honest with you. I am getting a lot of pressure put on me from my superiors in the Met for what they consider a lack of progress and, as is customary in such circumstances, since I'm getting my arse kicked, my immediate response is to gather you lot together and give you all an even bigger kick up the proverbial." She turned and waved her black marker pen at the mostly empty whiteboard. "This looks pathetic at the moment. I trust that, by the end of this meeting, we will have filled it up with some solid leads. So, Aisha. How about you kick us off. Any results from your investigations around the local area?"

Aisha Begum was standing at the back of the room partially hidden behind two burly male officers. She edged her way between them to stand in front of the rest of the team and face Maddy Rich.

"I'm afraid there's not much new to report, boss. We've had no luck with any of our interviews with the neighbours or other people in the locality. Lots of people said they knew Harry Felatu but, on closer questioning, it turned out that they knew him by sight but had never spoken to him. Of course, he was a very distinctive figure. Hard to miss. Likewise, we've had no luck so far with any CCTV footage although we're widening the search to cover a bigger area. We also put out requests to the public in the media for anybody who had any information to come forward. As always, we were inundated with responses but they've all been either the usual nutters wanting attention or people who had just seen him around."

"Thanks Aisha. So, it looks like we've drawn a blank so far but keep checking that CCTV," said Maddy. "Cowboy." She fluttered the hand clutching the papers at Ethan. "You've been following up on some possible leads. Perhaps you've got something a bit more positive to report."

Ethan stood and half turned towards his colleagues while still glancing at Maddy Rich. "My first area of investigation was Felatu's will which led me to interview his solicitor and his only remaining relative, his mother's ex-partner, Ana Geisler. She brought him up after his mother died when he was a teenager. What I discovered was that Felatu was a relatively wealthy man. He had been left a large trust fund by his mother which was managed by him and Ms Geisler. It provided Felatu with a regular income but also paid out money to lots of charitable organisations set up by the trustees, mostly educational charities. Neither Ms Geisler nor his solicitor had any idea who might have wanted to kill him." He paused briefly to flip open his notebook although it was more as a prop as he didn't once look at it while he was speaking. "However, when we investigated the trust fund, we found one payment which didn't fit in with all the rest. It was to a Dr Malcolm Harrison, formerly known as Dr Alexander Laxley-Young." Maddy turned to face the whiteboard and wrote the name Dr Malcolm Harrison inside the Dr Alexander Laxley-Young balloon and then drew an arrow line connecting it to the Sarah Weinstein Trust Fund. "He is now living and working in Vienna. The Austrian police interviewed him for us and he confirmed that he was the person who received the payment but refused to specify what it was for other than 'services rendered'. We've investigated him and he seems to be a bit of a dodgy character. He was struck off the medical register in this country for various misdemeanours including misappropriation of prescription drugs and accusations of sexual assault by female patients. I've asked the Austrian police to interview him again to see if we can get any more out of him. He's not a suspect as it can be verified that he was in Vienna at the time of the murder." Ethan nodded at Maddy Rich and sat down.

"Thanks Ethan. Not much there but still something to follow up. Colin." She turned towards a tall pot-bellied officer with a red face and sandy receding hair. "You've been researching Felatu's history. Come up with anything interesting?"

"Okay. I won't go back into his childhood as I don't think there's anything there of interest apart from the trust fund that Ethan's already mentioned. He's never been married, didn't have a partner and hasn't got any children. He doesn't seem to have had any kind of career or regular job. He was a writer – he published one novel. He also had a lot of connections with the art world. We're still piecing some of that together although we do know that for a period from the mid-1970s to the early 80s, he part-owned and ran an art gallery in Mayfair. His partner in this venture was a man called David Reznikoff who is still alive and seems to be about the only friend that Felatu had at the time of his death." While he was talking, Maddy drew another balloon on the board and wrote 'David Reznikoff' inside it, except she spelt it with a 'v'. Colin continued without bothering to correct her. "He took responsibility for clearing out Felatu's rooms after forensics had finished with them. Since he was the person who knew Felatu best, we've interviewed him a couple of times at length, but he's been unable to give us any useful information. He claims that he has no knowledge of any enemies that Felatu might have had or of any reason why anyone would want him dead. However, I think he might know more than he's telling us so we will definitely revisit him."

Maddy put a large red question mark next to Reznikov. "Is that everything, Colin?"

"Yes, ma'am."

"Okay. Carol. You've been looking at other aspects of Felatu's background and history. Give us a rundown on what you've found."

Carol James, who was sitting perched on the edge of a desk, stood up and opened a notepad. "I've mostly been checking to see if Harry Felatu had any sort of criminal record or history of involvement with the police. What I found was that, although he had no criminal record, he was arrested in 1967 and charged with aiding and abetting the Kray twins in demanding money with menaces. The charges were eventually dropped. He was also brought in for questioning the following year when the Krays were charged with two murders. One of the Krays' associates had said in a police interview that Felatu was at the party where one of the murders took place. But Felatu had an alibi for that night and there was no further evidence linking him with either of the murders."

Maddy added these details to the whiteboard in a spider diagram surrounding the Krays' bubble.

"So, this connection with the Krays," Maddy said. "Obviously worth following up. Have you discovered anything else, Carol?"

"Not much, ma'am. He definitely worked for the Krays and it's hard to believe that a man of his size and strength wouldn't have been used by them as muscle. However, we haven't been able to find any evidence that he was ever involved in any violence. We've interviewed some of the

Krays' ex-henchmen and none of them link him directly to the Krays' criminal activities. I spoke to an elderly Italian man, Mario Salvi. He and Felatu ran a nightclub in the East End owned by the Krays. He said much the same as the others – that he didn't think Harry Felatu had been involved in any violent activities. However, unlike the others, he had run across Felatu more recently and he said some quite interesting things. He said that Felatu had a number of connections with people very high up in the establishment. He wasn't very specific but when I pressured him about what sort of people he was talking about, he mentioned Members of Parliament, peers, wealthy businessmen and such like." Carol closed her notepad and sat down.

Maddy created another bubble on the board containing the words 'VIP associates'. Then she turned to face the team. "Okay. If that's all, then maybe I can now sum up where we're at."

"Actually that's not quite all, ma'am." Andy Ridgen pushed himself to the front of the room with his hand in the air like a school pupil eager to answer the teacher's question. He was the newest, and youngest, recruit to the team. Fresh faced and nattily groomed, he could have been mistaken for a school sixth former on work experience. "Sorry to bring this up at the last minute but I didn't get the chance this morning to report this to you. You could say it's hot off the presses." He glanced round the room with a smug expression on his face as if waiting for applause.

"Alright, Andy. Stop milking it and just spit it out," said Maddy.

"Yesterday I interviewed a woman called Anthea Sedley. I was looking into Felatu's connections with the art world – in particular, this gallery he owned in Mayfair. She was one of the assistants working in the gallery. She also hinted that she and Felatu were an item for a brief period around that time. She confirmed what Carol just reported. Namely, that he had a lot of contacts among the upper classes and she said that, after the gallery closed in 1982, he often did some work for some of these people. In particular, she mentioned an MP." At this point, he flipped open the ubiquitous notebook and carefully read out the name. "Sir Richard Delacourt. She couldn't tell me anything about what Felatu may have done for this man or for anybody else. It's just that this was the one name she'd heard him mention. Oh, and she also said that he'd told her that he was good friends with Princess Margaret."

"Ma'am." Colin interrupted, raising his hand and looking a bit sheepish. "I forgot to mention it but a couple of the people I spoke to also talked about his friendship with Princess Margaret."

Maddy gave him a withering look. "And you thought this was too insignificant to be worth mentioning?"

"Well," he said hesitantly, "none of them really knew much about it. It was just gossip. What they said was that there were rumours about him and the Princess – even the suggestion that he had had an affair with her. But none of them had any evidence."

Andy Ridgen raised his hand again. "If you think her Royal Highness is somebody we should be interviewing for the enquiry, ma'am, I'll be happy to volunteer to do it." There was a smattering of laughter in the room, as if the members of the team were not quite sure whether he was joking.

Maddy Rich obviously thought he was being serious. "I don't think that will be necessary, Andy. We'd need much firmer evidence linking her to this than a load of low-life gossip before we approached a member of the Royal Family. After all, we wouldn't want you being marched off to the Tower of London, would we?" Again, there was a ripple of laughter.

"Sorry, ma'am," said Andy, unabashed at being the butt of his colleagues' laughter. "It's just that I was remembering all those stories about the Duke of Edinburgh being involved in the death of Princess Diana."

"We don't deal in conspiracy theories here, Andy. We're only interested in facts. I'd advise you to spend less time trawling through dodgy sites on the internet. Okay, if nobody else has any last minute surprises to spring on us... " She paused and glanced round the room, "I will now sum up. On the minus side, we don't have any leads at present that we can follow up from enquiries among the locals although we will keep on looking. On the plus side, this connection with the Kray brothers, even though it's a long time ago, is worth pursuing. Maybe Felatu was more deeply involved in their criminal activities than we've so far been led to believe. Perhaps there was some sort of ancient grudge or vendetta still being pursued. So, Colin. You and your team need to see whether there's anything else you can find out. Also, there's this link to MPs and other influential people. Is this Sir Richard Delacourt still with us?"

"Yes, he is," said Andy. Maddy turned and created another bubble on the whiteboard with the MP's name inside it. "He lives in some stately pile in Buckinghamshire. He's not an MP anymore but he's still on the board of a couple of major financial institutions."

"Right then," said Maddy. "We need to interview him. Andy and Carol, I think you should do that together. I'm thinking that, perhaps there could have been some kind of blackmail involved. Just a hunch – off the top of my head. Anyway, see what he's got to say. Whether he can lead us to anybody else in his upper-class circles that Felatu was involved with. Okay. We'll meet back here in three days. I'm depending upon you all to have some more positive results to report back by then. If not, we're in danger of this case going cold on us."

Maltese Tony lived on the ground floor of a brutalist block of low-rise council flats in Camden Town. Becky and David Reznikoff sat opposite him as his wife, Maria, could be heard shuffling around in the kitchen making tea. The room appeared not to have been decorated or refurbished for at least twenty years. The white wallpaper with a large yellow and brown flower-pattern on it was peeling around the joins. The plain beige carpet was threadbare in places with large stained patches in front of the settee. The once white ceiling was yellowing. The walls were bare except for two large framed photographic prints of what looked like Mediterranean coastal village scenes.

Tony sat in an upright, heavily cushioned, chair, a plastic facemask round his neck attached to an oxygen tank at his side. He had a full head of wiry, steel grey hair forming a widow's peak above a very furrowed brow. His face was skeletally thin and sallow with a crooked nose and light blue watery eyes. There was just enough evidence in those eyes and the prominent cheekbones to show that, before his illness, he had been a handsome man.

Maria came into the room carrying a tea tray. She was as emaciated-looking as her husband with straggly, shoulder length, dyed blond hair. She had a tired, worn down appearance, walking unsteadily with a bent back, the tea things rattling precariously on the tray. Becky sprang to her feet and helped her to lower the tray safely onto the coffee table. Maria poured the tea from a large chipped brown teapot into china cups decorated with cornflowers and then placed them in front of Becky and David. Becky stared down at her cup. The tea was a milky beige, matching the prevailing colour scheme in the rest of the room, with leaves floating on the surface, like tadpoles in a murky pond.

Tony clamped the plastic mask over his mouth and inhaled deeply several times before starting to talk. "So, Harry Felatu. I was very sorry to hear about what happened to him. What can I tell you about the big guy?"

"Well it's about his murder," Becky said. "Of course, we know the police are carrying out their investigation but Mr Reznikoff and I – well, we've been trying to do some investigating for ourselves."

"You're right. The police have already interviewed me," Tony said, before being interrupted by a hacking cough. He inhaled some more oxygen before he could continue. "I told them about the old days when we were both working for the Twins but I couldn't tell them much else. Nothing about what Harry had been up to more recently. And, of course, I don't know anything about who might have killed him."

"Look, Tony," David Reznikoff interjected. "I know how you feel about the police. About talking to them. So, maybe there are things, you know, that you didn't want to tell them, but you might be okay talking to us about? Perhaps there's somebody from those days when you were both working for the Krays – somebody who still bore some sort of grudge against Harry? Or maybe Harry knew stuff from back then. Where the bodies are buried – if you get my meaning? And they were finally settling things with him?"

"No, no, no." Tony waved a finger demonstratively in front of his face. "That's all past history. Everybody from those days is long gone. Either dead or in prison or retired like me. And anyway, Harry wasn't involved in any of that sort of stuff. He didn't know anything." Tony took a few more deep breaths through the mask, more to buy some thinking time than because he needed it.

"Harry Felatu was a gentleman," he continued. "A gentle giant Despite his size, he wouldn't hurt anybody. He was very good to me and my brother, Nick, when we came out of prison. He always kept us in mind when there were any little jobs going. You know – security jobs. He hired us as doormen at his art gallery when they had big parties there. And then, after the gallery closed, he hired us to provide protection for this rich MP. He had this grand house in the countryside somewhere west of London. We manned the door for a couple of parties there. There were always a lot of bigwigs attending. Even Princess Margaret was at one of them." He was interrupted by another coughing fit.

Maria came into the room from the kitchen and stood with her hands on her hips staring disapprovingly at Becky and David. "He shouldn't be doing all this talking," she said to them. "You can see he's not well. This is not good for him."

"It's alright, Maria, I'll be fine. Stop treating me like a child," Tony said.

She frowned and was about to respond but David got in first. "It's alright, Mrs Lambros. We're very nearly finished. We'll keep it as brief as possible."

"You better had," she said waspishly before retreating into the kitchen.

Once she'd gone, Becky continued. "Do you remember who this MP was?"

"I know he was a 'Sir'." He paused and scratched his head. "Sir Richard something, I think. I remember he had some job in government to do with Northern Ireland. That's partly why Harry called on us. Because of all that trouble with the IRA. After that other MP got blown up in his car outside Parliament. Of course, after that, this Sir Richard had police protection but Harry thought he might need something extra so he called on us. This Sir Richard

251

also had a son who'd just finished university. We provided some protection for him as well. Funnily enough, I saw him on the television yesterday – the son, I mean. He's also an MP now. No surprise there, I suppose. They tend to keep these sort of things in the family, these toffs."

"And what exactly was Harry's connection with this Sir Richard?" Becky said.

Tony inhaled again. "I'm not sure. He seemed more than just a friend. I think he was more like a kind of assistant. He seemed to spend a lot of time at that big house."

"And how long did this go on for?" David said. "How long did you work for them?"

"Only a couple of years. After that, I didn't see or hear from Harry for a long time. And then I ran across him in a Soho boozer – must have been a few years after."

"And when was the last time you saw him?" Becky said.

Tony paused for thought. "Must have been a couple of years ago."

"I know you told the police you didn't know anything about his death but, as I said before, we're not the police. So, is there anything you can tell us that might throw some light on what happened to him?" David said.

"Not much, to be honest," Tony said. "All I can say is that I think something funny went on with that Sir Richard." He paused for another intake of oxygen.

"Funny?" Becky said, leaning forward on the sofa. "What do you mean?"

"Well, when I met him in that boozer a few years later – a few years after we done that security work at the country house – I asked him whether he was still working for this Sir Richard and why he'd stopped calling on our services. He said that he didn't see him anymore. He was a bit tight-lipped and didn't go into any details but, from what I can remember, I think he hinted that they'd had some big argument about something. It wasn't clear whether this Sir Richard got rid of him because of this or whether Harry himself just decided he wanted no more to do with him."

"And you can't remember anything more about this Sir Richard? His full name? The address of the big house?"

This time the coughing fit was even longer and more rasping, only ending when he doubled over and hawked into a plastic bucket by the side of his chair. Maria hurried back into the room and stood over Tony gently patting his back while looking daggers at Becky and David.

Maria hadn't needed to say anything further. They expressed their thanks and retreated to a coffee bar in Camden High Street to order something drinkable, after leaving Maria's insipid tea untouched, and to discuss what they had just heard from Tony.

"So, where does that leave us?" Said Reznikoff. "Another dead end?"

"Not entirely," Becky said. "It could be worth following up on this Sir Richard. Something obviously happened between him and Harry. Some falling out. Admittedly, it seems an awful long time ago to have anything to do with Harry being murdered now. When would it have been? The mid 1980s?" She looked David Reznikoff in the eyes. "Did you know anything about this Sir Richard? Surely Harry must have talked about him?"

"No, I can't say he ever did." Becky studied him closely. She had started to recognise some of his little mannerisms when he was lying or trying to conceal things from her. The slightly averted eyes. The licking of his lips. |The supplicating hand gestures. This time there were no obvious signs that he was hiding anything. "We had a bit of a falling out after the gallery closed. He blamed me for it. We didn't talk for a long time. I know nothing about what he was doing during that time. Of course, I heard rumours. His friendships with influential people and all those rumours about Princess Margaret, but I don't remember hearing any specific names or details."

"Okay." Becky sipped her cappuccino as she paused for thought. "The best thing is if I go away and do some research. Find out who this Sir Richard is, or was, and whether he's still around. If he is, then our next move will be to try and speak to him."

"And how are you going to do all that? Sir Richard. A big house outside London. It's not much to go on." He looked questioningly at Becky.

"Do you use a computer, David?"

"No. I'm too old for all that stuff."

"So, you've never used the internet?"

"I don't trust any of that. It's just another way for the government to spy on us."

Becky nodded. In this age of the computer, she mused, the generation gap was wider than ever. "I'm a researcher, David. I know how to find out about things. Just leave it to me. I can google him." She ignored his puzzled expression. "I've got enough information. Sir Richard. Presumably a Tory. Some sort of junior minister in the Northern Ireland Office. In Margaret Thatcher's government. It shouldn't be a problem to find out exactly who he was and whether he's still alive. I'll get back to you when I've got the information."

# Thursday 29th October 2001

Inspector Lukas Honig parked his car on a side street off Prince Eugen-Strasse and walked back to the wide boulevard which was relatively quiet now the early morning rush was over. He stood still for a moment admiring the impressive jungendstil-style apartment block on the opposite side of the road. The October sunshine glinted off the gold-painted, floral-patterned, wrought iron balconies. Between the windows on the top two floors of the block, there were attractive, oblong, green-painted panels with vertical black stripes entwined with pink flowers. If he could have afforded it, it was just the kind of historic Viennese building that he would have loved to live in rather than the anonymous modern house he and his family occupied in the suburbs.

He snapped out of this brief reverie and reminded himself that he wasn't there to admire turn-of-the-century art nouveau architecture. As he crossed the road and reached the carved vaulted wooden entrance to the block, he saw there was a woman standing in front of the brass mounted entry phone buzzers above which was a black plaque with white lettering advertising Doctor Malcolm Harrison's services and his apartment number, 34. The middle aged woman was smartly dressed in a knee-length dark grey skirt and emerald green jacket over a crisp white blouse. Her blond hair was cropped short. She was staring at the entry buttons with a perplexed look on her face. Lukas was just about to politely ask her if she would excuse him so he could move in front of her to get at the buzzers when she reached up and jabbed her finger several times in quick succession at the one for number 34, perplexity now replaced with irritation.

"I'm sorry, madam," Lukas said. "Is there a problem?"

She twisted around in surprise having not noticed him standing there. "Oh, I'm sorry, sir. I'm in your way." She stepped back to allow him access to the buzzers.

"No, it's okay," he said. "Forgive me, but I noticed that it's Doctor Harrison's buzzer that you were pressing. It's just that I've come to see him as well. Is he not in?"

"Well, he's not answering his buzzer at the moment," she said in exasperation. "But I'm sure he must be in. I have an appointment with him at eleven o'clock." She looked down at her watch and then held up her wrist to show Lukas that it was now two minutes past eleven. "I assumed he must be in the bathroom or on the phone, but I've been pressing the buzzer for several minutes now."

"Maybe he's forgotten about your appointment and gone out," Lukas said.

"I shouldn't think so," the woman said. "I've had a number of previous appointments with Doctor Harrison and he's never let me down. He's always been very professional." She turned around and pressed the buzzer several more times with violent jabs of her index finger as if the man in the upstairs apartment must simply be hard of hearing and this forceful repetition would eventually get through to him.

"Well, whatever the reason, he either isn't in or doesn't want to or can't answer," Lukas said. The woman stared angrily at him almost as if it was his fault.

"Have you tried phoning him?" Lukas asked.

"I don't have a mobile phone," the woman said.

"Let me try," said Lukas, taking his phone from his jacket pocket. He found Doctor Harrison's number and rang it but only got the answer machine message. He shrugged and put his phone away.

"I can't waste any more time here," she said. "It's most annoying. I've travelled all the way from Dobling this morning. Rest assured, I will be giving Doctor Harrison a piece of my mind when I next see him. Good day, sir." She turned and walked briskly away, her high heels clacking on the pavement.

Lukas was about to follow her lead, but he paused in thought for a moment. He had phoned Malcolm Harrison several times over the previous two days to arrange a follow up interview with him, but he'd only got his answerphone. He'd left messages for Harrison to call him back but had heard nothing so he had come anyway this morning in the hope that he would find him in. This failure to make contact with Doctor Harrison coupled with his failure to fulfil his appointment with the woman was suspicious. He changed his mind about leaving and, instead, pressed the buzzer for the concierge, situated just beneath the rows of apartment numbers.

"Hallo," said a female voice.

"Good morning. My name is Inspector Lukas Honig from the Vienna police department. I'm trying to contact Doctor Malcolm Harrison but he's not answering his buzzer."

"That's probably because he's not in," said the voice with no hint of irony.

"It's just that there was also a woman here just now ringing for him because she had an appointment with him."

"Well I'm sorry about that but I'm not sure what you think I can do about it. I've had several people complaining to me over the last few days that Doctor Harrison wasn't in when he was supposed to have an appointment with them. As I said to them, I am not responsible for Doctor Harrison's whereabouts." The voice had grown tetchy.

"I'm sorry to bother you," Lukas said, "but I'm here on important police business. Could I come in and have a word with you? I won't take up too much of your time."

There was a moment's silence before the voice replied, still sounding tetchy. "Alright. Wait there. I'll come and let you in."

A minute later, the heavy arched wooden entrance door opened and a small woman in a blue gilet with a red scarf tied round her dark brown hair, wearing pink rubber gloves, stood looking up at him. He showed her his identity card and she led him over to a plain wooden bench on one side of the high-ceilinged entrance hall. They both sat down.

"Thank you again for your time," Lukas said. "I'll try to be brief. You said there have been a number of people complaining to you about Doctor Harrison not answering his buzzer. Does this happen often, do you know? Is he often not in when he's arranged appointments?"

"No. I'm not aware of it happening before. I've been the concierge here for five years and I've never known this to happen. Or, at least, I've never had complaints about him not being here."

"Does he go away a lot, do you know?"

"No. Quite the reverse. He's nearly always here. Always working. His practice is very popular. I'm not sure exactly what he does but he seems to be very successful." She uttered the last sentence, leaning closer to Lukas and lowering her voice in a manner that suggested that there might be something suspicious about the doctor's activities.

"And when was the last time you saw him?"

"I can't exactly remember. Not for several days."

Lukas leaned forward and put his hands on his knees. I assume you clean and service Doctor Harrison's apartment?"

"Yes."

"And when did you last clean the apartment?"

"Well, I always do it on a Friday morning so it would be nearly a week ago."

"So, you have your own duplicate key?"

"Yes," she said, starting to look uncomfortable.

"I'm afraid I'm going to have to ask you if you could go and get it and then let me in to his apartment."

The woman looked doubtful. "Don't you need a warrant to do that?"

"No, madam. I'm not going to search the apartment. I just want to make sure that nothing is amiss seeing as his whereabouts are something of a mystery."

As they stood outside the door to number 34, the concierge rifled through her collection of keys on a large metal ring. Lukas stared at it with amusement. It was the kind of thing you saw in old movies of the thirties and forties. This one had probably been in use since the building was first inhabited. Once she had found the key and opened the door, Lukas walked past her into a long narrow hallway. The concierge started to follow him into the apartment.

"Excuse me, madam, but I think it would be better if you waited for me outside." She didn't look happy but, slowly and grudgingly, she retreated to the vestibule just outside the door to the apartment.

Lukas proceeded down the hallway, calling out, "Hallo. Is there anyone here?"

The apartment was hot and stuffy, the central heating turned up far too high for such a mild Autumn day. He passed open doors on either side of the corridor revealing a toilet and a kitchen, both empty. Further along was a small office, also empty. As he moved further down the hallway, he started to detect an unpleasant smell over and above the general fustiness. His shoulders tensed and his chest tightened. It was a smell only too familiar from previous investigations. A large reception room with a floor to ceiling window leading on to a balcony overlooking the main street was also uninhabited but, when he reached a bedroom at the far end of the corridor, the smell became more pronounced. He pushed the door fully open and calmly surveyed the scene inside. He felt no shock because it was what the smell had led him to expect. Malcolm Harrison's body lay sprawled across a rumpled bed. He was dressed only in a pair of pyjama bottoms. His torso was waxy pale and his eyes were wide open. There was a leather ligature tied tightly around his right bicep. On the bedside table was a small metal tray of the type used to hold instruments in an operating theatre. It contained a partly blood-filled syringe and two glass vials part-filled with clear liquids. Lukas moved closer but didn't bother to examine the body. Malcolm Harrison had obviously been dead for some time. He removed his phone from his jacket pocket and rang headquarters.

It only took ten minutes of googling for Becky to settle on the identity of the Sir Richard mentioned by Maltese Tony. There were fifteen Conservative MPs from the mid-1980s called Richard but only two were Sir Richards and only one of those lived in Buckinghamshire, west of London. She read quickly through a Daily Telegraph profile of him written in 1997 when he had announced his retirement from politics. He was first elected to the House of Commons in 1974 and immediately gave his support to Margaret Thatcher's bid for the leadership in 1975. After her victory in the 1979 general election, she appointed Sir Richard to the first of several minor government posts, culminating in him becoming under-secretary in the Northern Ireland Office. In the mid-1980s, he fell out of favour with Margaret Thatcher, becoming one of those Tory MPs labelled a 'wet', and was sacked from his under-secretary post in 1986. In

1988 he resigned the Tory whip but continued to take his seat in the House, initially as an independent, before joining the Liberal Democrats. In 1992, he was re-elected for his Dorset constituency as a Liberal Democrat MP. He lost his seat in the 1997 election and announced his retirement from party politics. Becky scrolled through the rest of the first two pages of references to Sir Richard but couldn't find an obituary for him so she assumed he must be still alive. She worked out that he would now be seventy-eight.

She made a note of the location and address of his family home, Hedley Hall, and was about to close down her laptop when she remembered an entry that had briefly intrigued her on the first page of google references for Sir Richard Delacourt. She clicked back to the page and scrolled down until she came to the item. It was another, more recent, newspaper article, this time from the *Daily Mail*, headlined 'Son of Dissident Tory MP to stand as Thatcherite in Leadership Election'. She recalled that, when Maltese Tony had talked about he and his brother providing protection for Sir Richard's son, he'd mentioned that he had recently seen him on television and that he was now an MP just like his father. The reason Becky hadn't recognised who he was talking about was because David Delacourt now went under the name of Billington. Becky already felt that she knew more than enough about David Billington, the MP the article was about. He had come to prominence in recent years as the founder of a right-wing thinktank and had been hotly tipped as a future leader of the Conservative Party. His public profile had risen over the past year as a result of his frequent television appearances where he could be relied upon to spout controversial right-wing populist opinions, mostly anti-immigration and the EU. Since the destruction of the Twin Towers in New York, he had upped the rhetoric with statements that were viewed as Islamophobic. His toffish good looks, dapper appearance and reputation as a womaniser only fuelled the growing support for him.

The one piece of information in the article new to Becky was that he was Sir Richard Delacourt's son or, as the *Daily Mail* journalist put it, the ex-MP Sir Richard Delacourt's 'estranged' son. When she had finished reading the article, she googled the name David Billington. Near the top of the page, just below the *Daily Mail* article, was a profile from *The Spectator* written at about the same time. Most of the information was familiar so she skimmed through it until she reached a section near the end describing David Billington's relationship with his father. It explained why he had jettisoned the Delacourt name some years earlier and called himself Billington – his mother's maiden name. The article stated that he was Sir Richard and Lady Anne's only child and that he had had a fractious relationship with his father ever since his teenage years when he had been involved in a juvenile prank at Eton which, but for the intervention of his father, would have resulted in him being expelled. He eventually severed all contact with his father after Sir Richard resigned from the Conservative Party and joined the Liberal Democrats. Although he remained close to his mother, the writer continued, he had not had any contact with his father for over ten years.

Becky decided there and then to draft a letter to Sir Richard asking if she could come to Hedley Hall and interview him about Harry Felatu. She took a while to decide on a pretext for this interview. She decided it would be best not to say anything about his murder and her amateurish attempt to investigate it but, instead, to tell him that she was writing a biography of Felatu and was trying to speak to as many people as possible who had had some connection to him. She ended the letter by suggesting that, if he was agreeable, she would like to interview him as soon as possible and, to that end, she included her email address and phone number as contact details.

Ethan poked his head round the door to Maddy Rich's office.

"Can I have a brief word, ma'am. I've just received some important news."

Maddy looked up from her computer screen. "Come in, Cowboy. Take a seat. Some good news at last, I hope."

Ethan pulled out the chair in front of Maddy Rich's desk and sat down, shuffling around awkwardly to try and make himself feel more comfortable.

Maddy stared at him but he avoided making eye contact. "Oh dear. So, not good by the look of you."

"Afraid not ma'am. I've just received a phone call from Inspector Honig of the Vienna police. He's just been to do a follow up interview with Doctor Laxley-Young, as we requested. Anyway, to cut a long story short, he found him lying dead in his apartment. A suspected drugs' overdose. He thinks it could be accidental as there's no sign of a suicide note. He'd been dead for a couple of days."

"Great. So that's another line in our investigation shut down." Ethan nodded. "Remind me, Cowboy, didn't he have a history of drug addiction?"

"We're not sure, ma'am. All we know is that he was struck off the medical register for the unauthorised sale of prescription drugs so we know he had been a dealer in his younger days, so I guess it's possible that he was a user as well. They're waiting for the autopsy report before making a final decision on the cause of death," Ethan said. "He'll let me know as soon as they have it."

"I've had a bad feeling about this from the start," said Maddy. "It's not just that we're getting nowhere, we seem to be going backwards. Anyway, let me know when you hear more."

Becky was shown into the drawing room at Hedley Hall by an attractive young woman with short red hair and a pale complexion. She was smartly dressed in a black trouser suit and high heels, giving Becky the impression that she was more of a secretary or personal assistant than a maid.

"Would you like something to drink? Tea or coffee?" The young woman said.

"Tea would be nice," Becky said.

She glanced around the room taking in the elaborate carved cornicing, the enormous white marble fireplace and the range of modernist paintings on the walls, all originals she presumed, one an obvious David Hockney from his Californian swimming-pool period.

Becky had been surprised to receive an email reply from Sir Richard two days after sending her letter. Surprised not only at the promptness of the reply, but also that such an elderly man was familiar with the use of email. In it, he said how sorry he had been to hear about the death of Harry Felatu. He had indeed known him well in the 1980s and would be happy to meet Becky and share his memories of Harry. Now that he had retired from all his political and business pursuits, he said, he had plenty of time on his hands. He included his phone number and asked Becky to call him to arrange a time for the interview.

Once it had been arranged, Becky, although reluctant, felt duty bound to inform David Reznikoff who immediately assumed that he would be accompanying her. She told him that wouldn't be necessary, but he was very insistent. Becky was equally adamant, explaining that she had told Sir Richard that the reason for the interview was for her research for a biography she was writing of Harry Felatu. How would she explain having him in attendance at such an interview? He continued to complain for a while before eventually giving in.

The red-haired woman re-entered from a door at one end with a tea tray just as Sir Richard came in through a door at the opposite end of the drawing room.

"Thank you, Jenny," he said to the young woman. "Efficient as usual." He walked over to Becky who stood up to shake his outstretched hand. "Sorry to keep you waiting, Miss Stone. I was on the phone. A bit of a coincidence as it happens. It was the police calling me from London about Harry Felatu. They're coming to talk to me this afternoon although I can't see how I can be of much help to them. I haven't seen or heard from Harry since…" He paused in thought as he sat down opposite Becky. "It must be about 1986 so I don't think there's anything I can tell them about his murder. Shocking business." He shook his head.

He was a tall, handsome man with a full head of wiry grey hair, a large nose and pale blue eyes. Apart from walking with a pronounced stoop, he was well preserved for his nearly eighty years. He was dressed in a pair of grey slacks and an open-necked check shirt with long sleeves buttoned at the wrist.

After he had poured the tea, Becky took notes as he started to give an account of his initial introduction to Harry Felatu by Lord Boothby at the opening of his gallery and then went on to talk about the period when Harry worked for him and lived at Hedley Hall. Becky reminded herself that she was supposed to be a biographer and plied him with supplementary questions to elicit more details about Harry's character and the work he had been doing, namely, writing the Delacourt family history; details which she didn't need to know.

"But he didn't work for you very long?" Becky eventually asked. "You said you last saw him in 1986. Had he finished writing the family history?"

"No. On the contrary. He was still in the early stages."

"Did something happen?" Said Becky. "Did you have some kind of falling out? Was he dismissed?"

"No. Not at all," Sir Richard said. "Quite the opposite. Everything seemed to be going well. He seemed happy here. The family history appeared to be going well. Despite his initial doubts about whether he was qualified for such a project, he told me that he was enjoying writing it. And he got on very well with my wife. She was very fond of him. Unfortunately, her sister's not very well and she's gone to stay with her up in Durham otherwise I'm sure she'd have had lots of stories she could have told you about Harry." He paused and rubbed the back of his hand across his forehead. "No, it came as something of a shock. One morning, out of the blue, he asked to talk to me and told me that he was going to have to leave. That he wasn't going to be able to complete the family history. I expressed my surprise and asked him why. He was rather hesitant to answer – like he wasn't sure what to say. Eventually, all he could tell me was that it wasn't anything to do with me or the work he'd been doing for me. It was just that problems had come up in his personal life and he needed to spend some time sorting them out. I told him that would be fine. If he needed to take some time out, it wouldn't be a problem. There was no deadline for completing the family history. He could always resume the work later on when he'd sorted things out. He was uneasy. Said it might take quite some time. He thanked me and said he'd keep in contact, but he never did. I didn't hear from him again." Sir Richard's hand moved from his forehead to scratching his ear.

Becky had watched him very closely while he was talking, trying to detect whether he was telling her the truth. She tried to recall things she'd read about people's mannerisms when they were lying. Not making eye contact. Rubbing his head and scratching his ear. Were these signs? Despite all the recent interviews she'd conducted surrounding the mystery of Harry Felatu's death, she wasn't a police officer and had never been very good at detecting when people were not telling the truth. The ease with which David Reznikoff had bamboozled her on occasion was proof of that.

"So, you think these alleged 'personal problems' might have been an excuse? Can you think of any other reason why he might have decided to leave?"

"No. He was definitely on edge that morning. I'm sure there was something troubling him but I've no idea what it was." Again, Becky studied Sir Richard as this time, he rubbed his nose with his thumb and index finger. He might have been lying but she couldn't be sure. After all, he was an ex-senior politician so he was bound to have had plenty of practice at telling convincing lies.

"And can you think of any reason why someone would have wanted to kill him?"

"No, I can't – which is what I will have to tell the police this afternoon. As I'm sure you must already know from your research, Miss Stone, Harry had quite a shady past. He never talked about it, but Bob Boothby told me all about the time he worked for the Kray brothers. And I know he still had contacts with that world because he hired a couple of ex-gangster brothers to provide security for me and my family.

"Well, thank you very much for your help," said Becky, putting her pen and notepad back in her bag.

"It's been good to talk to you, Miss Stone. I hope I have been of some help. I will look forward to reading your book when it comes out."

Becky was on the train back to London when her mobile phone rang. It was David Reznikoff. She was about to let it go to voicemail but then changed her mind. There was no point in putting it off. It would be the same conversation she'd had with him several times before only this time she was determined to hold firm. It was over, she told him. She'd got nothing useful or interesting from Sir Richard. It was another dead end. It was definitely time to give up. Leave it to the police. The expected protestations from Reznikoff did not materialise. She was fully expecting him to throw some new angle at her to keep her sucked in but all he said was that he was sorry to hear it. He had enjoyed the time they had spent together and, even though their investigation was over, perhaps they might still meet up again some time.

As she put away her phone, Becky felt a mixture of relief and disappointment that it was all over. She had enjoyed her little adventure as a private investigator. Admittedly, she was no Philip Marlowe or Miss Marple, but it had been fun. A dash of excitement in her otherwise mundane life.

# Extracts from
# The Autobiography of an Invisible Man

## MR FIXIT FOR THE RICH AND INFLUENTIAL

Sitting in a high-backed black leather armchair in the reception area of Brooks's Club in St. James Street, watching the pin-striped, club-tied, elderly members walking by, hands clasped behind their backs, braying greetings at one another like donkeys in pain, I felt as conspicuous as a turd in a jacuzzi. The antique escritoire next to me contained a silver tray full of embossed, headed notepaper, an elaborate brass lamp and a glass case full of fat Havana cigars. On the wall above the reception desk was a large framed roll of honour of Brooks's Club members who lost their lives in the service of their country during the Great War. Most of the members passing through reception cast me a sideways querulous glance. It was obvious that large dark-skinned men like me were not a common sight in Brooks's. If it wasn't for my suit and tie, I'm sure they would have assumed I was there to carry out some menial task. And what if they had known I was Jewish as well? I was reminded of a joke I'd heard about Sammy Davis Junior. He sits down at the front of a bus in Mississippi. "Niggers have to sit at the back, boy," the driver says to him. "But I'm Jewish," Sammy Davis replies. "Then get off," says the driver.

Apologies for the digression, dear reader, Here I go disorientating you once again. But you'll be used to it by now. I have a penchant for it. Yes, I am sat in the foyer of the exclusive Brooks's Club in Mayfair because I have been invited to meet a member, Sir Richard Delacourt MP. Despite the fact that, since I had been running the Sarah Weinstein Gallery just around the corner from Brooks's, I had become used to mixing with the kind of people who are denizens of exclusive West End private members' clubs, I still could not feel comfortable sitting in one myself. During my time at the gallery, I had made the acquaintance of many of the super rich upper classes. Having achieved recognition as something of an expert on modern art, particularly modern British painters, I was often invited to their palatial mansion flats to provide them with a valuation of one of their works of art.

So, why am I sitting in these unfriendly surroundings waiting to meet Sir Richard? Let me backtrack. The gallery had initially been a huge success. The early exhibitions attracted wealthy crowds and made us plenty of money. I became very adept at buying and selling modern paintings, rarely putting a foot wrong. But, after six years, we went into a gradual downward spiral. In the difficult financial circumstances of the late 1970s and early 1980s, with the stock market faring poorly, the wealthy looked to invest their money more profitably elsewhere and the art market was seen as a good, although not entirely risk-free, place to invest. However, once the economy started to pick up, there were much safer places to put their money and we began to suffer. The death blow came when Nathan Myerson, our philanthropic business partner, decided it was time to withdraw his investment. David Reznikoff's efforts to dissuade him failed and we staggered on for a further six months, struggling to pay the rapidly rising rent, before we were forced to close. Once again, I found myself marooned and rudderless. Until, that is, this invitation to meet Sir Richard. I had reluctantly accepted his invitation six years earlier, when I was introduced to him at the gallery opening by Robert Boothby, to his birthday party for Princess Margaret. When the formal invitation had arrived at the gallery, I immediately started to feel the full weight of my mother's disapproval as it became the chief topic in our imaginary conversations. I was about to send my apologies to Sir Richard, when David Reznikoff heard about the invitation. He was adamant that I should go; that I should put the future of the gallery above my personal feelings. The more I was able to mix with this wealthy elite, the more likely we were to get commissions for the gallery.

I won't get into the details of the birthday party, other than that my conversations with the Princess were truncated by calls for her attention from the other far more stellar guests than me. It would have been a very lonely evening for me if it had not been for Sir Richard's wife, Lady Anne, taking me under her wing. Both she and Sir Richard were charm personified and went out of their way to make me feel welcome, unlike most of their other stuffed-shirt guests. They belied all my mother's vitriolic assertions about the racist obnoxiousness of the English upper classes. So, I went away feeling that I had done my bit for the gallery and, from then on, I would limit my contact with the rich and aristocratic crowd to strictly professional necessity. The first test of this resolution came a week later when I received a letter from Kensington Palace. It was an invitation from Princess Margaret to accompany her, with a group of other friends, for a two week stay at her retreat on the Caribbean island of Mustique. I didn't need to think about it or even waste any time debating it with my mother, but immediately dispatched a polite reply, thanking her for the offer but sadly declining it as I was far too busy at the gallery.

When I subsequently saw all the newspaper gossip and the paparazzi photos of the Princess cavorting on the

Caribbean beach with Roddy Llewellyn and John Bindon, a part-time actor and full-time villain I'd briefly met during my time with the Krays, I knew I had made the right decision. Despite my associations with the likes of Lord Boothby, Sir Richard Delacourt and Lady Anne and Princess Margaret herself, the last thing I would have wanted was to see myself the subject of scurrilous tabloid newspaper gossip.

But, as I previously intimated, I continued to mix with these people at the gallery and offer them my services. After my attendance at his party, Sir Richard continued to visit the gallery and bought a number of paintings from us. And then, my relationship with him developed further when he invited me back to his mansion in Buckinghamshire to advise him on the sale of some of his collection of old family portrait paintings so that he could free some wall space for the purchase and display of more modern art. However, this was the first time he had invited me to Brooks's. Although he hadn't given me any reason for the meeting, I assumed it was something to do with his art collection.

"Harry. Thank you so much for coming," Sir Richard barked as he descended the curved, plush, red-carpeted staircase with its curlicued wrought-iron balustrades. "Long time no see." I stood up and we shook hands. "I'm sorry to have kept you waiting. Let's go upstairs and have a drink."

I followed him back up the staircase past a line of alcoves filled with marble Romanesque busts. We entered a drawing-room on the first floor, large and airy beneath a huge glass dome which cast beams of sunlight on to the red leather sofas. The walls were covered in imposing portraits of bewigged eminent looking men.

"Arthur!" Once we'd sat down on one of the sofas, Sir Richard waved an outstretched hand to call over a slightly stooped, grey-haired attendant in a shiny suit and black bowtie. "We'll have two glasses of the Palo Cortada de

Anada please." He turned back to me as Arthur nodded and headed back across the room. "I hope you don't mind me taking the liberty of ordering for you, Harry, but it's exquisite stuff. The club has its own wine cellar specialising in vintage sherries."

He watched me as my eyes took in the rest of the room. "Impressive, isn't it? I rarely spend any time here these days. Too busy with government business, but it's a useful place to get away from all that. And it's a good place to get a bit of gossip and make a few contacts. And the food's very good as well. I'm a bit busy today. Got to be back in the House this afternoon but another time you must come for lunch. Plus there's also the gaming tables next door. Not that I'm that way inclined myself. A lot of money gets frittered away in there. And there's a lot of private betting. If you get a chance to go in there, have a look at the big leather-bound book on the mahogany table at the far end of the room. It's the club's betting book. A very interesting historical document. It's where the members enter their private bets with each other. Quite fascinating some of them. The most famous is one lordship betting another that he would fuck a woman in a hot air balloon half a mile above the Earth. Anyway, I haven't got time to show you round today. We need to get down to business."

Arthur arrived with the drinks and a dish of assorted nuts.

"I'm sorry to call you up out of the blue like this. It must have seemed a bit mysterious."

"You could say that," I said, sipping my sherry and giving Sir Richard an approving nod. Sherry was far from my favourite tipple so I can't say that this one struck me as particularly special.

"I heard about the gallery closing," he continued, "and I presumed you might be at a bit of a loose end."

"Yes, that's true. I'm not doing anything else at present. Just considering my options."

"Of course. I was sorry to hear about the gallery, but opportunity often comes about after misfortune. I'd like to offer you some work."

"Okay," I said. "I'd be happy to look at some paintings for you. Despite the gallery closing, one of my options for the future is to keep my hand in as an expert valuer."

"Actually Harry, what I'm offering you has nothing to do with art." He paused to take a sip of his sherry. "For some years now, I've had someone working for me in a general capacity. In past, less egalitarian times, you might have called him a butler. I tended to refer to him as a major-domo. Anyway, he recently left me. Moved on to pastures new. I've had a hard time finding a replacement – and then I heard about the gallery closing and thought of you."

I'm not sure what I had expected from this meeting, but it certainly wasn't this. I had taken on some strange jobs in my time, but I was finding it hard to picture myself as a faithful retainer to an aristocratic Tory MP. Once again, I felt my mother's disapproving ghost hovering over me.

"No offense, Sir Richard. It's very good of you to think of me," I said, "but it doesn't really sound like my sort of thing. I don't think I've got the kind of attributes needed for such a job."

"Before you rush into making a decision, Harry, let me explain in a bit more detail. I think I might have given you the wrong impression. You've probably got an image in your head of those wizened old servants bowing and scraping in old black and white British movies. This job's nothing like that. The reason that I thought of you was precisely because of what I know about your past and how it fits in with some specific tasks that I'd want you to do for me." He paused to signal Arthur over and order two more sherries.

"I understand that you're a writer. One of the things I'd like you to do is to write a history of the Delacourt family. We've got an extensive family archive at the house. It needs a lot of sorting through but it contains some fascinating stuff. Needless to say, we Delacourts go back to the Norman Conquest. I can put you up very comfortably in the house while you're working on it and…"

I raised my hand to interrupt him. "Whoa, Sir Richard. I think you've been slightly misinformed. I have been a writer but I've only written fiction. I'm not a historian and I don't have any qualifications to write a family history."

"No, I already know that. It doesn't matter. If you fancied giving it a go, I would trust you. A few years ago, I made a deal with a well-known academic historian to write our family history, but it didn't work out. We didn't get on. He was a bit of a drinker. And had some other disgusting personal habits which I won't go into. I got rid of him." He leaned forward and looked me straight in the eye. "Although I wouldn't call us close friends exactly, over the past few years we've got to know each other pretty well. I like and trust you, Harry, and that's far more important to me than any academic credentials you may or may not have."

"Well, I don't know…"

This time it was his turn to interrupt. "But the job's not only about writing the family history. I hope you'll forgive me. I didn't mean to pry into your background, but Bob Boothby has told me all about your past association with the Krays. You're an imposing man yourself and I'm sure you still have some connections with that world. You see, I need some extra security around the place and I think it's something else you could help me out with. Since the Prime Minister's given me this under-secretary job at the Northern Ireland Office, I've been given some extra police security as me and my family could now become IRA targets. It's made my wife, Anne, feel very uncomfortable. She was very taken with you, Harry, when you spent time together at the party. I think she would feel reassured to have your presence around the house, especially as I have to spend so much time away from home. So, there you have it. Two roles that I think you could combine really well."

For the next few minutes, I prevaricated, giving Sir Richard a range of reasons why I wasn't as suitable for these tasks as he thought I was. My association with the Krays had been nearly fifteen years ago and it had chiefly been as a manager of one of their nightclubs. And I had had very little contact since then with any of the men the Krays had used as 'security'. Also, I was very much a Londoner and I wasn't sure whether I would be able to adapt to living in the 'sticks'.

Eventually, he glanced down at his watch and said that he would have to cut our conversation short as he had a meeting at the House of Commons. Why didn't I give myself a couple of days to think over his offer? Then he'd come back to me for my answer.

I'm sure you know me well enough by now, dear reader, to have guessed what is coming next. To picture exactly where I am going to be. And you would be right. Here I am, four weeks later, ensconced in the oak-panelled library at the Delacourt's palatial home, Hadley Hall, just outside Chalfont St. Peter. To say it felt strange, sitting at the voluminous satinwood antique desk sorting through dusty yellowing manuscripts, would be an understatement. One of my unstated reservations about accepting Sir Richard's offer had been the thought of living in a place that was adjacent to my old, and not very happy, childhood stamping ground of High Wycombe. But, as with so many of the big decisions I have made in my life, I am hard put now to explain why, despite my long list of reservations, I finally accepted Sir Richard's offer.

Whenever I have had to make big decisions in my life, I have tended to follow the same process. An immediate, apparently firm, decision. But then I go away and start to think about it. I compile two columns in my head – arguments for accepting the offer and those against. Invariably, the against column would be long, the arguments for very short. But I still can't let it go so I carry on thinking about it. I start to waver and then, when the person who has made me the offer comes back for an answer, I unaccountably allow myself to be sucked in. It was the exact same process I went through when I was asked to join the 43 Group; when Francis Bacon wanted my services; when the Krays made me their offers; when David Reznikoff asked me to join him in setting up the gallery.

To add to this habit of indecision, there was what I used to refer to as my *Waiting for Godot* syndrome. My unending search for a goal in life. That, just awaiting around the corner, would be the one great opportunity in my life. And so, I tended to see everything else I ended up doing as only being temporary – filling in time until that one big opportunity would come along. So, perhaps this was another example.

And yet, despite going through all my usual vacillating processes over Sir Richard's offer, this time I remained intent on declining it. However, when Sir Richard phoned me three days later, he gave me no chance to turn him down, instantly issuing an invitation for me to come to Hedley Hall on the following Saturday so that I could see for myself where I would be working and what I would be working on. Yet again, I succumbed and accepted his invitation, reasoning, as I always did, that I wasn't committing myself to anything. I could still say no.

Much to my surprise, I enjoyed the lifestyle at Hedley Hall. What's not to like, you must be asking yourself, dear reader. I was very well fed and watered. My room was luxurious, with my own private bathroom and a magnificent view from my window of the Italianate garden. Sir Richard's wife, Lady Anne, was charming and treated me more like a long lost relative than a paid employee. Even though I had little idea what I was doing, I loved working in the library. The smell of musty old books and lingering cigar smoke. Sunlight streaming through the stained-glass, leaded windows. The comforting embrace of kid leather armchairs. Maybe, somewhere deep within my DNA, I had inherited a feel for that period in my mother's young life when she used to spend so much of her time in the British Museum Reading Room and the London Library researching and writing her newspaper and magazine articles.

My life had been about constantly taking on new challenges – challenges that I initially deemed myself unsuited to. But, now that I had passed my fiftieth birthday, this seemed like an eminently suitable occupation for a middle-aged man: spending my days in the galleried library of a stately home delving into ancient texts while my every need was catered for.

The only downside was the occasions when Sir Richard asked me to act as a bodyguard to his son, David, and accompany him to various social gatherings. Sir Richard was a traditional patrician Tory politician – one of those later referred to as a 'wet' when he fell out of favour with Margaret Thatcher. Nevertheless, I liked and respected him. He showed no signs of racism and treated me more like a friend and confidante than a paid employee. Young David and his friends, however, were every inch the product of their privileged upper-class Eton and Oxbridge education and, now in their mid-twenties, their lavishly remunerated sinecures in City financial institutions. Any historian, looking back at the mid-1980s, could cite them as perfect examples of those labelled 'Thatcher's children'. Their drug and drink fuelled parties were raucous; their conversation replete with disparaging comments about oiks, blacks and Jews. Unlike his father, David always made our relationship clear – it was master and servant. I was either made to wait and sit guard in drafty corridors or vestibules or, at house parties, in the kitchen. It was a relief when I managed to establish contact with ex-Kray brothers' henchmen, Tony and Nick Lambros, who had recently been released from prison, and hired them to provide extra security for Sir Richard. Once they had gained his trust, whenever possible I passed on the bodyguard duties for David Delacourt to them.

To my surprise, I also found myself starting to enjoy writing the Delacourt family history. The historian Sir Richard had previously employed had left behind early drafts of the work he had started which provided a useful template for me in terms of the appropriate tone and style for writing such a history.

Not for the first time in my life, I had landed on my feet. That was until I had the rug pulled out from under them.

# Monday 2nd November 2001

"You're in this office so often, Cowboy, it might be easier if we just moved your desk in here," Maddy Rich said when she saw Ethan hovering in the open doorway.

"If you're suggesting a promotion, ma'am, I'd be up for that," said Ethan.

"Don't push your luck. Although, if you've come to tell me you've cracked the Felatu case then there could definitely be a promotion in the offing."

Ethan walked up to her desk and sat down without waiting for an invitation.

Maddy peered at him intently over the top of her computer screen. "This looks a bit more encouraging, "she said. "I wouldn't go as far as to say that you're looking cheerful but at least it's not your usual hangdog expression. Okay, spill the beans."

"I just had another call from Inspector Lukas Honig in Vienna. He's got the initial results from the autopsy. It's not conclusive. They've still got to wait for the full report."

"Alright. Spare me the technicalities, Cowboy. I'm aware of how autopsies work. Just cut to the chase. It's obviously interesting."

"They don't think it was suicide or an accidental overdose. They think it's likely that Doctor Harrison was murdered." Ethan pulled a notepad from his inside jacket pocket, flipped it open and started to read from it. "He died from an overdose of heroin mixed with a barbiturate – amorbarbital. They say that heroin and amorbarbital are a fairly common drugs combination. Addicts take the barbiturate because it helps to reduce the downs they get as the heroin wears off. One of the reasons they're suspicious is that amorbarbital is normally taken orally but, in Doctor Harrison's case, it was injected. What they think might have happened is that, if he had been forcibly injected with the heroin and was incapacitated, it would have been easier to inject the barbiturate rather than trying to force him to swallow it. The other reason they think it wasn't an accidental overdose is that there was no other evidence on his body that he was a regular intravenous drug user."

"That does sound interesting. If he was murdered, do they have any idea who might have done it?"

Ethan flipped over a page in the notepad. "Possibly. After he got the interim report, Inspector Honig revisited his apartment block and re-interviewed the concierge. One of the things she remembered was that, a couple of days before his body was found, she'd been cleaning in the lobby when two men arrived to see Doctor Harrison. They only spoke to her briefly in basic German, but she was fairly certain that they were English. She gave him a description of them." Ethan read from the notepad. "They were in their mid to late thirties and were both smartly dressed in almost identical dark grey suits. They were both clean-shaven with short dark hair. She couldn't remember them having any other distinguishing features. One of them was carrying a black leather holdall. She doesn't know how long they stayed. She didn't see them leave. Unfortunately, there's no CCTV at the front of the building or in the lobby. So, the next thing the Vienna police are going to do is to study camera footage at Vienna airport for the period just before and just after Doctor Harrison's death to see if they can spot two men who fit the concierge's description either getting off or getting on a flight to or from the UK."

Maddy stared into space for a moment before turning her attention to her computer to bring up the Felatu case notes. "Didn't that old Polish couple in the house where Felatu lived say something about him being visited by two smartly dressed men?"

"It's okay, ma'am. That's well-remembered but I beat you to it. I've already checked out the description that the Kaplanskas gave of the two men and it near enough fits with the men the concierge described. Obviously both descriptions are a bit vague but they're not dissimilar. If we can get any camera images from Vienna airport, then we can show them to the Kaplanskas as well as the concierge."

Maddy sat back and drummed her fingers on the desktop. "Well, let's hope the Vienna police come up with something. You never know. We might be getting somewhere at last."

Ethan stood up and was about to leave when Maddy stopped him. "Oh, Cowboy. Before you go. Any news from Andy and Carol about that interview with the ex-MP?"

Ethan turned around. "Oh yes. Sorry ma'am. I meant to tell you but it got pushed into the background once I got that news from Vienna." He hovered in front of the desk not sure whether to sit back down before deciding to remain standing. "Sir Richard Delacourt. He was the MP. Andy and Carol went to see him but I'm afraid it wasn't very productive. Felatu did work for him back in the 1980s but he hadn't had any contact with him for the past fifteen years and had no idea who might have killed him or why anyone might have wanted him dead. Anyway, they'll have a copy of their report on your desk later this afternoon."

Once again, he turned to go but then changed his mind. "One thing Sir Richard did confirm was Felatu's friendship with Princess Margaret. I still think that might be worth following up, ma'am."

"And why would that be necessary, Cowboy?" She gave him a sceptical look.

"Well, I was just thinking about those theories that someone in the Royal Family – the Duke of Edinburgh to be precise – maybe had something to do with the death of Princess Diana. And the reason they thought that was because she was having relationships that were felt to be unsuitable for a mother of the future King – like the one with Mohamed Al-Fayed's son. And so, on that basis, I shouldn't think they would have been very happy about the Queen's sister consorting with a character like Harry Felatu."

Maddy had returned her attention to her computer screen. "As I told everybody the last time this was brought up, we do not buy into conspiracy theories here. If you find any evidence of murderous mayhem among members of the Royal Family, then let me know. Otherwise, Cowboy, let's hope for something positive from the Austrians."

"Sorry to interrupt but is there a Becky Stone in here?"

It was a young man from the reception desk at the Museum of London, standing in the open doorway of the research department, looking around at the six people working at their desks.

Becky looked up from her computer screen. "Yes, that's me," she said.

"There's a woman at reception asking to speak to you." He looked down at a slip of paper in his hand. "A Magda Simkova."

Becky looked blankly at him. The name Magda was vaguely familiar but she couldn't quite place it. "Did she say what it was about?"

"No Miss, but she had one of your cards."

"Okay. Tell her if she could just wait a couple of minutes, I'll come through and speak to her."

Becky finished typing the sentence she was on and then clicked to save the document. As she walked through to the museum foyer, she tried to think who the visitor could be and what it could be about, but the name didn't register. Her immediate thought had been that it was the police who had finally caught up with her over her involvement with the Harry Felatu case, but then she realised that they would have shown their identity cards at the front desk.

As soon as she turned the corner past the gift shop and saw the middle aged, stockily built, blond-haired woman standing near the ticket desk, she recognised her instantly, even though her long hair had been cropped short since she last saw her. Of course. Magda. Now she knew why the name was familiar. Ana Geisler's partner. She looked a far less forbidding figure than when Becky had interviewed Ana. Then, Magda had taken on the role of protector of her ageing partner; a brooding, hostile presence trying to make Becky feel as unwelcome as possible. Now she looked smaller and more nervous, glancing uneasily round the foyer until she saw Becky walking towards her and gave her an awkward half-smile of recognition.

"Miss Stone. Thank you so much for agreeing to see me." They shook hands.

"It's good to see you, Magda," said Becky, trying to sound sincere. "How's Ana?"

Magda frowned. "Oh dear. I thought you must have known. She passed away last week. There were obituaries in some of the newspapers."

"I'm so sorry. You have my deepest sympathies," said Becky, this time with genuine emotion. "I'm afraid I haven't had time to read the papers recently."

"She had cancer. She refused any treatment. She said she had lived long enough and wanted to enjoy what life she had left. It was very quick in the end. There wasn't much pain."

"I know I only met her the once but she struck me as being a very impressive woman. And she'd had such a full and productive life."

"Yes, she had," Magda mumbled. She stood in silence for a moment looking down at her feet.

"You obviously didn't come to inform me about her death, so what can I do for you?" Becky said, hoping that she wasn't sounding heartless.

Magda snapped to attention as if only just remembering why she was there. She reached down into a scuffed brown leather satchel dangling from her shoulder and extracted an A4 jiffy bag and clutched it to her chest.

"I brought this for you but I need to explain. Is there somewhere we can go to talk?"

"There's a café down in the basement. It's usually not too busy at this time of day."

Becky insisted on paying for their two coffees and they sat down as far away from the two other occupied tables as they could get as Magda had expressed the need for privacy.

She was still holding the envelope. She pushed it towards Becky without saying anything. Becky saw that it was stamped and addressed to Ana Geisler and was unopened. She picked it up carefully as if it might contain some noxious substance. It felt light. She turned it over. Written on the back, at the top of the envelope, just underneath the seal, in black felt pen and block capitals, was the name HARE YEHUDA FELATU. Underneath, in smaller writing, he had written 'not to be opened until after my death'. Becky put it back down on the table and stared expectantly at Magda.

Magda took a deep breath before starting to explain. "It came about a month ago. Before Harry's death. I just put it away in a drawer. I didn't mention it to Ana. I didn't want to worry her. She knew she was dying. She hadn't told Harry about the cancer. She didn't feel she needed to. So, as I'm sure you can imagine, when I saw what he had written on it, I thought it sounded a bit dramatic. A bit ominous. Why bother her with it? No point in her knowing about it because she was almost certainly going to die before Harry. And then, when he did die a couple of weeks later, she was so upset, that I still didn't want to risk upsetting her further and making her illness worse by giving it to her. After that, I was so busy caring for her in her final days that I forgot all about it. After her death, I decided that the flat was too big for me and held too many painful memories, so I decided to move out. It was only when I started clearing out the flat in the last few days that I found the envelope and then I had to decide what to do with it. It was addressed to Ana, not to me. I didn't want to open it. And then I thought of you, Miss Stone. That it might be something of interest to your research. You'd given Ana a card with your contact details at the museum – so, here I am." Magda still spoke in a pronounced Eastern European accent but her English was near perfect.

Becky picked up the envelope again and held it hesitantly before putting it back down in front of Magda.

"Magda." Becky paused, thinking carefully about what she was about to say. She barely knew this woman and wasn't sure if she could trust her. She quickly decided that she would have to. "I wasn't totally honest with Ana when I spoke with her. It's true that I've been researching this Soho exhibition for the Museum of London and it's also true that Harry Felatu has some relevance to that, but I was more interested in being a kind of amateur detective and seeing if I could discover who had murdered him. It was a stupid thing to do and I've given up on it now. I'm leaving it to the police, as I should've done in the first place."

Rather than dampen down Madgda's determination, what Becky had said only increased it. "But that means this letter could be of even more importance to you. He has written that it's not to be opened until after his death and then, almost immediately after, he dies. So, maybe inside here are the clues about his death. Don't you see – this means that my decision to give it to you makes even more sense now." Like a game of pass the parcel, Magda gently edged the padded envelope back towards Becky.

Becky sighed deeply. "No, Magda. As I just said, I was stupid to allow myself to get mixed up in this in the first place. What you need to do is take it to the police."

"No, I can't do that." Magda shook her head vigorously.

"Why not?"

Magda looked around the café as if checking to see that they weren't being overheard. "I don't want anything to do with the police." She paused as if the implication of what she had just said was obvious.

Becky gave her a quizzical look, waiting for her to elaborate.

Magda leaned closer to Becky and lowered her voice to just above a whisper. "I first came to England from Czechoslovakia in the 1970s on a student visa. That's when I met Ana. She came to my university department to give a lecture. Once my course was finished, we moved in together. We've lived together ever since. I've never had a proper job. I looked after Ana and was her assistant, helping her with her work." She paused. She had averted her eyes from Becky's during this monologue but now she stared straight at her. "I'm illegal. I overstayed my student visa. I kept putting off doing anything about it until I decided it would be too late and it was best to carry on with things as they were. By then, I thought that, if I went to the authorities and owned up and tried to make myself legal, they'd deport me. I had no automatic right to stay." Becky stared at her. She suddenly looked very tired and anxious. "I'm scared about what's going to happen to me now. I can't go back to Prague. My family are strict Catholics. They disowned me when they found out I was a lesbian. And I no longer have any friends over there."

Becky took a moment to think this through. She didn't know enough about the immigration laws to argue with Magda although she wanted to say to her that, surely, she must have a right to stay having lived here for such a long time.

"You could send the letter to the police anonymously," she eventually suggested.

"It's addressed to Ana. They would guess who must have sent it. And then they'd come to question me."

"Well that's easily solved. We can take out whatever's in there and repost it to them anonymously. Then they won't be able to trace it to you."

Magda's response was to push the envelope even closer to Becky so that it hovered on the edge of the table, almost toppling into her lap. "No. I don't want anything more to do with it. I'll be honest. I never really liked Hare. Every time he visited Ana, she would be upset for days afterwards." She paused and gave Becky a long hard stare. "I will leave it up to you to decide what to do with it. If you want to open it and then send what's inside to the police, then that's up to you."

Becky put both hands on the envelope in a gesture halfway between picking it up and pushing it back to Magda.

"Admit it," Magda said, still staring intently into Becky's eyes. "You are very tempted to open it up and see what's inside?"

Becky gritted her teeth and looked down at her hands resting on the envelope as if they belonged to somebody else. Magda was right. If the package could emit sounds, it would be a siren song calling out to her. There might, of course, turn out to be nothing of significance inside but the temptation to find out had been growing ever since Magda had first shown it to her. This was far worse than all those temptations that David Reznikoff had dangled in front of her to keep her on board.

There was no point in giving it any more thought. Her impetuosity took over. She picked it up, tore off the tab at the top and pulled out a bundle of hand-written pages. As Magda looked on, she flipped hurriedly through the separate sheets to confirm what they were and to check whether there was any letter of explanation. There wasn't. She pulled open the envelope and peered inside but there was nothing else in there.

Magda looked at her expectantly.

"It's two more chapters of his autobiography," Becky said. "I've already read the rest of it."

# Extracts from
# The Autobiography of an Invisible Man

## MY DARK NIGHT OF THE SOUL

I am sure you will agree, dear reader, that one of the most important things when writing one's life story is complete honesty. There will always be the temptation to present only the very best side of oneself by emphasising one's best moments and downplaying, glossing over or even omitting the worst. I hope that, so far, in this autobiography, I have been totally honest. I may have gone too far in trying to carry out my original purpose of establishing my important, although largely invisible, role in so much of the cultural life of mid-twentieth century London but I have not made anything up or left anything out.

Looking back on one's life by writing an autobiography can, I am sure, be a disheartening experience. Up to this point, I am not sure whether it has been for me. I've tried to depict an unconventional life of adventure and intrigue, but I fear that you, dear reader, may by now simply see me as a dilettante or, less politely, a layabout. Somebody who has lived his life through an association with other people's achievements whilst achieving nothing at all himself, while having the luxury of being able to live off an inheritance. So, as I approach the final years (or more probably days) of my life, can I sum myself up either as a success or a failure? I guess my answer is that it's a stupid question to which very few of us would be able to give a definitive answer. Most of our lives are mixtures of the two. To use that tired old cliché, our lives are like rollercoaster rides – a mixture of ups and downs.

As I write the above, I am only too aware that I am prevaricating; delaying the inevitability of having to start to tell the story of this next stage of my life. The one I am least proud of. No, that's too mealy-mouthed. The one I am most ashamed of. And the one that will prove to be my nemesis. Anyway, here goes.

I had been working for Sir Richard at Hedley Hall for almost a year when it happened. By then, I was dividing my time between the mansion in Buckinghamshire and my very modest flat in Paddington, usually spending the weekdays at Hedley Hall and the weekends in London. I had a new girlfriend, Rachel Lehrer, a sculptress who I had met through my continuing association with the London art scene. Like almost all my relationships with women, it was something of an on-off affair which seemed to suit both of us. If we were in London simultaneously, we would spend time together. But that also meant that there were weeks at a time when we did not see each other at all. Rachel was twenty years younger than me, a vibrant and attractive young woman whose career was just beginning to take off. The reason that she was so frequently away from London was that she had started to get commissions from around the country for new public art installations.

It was a Saturday night and we were in bed together in my flat, just drifting off to sleep, when the phone rang. It was Maltese Tony.

"Sorry to disturb you so late, Harry, but there's a problem. A big problem. It's David Delacourt. He phoned me this evening in quite a panic. I would deal with it myself but it's too serious for that. I'm afraid I need your help."

There was a strange mismatch between what he was telling me and his tone of voice. He sounded unnaturally calm.

"Okay, Tony. You need to tell me exactly what this is all about because I've just gone to bed and I don't want to have to get up and go gallivanting about in the middle of the night unless there's a very good reason."

"I'm sorry, Harry, but I don't want to talk about it over the phone. I'm with David now. He's in a friend's apartment in Knightsbridge. I need you to get over here and then, you can see for yourself what the problem is."

I took a deep breath. In hindsight, I wish I had followed my initial instinct and told Tony that, whatever the problem was, he'd have to look after it himself, but I couldn't and didn't. I was being looked after, and generously paid, by Sir Richard, both to write the family history and to be responsible for the safety and security of his family. If something had happened to his son, there was no way that I could keep myself out of it.

I wrote down the address Tony gave me over the phone and told him I would get there as quickly as possible. I told Rachel I had to go out for a while and that it was nothing to worry about. I would be back soon and, of course, she was welcome to stay. I got dressed, left the flat and walked down the street to Paddington Station where I was able to pick up a taxi.

The apartment was on the second floor of a mansion block in one of the smart squares behind Harrods. Tony buzzed me in through the front entrance and was waiting at the open door to the apartment when I got out of the lift. He didn't say anything. He turned and walked down the hallway to a door at the far end which led into a bedroom. I followed close behind. Lying on top of rumpled sheets on a double bed was a young woman dressed in black lacey underwear. Her long dark hair was splayed around her shoulders and across the pillow. She was staring open-eyed at the ceiling, her tongue poking out of the side of her mouth. I didn't need to take her pulse or go any closer to examine her. As soon as I saw her lying there, I knew she was dead, even though this was the first time in my life that I'd seen a dead body.

Tony looked at me looking down at the dead girl. "I told you it was bad," he said.

"What happened? Who is she? Who did it?" Unlike Tony, I couldn't keep the panic out of my voice. "Where's David?" I added.

"He's in the sitting room," said Tony. "There's three of them. The flat belongs to a friend of his. A doctor. His name's Alexander Laxley-Young. And there's this other friend, Angus McNair."

"So, which one of them did this?" I pointed at the young woman.

"They wouldn't tell me anything at first. They've all had quite a bit to drink and I wouldn't be surprised if there's also been a bit of cocaine snorted. I had to be a bit firm with them before I could get anything out of them," said Tony, emphasising the word 'firm'. "She's an escort. A prostitute. This guy, Doctor Alexander, hired her for the night. Apparently, it's David's birthday and she was his present." Tony raised his eyebrows.

"Fine," I said. "But she's dead. What the fuck did they do to her?"

"I told you, I couldn't get much out of them. They're all in shock. They just want me to get rid of the body."

I moved to the edge of the bed, bent over the young woman and examined her more closely. I was trying to avoid touching her. She was very young, perhaps eighteen or nineteen, with a pretty face and a slim figure.

"What was it? A drug overdose?" I knew from previous attendances at their parties that David and his friends were partial to cocaine and, more than likely, other illegal substances as well.

"I don't think so," said Tony.

I bent over to look more closely at her chest. There was a reddish purple patch just above her breasts.

Tony saw what I was looking at. "That's where the Doc, Alexander, tried to resuscitate her. Gave her mouth to mouth as well. Obviously to no avail."

Tony moved next to me at the side of the bed, bent over and brushed her hair away from her neck and shoulders to reveal livid red marks on either side of her neck. "I'm no expert," he said, indicating the marks, "but I would guess that those are the cause of death."

"So, was it him that did it? This Doctor Alexander?" I said.

"He won't say. None of them'll say who did it."

"Oh, for fuck's sake. What is this? A game of tell-tale tit in the school playground?"

I turned around abruptly and strode out of the bedroom and along the hallway, pushing open doors on either side, the first one leading into a bathroom and the second into another bedroom, before I reached the door to the sitting room. The three men were seated round a glass-topped dining table, staring in silence at half-filled glasses in front of them. They looked up in unison as I came into the room. None of them, including David Delacourt, showing any emotion on seeing me. There was a nearly empty bottle of brandy in the middle of the table next to a glass ash tray overflowing with cigarette butts. All three of them were smoking. David Delacourt held my angry stare for a moment or two before averting his eyes and swallowing the contents of his glass. He looked a mess. There were beads of sweat on his forehead: his normally abundant wavy fair hair was flattened greasily across the top of his head: his white shirt was open to halfway down his chest and the tail was hanging out of his trousers.

"I need to know what's going on here, David. You need to tell me exactly what happened."

The man with curly red hair and a thin fuzz of beard looked imploringly at David. His eyes were red-rimmed as if he'd been crying.

"You can see for yourself," said David, still not making eye contact with me. "The girl's dead. What else is there to know? We just need your help to get rid of the body."

"It's not that simple, David, and you know it," I said. "You're asking Tony and me to be accessories to a murder."

"Who said anything about a murder? There's been no murder." It was the panicky voice of the man sitting next to David. He also looked dishevelled, his long fair hair standing up in unruly tufts, his forehead dripping beads of sweat.

"And you are?" I asked.

"Alex. Doctor Alexander Laxley-Young."

"Okay, if none of you killed her, you're still going to have to tell us exactly how she died before we do anything – if we do anything." It was Tony speaking. I hadn't noticed him follow me into the room, but now he was standing next to me.

"All that you need to know," said David Delacourt in a slow deliberate tone of voice, as if giving orders, while pouring himself another shot of brandy, "is that you will both be very well rewarded for helping us."

"Fucking hell, David. A young woman is dead. You can't just buy your way out of this," I said, wondering what on earth I was doing there when I could have been tucked up in bed with the lovely Rachel.

"Can't I?" He looked up at me and then at Tony. "It's not as if you two haven't done this sort of thing before. You worked for the Krays, for Christ's sake."

Tony was about to say something but I put a restraining hand on his arm. "Look, David. I'll say this for the last time. We are not going to do anything until you tell us exactly what happened. Exactly how this girl died. Except, maybe, to call the police."

Alexander, the young doctor, looked at me in alarm as I said this and sprang to his feet, knocking into the table, rattling the glasses and tipping over the brandy bottle.

"Mr Felatu. Harry. That is your name, isn't it?" He said. I didn't respond. "Could I have a word with you in private?"

David Delacourt gave him an angry look. "Alex. You don't need to tell him anything. Remember, we're all in this together."

"It's alright, David. You can trust me," he said and then turned away and walked out of the room into the hallway. Tony and I followed him. He led us through a door into a dark green tiled bathroom where he perched himself on the edge of the bath, leaned forward and put his head in his hands.

"It wasn't murder," he said. "It was an accident."

"Of course it was," said Tony in a gently chiding voice. "Somebody accidentally strangled her to death. Which of you was it?"

"It was David, wasn't it?" I said. "She was his birthday present. It must have been him."

Alex balled his hands into fists and started banging the sides of his head with them. "He didn't mean to do it. They were having sex. It just got a bit too..." He paused, searching for the right word. "... boisterous."

"Shut the fuck up, Alex." It was David, standing behind us in the bathroom doorway. He was looking much less

296

composed now, and even more dishevelled. Now that he was standing, I could see that his flies were wide open. "This is not going to ruin my life. I'm not going to prison for this. And, as for you, Alex, what do you think will happen to you? You're an accessory. If this comes out, what do you think it will do to your medical career?" He stood still for a moment, taking deep breaths. His face was deathly pale as he put his hands to his mouth and started to wretch. He pushed Tony aside, rushed to the toilet, knelt down and threw up.

As Tony and I looked away, Alex stood up and left the bathroom. We followed him back into the sitting room. He sat back at the table and took a swig from his brandy glass before continuing with what he had been telling us before David interrupted.

"David is into erotic asphyxiation," he said, in a tone of voice that he might have used in his surgery to explain a diagnosis to a patient. "He does it a lot. Not just with prostitutes – also with girlfriends. He usually knows what he's doing. I guess it must have been the effect of the drink plus the cocaine. He must have lost control. Overdid it." He paused. After all those years I had spent with Francis Bacon and his debauched chums, nothing should have surprised me concerning people's sexual practices, but this was a new one to me. He gave a sardonic laugh before continuing. "Try telling that to the police. I don't know much about the law but, even though he didn't intend to kill her, I imagine he'll still be charged with manslaughter. And then, taking into account that he was under the influence of drink and drugs, they'll throw the book at him. And I don't suppose that Angus and I will get off too lightly either."

David came back into the room and walked unsteadily to his seat. He had flecks of vomit round his mouth. Try as I might, I couldn't feel the smallest iota of sympathy for him.

He was an overprivileged shit and, although I didn't know them, I was sure his friends were just as bad. They believed that they were superior to most other people and that money could get them anything they wanted. I turned and started to walk towards the telephone on a small console table next to the door. Tony immediately saw what I was intending to do and moved swiftly to block my path, grabbing both my arms.

He shook his head and said, "Before you do anything hasty, can I have a word?"

Reluctantly, I followed him outside into the hallway. He pulled the sitting room door closed behind us.

"Listen, Harry. If you call the police, how am I going to explain what I'm doing here? I've got previous. I've already done a long stretch inside. I'm not going back to prison."

"You won't need to," I said. "You can leave now and then I'll call the police. There's no need for you to stay here."

"And what about you Harry? The police will know all about you and the Krays. You think they won't be suspicious that you were also involved?"

"That's a risk I'll have to take," I said. I tried to sound confident, but Tony had sowed a seed of doubt.

"I don't mean to sound heartless, Harry, but she was a prostitute. It's an occupational hazard."

I glared angrily at him. "Oh, so she deserved to die. You think her life is worth less than the lives of those three in there."

"Keep your voice down," Tony said. "No, I don't think that. But what's done is done. We can't bring her back. Whereas, those young men – it's going to ruin the rest of their lives."

"And I should care about that?" I said in a rasping whisper.

"Harry. Just stop and think for a minute. You're employed by David's old man to look after him. How're he and David's mother going to feel when this comes out? You think they're gonna thank you for turning him in?" He was looking straight into my eyes, his face up close to mine. He could see he was having an effect. He pushed on before I could respond. "His father, Sir Richard. He's an MP. He's some kind of minister in the government, isn't he? What's it gonna do to his career when this hits the newspapers?"

I leaned back against the wall and rubbed my hand across my head. "Okay. It's going to be awful for everybody. But there's a girl in there who's died through no fault of her own. She's a human being, not some piece of rubbish that can simply be tossed away with the garbage."

Tony didn't respond but looked over his shoulder towards the open doorway to the bedroom. He was silent for about thirty seconds.

"There's something else to consider, Harry. I didn't want to bring this up but I feel I've got to." He paused, thinking carefully about what he was about to say. "When the police come and those young men are taken away for questioning, what are they gonna say? He's a cunning piece of work, that David. I'll bet you, right this minute, he's thinking of all the ways he can worm his way out of this. He's a toff. The son of a wealthy government minister. He's in a flat with one ex-con and an ex-associate of the Krays. It wouldn't take much for him to find a way to blame this on us. And his two equally posh mates will back him up. I can picture it now." He switched to a wheedling impersonation of David Delacourt's upper class accent. "Yes officer. I'll have to come clean. We asked them to go out and procure a prostitute for us. And when they brought her back, they said to us that, as part payment for their services, they'd like to have a turn with her first themselves. And then, the next thing we knew..."

"Alright, Tony. That's enough. You've made your point." My mind was whirring. A voice inside my head was saying 'you know what the right thing to do is. Stick to your guns. Do what you have to do'. But it was growing fainter.

Tony held both my arms and pulled me towards him. "Look," he said. "This is what we're going to do. In a minute, you're going to walk out of this flat and head off home. You were never here this evening. Okay?" I didn't say anything. "I'm going to call my brother, Nick, and get him over here and we will dispose of the body. We're professionals. We know how to do this. It'll just be another prostitute, murdered by a punter and found in some bushes by a man out walking his dog. There'll be nothing to link her to those young men or this flat. I've already checked with them. They picked her up off the streets. They're sure no-one saw her getting into their car." He shook me by the arms. "The only thing I need you to do, Harry, is to tell Sir Richard what's happened. What me and my brother have done to save his son's neck. Because we'll want paying big bucks for this."

"No. You're not going to tell my father anything. He mustn't know about this." It was David Delacourt. We hadn't noticed him opening the sitting room door and edging into the hallway. "We've got access to plenty of money between the three of us. We'll pay you whatever you want to make this go away."

I wish I could say, dear reader, that, at this point, I put up a fight. That I argued long and hard with Tony and David about what was the right thing to do. But I must be totally honest with you. I did no such thing. Tony's plan was immoral as well as illegal. It was plain wrong. But it made sense – and it would probably work. And, at that moment in time, all I could think about was that it would enable me to get out of that flat, which is what I wanted more than anything. Far away from that poor dead girl with her staring eyes and lolling tongue. I half-hoped that David Delacourt would make some facetious comment in support of Tony's plan and confirm what a despicable person he was, which would provoke me to stick to my guns and do what I knew was right, but he didn't say anything. And so, as if in a trance, I allowed Tony to usher me out of the apartment and I walked into the street and carried on walking, barely conscious of where I was going. It had started to rain and I turned my face up to it as I headed towards Park Lane, as if trying to wash away my guilt. I didn't bother hailing a taxi. I needed the fresh air and the cleansing rain. I walked all the way back to my flat in Paddington, got out of my damp clothes, had a long hot shower and climbed into bed, being careful not to wake Rachel.

On the Monday morning, I returned to Hedley Hall. I didn't go to my desk in the library but, instead, went into the drawing room where Sir Richard was sitting reading *The Times*. I asked him if I could have a word. My mind was still in a whirl. I couldn't get the events of the previous Saturday night out of my head, which meant that I hadn't properly thought out what I was going to say to Sir Richard. It must have come out as a barely coherent jumble. I told him I would have to stop working for him and leave Hedley Hall. I made up some vague excuse about personal problems that I needed to sort out. He expressed his disappointment and tried to dissuade me; told me that I could take as much time off as I needed and then return to my work when I was ready. I didn't disabuse him; didn't tell him I was never coming back. Throughout those few minutes, I had an overwhelming desire to blurt out the truth. To tell him exactly what had happened that Saturday night in the Knightsbridge apartment. But I didn't, especially as Lady Anne chose that moment to come into the room. Sir Richard told her what I had just told him and she was so gracious to me, expressing her gratitude for all I had done for their family, that I felt like crying. If only she knew the truth about what I had done, I thought, as I shook her hand. If only I had had the courage to tell her the truth about her beloved son.

When I returned to Paddington that evening, I was just in time to catch an item on the BBC London News about the body of a partially clad young woman being found hidden in undergrowth in a park in Croydon. To add to the horror of it, her body had been found by some children playing football. I switched it off and avoided watching or listening to any News bulletins or reading the newspapers for the rest of the week. I didn't want to know her name or see interviews with her grieving family or friends. Tony's plan was working. It would be yet another unsolved murder of a prostitute. Not worth the police mounting a more serious investigation as they would have done if she had been a so-called 'innocent' victim.

It was also the first time in my life that I completely shut out my mother's voice. I had frequent visions of her staring at me and shaking her head in dismay, but I instantly forced the vision from my mind and distracted myself in whatever way I could. It was obvious what she would tell me to do, but it was too late. Yes, I felt remorse, but there was no question of my seeking redemption and going to the police.

I tried to expunge all memories of that night from my mind and get on with my life but, no matter how much alcohol I consumed, it proved impossible. I had trouble sleeping. Almost every night I dreamed about it, dreams that mostly involved the police knocking at my door once the whole incident had come to light. We would all be arrested and then it would end with David Delacourt walking away scot-free while Tony, his brother and I were dragged off to prison.

And then, almost exactly a year after that fateful night, it caught up with me in real life. It started with a phone call from Maltese Tony. I had had no contact with him since that Saturday night in Knightsbridge. He asked me to meet him at his Camden Town flat. It would be an understatement to say that I was not keen. I told him in no uncertain terms that, after what had happened a year ago, I had vowed never to have anything more to do with him or David Delacourt and his chums. He said he understood my feeling that way, but he wouldn't be contacting me if it wasn't unavoidable. In that case, I said, you will need to tell me what it's about. You know what it's about, he replied. Yes, but you're going to have to be more specific, I said. Like an echo of that late night call the previous year, he said he couldn't talk about it on the phone. Suffice it to say that there was a problem which he needed my help to sort out. A problem that threatened to land both of us in serious trouble.

Like all those other times when I was faced with a dilemma, the Robert Frost poem *The Road Not Taken* came into my head, although I always saw it as a choice between footpaths rather than roads. Do I take the clearly delineated wide track leading across open fields or the barely discernible overgrown one leading into a dark forest? I knew which one my mother would choose, but I would prevaricate, wishing that another one would somehow appear – not as safe as the first but not as dark and dangerous as the path into the forest. But, of course, there never is a third way in life just as there can never be a magical third path.

I arrived at Tony's flat the following afternoon to find David Delacourt sitting in a high-backed armchair in the living room looking far more elegant and composed than he had done the last time I had seen him. He no longer had that boyish fringe flopping over his forehead or the wisps of hair straggling over his ears. His hair was short and neatly cut and his face had filled out. He wore an expensive-looking dark grey suit and his black shoes shone. As I entered the room, he gave me a wry smile. I immediately turned round to walk back out of the door. Tony must have anticipated my reaction because he was standing close behind me and barred my way.

"Sorry Tony," I said, trying to push my way past him. "I only very reluctantly agreed to come here and talk to *you*, but I want nothing more to do with that little shit."

"I understand that, Harry, but beggars can't be choosers. You need to hear what he's got to say. Whether we like it or not, we're all in this together."

"Listen Harry. I never had the chance to thank you for what you did that night," David said. "Like you, I hoped that it was all over and we'd never have to see each other again but these things have a tendency to come back and bite us on the bum."

"You can stuff your thanks up your arse." I turned to face him. "It was stupid of me not to go to the police at the time. Maybe I still should."

"Take a seat, Harry," Tony said, putting a hand on my shoulder. "You need to listen to what he has to say. It's something that has to be sorted out between the three of us."

I wouldn't be surprised, dear reader, if, as you read this, you are screaming 'walk away', 'walk away'. It's what a voice inside my head was screaming. The voice that had screamed the exact same thing at so many other crucial moments in my life. The voice that I had always ignored, much to my subsequent regret, and yet here I was, ignoring it once again. How to explain it. I guess it's a mixture of vestigial politeness and that other voice which says 'what have you got to lose? Hear him out. You can still walk away whenever you want.'

"Tony's right," David said, once Tony and I were sat on the sofa opposite him. "We do have a problem. And I do mean 'we'." He paused, as if giving me the opportunity to contradict him. I said nothing. "It's Alex. Alex Laxley-Young. The doctor. The guy whose flat we were in." He didn't need to elaborate. I knew who he was talking about as soon as he said 'Alex'. "He's in a lot of trouble. His career's over. He's been struck off the medical register. It means he can no longer practice…"

"I know what it means," I said. As well as treating me like a servant, David had always talked down to me, assuming I was thick.

"It's nothing to do with the girl's death," he continued. "I don't need to go into it now. The reasons are not important. What is important is that he's in a dreadful state. His head's all over the place. He's asked me for help. He needs money. Since his professional career is over in this country, he wants to go abroad and start up somewhere else but he hasn't got the funds to do it. He wants twenty-five thousand pounds." He paused again.

"So, how does that have anything to do with me and Tony?" I said. It was a stupid question. I could already start to guess the answer.

"I told you he was unhinged," David said. "He's threatening blackmail to get the money out of me. He says he's only got himself into this mess because of the girl's death and his part in covering it up. He claims he can't get rid of his guilt feelings. It's driven him to drugs – which is partly what got him struck off. Anyway, now his life is in ruins, he feels he's got nothing to lose. If I don't give him the money, he says he'll go to the police. At least then, he can salve his conscience."

"And you think he'll do it?" I said.

David smiled sardonically. "Probably not, but it's a risk that I'm not willing to take." He looked from Tony to me. "That *we* shouldn't be willing to take. Unlike Alex, things are going really well for me. I'm not willing to risk him dragging me down with him. I can get the money. That's not a problem. My worry is that Alex is a loose cannon. I've known him since schooldays. He's always been unstable. I'm not sure I can trust him even if I give him the money." David Delacourt exuded that air of smug confidence born of upper-class privilege. As I listened to him, I searched for something to say that might unnerve him, bring him down a peg or two, but I couldn't come up with anything.

"There is an alternative," Tony interjected. "David has suggested that he could use that money instead to pay me and my brother to dispose of Doctor Laxley-Young."

I felt numb. I heard what they were saying but the words were barely registering in my brain. I felt no sense of shock or panic, just a stultifying inevitability, as if I had already foreseen all of this.

"I still fail to see what all this has to do with me," I said, knowing that I was wasting my breath. They were about to tell me. "You don't need any advice from me. You do what you want."

"You're right, Harry. I don't need your advice, but I do need your help. Tony and I are agreed that it's not a good idea to have Alex bumped off. After all, I'm not some criminal hoodlum." He avoided looking at Tony when he said this. "As I said, I can pay him the money. The problem is that I need some way to make sure that the payment can't be traced back to me. I can't risk this coming back some day to incriminate me. That's where you come in, Harry."

He paused again and looked me in the eyes. "I suddenly remembered that, when you were working for my father, you asked him if he would attend a charitable award ceremony. You wanted him to be the guest of honour to hand out grants and scholarships from your mother's trust fund. I believe that trust fund is still going strong and gives out lots of grants every year?" He looked at me and I stared back impassively. "Well, my idea is for you to set up some imaginary award as a one-off payment to Alex – although, of course, it wouldn't be to him personally – and then I could secretly reimburse you. That way the money would be difficult to trace back to me."

There was a momentary silence before I responded. "So, it gets you off the hook and leaves me in danger of being implicated instead."

"No, Harry. I've got a very good accountant friend who will arrange it. He'll make sure it will be very difficult to trace it back to either of us."

Walk away. Walk away. It was ringing in my ears again.

I'm going to bring the curtain down on this. You know what happened, dear reader. I won't attempt to justify myself. There is no justification. I resisted, of course, at which point, David said that would mean they would have to resurrect the plan to permanently dispatch Doctor Alex. So, you could say, in my favour, that I saved his life. Except I didn't give a damn about Doctor Alexander Laxley-Young's life.

I very much doubt, dear reader, that I will write any more of this autobiography even though I have another fifteen years to go to bring it up to date. Partly, this is because I am doubtful about how much longer I have to live, but mainly it is because there's not much more to tell. If I was to write a final chapter, it would most appropriately be sub-titled

'The Wilderness Years' – a story of Soho pub crawling and heavy drinking. Those years have raced by in an alcoholic haze – a welter of wasted time. Apart, that is, from writing this autobiography.

So now, all I can do is sit here in my room and wait for the inevitable arrival of the men who will put an end to my life – deserved retribution for my night of shame.

# Wednesday 4th November 2001

Ethan sat hunched over in front of his computer screen, transfixed. He had been re-running the clips from the security cameras at Vienna International Airport sent to him by Inspector Lukas Honig earlier that morning. Each time he replayed them, he found himself inadvertently leaning closer into the screen. Like all such footage, they had been taken from above head height, looking down on the two men dressed in almost identical dark grey suits, one of them with a full head of short brown hair, the other with black hair surrounding a bald patch on the crown. They were both pulling small wheeled cases and the balding one carried a leather holdall in his other hand. As well as the original camera footage, the inspector had sent him several enhanced close up images of the two men's faces as they stood in front of the airline check-in desk. None of the images were crystal clear but Lukas Honig said he hoped they would be good enough to enable the men to be identified. He had also sent details of the incoming and outgoing flights they had been on and their names from the flight registers.

Ethan was just about to get up from his desk and head for Maddy Rich's office to relay the good news when an incoming email alert pinged in the top right-hand corner of his screen. It was from Lukas Honig. As he skim-read the brief message, he pumped his fist in the air and hissed 'yes' out loud. Two of his colleagues at nearby desks looked up at him enquiringly but he was too excited to take the time to explain. He was impressed by the Austrian policeman's speed and efficiency. In the message, Lukas Honig said that he had called the concierge from Doctor Harrison's apartment block into his office that morning to view the images. Although she couldn't be one hundred per cent certain, she was fairly confident that the men captured on the CCTV were the same two men she had seen visiting Doctor Harrison on the day of his murder.

Although he was itching to tell Maddy Rich the good news, he restrained himself, instead writing and sending a brief thank you reply to Lukas Honig and then clicking on the database for the Felatu investigation and retrieving the phone number for Mr and Mrs Kaplanska. He wanted to show that he could be equally as efficient as the Austrian by getting the elderly couple into Paddington Green Station as quickly as possible. If he could get a positive identification of the two men at Vienna Airport from them, it would be the icing on the cake.

After Becky had finally allowed herself to be persuaded by Magda to keep the contents of Harry Felatu's envelope, she accompanied her to the Museum's main entrance, expressed her condolences once again and said goodbye. Back at her desk in the research department, she sat for what seemed like an age staring at the sheath of handwritten papers lying on top of the opened jiffy bag. Magda was right. She was desperate to read the two chapters but, at the same time, fearful. It had been such a relief when, after her meeting with Sir Richard Delacourt, she had finally decided to wash her hands of her misguided amateur investigation. And now, here she was being dragged back into it. Perhaps the best thing to do was what she had suggested to Magda. Not read it at all but put it in another envelope and send it anonymously to the police. Then she would have fully washed her hands of the whole thing. She wouldn't have to tell them about the rest of the autobiography and how she had got hold of it or explain why she had withheld evidence from a murder inquiry. After all, interesting as it was, she couldn't see that there was anything in what she had read so far that would provide any clues for the police about Felatu's murder. Not that the police would necessarily agree with that. She was sure that they would tell her, in no uncertain terms, that it was evidence and it was up to them, and not her, to decide whether it was important. No: however she decided to do it, there was no question that the police had to be given Harry Felatu's autobiography, including the two chapters on the desk in front of her. Even though she hadn't read them, they must be significant, she thought, otherwise why the melodrama of separating them from the rest of it and sending them to Ana Geisler with that message on the envelope?

Finally, Becky made a decision to delay making a decision. She stuffed the chapters back into the envelope, put it in her bag and headed home. The journey was interminable. At every stop on the underground, she felt the urge to open the envelope and start skim reading the contents, but she resisted. She needed the peace and quiet of her own flat if she did decide to read it rather than send it unread straight to the police. Although, the closer she got to home, the more she knew that it was no longer an 'if'. She would have to read it.

By the time she arrived back at the flat, it was four-thirty in the afternoon and she knew she wouldn't be disturbed for at least another hour. Richard never left school before five o'clock. Her stomach ached and her mouth was dry. She went into the kitchen, poured herself a glass of water and gulped it down in one go. It made little difference. Her throat still hurt. She resisted the magnetic pull of the envelope in her bag for a little longer and made herself a cup of tea.

A half an hour later, she was sitting in the wicker chair by the side of her bed with the contents of the envelope spread out on the duvet. It hadn't taken her long to read the two chapters. Her stomach no longer ached. It now felt not dissimilar to the way it had at school when she had had a bad attack of exam nerves before sitting a French A level paper. Not so much butterflies, more a flock of small birds flying around inside her. She didn't know what she had expected before she started reading but it was nothing like this. There was now no more room for any evasion. Whatever doubts she had had before, now that she had read and fully digested Harry Felatu's confession, there was no question that it had to go to the police. And not even sent anonymously to keep herself out of trouble. She would have to take it to them herself and offer her full cooperation no matter what consequences there might be.

She was still thinking all this through when she heard the sound of the front door opening and closing. She looked at her watch. It was around the time Richard normally arrived home from work. She heard him going into the living room and then, thirty seconds later, he pushed open the bedroom door.

"Hi Becky. You're home early. Makes a change for you to be home before me. I thought it was all hands to the pump at the Museum what with it getting so close to the opening of the exhibition."

Becky hurriedly scooped the pages up from the bed and stuffed them awkwardly back into the padded envelope. She hadn't yet thought about what to tell Richard. Or even whether she would tell him at all.

"Is everything okay You're not sick, are you?" Richard was staring closely at her. She must look dreadful, she thought. She certainly felt dreadful.

"I'm fine," she said in an overloud voice, trying to sound upbeat. "I decided to do some work from home this afternoon."

"Do you want something to drink?" Richard said. "I was just about to make myself a gin and tonic. I've had a pretty heavy day myself."

"No, you're alright. I've just had a cup of tea."

After he'd gone, she sat thinking for several minutes. She had to tell Richard everything and she had to tell him now, she decided. Once she went to the police, it would all come out anyway. She needed to talk to somebody about it and she felt confident that Richard would be calm and supportive. He would reassure her that she was doing the right thing.

He was sitting on the sofa with his gin and tonic watching the BBC *Six O'Clock News*. Becky was about to ask him to turn it off as she had something important to tell him when she was transfixed by the face on the screen. It was a very smooth looking David Delacourt, or David Billington as he now called himself. A lick of blond hair hung across his forehead. There was a broad smile spread across his fleshy handsome face. The shock of seeing him so soon after what she had just read left her momentarily stunned. She couldn't take in what he was saying to the interviewer or what the female newsreader was talking about when she came back on to the screen.

"Hi." Richard gave her a puzzled stare. "You look like you've seen a ghost."

"That's probably because I just have," Becky said.

Richard waited a second and then laughed. "Yes, I know. Shocking, isn't it? Just think. That bastard could be our next Prime Minister."

Becky managed to take her eyes off the screen and sat down next to Richard on the sofa. "Sorry. I wasn't paying attention. Why was he being interviewed? What's happened?"

"He's just been made the Shadow Home Secretary," Richard said, "and since they think there's about to be a challenge for the leadership of the Conservative Party, they were asking him if he'd be a candidate. Of course, he was non-committal, but everyone agrees that, if there is an election, he's a shoe-in."

Becky picked up the remote control and turned the television off.

"I've got something important I need to tell you," she said, "and, weird as it may seem, that 'bastard' as you rightly call him, is very much a part of it."

Once he had escorted the Kaplanskas to the lift and thanked them for coming in so promptly and being so helpful, Ethan returned to his desk to mull things over. Mrs Kaplanska had studied the CCTV footage for a long time, asking Ethan to replay it several times and then spending an age peering at the still images of the two men. The best she could say was that they looked very like the men who had visited Mr Felatu but she couldn't be one hundred per cent certain. Her husband, on the other hand, only needed a brief glance at the images before pronouncing authoritatively that they were the same men. It was hard to take him seriously, Ethan thought. He was the kind of dogmatic character who had no time for prevarication. Once his wife had expressed her hesitantly qualified opinion, he was always going to give his view with one hundred per cent certainty. All Ethan could do now was to wait as patiently as he could for his colleagues to track down the men identified on the flight register and bring them in for questioning. It was far from cut and dried. They were still some way from solving the case, but at last they were getting somewhere.

And then the internal phone on his desk buzzed. It was the reception desk downstairs. There was a young woman called Becky Stone asking to speak to somebody about the Harry Felatu murder investigation. She claims she has some important information, the desk sergeant said. Ethan said he'd be right down. As he walked back towards the lift, he couldn't help thinking that conducting a murder case was rather like waiting for a bus. You wait for ages to get any leads at all and then several come along at once.

Becky sat in the police station waiting area, a black holdall at her feet containing the initial manuscript of Felatu's autobiography and the jiffy bag with the two extra, incriminating chapters. Richard sat next to her, holding her hand. As the lift doors opened at the far end of the foyer, she saw two familiar figures getting out and walking towards the exit. The very much shorter woman was clinging to the arm of the tall upright man. It was the couple that Harry Felatu had been renting his apartment from. She couldn't remember their names. Mrs Kaplanska glanced briefly in Becky's direction but gave no sign of recognising her.

There was a flat screen television high on the wall to the right of where Becky and Richard were sitting. The sound was off but there were subtitles across the bottom of the screen. It was a midday politics programme and on screen was the ubiquitous figure of David Billington making a speech to a national conference of police officers. Becky and Richard were both glued to the screen.

The newly appointed Shadow Home Secretary was castigating the Labour Government for its soft stance on crime. It was all very well to drone on about the causes of crime, he was saying, but the important thing was to come down hard on it. Serious crime needed to be met with serious custodial sentences. Police powers of stop and search must be re-instated. And it was now time, with the increased terrorist threat since 9/11, for the re-introduction of capital punishment.

"Hi. I'm Sergeant Ethan Edwards."

Becky and Richard had been so glued to the screen that they hadn't noticed him approaching.

"I believe you have some information for me concerning the Harry Felatu investigation. If you'd care to follow me, we'll go to an interview room."

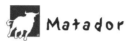 **Matador**